PRAISE FO
IN THE *SF*

"Nina Lane has written an amazing story that will resonate with every reader... A journey of one couple's spiral into a world of jealousy and betrayal, hidden secrets, and the raw purity of first love."

—*Sandy, The Reading Cafe*

"5 breathtaking stars... It was moving, emotional, warm, tender, funny, sensual, gut-wrenching and I became absolutely and completely invested in Liv and Dean."

—*Jenny, TotallyBooked Blog*

"5 amazing stars... I loved this author's style of writing; it was beautiful and vivid and made for compulsive reading... Be ready to feel every single emotion possible."

—*Gitte, TotallyBooked Blog*

"Arouse is achingly beautiful in its intensity... If you are on the lookout for a read that provides a great, thoughtful story combined with enticing as well as fierce sex scenes then look no further. You have found it."

—*Baba, Goodreads*

"The author completely drew me into Dean and Olivia's story, as well as their lives... From beginning to end, the journey is riveting."

—*Yesi, Reviewer with Literati Literature Lovers*

"Nina Lane knows how to create characters whose actions and feelings make a lasting connection with the reader."

—*Bridget, My Secret Romance Book Reviews*

*I want to do with you what spring
does with the cherry trees.*
—Pablo Neruda

AROUSE

Arouse

A SPIRAL OF BLISS NOVEL:

Book 1

NINA LANE

SNOW QUEEN
PUBLISHING

Cover Design & Interior design by VMC Art & Design, LLC

Published by Snow Queen Publishing

ISBN: 978-0-9887158-3-7

PART I

CHAPTER ONE

OLIVIA

*H*e didn't touch me. He could have—he had the perfect reason to—but he didn't.

Instead he bent to collect my papers before the breeze could whisk them away. Instead he picked up my satchel from the sidewalk and asked if I was okay. Instead he stood between me and the busy street while I brushed the dirt from my palms and tried to swallow the knot of frustration stuck in my throat.

Instead he just waited. I had the strange thought that he would wait forever.

August 7

Adhesive sandcastles, flip-flops, and smiling suns cover the windows of the shops lining Avalon Street. The bed-and-breakfasts are filled with guests, and boats dot Mirror Lake like stars in the sky. University students crowd the coffeehouses, and both tourists and locals stroll through downtown with ice-cream cones or sodas in hand. Children, skin browned from the sun, scurry along the paths leading to the shore.

"Sorry, miss." The shaggy-haired fellow at the outdoor drink stand gives me a smile of apology. "We're out of lemonade."

Of course they are.

I push a damp tendril of hair away from my forehead and look at the chalkboard menu again.

The sun has started to set, but it's still roasting out. My pantyhose are shrink-wrapped to my body, and the elastic band is gouging my waist. My toes ache from being crammed into heels all day. And though I refuse to look, I'm quite certain there are sweat stains under the arms of my silk blouse.

"Okay. An iced tea, then." I push two dollars at the guy and take the plastic cup, poking a straw into the hole. I don't much like iced tea, but the cup is cold and wet, and the liquid feels good going down my dry throat.

I scan for an outdoor table, but they're all filled with clusters of people enjoying their drinks.

I grab my paper bag of groceries, pull up my satchel strap, and trudge down the sun-baked street, feeling like a bone-weary schoolmarm amidst the happy, relaxed summer crowd. My ponytail slips farther from the loose clasp, welding more strands of hair to my neck.

Home. Our small, two-bedroom apartment sits above a row of shops overlooking Avalon Street. The sight of the wrought-iron balcony, laden with plants in fat, colorful pots, elicits a welcome sense of relief.

I increase my pace despite the blister forming on my heel. The minute I step into the building foyer, I drop the bag, kick off my shoes, and sink onto the bottom step of the stairs. I suck in another mouthful of iced tea. Sweat trickles down my spine.

"Hey, beauty."

The deep, masculine voice resounds inside me. I look up at the top of the stairs where Dean is standing. His dark hair is messy from him dragging his hand through it, his shirt is wrinkled, and the sleeves are pushed up to his elbows. His tie is unknotted and loose, the buttons of his collar unfastened to expose the tanned V of his throat.

Warmth, both spicy and sweet, curls through me at the sight of him. Dean's seamless combination of Brilliant Professor and Hot Hunk never fails to quicken my blood.

"Hi." I duck my head and sip the iced tea.

"Thought you were working late." He descends the stairs to where I'm sitting and picks up my satchel.

"Yeah, well." A lump forms in my throat. "I got fired."

Jesus, Liv. Don't *cry*.

"Fired?" Dean drops the satchel and sits beside me on the step. He reaches out to brush my hair away from my sticky neck. "What happened?"

"A screw-up with the printer for tonight's opening. They got the names of a couple of the big donors wrong, even though I emailed them the information twice and sent a hard copy. Mr. Hammond blamed me anyway."

I hate sounding like a victim, even if that is the truth.

"That's not right, Liv. Wrongful termination is—"

I wave my hand to stop him. "Forget it, Dean. It wasn't that great a job. Hammond was always complaining that I made too many mistakes. Which I did not."

"Want me to go beat him up?"

"Kind of." *My white knight…*

"C'mere." He slides an arm around me and pulls me closer.

Even though I'm hot and gross and probably smelly, I burrow against him with a sigh. Just the feel of his strong chest beneath my cheek is soothing.

When he eases the clasp out of my long hair and finger-combs the tangles, then moves his hand up to knead the muscles of my nape, I think I could quite happily sit there for the next hour or three.

"I offered to try and fix the problem, but he told me to pack up and go," I say.

"Their loss." He brushes his lips against my temple. A tingle sweeps clear down to my toes. "Besides you said the artwork was crap anyway."

"It was." I take another sip of tea. "Bunch of junk glued onto canvases. I could make us a fortune doing that. Hell, maybe I will. Olivia West, the Dumpster-diving artist."

"That's my girl."

"Ah, well. Mr. Hammond was kind of a creep anyway."

"What do you mean?" Tension ripples through Dean's solid frame. "Did he—?"

"No, no. I mean creep as in oily. Groveling to the customers, you know, like a medieval surfer."

"Serf." Dean tweaks my nose.

"I know." I grin at him and push to standing.

Dean picks up my satchel and the wrinkled grocery bag. I grab my shoes and trudge after him into our apartment. My anxiety settles a little more as soon as I close the door behind us.

The windows are shut and the air conditioner is running, so it's cool and quiet inside. When we first moved in, I put pale blue curtains on the windows, which complement the navy sofa and striped pillows. With the cream-colored walls, blue-and-white quilts, and wood trim, our apartment has the feel of an open, airy beach house.

I toss my shoes in the front closet and go into the bedroom to peel off my clothes. I take a quick and lovely cool shower, then dress in yoga pants and a T-shirt.

The knots in my shoulders loosen. Being at home always makes me feel better. I love our pillowy bed with the thick, flowered comforter, the tiny kitchen with the white wooden table I sanded and repainted myself, the living-room shelves stuffed with books, the curved balcony overlooking Avalon Street.

I towel-dry my hair and grab a brush to work out the tangles. My hair is straight as straw, but long, thick, and a deep brown that matches my eyes ("the color of coffee with cream," Dean told me during one of his more poetic moments). I don't bother drying it further, but leave it loose because I know that's the way he likes it.

After heading to the kitchen, I lean against the doorjamb and watch Dean set out plates for dinner. He's changed into jeans that hug his long legs and a T-shirt emblazoned with a San Francisco Giants logo.

My husband is a handsome man, built like an athlete rather

than a scholar. Nine years older than I am, he's tall with hard muscles and broad shoulders, his dark brown hair threaded with a few distinguished strands of gray.

He has beautiful eyes, chocolate-brown and framed with thick lashes that offset the strength of his cheekbones and jaw. He also has a great deal of self-confidence and dignity, which show in his straight posture and in the measured way he speaks.

No wonder, considering the man's impressive pedigree. Bachelor's degree from Yale, PhD from Harvard, postdocs at the University of Wisconsin and UPenn, fellowship at the Getty Institute, guest lectures at European universities.

Two years ago he was offered a tenure-track position at King's University, a private, prestigious university in Mirror Lake. He's spearheading a new Medieval Studies program, which is the reason King's enticed him to their faculty with a top-level salary and promises of project funding.

I wasn't remotely surprised by how much they wanted him.

Dean glances up and smiles. My heart gives a pleasant thump. When he looks at me like that, his eyes creased with warmth, all his illustrious distinctions fall away and he's only the man who loves and wants me.

"How was your day, professor?" I ask, moving in for a proper hug. "Did you finish your paper on the medieval sins of passion?"

He kisses the top of my head. "Excavation and archeology of a town originated by a castle of the Teutonic Order."

Of course.

I tighten my arms around his waist. "Mmm. Dirty talk."

"Urban hierarchy." He slides a big hand down to squeeze

my rear. He could say anything in that deep voice of his and I'd go all fluttery inside. "Vernacular architecture. Topographical analysis. Flexible growth."

He bends to nuzzle my throat, his stubble scraping my skin rather deliciously, then slides his mouth up to capture my lips.

Ah, good. His kisses are always so good. He cups a hand behind my neck to angle my head so he can fit his mouth across mine. Arousal blooms inside me swift and hard, banishing my earlier frustration as I part my lips underneath his and accept the hot sweep of his tongue.

With a mutter of pleasure, he slides his other hand to the small of my back and pulls me closer. I press my palm against his flat belly, easing my fingers into the waistband of his jeans. When I start to explore farther down, he catches my wrist and gives a husky laugh.

"Watch what you start, beauty," he murmurs.

"I intend to." But I'm also hungry for dinner, so I reach up to kiss his chin and then ease away. "So what else did you do today?"

"Worked on a conference presentation and summer lectures."

"What conference?"

"Didn't I tell you?" He frowns. "Atlanta. October. I'll be gone for three or four days."

He reaches up to take a glass from the cupboard. The material of his T-shirt stretches over his upper arm. I slide my gaze to where the shirt rises slightly to reveal his muscular lower back.

"Sorry, Liv," he says. "Thought I told you."

I shrug. "Doesn't matter."

It doesn't, except that we're not apart often, save a couple of times a year when he goes to a conference or on a research trip. Neither of us likes the short separations, but they're good for us—gives me a chance to be alone, gives Dean a chance to learn what else is going on in the field. If you're into Visigothic Iberia and Old Norse poetry.

Which he is.

"What're you talking about at the conference?" I ask.

"Visual culture in the Crusades. I'm thinking of constructing a course around the topic."

I turn to open the containers of Chinese take-out he must have picked up on the way home. He's still talking, and while I like the sound of his baritone voice—as, I'm quite certain, his female undergrads do—I don't understand much of what he's saying since I've never taken a medieval history course.

Still, Dean has said before that talking helps clarify his thoughts and ideas. So I'm happy to let him ramble, and he's happy to have an audience.

We sit down to eat sesame chicken and fried rice, and I give him a play-by-play of the events that ended up with me getting fired. When he starts in with the whole "wrongful termination" thing again, I lean across the table to kiss him and stop his tirade.

"We have better things to do with our time," I say before shooing him out of the kitchen so I can clean up.

After putting away the leftover food and doing the dishes, I head into the living room. Dean has taken over the second bedroom as his office, so my own narrow desk sits at the living room window and looks out over the rooftops to the mountains and clear expanse of the lake.

I power up my laptop and scan a few job sites. *Web designer.* No. *Paralegal.* No. *Real-estate agent.* No. *Spanish teacher.* No. *Welder.* Lord, no.

"What about the library over at SciTech?" Dean suggests. He's lying on the sofa, an intricate web of string like a cat's cradle pulled taut between his palms.

"Already applied. They turned me down because I don't know whatever database system they use."

"I can ask about job openings around the university." Dean tucks his forefingers into the string to create another pattern.

"No." I rest my chin on my hand and click another job site. "I'll find something."

Sales associate. Cashier. Stock clerk.

I've been hoping for more than retail, a job that will start me on a path toward *something*, but my lack of work experience makes that a daunting prospect.

"There's that bookstore over on Emerald Street," I say, injecting a breezy *it'll be fine* tone into my voice. "I'll stop by tomorrow and see if they could use some help. And I can pick up a few more volunteer hours at the Historical Museum."

"With all the work you're doing for the museum, you'll be their first pick when a job opens up," Dean says. "Same with the public library."

"You think so?"

"I know so. And remember that college kids have most of the summer jobs now. You'll have more options when the fall semester starts."

Maybe. Feeling sort of down again, I close the laptop and push away from the desk. Dean unravels the string from his fingers and tosses it onto the coffee table.

"Come here, beauty," he says. "You need to be kissed."

I go to the sofa and sprawl out on top of him with a sigh. He feels so damn good. He has a gorgeous body—he's all lean, tensile strength with a solid chest that makes me want to stretch against him like a cat in the sun. He puts his hand on the back of my neck and brings my mouth down to his.

The disappointment drains from me. He's right. I need to be kissed, and he's the one who needs to kiss me.

His lips are warm and firm against mine, and shivers race over my skin as his hands slide down to grasp my hips. I part my lips on a sigh and let our tongues tangle together. He closes his teeth gently on my lower lip, eliciting a delicious little twinge that shortens my breath.

I wiggle around, rubbing my breasts against his chest. He tightens his grip on my hips before moving his hands to the waistband of my pants. With a smooth stroke, he delves inside and spreads his palms over my bottom, pressing his fingers into the crevice. An ache pools through my lower body.

"I think..." I lift myself to look down at him, my blood heating at the sight of the lust brewing in his eyes. "I think I need to be more than kissed."

"Yes, you do." Dean pushes his hands underneath my T-shirt and opens the clasp of my bra with one twist, then rubs a hot, friction-laced path over my naked back. "I'll take care of you."

"I know you will." I sink against him and lower my mouth to his again.

Our kiss grows urgent, Dean's body tightening beneath mine. He eases a hand between us to work the buttons of his jeans. I uncoil to sit back on his thighs and watch the quick movements of his fingers. My heart hammers at the sight of the bulge pressing against his jeans, especially since I know well what's underneath.

"You've been waiting for me, huh?" I ask breathlessly.

"Always."

I move off him to tug the jeans over his long legs. His erection tents his boxers, and I palm the hot, heavy length. Sparks fly through me with the anticipation of his tight flesh embedded inside me, stroking and pulsing.

I inhale sharply and look up at Dean. His eyes are glazed with lust, his chest heaving with the force of his breath. He gestures toward my breasts.

I grasp the hem of my T-shirt and pull it over my head, tossing it on the sofa along with my bra. His gaze rakes over me, and my nipples harden in delicious response. In one movement, Dean grabs me around the waist and brings us both to the floor.

Even better than lying on top of him is the sensation of his weight on me, strong and powerful. He splays his hands over my breasts, rubbing his thumbs across my nipples before he bends to capture one in his mouth.

I gasp and clench my fingers into his hair. Heat cascades through me, centering in the core of my body. I twist beneath him until he tugs at my pants and lowers them over my hips along with my underwear.

"Ah fuck, Liv, you're so ready."

His fingers brush against my damp sex, his cock pressing against my thigh. A flush sweeps me from head to toe when he kneels between my spread legs and pulls off his shirt, then shoves his boxers down.

His erection is beautiful—long and thick, the heavy sac pulled tight. He opens a drawer of the end-table and takes out a foil packet. My pulse pounds as I watch him roll on the condom.

He glances up at me, his eyes tracking over my naked breasts to my face. He puts his hand against me again, dipping one finger into the slick opening of my body.

"Dean." I push upward to deepen his immersion.

A slight smile curves his mouth as he explores farther. His thumb swirls around my clit, his forefinger moving up one side and down the other. He knows exactly how to touch me, and within seconds I'm panting and gasping as the spool of bliss winds tighter.

"Dean, I'm…"

"What, beauty?" A teasing note underlies the lust in his voice.

"So close…" I breathe.

He lowers himself over me, his mouth coming down on mine, his tongue sliding across my lips. I grip his biceps and arch against him, craving that explosion of pleasure dangling just beyond my grasp. One press of his fingers and I come with a cry, my inner flesh tightening around him.

With trembles still coursing through me, I wrap my legs around his hips and pull him closer. He thrusts into me hard and deep, his groan rumbling against my neck.

"Oh!" I clutch his back and lift my thighs, swimming in the heat and sensation of him driving into me.

I fall, swirling, swept into the exquisite pleasure of us rocking together, his flesh slamming against mine, the push-and-pull cadence of his hard plunges. My arousal spikes again, the friction lighting my nerves as his thrusts slow into the rhythm of his impending release.

I edge my hand between our bodies to rub myself to another sharp orgasm, then glide my fingertips against his pulsing shaft. Our eyes meet with a sizzle in the instant before he slides out of me, rolling the condom off before grasping his cock.

I'm hot all over watching the slick, easy movement of his hand, the tensing of his muscles and the way his thumb brushes the damp head of his cock. To ratchet up his urgency, I squeeze my breasts together and twist my nipples, then writhe around with shameless little movements that I know will send him over the edge.

He groans deep, thrusting heavily into his fist as he comes long and hard over my belly. Panting, I push to my elbows to watch him finish himself off. After riding the final pulses, he braces his hands on either side of me and leans in to press his lips to mine.

"You were right," I murmur against his mouth. "I needed to be kissed."

"Very glad to help."

He lowers us both to the floor again, our mouths still locked together, then eases to the side so I can fold myself against him. A lovely, warm feeling like melted honey slides through me—a feeling I have only ever experienced with this man of mine.

Once upon a time I didn't know people like Professor Dean West existed. There had been no one like him in the tangled woods where I once lived, a place in which night fell too early and ogres lurked behind skeletal trees.

He pulls me closer, his arm around my shoulders. His body is enveloping, protective. I fit perfectly, as always, into the space against his side.

CHAPTER TWO

AUGUST 9

*A*fter Dean leaves for work, I clean the apartment and water the potted plants on the balcony, which is a lush little jungle of pansies, geraniums, daisies, and lantanas. Then I spend an hour curled up on a chair by the window, leafing through the *Help Wanted* sections of a couple of newspapers.

Exotic entertainer. Plant manager. Sandwich artist. I circle "marketing assistant" and "animal care attendant," even though I know nothing about marketing or animal care.

It's discouraging, this spread of black-and-white rectangles that each announce a profession I either can't do or didn't know existed *(mold setter?)*.

I toss the paper aside with a sigh. After Dean and I got married, I wanted to support him, wanted to be his solid ground while he established his career. I've been happy to do that for the past three years—I've enjoyed making warm, pleasant homes out of the utilitarian apartment we lived in during his fellowship position and now our little above-shop place in Mirror Lake.

I've loved being Professor Dean West's wife, watching his success and growing renown in academia. And I haven't minded my temporary part-time jobs, because I'd planned to start a career path as soon as Dean settled into a tenure-track position.

Except now we've been in Mirror Lake for almost two years and I've hit barriers at every turn: I freelanced for a local magazine that went under, I've been rejected for several jobs due to lack of experience, the King's agriculture majors do all the work at gardening centers, and I quit a cashier's job at a clothing store so I could take the assistant position at the art gallery.

So much for that plan.

After changing into shorts and a T-shirt, I walk several blocks to the gym where I work out five… okay, two times a week. I sweat through an aerobics class, shower, and go to meet my friend Kelsey March for lunch.

Kelsey is an atmospheric scientist at the university, and of course I met her through Dean because they're academic soul-mates and have known each other for years. She is one of the few people who refuses to fawn over him, which is just one of the reasons we both like her so much.

She's pacing in front of the Italian restaurant where we

agreed to meet, her thumbs working the buttons of her smart-phone, her stride brisk.

As is her style, she's wearing a tailored suit and button-down shirt, but she has this vibe that makes you think she's sporting sexy lingerie beneath. Her frosted blond hair is cut in a sleek pageboy and embellished with a single streak of navy blue, which she flips back as she watches my approach.

"You're late," she says, blinking at me through her rimless glasses.

"Am not. Your watch is fast."

She punches a few buttons on her phone and holds it up. "Greenwich mean time."

"Because *you* would never consult Greenwich nice time."

"You got that right." Kelsey smirks and shoves her phone into her bag as we head into the restaurant.

We get settled into a booth, peruse the menus, and place orders of chicken marsala for Kelsey and butternut squash ravioli for me.

"Hey, sorry about your job," Kelsey says, poking a straw into her soda. "I can get you something at the AOS department if you'd let me."

"No, thanks." I always balk at her and Dean's suggestions that they can "get me" a job at the university. I know they don't think I can't find something on my own, but accepting their help might make *me* think that. "I have a few leads I'm looking into."

"Let me know if you change your mind," Kelsey says. "The professors are pains in the ass, but overall the department's not horrible to work for."

"Well, with that kind of resounding endorsement, it's a

wonder the AOS department doesn't have applicants lined up around the block."

Kelsey shoots me one of her "don't-fuck-with-me" looks. I respond with a smile because she knows I would never seriously fuck with her. I'm not stupid.

"Hey." She sits back and frowns. "Really. You look under the weather."

"The fact that you just made a weather joke cheers me up immensely."

"You know, Liv, you don't have to find the perfect career right away," she says. "Give it a little time, you know? Weren't you a library sciences major in college?"

"Yeah. I worked at the art library at the UW for a while, but then Dean and I got married and moved to L.A. I just worked part-time retail when he had the Getty fellowship. And the libraries at King's haven't had any openings since we moved here." I poke at my salad. "I did see an ad this morning for an exotic entertainer position."

Kelsey snorts. "Missionary or doggy?"

I choke on a gulp of water and laugh. "Probably both."

"I'm sure your husband would provide you with great references."

I swat her with my napkin, then admit, "Well, that's true."

Kelsey grins, and we turn our attention to the arrival of our entrees. She slathers butter on a roll and says, "So, Liv, can I steal Dean on Saturday the twenty-fifth? I wouldn't ask if it weren't an emergency."

"Sure. What's up?"

"There's a faculty banquet for some old fart who's retiring." She stabs a green bean with her fork. "I wouldn't normally go, but I'm trying to get funding for a modeling program, and I need to pretend I'm a team player."

"By eating dry beef medallions?"

"By showing up. At least if Dean's there, I won't have to make too much small talk. I hate small talk." She shakes her head at the indignity of it all. "You guys have any plans this weekend?"

"Going to the movies Friday night. Otherwise, nothing."

I steer the conversation to her latest project, then we ramble about novels we've read and what movies look good, and what we're planning for the rest of the summer.

After we part ways, I walk through downtown toward Emerald Street, enjoying the breeze rustling in from the water. I stop and get an iced cappuccino to go from one of the coffeehouses.

Even though I've been at loose ends since we moved to Mirror Lake, I'm glad this is where Dean and I have ended up. It's a medium-sized, Midwestern town with a crystalline lake surrounded by mountains. In winter, the lake freezes, snow and ice fall, and the college kids keep the town busy. In summer, tourists descend on Mirror Lake to swim, hike, kayak, canoe, and camp.

There's a theater festival in the spring, numerous farmer's markets and art fairs. It's a town with good energy and plenty to do—a pretty little egg tucked away in a nest of mountains.

I stop in front of a shop squeezed between a fabric store and a yoga studio. A crooked wooden sign above the door announces *The Happy Booker* in flowing pink script and is embellished with a picture of a voluptuous, leggy blonde holding a stack of books. A bell rings as I enter.

Dusty silence greets me. Shelves line the walls, cluttered with books, and cardboard signs announcing new releases dangle from the ceiling. The front tables are stacked with book displays, and a magazine rack sits near the cash register. A vinyl runner made to resemble yellow bricks snakes toward the back of the store.

"Lions and tigers and bears, oh my!" A gnarled, scary tree leaps out suddenly from behind a bookshelf, wielding spiky, leaf-covered branches.

I shriek and drop my coffee.

"Oh, shit." The tree lowers its branches and stares at me from behind large purple glasses. "Sorry about that."

"No, it's my fault." My heart pounding, I grab some tissues from my satchel and kneel down to sop up the mess. "Shouldn't have brought coffee into a bookstore."

The tree waddles over to the front counter and pokes out a hand, then returns with a roll of paper towels. "You're not here for the Wizard Party, are you?"

"Uh, no." I glance up and encounter a round, pink face peering at me from a knothole in the trunk. Red foam apples dangle from her branches.

She extends the paper towels. "I can't kneel in this thing, or I'd help you."

"No problem." I soak up the coffee as best I can, then pick up the cup and lid. "Where can I…"

The tree waves a branch. An apple plops to the floor. "Behind the register."

"I'll pay for the cleaning." I toss the cup away and wipe my hands. "So… Wizard Party?"

"Yeah." She looks at the clock and sighs, her leaves drooping. "I started advertising, like, last month. Told kids to come dressed as their favorite character from *The Wizard of Oz*. We were going to read a couple of stories, play games, have some treats. You know, a party."

"Sounds great."

"It would've been, if anyone had shown up." She shoves the knothole away from her forehead. She looks so dejected that I can't help feeling sorry for her.

"When's it supposed to start?" I ask.

"It was supposed to start an hour ago. I thought maybe there'd been a misprint on the flyer, but no." She flaps her branches toward the window. "Two o'clock on Thursday, it says. Hey, could you help me out of this thing? I've been in it for over two hours, and I'm about to have heat stroke."

"Sure."

We maneuver around a little while trying to figure out the best method of liberating her from the trunk. Finally she bends forward as far as she can, sticking her branches out. I grab hold of them and pull. A few yanks, a few more curses, both of us pull in opposite directions, and then she pops out like a cork from a bottle.

"Dang." She pushes a mess of damp curls back. "Now I know what a sausage feels like."

I grin and put the costume on a chair. "You're the owner?"

She nods and sticks out a hand. "Allie Lyons."

"I'm Olivia West." I shake her hand. "Everyone calls me Liv."

"Welcome to the Happy Booker, Liv." She takes a water bottle from behind the counter and downs a few gulps. She's cute and petite with floppy red hair and green eyes behind her purple-framed glasses.

"Sorry no one came to your party," I say.

"Yeah, well, I should be used to it by now. No one came to

the Winnie-the-Pooh party either, and I had a real beekeeper here with real bees." She shrugs. "Do you like *The Wizard of Oz*?"

"Not really. The flying monkeys scare the crap out of me."

She chuckles. "Me too. Want to come to the party anyway? I have cupcakes."

"I love cupcakes."

"Come on in, then. Stay on the yellow brick road."

I follow her on the vinyl runner to the children's section at the back of the store. She's got little round tables all set up with matching chairs, a "yellow brick" rug in front of a rocking chair, and another table covered with plates of food.

"Help yourself." She nods toward the food. "Or I'll have to donate it… somewhere."

I take a plate and pile it with a rainbow cupcake, a cookie shaped like a hot-air balloon, and a frosted cake-pop glittering with red sprinkles. To complete this sugar buffet, Allie pours me a cup of lime-green punch.

"Have a seat." She gestures to one of the tables.

"Why'd you decide to be a tree?" I ask, adjusting my rear on the diminutive chair.

"From the Forest of Fighting Trees." Allie sits across from me with another plate. "You know, the apple trees that get mad when Dorothy picks their fruit?"

"Sure, but why a tree?" I peel the paper away from the cupcake. "Why weren't you Dorothy or the witch?"

"Oh, I wanted to save those for the kids, so I picked a costume that was less obvious. I figured we'd have a dozen Dorothys and witches running around."

"Did you advertise over at the library?" I ask. "I volunteer there once a week. They've always got kids' programs going on."

"Yeah, but I think that's the problem. Everyone goes there instead of coming here. I even spent three afternoons last week down by the lake wearing that stupid costume and handing out flyers."

"Maybe no one realized you were supposed to be from *The Wizard of Oz*," I suggest. "They might've thought you were advertising some freakish tree party."

"Maybe." Allie munches on a cookie. "So, anyway, sorry for bitching about it. What can I help you with? Are you looking for a book?"

Although I have concluded my chances of employment here are slim to none, I figure I have nothing to lose. "Actually, I'm looking for a job. I was wondering if you need any help."

"Oh. Business is pretty slow, unfortunately."

"I have a lot of retail experience. I could hold down the fort while you… advertise."

"Not a bad idea." Allie pops the last of the cookie into her mouth and gives me a considering look. "I have been thinking about staying open later on weekends. Try to catch some of the theater and restaurant foot traffic. If you're looking to work random hours, plus weekends, for very little pay, then you've hit the jackpot."

Hardly ideal, but I like Allie Lyons. I like her shabby shop and her scary apple-tree costume and the pink calligraphic sign that's better suited for a questionable massage parlor than a bookstore.

"Great." I push to my feet. "When can I start?"

"Heart, courage, home, or brains?"

"What?"

I hold out the plate of cookies that Allie insisted I take home. They're rectangular sugar cookies frosted with the words *Heart, Brains, Home*, and *Courage*.

I dangle a *Brains* cookie in front of Dean. "I suppose I didn't need to ask."

He takes the cookie and bites into it. "Doesn't this mean I don't have brains?"

"Like I said, I didn't need to ask."

He gives me a swat on the rear, which then turns into a very nice caress. I nibble on a *Courage* cookie and settle in beside him on the sofa. He's supposed to be watching a baseball game, but apparently the butt-pat got him thinking in another direction because he curves his hand around me to fondle my breast.

"Shouldn't you be working?" I ask, shifting around so he can get a better hold on me. "Summer classes end next week."

"Work's all done. Give me a kiss, beauty."

I turn my head and surrender to his warm, sugary mouth. Heat shoots across my skin. He tucks a hand underneath my shirt and flicks the clasp on my bra, then cups the weight of my breast in his palm.

"Oh, wait." I've had the dates of the summer session in my head because I was hoping some jobs might open up if students leave town before the fall semester starts at the end of August. Now something occurs to me, and I ease away from Dean. "Hold on. I need to check…"

I head into the bedroom, pressing a hand to my stomach. As much as I'd like to start stripping naked right away, I don't want to be unpleasantly surprised. I pull down my pants and underwear to check things out. Nothing. Good.

I head back to the living room, then stop. I turn into the kitchen and look at the calendar, do a quick calculation in my head.

My stomach flutters hard.

"Liv?"

"Coming." Tension tightens my spine as I return to the living room. Dean's sprawled on the sofa, looking entirely edible with his stubbly jaw and thick, wavy hair. His T-shirt has ridden up a couple of inches to expose the hard ridges of his stomach. His hand hovers over the button-fly of his jeans.

"Ready?" he asks.

"Um."

He lowers his hand and pushes to sitting. "Um what?"

"I didn't get my period." I rub my palms on my thighs. "Or I... I haven't gotten it, at any rate. Yet."

Something flickers in his eyes, but I can't read what it is.

"How late are you?" he asks.

"A week and a half."

"That's not much."

"I'm pretty regular. I didn't think of it with getting fired and starting the job search again, but when I realized the date..."

We look at each other. The silence is weighty.

"The condoms haven't broken or anything," I finally say.

"They don't have to. And I'm not always wearing one when I come."

"You're not inside me then either."

"I don't necessarily have to be, if it's close enough." He

stands, fastening the top button of his jeans. "I'll run to the drugstore and get a pregnancy test."

"Wouldn't it be too soon to register?"

"Won't hurt to take one." He pulls on his shoes, grabs his keys, and heads out.

I press a hand to my stomach again. We've been careful about condom use. Even during my brief, nausea-inducing attempts to take the pill, Dean wore a condom when we had sex. I told him before we got married that I didn't want to have children. He understood why and has never tried to convince me otherwise.

I pace to the window and stare down at the street. A group of teenagers passes by, laughing as they head down the path toward the lake. A couple with two kids goes into an ice-cream shop. An older man shuffles past, led by a leashed dog.

After about fifteen minutes, the door clicks open. Dean hands me a paper bag. I peer inside at the boxed pregnancy test.

"Says it can detect results six days after a missed period," he says.

"Guess I should go take it, then." I glance at him. Why is his expression so unreadable? "What if it's positive?"

"Then we'll talk." He squeezes my shoulder, then tilts his head toward the bedroom. "Go ahead."

I go into the bathroom and close the door. There are two tests inside the box. I take one out and put the box in the cabinet beneath the sink. My hands shake as I peel a plastic test stick from the foil wrapper and unfold the instructions.

It's pretty straightforward, and because I'm so nervous I need to pee anyway. After I'm done, I cap the stick and put it on the counter.

Three minutes, the instructions say. I try not to look at the results window, but end up staring at it like it's a crystal ball. A faint pink line appears. My heart thuds.

Two lines mean positive.

I keep staring. The single line darkens.

One line. Not two.

My heart is still pounding hard.

"Liv?"

I take a breath and crumple up the empty foil and instructions. After tossing them in the trash, I open the door. "Negative."

Relief flashes across his face. "Good."

Good?

I check the test again. Definitely one line. I throw it in the trash and dust off my hands. "Well, that was something, huh?"

I push past Dean, feeling his gaze on me as I go into the kitchen. I pull a frozen pizza from the freezer and turn on the oven.

"Hey." Dean's hand settles warm and heavy on the back of my neck. "You okay?"

"Fine."

But I'm not entirely sure that I am, and I don't understand why.

I take a long walk through town this morning. Dean's usually the one up at dawn, but the morning after taking the pregnancy test, I wake before him. Can't remember the last time that happened. I dress in sweatpants and tennis shoes, pulling on a fleece jacket as I head downstairs.

I've never gone for a walk when most of the town is still asleep, but I like the stillness, the reddish light of dawn skimming over the lake, the burgeoning chirp of birds. I also feel relatively safe, though I stick to the downtown area where lights shine in a few of the houses, bed-and-breakfasts, and bakeries.

I walk down Avalon, turning onto Emerald and Ruby Streets, and then back around the block to Avalon again. I increase my pace, enjoying the flex of my muscles, the brisk air filling my lungs.

Negative. That's what I was hoping for, right?

I've never wanted kids. I'm not maternal. The shit-storm of my childhood was enough to put me off people in general, so it's a wonder I'm even married.

I'm almost thirty years old, and in my entire life Dean has been the only man I've trusted with bone-deep certainty. He's the only person I've ever really loved. We've built a life together—a lovely, normal, secure life.

I'm happy with just the two of us. I don't want a baby.

I stop and look in the dimly lit window of a baby boutique shop. Cute, overpriced clothes, hats, puzzles, blankets, and a few things I can't quite identify.

I remember a baby I once knew. I haven't thought of her in years. Penny. Round face, long eyelashes, fuzzy tufts of blond hair. I was thirteen and took care of her on occasion when her mother had something to do.

Penny was almost a year old then. She must be sixteen now. Probably driving. I wonder if she's had her first date, what her favorite subject is, if she plays sports or likes to read. I hope she's happy.

I stare at a pink, knitted hat. The memory of Penny clouds over with images too black to be transparent. A cold, icy ball tightens in my throat.

"Liv!" The sound of Dean's voice breaks the still dawn air.

I look up with a start. He's hurrying toward me, his expression dark with concern. A strange fear grabs me suddenly. I run to meet him and fold myself against his strong, warm chest.

"Jesus, Liv." He closes his arms tight around me. His breathing is hard against my ear. "I woke up and you were gone. Your cell was off."

"I forgot to bring it." I pull back to look at him. It takes me a second to process the fact that he was scared. "I went for a walk. What… where did you think I'd gone?"

"I didn't know." Dean lets out his breath and scrapes a hand through his damp, messy hair. "You're never up before seven. I thought you were in the kitchen, but when I got out of the shower…"

"I'm sorry." I put my hand on his chest, feeling the beat of his heart. Unease roils in my stomach. "I didn't mean to worry you."

"Just… next time, tell me, okay?"

I nod, unable to shake the edgy sense of fear surrounding both of us, the stretching reach of old shadows.

Dean wraps his arm around my shoulders as we head home. Once inside, he slides his hand to the back of my head, a slight pressure that turns me toward him. Tension still ripples through him as his lips come down on mine.

I curl my fingers into the front of his shirt and tug him

down harder. His mouth is cold and minty. Heat burns through the morning chill clinging to our clothes.

A sudden, hard rush of longing fills my chest. My eyes sting. I put my hand on his stubbled cheek and part my lips under his. He works the zipper on my jacket and pushes it to the floor, then slides his big hands under my bottom to lift me against him. I fold my arms around him as he goes into the bedroom and lowers me to the bed.

I grab his shirt and yank him down to me.

"Hurry," I gasp.

A burn flares in his eyes. He levers himself over me, planting his hands on either side of my head before descending for another kiss. I arch upward to meet him and wrap my legs around his hips.

He is the one who once rescued me from bitter isolation. I need him to defeat it again now.

I pull his lower lip between my teeth, drive my hands into his thick hair. He matches my swift urgency without hesitation, tugging off my shirt and bra, then pulling my sweatpants and panties off and dropping them to the floor.

He's hard already. I can feel his cock pressing against me beneath his jeans. A tremble quakes through me, centering in the throb of my heart. Dean's breath skims over my neck, his tongue dipping into the hollow of my throat as he slides a hand up my inner thigh and into my cleft.

"Open," he whispers, brushing his mouth across mine.

I part my legs to give him access and fist my hands in his shirt. He strokes a path over my folds, his adept touch wrenching a gasp from my throat. I twist underneath him, tears blurring my vision, heat surging across my skin. When his forefinger slides into my body, I push upward and grasp his wrist to keep him inside me.

He's saying something, a steady stream of murmurs in my ear, but I can't make out his words past the sound of my heartbeat. He circles his thumb around my clit, pressing against a spot he knows is especially sensitive.

My nerves stretch hard, a rubber band close to snapping. I fumble for the button-fly of his jeans. My hands shake.

"Dean."

"Easy, beauty…" He presses his mouth to the tears that have slipped from the corners of my eyes and down my temples. His breath rasps against my ear. "Come first, and then I'll fuck you."

A wave of heat pours over me. I turn toward him, and our mouths collide hot and wet. Our arrested lust and the strain of the previous night suddenly explode into crazed need. He splays his fingers over my clit and with one stroke, I come hard, bucking up against him and crying out his name.

When the sensations ebb, he moves away just long enough to take off his clothes before descending over me, his body hard and straining with urgency. Gasping, I wind my arms around him, crushing my breasts against his chest, pushing my tongue into his mouth.

His cock throbs against my thigh, and I writhe around to try and nudge him into the right position, aching to feel him immersed deep inside me.

"Wait." He pulls back to grab a condom from the bedside table. Then he slides his hand down my side and kneels between my legs. His eyes smolder as he strokes his gaze over my damp, naked body, lingering on the swells of my breasts and taut nipples. "You're so damn sexy, Liv."

Renewed arousal flares in my blood at the desire-thick tone of his voice, the heat in his expression. Dean presses his hands to my knees to urge them farther apart, running his finger over my folds. He rolls the condom on before putting the swollen head of his erection against me, then grabs my hips and pulls me onto his shaft.

"Oh, God, Dean..." It's a delicious shock, the sudden pulse of his long, hard length filling me. I tighten around him the instant he starts to thrust, and then everything disappears in the face of his heavy, repeated plunges, his eyes still raking my body, his hands gripping the undersides of my thighs.

I want it to last forever. I want him slamming into me hard and fast, want my body rolling under the force of our fucking. I splay a hand over my breasts and push upward to match his movements.

Tension spools inside me, a thread pulled too tight, and then convulsions tremble through me from head to toe all over again. My inner muscles clench around his cock. Dean braces his hands on the bed, sweat trickling down his jaw.

"Liv." His voice is strained, taut.

"Wait. I want to..."

Gasping, still shuddering, I push upward as his thickness slides out of me and he shoves to his feet. I close my fingers around his shaft and roll the condom off, then wiggle to the edge of the bed and open my mouth.

"Ah, fuck..." With a groan, he grasps the sides of my head and nudges his cock past my lips.

My chest heaves. I lean forward, closing my eyes and putting my hands on his hips. He's big, and I have to remind myself to breathe slowly as I take him in. The salty taste of him fills me. His grip on my head tightens as I press my tongue to the vein throbbing on the underside of his shaft.

For a moment, he stills. Above me, his breath saws through the air and restraint cords his muscles. He fists his fingers in my hair. I slide my hands to grip his buttocks and encourage him to move. Then he does, gently at first, then faster.

Even in the heat of lust, he's careful not to thrust too deep. I draw back to lick the hard knob and slacken my jaw, my mind filling with images of how we must look, sweaty and disheveled with him fucking my open mouth.

When he presses the sides of my head in warning, I pull back at the same time he does. I dart a quick glance at him, my blood swimming with heat at the sight of his raw, lust-filled expression and burning eyes.

I grasp his shaft again, sleek, pulsing, and begin to stroke. The air vibrates with his groan as he creams over my breasts, warm liquid dripping down my cleavage and tight nipples.

"God, Dean, that's so hot..." I shudder, pressing my thighs together as the sight elicits a surge of excitement.

I fall back onto the bed and cup my breasts, smoothing my hands over them until my skin is glossy with his release. Dean sinks onto the bed beside me and reaches out to rub my abdomen. Our bodies ease into relaxation, our breath gradually slowing.

I roll to my side, loving the scent of him on my skin, the delicious soreness between my legs—evidence of his complete possession.

He pulls me closer. I slide against him, my bare leg falling between his as I press my face into his shoulder and run my hand over his damp chest.

"Don't leave, beauty." His voice is a rough whisper.

"Never."

CHAPTER THREE

AUGUST 16

"*O*kay, so that's pretty much it." Allie chews on a pen and slams the cash register drawer closed. "I get shipments about once a week, but they vary in size. Invoices go in that basket over there. I run a weekly ad for a fifteen-percent discount on one item, so if someone comes in with one, give me a holler and I'll show you how to run it through. Any questions?"

"Nope."

"I'm not going to extend my weekend hours just yet because I've got a... thing this Saturday."

"A handsome thing?" I ask.

Her face gets pink, but she returns my smile. "Brent.

He's an assistant manager over at the Sugarloaf Hotel. He's very cute."

"Nice. Where's he taking you?"

"We're going on that dinner boat out on the lake. Ever been?"

"No, but I heard it's great, especially at sunset."

"It's my first date with Brent, but if things work out maybe we could double sometime," Allie suggests. "It would be fun." She glances at my left hand, where I wear a platinum wedding ring. "I mean, if you're…"

"I'm married," I say, "but my husband occasionally likes to have fun."

"Occasionally, huh?" Dean's deep voice rumbles across the bookstore.

Allie and I both look up to see him strolling toward us, carrying a paper tray with two covered cups from a coffee joint.

He's in full-professor mode, wearing a gray suit that perfectly sheathes his muscular body. His hair is brushed away from his forehead, framing his strong, clean-shaven features, and his brown eyes are creased with amusement.

I can feel the awe radiating from Allie as he approaches, and frankly I get a little tingly myself. The man not only looks gorgeous, he has a commanding presence that exudes both authority and sex appeal.

He sets the tray on the counter and addresses Allie.

"More than occasionally," he assures her, "do I like to have fun."

She smiles. "I don't doubt it."

He extends a hand. "Dean West."

"Allie Lyons. Welcome to the Happy Booker."

"I brought you both coffee, but had to guess what you'd

like." He pulls a cup out and hands it to her. "Two mochas with whipped cream."

"Perfect." Allie leans toward me and announces in a stage whisper, "I love him."

I grin at Dean. "He's okay."

He winks at me and hands me the second cup. "You're here all day?"

"No, just for the morning so Allie can show me the ropes. I'm volunteering at the library this afternoon. I'll pick up something for dinner on the way home."

"Call if you need me." Dean glances around the area in front of the cash register and buys two magazines, a bar of gourmet chocolate, and a hardcover history of the Civil War.

After handing him the bag, Allie cranes her neck to watch him leave. I do too because the back of Dean is as appealing a sight as the front of him.

"I mean it," Allie says. "I love him. Where'd you meet?"

"Madison. I was going to the UW." I twist my wedding ring around on my finger. "He's a professor at King's. Medieval Studies."

"No kidding? Like romances of knights in armor and courtly love and all that? Wow." She gives a dreamy sigh.

I decide not to burst her bubble by explaining that Dean is more interested in the concentric fortification of a castle. There was a time, however, when romances of knights captured his imagination. And courtly love… he is quite the expert on that.

I rub my arms against a shudder, remembering our hot encounter last weekend. Another tingle sweeps through me, and I'm already anticipating getting home to him tonight.

I started my period two days after I took the test, so I'm

definitely not pregnant. And even though I've been unsettled by the pregnancy scare (why is it called a *scare*?), my new job and Dean's work routine have settled things back to normal.

I think.

When Allie disappears into the backroom with instructions to "holler" if I need help, I make my way to the health section. Two shelves are filled with books about pregnancy and birth, while the shelf below is dedicated to child-rearing. I leaf through a couple of the *I Want to Get Pregnant* and *I Am Pregnant—Now What?* titles.

Then with a mutter of irritation, I push the books back onto the shelf and return to the front counter.

"A Miss Spider tea party!" Allie bounds out of the backroom, shoving her glasses up the bridge of her nose. "Isn't that a great idea? The kids can come dressed as their favorite insect and we can serve juice in tea cups and, like, bee-shaped cookies and gummy worms. Oh, and we can get some of that Halloween cobweb stuff for decorations."

"Do you have kids, Allie?" I ask.

The suddenness of the question makes her stop. "Kids? No, not yet. Why?"

"Just curious. You're really good at all this kids' stuff."

"Oh, yeah, I love thinking up things like this. My mom and I always had these elaborate birthday parties when I was growing up. My favorite was our *Alice in Wonderland* party when I turned ten. We had little cups with 'Drink Me' on them and a Red Queen cake. We played croquet, of course, and my uncle dressed up as the Mad Hatter. My dad even built this rabbit hole out of plywood and shrubbery, and the kids had to go through it to get to the party in the backyard."

"Sounds nice." It sounded more than nice. It sounded like a freaking Disney movie.

The memory of my own tenth birthday stabs the back of my head. I suppress a tide of nausea and focus on straightening the piles of bookmarks on the counter.

"Do you and Dean have kids?" Allie asks.

"No." I'm not sure whether I should add *not yet*. "No kids."

"Pity. You really need to ensure the propagation of your gene pool."

Although she's teasing, I think about what she said for the rest of the afternoon. Maybe that's all it is, this weird preoccupation I have now. Maybe I just have a sudden urge to propagate Dean's and my lineage.

When I get home, I set the table for dinner and divide portions of a store-bought roasted chicken and a green salad from the deli.

Dean comes home around seven and drops his briefcase and keys on the counter. He sheds his suit jacket, loosens his tie, and drags a hand through his hair.

He's got that rumpled, *"I have been thinking very, very hard about something esoteric"* look to him. It's a look he wears extremely well.

As self-possessed as he is, when he's tired from working too hard, his whole demeanor softens with vulnerability... which makes me want to tuck him right beneath my heart and hold on tight.

The way he has always done with me.

He crosses to the kitchen and curves one arm around me, pressing a warm kiss to my temple. He pulls a glass from the cupboard and pours a couple fingers of scotch—his one vice, and only when he's beat.

"How was your day?" I ask.

"Long. Yours? Bookstore job was good?"

I nod. "I like Allie a lot, despite the massive crush she has on my husband."

"A crush, huh? She has good taste." He winks at me and tilts his head back to take a drink. I watch the column of his throat as he swallows, the ripple of scotch sliding to his chest.

"She does, indeed," I murmur.

Heat simmers through me, though I tamp it down because Dean and I need to talk first. I occupy myself with cleaning the living room and give him an hour or so to wind down before we have dinner.

As I spoon out a portion of seasoned rice, I glance across the table at him. "So I gave Dr. Nolan a call."

A frown creases his forehead. "About what?"

"My period being late. Just because I'm usually so regular."

"Did she think it was a reason for concern?"

"No. She said to keep track of my cycles and let her know if the irregularity continues. She said she could put me on birth control pills to regulate them, if it becomes an issue."

"The pills made you sick, remember?"

"Yeah, well, I… I was wondering if maybe you wanted to give it a go without any birth control at all."

That didn't come out quite the way I'd expected.

My heart is pounding hard as Dean looks up. That shutter descends over his face again, like a transparent shield that allows me to look at him without really *seeing* him. My insides twist.

"You want to try and have a baby?" he asks.

I haven't even explicitly asked myself that question yet. I poke at a grain of rice.

"Liv."

"I don't know," I admit.

"If you don't want to use birth control, you *should* know."

Of course he's right. Silence stretches taut between us.

"Liv." Dean reaches across the table and tilts my head up to look at him. "You told me before we got married that you didn't want children."

"That means I can't change my mind?"

"Have you?"

"I don't know." For some inexplicable reason, tears spring to my eyes. I push away from the table and stalk to the living room, tension coiling through me. "What if I did?"

"Then we'd have a lot to discuss." Dean follows me and stops in the doorway, his gaze level. "Is this all because your period was late?"

"It's not *all* because of that."

"Then what?"

"I just want to talk about it." I turn to face him. "Haven't you thought this might be a good time to consider starting a family?"

"No, because we'd never intended to have children."

"But we've been married for three years, we're settled here for the foreseeable future, you're financially secure, you have a tenure-track job, and I—"

My voice breaks like a dry twig. I… *what?*

"You what?" Dean asks.

His question is low and quiet. I look at the floor.

I'd be a good mother? My doubts about my abilities are just one of the reasons I've never wanted children. I spent most of my own childhood yielding to my beautiful, self-centered mother, who was anything but nurturing.

"I was just thinking about it," I mutter.

"Because you're looking for something to do?"

I'm so shocked by this question that I can only stare at him. I can't even speak. He continues looking at me, and worse than the actual words is the fact that he doesn't try to apologize or take the question back—not that that would do any good.

"I'm…" My throat tightens. I force the words past the constriction. "That's what you think?"

"I'm asking if that's what you think."

"No! No, of course not." I can't stop the rush of tears, the ache spreading through my entire being. "God, Dean, you think I brought up the idea of a baby just to give me something to *do*? What the hell?"

"You've never mentioned it before, Liv," he says gently, but with annoying reason. "And I know you've been at loose ends, that you—"

"So I must think of a baby as a *hobby*? Something to pass the time in between soap operas and grocery shopping?" Anger erupts in me and I stride across the room to shove him in the chest. "I might not have an illustrious academic career, but I'm not an airhead, dammit. I've been thinking about a baby because I fucking love you and I thought we had a good life, and it'd be something we could go through, you know, together—"

"Liv, you don't *go through* having a baby. There's no end to it."

"I meant…" *What the hell did I mean?*

I take a breath. "Look, we've *gone through* a lot already, right? You and I? But we're happy now. Secure. Isn't this the next logical step?"

Dean shakes his head. "Liv, I don't think of having a baby as a step in some process. A baby would change everything, change *us*, forever. If that's what you want, then yes, we need to talk. But stopping birth control and leaving things up to chance is a lousy way of going about it."

Of course he's right again. That makes it no easier for me to contend with this sudden tangle of emotions.

"Liv, you need to be sure about what you want and why you want it," Dean says, his voice softening as he approaches me. "But there's no hurry. The timing's bad anyway."

"Why is the timing bad?"

"I just started this job."

"Almost two years ago."

"Yeah, but I'm spearheading a whole new program with half-a-dozen other departments," he says. "I'm organizing an international conference, I've got a book deadline, classes, journal editing. It's a lot of work."

"It's not going to get easier, Dean," I say, "if that's what you think has to happen before we even consider having a baby. We're settled here, right?"

"If the establishment of the Medieval Studies program goes well," he replies. "If I'm not offered something better some-where else. If I get tenure."

"So we just put the idea on hold until you know the answers to all those *ifs*? That could take years."

"It won't take years." He brushes my hair back from my forehead.

"Then how long?"

"I don't know."

That is not a phrase Professor Dean West often uses.

For a minute, we just look at each other. And then, because it seems like an earthquake is starting to tremble beneath our feet, I lean my forehead against his chest and spread my hand out to feel his heartbeat.

Ugly thoughts pop and blister in the back of my mind. A shudder splits my heart. I try to breathe. Dean tightens his arms hard around me.

"Okay?" he asks.

The word *fine* sticks in my throat. This time, I can't respond.

CHAPTER FOUR

AUGUST 20

*T*he promise of autumn is in the air. Breezes sweep from the surface of the lake, trees rustle, and ducks waddle along the beaches. The tourists are leaving town, and university students bustle around with their backpacks and laptops. Dean is mired in planning fall semester classes, advising, department meetings, committees. We talk, but not about anything important. Not about us.

I've agreed to work three days a week at the Happy Booker, and I volunteer for a few hours at the public library and the Mirror Lake Historical Museum. After an afternoon spent organizing an exhibition on colonial currency, I stop at a coffeehouse for a mocha. The scent of roasting coffee beans makes me think of my first few months with Dean.

I was twenty-four years old and had been accepted to the University of Wisconsin-Madison as a transfer student. I'd spent the previous three years in rural Wisconsin, working at a clothing store and taking night courses at a community college to earn transfer credits.

When my application was accepted at the UW, I'd packed up everything I owned and moved to Madison to start what I hoped would be a new life. The day I registered for classes, a woman at the registrar's office gave me a hard time about the transferability of my community college work.

I was upset, trying not to cry while pleading with Mrs. Russell to work out a solution.

"There must be something we can do," I said.

"Miss Winter, the courses you took won't cover the requirements," she informed me.

"But I wouldn't have taken them otherwise. If I can't get them to transfer, it puts me behind an entire semester."

"Look." Mrs. Russell swept the papers into a stack and pushed them toward me. "It's all in the catalog, if you have questions. We can't retroactively allow the credits to transfer."

"I'm not asking you to do it retroactively!" I said. "This is my first semester here, and I'm trying to get my courses in order. If I have to take another foreign language translation class, then I'm already behind. And those classes are full already anyway."

"The courses you took aren't equivalent to the requirements for your academic program." Mrs. Russell glanced pointedly at the line of students behind me. "I'm afraid I can't help you."

I blinked back tears, refusing to budge. "Why would they have told me the credits would transfer if they're not equivalent?"

Then a tall, handsome man approached from another section of the office, his dark eyes fixed on me, his deep voice rolling over my skin like a wave of heat on a cold winter night.

"Can I help with this?" he asked.

My breath stopped in my throat. The sight of him jolted something loose inside me, and for an instant I could only stare at him, struck by the sharp, masculine planes of his face, the steadiness of his expression, his aura of complete control and self-possession.

He was wearing black trousers and a navy blue shirt open at the collar to reveal a V of taut, tanned skin. His hair shone under the fluorescent lights, and I was seized by a sudden urge to tunnel my fingers through the strands to see if they felt as thick and soft as they looked.

Unnerved, I jerked my attention back to Mrs. Russell, who was explaining the situation to him. She called him "Dr. West." Likely a professor, then. I wondered what he taught.

Dr. West listened patiently, glancing at me every so often. "What classes are you trying to take?" he asked me.

"She's a library sciences major, and she has to register for foreign lit translation and intro to biology," Mrs. Russell said.

"But I shouldn't have to take those because my credits should transfer," I persisted.

"Make an appointment with a guidance counselor, Miss Winter," Mrs. Russell suggested. "That's all I can tell you."

"By the time I do that, classes will already have started."

"You have a couple of weeks yet to finalize your courses," she continued. "I'm sure they'll help you sort this out."

I knew by the tone of Mrs. Russell's voice that she wasn't going to give in, and the hopelessness of the situation crashed over me.

"The professors can—" Dr. West started.

"Never mind." Because I didn't want to start crying in front of *him*, I grabbed my bag and left the office.

Halfway down the sidewalk, my vision blurry with tears, I tripped on an uneven piece of concrete and went sprawling onto my hands and knees. My open satchel thumped onto the ground, papers spilling out.

"Are you okay?" Then he was there, crouching beside me to pick up the papers before the wind caught them. He reached out a hand but stopped an inch from my arm, his fingers brushing the sleeve of my gray sweatshirt.

"I… I'm okay," I said.

He could have touched me. He was close. Close enough that I caught a whiff of him, a clean, soapy smell that settled in my blood and loosened the knot of frustration stuck in my throat. Close enough that I noticed the size of his hands, his long fingers and the dark hairs dusting his forearm where his sleeve inched up.

Awareness shot through me. I dusted the grit from my palms and straightened. He stood between me and the street, waiting in silence for me to collect my composure. A few people passed behind me, forcing me a few steps toward him.

He held out my satchel, his gaze moving over me, eliciting a surge of heat. I pushed strands of hair away from my face and looked at him. My heart hammered, my chest pooling with warmth. I was shaken all over again by the way my body reacted to him, with this hot pull of attraction I had never experienced before.

Not for any man. Ever.

"Thank you." I took my satchel from him and straightened the papers. All I had to do now was turn and walk away.

I didn't. He was still looking at me, his hands in his pockets, his hair ruffled by the breeze.

"Are you a professor here?" I asked.

He was big. Not all bulky and heavy, but tall with broad shoulders, long legs, and that air of self-control that made him seem in total command. The wind flattened his shirt over his muscular chest, and I had a sudden image of folding myself against that chest and feeling his arms close around me. Safe. Protected.

Nothing to fear. Not from him.

I stepped back, not having felt this way before and not knowing where it was all coming from.

Why him? Why now?

"I'm a visiting professor for the year," he said. "Medieval history."

He was a medieval history professor. For whatever reason —the sheer dorkiness of the field?—this admission eased some of my tension.

"Oh." I hitched the satchel over my shoulder and folded my arms across my breasts. "Well, thanks for your help back at the registrar's."

"The professors of whatever classes you need to take can approve your transfer credits," he said. "You don't need to go through the registrar's office first. Get the course syllabus and bibliography from your previous college, and bring them to the professors to see if it fits their curriculum. If it covers the same ground, they should approve the transfer as a direct course equivalent."

"Why didn't Mrs. Russell tell me that?"

"She probably didn't know. Professors have a lot of power."

I almost smiled. "Even medieval history professors?"

"Especially medieval history professors," he assured me.

"Knights on horseback and all that?"

A responding smile tugged at his mouth. "And damsels in distress."

My heart constricted. *Ah, fairy tales.*

"Hey, Professor West!" A young man jogged up to him. "I heard you were teaching here this year. I was at Harvard when you were a grad student. Tom Powell."

The kid stuck out a hand. Professor West shook it and made a few appropriate comments. I backed up a step, not wanting to leave him and yet not knowing how to stay.

The other guy kept talking. Something about a paper he was working on.

Professor West glanced at me. I had the sense he was about to make an excuse, extract himself from the conversation so that he could turn back to me.

So we could finish what we'd started.

I retreated another step, staring at the sunlight glinting off his hair, the sharp edges of his profile, the muscles of his neck, and the confidence of his stance.

Professor West was beautiful. He was beautiful and warm and wanted to help a distraught girl in a ragged gray sweatshirt. Even though his eyes seared me like a caress he hadn't made a move to touch me or invade my space. If anything, he seemed to restrain himself from doing so.

If I could trust myself with anyone, I thought, it might be him.

Before he looked at me again with those penetrating eyes, before I could think of an excuse to stay, I surrendered to my fear and hurried away. I had to force myself not to look back.

I thought I'd never see him again. If I'd been another kind of woman, I could have sought him out, taken one of his courses, dropped by his office.

But I wasn't the kind of woman who did things like that. I couldn't be, even if I'd wanted to. I'd worked hard to get into the UW, and I had a very strict schedule of classes I needed to take to graduate.

I had a part-scholarship and a job at a coffeehouse on State Street, a tiny one-bedroom apartment, and an unwavering notion that graduation would put me on a path toward something *normal*.

While I nourished a secret hope of one day finding a man who would help rid me of my inhibitions, I had to focus on other things first. I'd spent years figuring out what I needed to do, and I couldn't deviate from that course now that I was finally accomplishing something. Seeking out a medieval history professor who made my heart race certainly wasn't part of my plan.

Two weeks after our encounter on the sidewalk, the semester started. I managed to get my transfer credits approved by appealing to the professors of two courses. I immersed myself in classes on digital communication, international studies, database management, and American literature.

When I wasn't in class or at the library, I studied or worked. I forgot all about Professor West—or tried to tell myself I had.

Until he walked into Jitter Beans one morning.

I was helping another customer, answering a question about the difference between a cappuccino and a caffe latte.

"So a cappuccino has a stronger coffee flavor?" the guy asked, peering at me intently.

"That's correct." I looked over his shoulder to check how many other customers were waiting.

My gaze collided with Professor West's.

I drew in a sharp breath, my pulse thudding a stream of heat through my blood. How had I not known the instant he stepped inside?

I couldn't stop staring at him, tracking my gaze over his ruffled, dark brown hair, the angles of his features, the curve of his beautiful mouth. He was all-professor in a tailored suit and a perfectly knotted tie, his briefcase in hand.

A smile crinkled his eyes as he looked at me, then he tilted his head slightly toward the guy I was supposed to be helping.

"Oh." I swung my attention back to the customer, who looked a little annoyed at having been dismissed. "Sorry, what?" I said.

"I asked if you could make the latte with an extra shot of espresso," he repeated.

"Sure." My hands trembled as I rang up the order and conveyed it to the girl who was making the drinks. "It'll be ready in a sec."

The guy took ten years to get out his wallet and pay for

the latte. By the time Professor West approached the counter, my stomach was taut with nerves.

"Um…" I gripped the edge of the counter. "Hi."

Amusement flashed in his expression. "Hi."

"Can I help you?" I tried to muster a professional tone, aware of my coworkers bustling around behind me, the hum of conversation from other customers.

"Medium coffee, please." He slid a hand into his pocket. "For here."

I turned to grab a cup and pour the coffee. "Room for cream in your coffee, sir?"

"No, thanks. Did you get everything straightened out with the registrar?"

I looked at him in surprise, wondering why he cared. "Yes, I did what you suggested. A couple of professors filled out the right forms indicating I'd already covered the curriculum."

"Good."

"Thanks for the help… Professor West."

"Dean."

I put the cup on the counter, painfully aware of the beat of my heart, fast as a hummingbird's wings. "Dean?"

"My name. Dean West."

"Oh. I'm—"

"Olivia," he said.

The sound of my name in his deep voice rolled through me like a breaking cloud.

"How did you know?" I asked.

"I saw your name on the papers at the registrar's office." He handed me a couple of dollars. "I remembered it. Olivia R. Winter."

I rang up the order and counted out his change. "Why did you remember my name?"

"Actually…" He lifted the cup and turned to the tables. "I remembered *you*."

I stared after him as he sat at a table beside the window and opened a newspaper. We didn't speak again that day, but I saw him leave and gave him a little wave of farewell. I had the instinctive sense he would come back. I wanted him to.

And he did. He always ordered a medium coffee, no room for cream, and sometimes a muffin. It was my favorite time of year—early September with crisp, clean air and warm colors and a touch of fall.

I couldn't help it. Every time I went to work, I hoped I'd see him. I didn't want to hope for it, didn't think anything could come of it, but a thousand happy sparks twirled through me whenever he came into Jitter Beans.

I liked everything about him—his masculine features and thick-lashed eyes, his jaw sometimes dusted with a hint of stubble. I liked his dark hair, his tall, strong body, his smile, and the twinkle that shone in his eyes when he looked at me.

I started to welcome the feelings he aroused in me, all so utterly different from the narrow practicality that had driven my life for years. One morning he pushed a folded piece of paper across the counter along with his dollar bills.

Half-expecting it to be his phone number, I opened the paper. There was a library call number written in scrawled, masculine handwriting: PR9199.3 R5115 Y68.

I looked at Dean in confusion.

"Memorial Library," was all he said before taking his coffee and going to his usual table by the window.

I tucked the paper safely into my pocket. As soon as my shift ended, I hurried down State Street to the massive campus library. I took the stairs to the second floor and checked the numbers on the ends of the stacks that stood like sentries throughout the floor.

PR9199.3 R5115 Y68. I ran my finger along the rows of dusty, old books before I came to the correct volume. My heart thumped as I pulled it off the shelf and looked at the title.

Your Mouth Is Lovely.

I smiled.

When Dean walked into Jitter Beans the next day, I pulled the book from beneath the counter and handed it to him. I'd stuck a Post-It on the front with another call number: Aston 552.

"Cooperative Children's Book Center," I said. "What can I get for you, sir?"

"Medium coffee, please." He put the book under his arm. "No room for cream."

He returned two days later and held up a children's picture book titled *A Rock Is Lively.* I grinned.

His eyes twinkled. "Lots of stuff buried beneath the surface of a rock, the book says. Very turbulent. Molten, even."

"The book is right."

Our gazes met. A bolt of energy arced between us, one that made my heart hum with warmth and excitement.

"Medium coffee, no cream?" I asked, turning to the dispenser.

I pushed his cup across the counter at the same moment

that he reached for it. Our fingers met, and a shiver of aware-ness jolted clear up my arm.

I jerked my hand back, my breath shortening. "Sorry."

"It's okay." His eyebrows drew together, faintly puzzled by my reaction.

My face grew hot. *Now he must think you're a freak.*

I wiped my damp palms on my apron and tried to regain my equilibrium. "We... uh, we have some fresh scones in."

"No, thanks." He continued looking at me, one hand curved around the cup, a frown tugging at his mouth.

Yeah. You should probably stay away from me, Professor West.

"Olivia, I'm giving a lecture at the Chazen Museum on Friday night," he said. "I'd like it if you'd come. We can go somewhere afterward."

I blinked. "Are you asking me out?"

The bluntness of the question made him smile. "I am."

"Oh." *Oh!*

He waited. I flushed. Panic fluttered in my chest.

"I don't... I don't really date," I stammered. "In fact, I don't date at all."

"Okay." He scratched his chin. "Well, we don't have to think of it as a date, if you don't want to. We can just go out."

The tight knot of dismay inside me loosened a little. I badly wanted to spend time alone with him, this medieval history professor who was luring me with library call numbers.

"Isn't us going out against university policy?" I asked. "Since you're a professor?"

A shadow eclipsed his expression for an instant, as if I'd reminded him of inviolable rules. Then I got worried he would retract the invitation.

What the hell is wrong with me?

"It's not against policy if you're not a student of mine," he said. "But if you'd rather not—"

"No, that's not it," I interrupted. "I just… I was just making sure."

"Do you plan to take any medieval history classes?" he asked.

"Actually, I plan to stay far away from the medieval history department," I admitted.

"Good idea." He paused. "So what do you think?"

I took a breath. *For God's sake, Liv. It's a lecture and maybe coffee afterward. That's it.*

"Okay," I finally said. "Friday night."

"Good. The lecture starts at seven."

"What's it about?" I asked.

"Monastic architecture and sarcophagi." He lifted his cup in a salute and winked at me. "Prepare to be dazzled."

I already am, I thought as I watched him walk away.

I arrived at the Chazen Museum an hour before the lecture and spent the extra time looking at the exhibits. I was still a little nervous about the evening, but in a good way. After two days of wrestling with the whole issue, I'd firmly told myself that I liked Professor Dean West and I was looking forward to seeing him outside of Jitter Beans. It was exactly the kind of nice, normal evening that I wanted.

A large crowd filled the lecture hall of the museum, the buzz of conversation fading as a woman came out to announce the other museum events and introduce Professor West. I was sitting in the fifth row, and my heart gave a little leap when he approached the podium and began speaking.

Warm and rich, Dean's voice flowed over the audience and seemed to settle in the core of my being. I welcomed the opportunity to stare at him without reservation, drinking in the sight of him in a crisp, navy suit and striped tie, his hair burnished by the lights.

I remember him talking about a medieval church in France, the structure of a town, Roman sculptures, but more than the subject matter I was enraptured by the sound of his deep voice, the authoritative way he spoke and discussed the images on the screen behind him. I loved the gracious way he answered questions and listened to people's comments. I loved that he knew so much.

There was a reception after the lecture was over, and people kept vying for the distinguished professor's attention. I drank a glass of cherry-flavored mineral water and ate about twenty grapes before I finally found a chance, and worked up my courage, to approach him.

He gave me an easy smile, one that made my heart flutter. I had *such* a crush on him.

"Hello, Olivia," he said. "I'm glad you came."

"So am I. It was a really interesting lecture."

"Thanks." He curled his hand beneath my elbow in a gesture that seemed utterly natural. I felt the warmth of his palm through my sleeve, and this time I didn't pull away. I didn't want to.

"I need to go and thank the curators," Dean said, his voice a low rumble over my skin. "Then if you're free, we can go somewhere. Will you wait for me?"

I nodded. I thought he might be the only man I would ever wait for.

After ten minutes, he returned and we went to get our coats from the coatroom. Dean held out my coat while I slipped into it.

I reached back to tug my hair from the collar, but he got there first. His fingers brushed the back of my neck as he eased my ponytail free of the coat. A waterfall of shivers ran down my spine, and my breath caught in my throat.

"Thanks." I quickly stepped away from him, ducking my head as I fastened the buttons.

"Sure." A slight tension ran through his voice.

Shit. I turned back to him and forced a smile. "So where should we go?"

"There's a place over by the Capitol where we can get a drink or something to eat," he suggested, hitching up the collar of his coat. "We can walk, if you don't mind that it's a little cold."

"I don't mind."

He seemed to make a conscious effort not to touch me as we left the museum. I felt like I should apologize, knowing I was sending him mixed signals, but I didn't know how to without getting into treacherous waters.

We walked the length of State Street to a restaurant called The White Rose situated in a corner of the square. He held open the door of the restaurant for me, then spoke to the hostess. She smiled at him and led us past a crowd of waiting customers to a secluded, linen-covered table in the corner.

"How'd you manage that?" I asked as Dean pulled my chair out for me.

"Magic."

I didn't doubt it. One look from him probably turned the hostess into a puddle of goo.

"Actually…" He flashed me a grin. "Reservation."

Nice that he'd planned in advance where we would go. Made me feel like he'd been thinking about me.

The waiter handed us leather-covered menus. Shadows and candlelight cascaded over the intimate tables, voices rose in a low hum, silver clinked against china plates.

I studied Dean as he looked at his menu. The flame of the candle cast warm, dancing light over his face, illuminated the flecks of gold in his chocolate-brown eyes. The perfect, smooth knot of his tie nestled at the hollow of his throat. A swath of hair tumbled over his forehead. I curled my fingers into my palm against the urge to brush it back, to feel the sweep of the thick strands beneath my hand.

Was he the one?

I had no illusions of great love and romance. I never had. My mother's relationships with men were restless and sometimes violent. I'd learned early on that it was easier not to count on anyone.

But during the past few years, I'd come to certain conclusions about myself and relationships. I wanted to learn how to trust a man. I wanted to know what true, physical pleasure felt like. I wanted to find the courage to be vulnerable on my own terms, as my own choice.

No, I hadn't expected to find *that* man anytime soon, but I had an unnerving feeling he might be sitting across from me now.

Dean looked up and caught me staring. His gaze held mine. Electricity crackled in the air between us, sparking red and blue. Heat flooded my cheeks.

"Sorry," I whispered.

Confusion creased his forehead. "For what?"

"For being... weird."

His smile flashed. "I happen to like weird."

"Well, then, you hit the jackpot with me," I muttered.

"I know."

I glanced at him, arrested by the warmth of his gaze, my blush deepening. A streamer of pleasure mixed with trepidation wound through me.

He nodded toward the menu. "Are you hungry?"

"Very. The grapes I ate at the reception weren't exactly filling."

We both ordered spice-crusted salmon with wild rice, and the waiter sent over a sommelier to discuss the wine choices. Dean seemed to know what he was talking about, and they eventually decided that some certain vintage of pinot noir would go well with our meals.

"Where are you from?" I asked when our food arrived.

"Originally California. San Jose area. My parents and sister still live out there."

"You have one sister?"

"And a brother." He speared a slice of fish with his fork, his mouth tightening. "I don't know where he is." He shook his head as if to dismiss the thought. "You?"

"No brothers or sisters."

"Where did you grow up?"

I hated that question. I reached for my wineglass in an attempt to stall my answer. "Oh, all over," I finally said. "We traveled a lot."

"Was your dad in the military?"

"No. My parents split up when I was seven." I concentrated

on forking up a portion of rice, not wanting to know if he was looking at me with pity.

"And what brought you to Madison?" he asked, almost as if he sensed I didn't want to go down the path of my childhood.

"I'd been wanting to attend the university," I explained, "but couldn't afford the full tuition. My aunt lives up in Pepin County, so I moved to a nearby town and went to a community college while saving my money. Then I got a part-scholarship so I could go to the UW. If everything goes as planned, I should graduate in two years."

He looked at me, something indefinable passing across his expression. "That's very admirable."

I smiled wryly. "It's why I'm an old undergrad. I didn't enroll in community college until I was twenty-one, then I took classes part-time for a few years because I had to work."

"You're not old."

"You probably had a master's degree by the time you were twenty-four." I reached for my wine again. "Took me a while to get here."

"But you did."

"I did."

We ate in silence for a few minutes, casting occasional glances at each other, the air sparking with heat whenever our eyes met. I liked the way he ate, his movements sharp and precise. I watched the muscles of his throat as he swallowed, the way his hand curled around his fork. The sight of his mouth closing around the rim of his glass sent a rush of arousal through me.

I'd never felt this way before. About anyone.

"So what exactly is it you teach, Professor West?" I asked.

"Mostly medieval archeology and architecture, though that ties into other things. Town planning, political structures, religion. I'm going to France over winter break to do some work on the architecture of Sainte-Chapelle."

I should have been intimidated by the illustriousness of his work, but he was so matter-of-fact about it that any potential breach between us—a renowned professor and a girl struggling to get a bachelor's degree—faded into insignificance. And I loved listening to him talk, his smooth baritone voice thudding right up against the walls of my heart.

After dinner, we had coffee and shared a sinfully rich chocolate torte. He took a couple of bites, then sat back and watched me. Warm tension tightened my belly. I swiped a dollop of chocolate from my lower lip.

"You, ah… you look at me a lot," I remarked.

"You're very pretty."

I didn't know about that, but the compliment poured through me like honey. "I like the way you look too."

That was an understatement. One glance at him and I went all hot and fluttery inside.

He leaned forward, resting an elbow on the table. Curiosity and heat simmered in his expression.

"What is it about you, Olivia?" he asked.

"What do you mean?"

"Why are you so sweet and determined and guarded all at once?"

"I didn't know I was all those things."

"You are. Why?"

I shrugged and sank my fork into the torte again. If I was eating, I couldn't talk much.

I ate another bite and spoke around the mouthful. "This is really good."

Dean's mouth twitched with a smile, but his eyes were still curious as he sat back again. He continued watching me as I polished off the torte and scraped the plate clean.

By the time he paid the bill and retrieved our coats, I'd realized the danger of Professor Dean West. If I let him, he would slide right past all my defenses. No one had ever done that before.

We went outside into the cold. He didn't touch me. This time, though, I wanted him to. I nudged his elbow. He looked at me, then extended his arm and waited. I moved closer, falling into step beside him as we walked back to State Street.

It felt exactly the way I'd imagined it would, pressed to his side with his body heat flowing into me and his arm strong and tight around my shoulders. I fit against him like a puzzle piece locking into place.

"Where do you live?" he asked.

"Off Dayton Street, not far from the Kohl Center. I walked."

"Next time I'll pick you up."

My pulse leapt at the idea that there would be a *next time*.

"And this time," Dean said, "I'll drive you home. I'm parked by the museum."

When we reached the parking lot, he unlocked the door of a black sedan and ushered me inside before getting into the driver's seat. I told him my address, and we fell silent on the short ride home. The buildings of downtown passed by in a blur of light and shadows.

When he pulled up in front of my apartment, my damned nerves got tense again. I fumbled around collecting my bag and buttoning my coat.

"So, thank you," I said. "That was really nice."

"Yes, it was. Thank you too."

I took hold of the door handle. "I'll just..."

"Olivia."

I turned to face him. His eyes glittered in the light of the streetlamps. He reached out slowly, as if he were trying not to startle a kitten, and curled his hand around my wrist.

His touch spiraled heat into my blood, igniting flashes of unbearably intimate thoughts—me in his arms, his lips sliding over my throat, his hands on my bare breasts. The air grew hot, compressed.

"I'm going to kiss you now," Dean said.

My heart crashed against my chest, and a hard tremble swept through me. I parted my lips to draw in a breath.

"I... okay."

He leaned across the console and lifted his hands to cup my face. His touch was gentle, still cautious, but the heat brewing in his eyes left me in no doubt as to his desire. We were closer than we'd ever been before, so close that I could see the darker ring of brown surrounding his irises.

For a moment, we just stared at each other. Then his hands tightened on me as he lowered his mouth to mine. And the world fell away the instant our lips touched.

CHAPTER FIVE

AUGUST 22

Six days have passed since I mentioned the idea of having a baby. A million thoughts are flying and twisting through my mind, but they don't have anywhere to go. I've never been one for discussing personal details with my few girlfriends, and my mother would dispense lousy advice, even if I did know where she was. Not that I'd ever tell her anything either.

What sucks is that the one person I really want to have a conversation with—the man I've always been able to talk to about anything—is unapproachable right now. When he's even home. He's not outwardly cold or forbidding, but I sense his reluctance to discuss it further. And truth be told, I'm not all that eager to have a repeat of our previous conversation anyway.

Plus, that *question* ("Because you're looking for something to do?") is still running through my mind like a looped tape.

At breakfast, we stick to safe subjects like a news story about an art forgery that we've both been following, Dean's upcoming semester, and my new job at the bookstore.

"Did Kelsey tell you about the banquet?" I ask after refilling our coffee.

"The one on Saturday?" Dean asks, as if he's got a dozen banquets lined up. "Yeah. She said you don't mind if I go. Of course, she didn't ask if *I* mind if I go."

He sounds a little affronted, which makes me smile. He doesn't care for academic socializing, but he's good at it and he'd do anything for Kelsey.

"At least now she'll owe you one," I remark.

Dean grunts into his coffee and flips a page of the newspaper. I focus on my own section of the paper, but the lines blur before my eyes.

The sudden distance between us is unsettling. Dean and I have always made each other feel good physically, and the fact that almost a week has passed without one of us making a move is... unusual.

I stretch my leg beneath the table and run my foot up to his inner thigh. He glances at me. I wiggle my toes against his crotch.

"Time before work?" I ask.

"Sorry." He closes the paper. "Couple of meetings this morning."

"Too bad." I stare down at my coffee.

"Yeah." He glances at the clock, then leans across the table to kiss my forehead. "I've gotta go to work. I'll see you later."

After he leaves, I sit at the table for a few more minutes. I wonder if he's now worried that I'll get all upset if he reaches for a condom when we have sex.

I go to put my cup in the sink. Okay, so I didn't handle that whole "stopping birth control" conversation well at all. But I also don't quite understand Dean's evident relief over the negative pregnancy test. Wasn't he the tiniest bit disappointed?

I head toward the bedroom, then stop in Dean's office. I go in there to dust and straighten up every now and then, but mostly I leave it alone. Today, though, I look at the stuff on his desk—a stack of printed lectures, photos of Chartres Cathedral, a yellow legal pad covered with notes in his scrawled handwriting. There's a framed picture of me next to the computer, and a photo of us together is on the bookshelf.

His computer is on, and I scroll through the contents of the hard-drive, then his Internet history. I've used his computer before, and neither of us has given it a second thought. Anyway, there's nothing interesting—lectures, papers, PDF files, email, news websites.

I push away from the desk and go to get dressed. Outside, there's a sense of late-summer melancholy in the air, as there always is when the tourists leave and take their vacation excitement with them. I drive to the university, a sprawling collection of brick buildings dotting an expanse of grass and trees.

The history department is nestled in a classical-style building at one end of campus. I park in the visitor's lot and take the worn stone steps leading to the offices. I greet a few staff members and professors whom I've met before, then go down the hall to Dean's office.

Several voices emerge from the open door, and I catch snippets of conversation about city-states, *Beowulf*, some Italian cathedral, and the tapestries of medieval Dominican nuns (really).

"I'll get that outline to you by the end of the week, Professor West," a young man says, his voice getting clearer as he moves toward the door.

"Thanks, Sam. And Jessica, send me the list of grad students who have submitted papers for the conference presentations."

"We've gotten a ton of proposals already," Jessica says. "It's kind of cool that we'll be able to pick the cream of the crop. We've only sent out two calls for papers so far, and we'll have more in the spring."

"King's students get priority, right?" asks another girl. "For presentations? I want to submit a proposal. It'd be good for my résumé."

"The most original work gets priority, Maggie," Dean says. "And most of the proposals are based on theses and dissertations."

"Well, mine would be too," Maggie says.

There's a momentary silence before Jessica says brightly, "I need to get to the library. Thanks for your time, Professor West."

"Yeah, thanks," Sam adds.

The door opens farther as the two depart, hefting their backpacks over their shoulders.

"Can't believe Maggie thinks she can..." Jessica mutters to Sam, her voice becoming inaudible as they pass me and walk down the hall.

I wonder if I should let Dean know I'm here, but then he and the girl Maggie start talking again. Should I leave? The office door is wide open and anyone in the corridor can hear his conversations. Nevertheless, I move a little farther away to try and give them some privacy.

"You need to sharpen your methodology, Maggie, before you submit a proposal," Dean says, his voice carrying into the hall. "I told you that I'd help you, but you have to narrow your focus first. Have you looked at the bibliography I gave you?"

"Some of it," the girl replies. "It's, like, twenty pages long."

"If you're interested in Trotula of Salerno, you need to start with medieval women's history and the history of medicine. After you look at the research, write down some questions you want to tackle and we'll talk about them."

She lets out a sigh. "Okay."

"Okay. Now what about your coursework?"

"Well, because I'm also supposed to take the LSAT next semester, I can't take Latin because it conflicts with a prep course."

"What about an independent study?"

There's more talk about requirements and credits before they leave the office.

"Liv." Dean looks faintly surprised to see me. The young woman stops just outside the door. She's a pretty girl with blond hair pulled back by a headband, wearing shorts and a tank top that do justice to her toned figure.

"Maggie, this is my wife Olivia," Dean says.

"Oh." The girl blinks at me, then glances back at Dean, as if she's surprised by the fact that he's married.

"Liv, this is Maggie Hamilton, one of our grad students," Dean continues.

Maggie and I shake hands and exchange pleasantries. "What's your thesis research?" I ask out of politeness rather than genuine interest.

"Well, Professor West suggested something about the perception of women through the writings of Trotula of Salerno." She shoots him another glance. "Because I'm interested in medieval views of women's sexuality."

"Interesting," I remark.

"Maggie, check with the registrar about those classes and get back to me," Dean says. "You'll have to have your thesis proposal approved before next semester, then you can submit a paper for the conference."

"Okay. Nice meeting you, Mrs. West." She heads off down the hall.

Dean looks at me. "What're you doing here?"

"Thought I'd see if you wanted to grab lunch."

"It's ten-thirty."

"Or brunch."

He frowns, then gestures me into his office and closes the door behind us. "What's going on?"

I sigh and flop into the chair in front of his desk. I've never brought our personal stuff into his workplace. But now I plunge ahead, like a rock rolling downhill.

"I looked at the stuff on your computer this morning," I admit.

"What for?"

I shrug and chew on my thumbnail, nettled by the sense that there is something I don't know about him when I thought I knew everything.

"You don't even look at porn, do you?" I ask.

"Why would I look at porn?"

That makes me laugh. "You don't know?"

"I've got you. I don't need porn." He scratches his head, looking baffled. "Where are we going with this? Do you want me to look at porn?"

"No."

"Do *you* want to look at porn? Because there's plenty of it, from what I gather."

I study him for a moment. I don't care about porn, but I'm curious about what one of us might do if the other one isn't around sexually, whether because of physical or emotional separation.

Sex has always been a big part of our relationship, both for the usual reasons—pleasure, to connect, because we're in love—and for intensely personal reasons that belong to us alone.

"Would it bother you if I did look at porn?" I ask.

"No. If you want to, go ahead."

"I don't want to."

"Liv." Dean gestures to his desk, which is piled with papers. "I've got a shitload of work to do. Whatever you're here about, can we discuss it at home?"

"You haven't been home much this past week," I remind him. "And we tried to discuss it, but we never reached any conclusions."

He folds his arms. "The baby you're thinking about."

"And you're not."

"Liv, you haven't even reached a conclusion about what you want. What is there to reach a conclusion about together?"

"How would you have felt if that test was positive?" My

heart thumps. He's watching me, his arms still crossed, his expression wary.

"I don't know," he says. "But that's a pointless speculation."

"You didn't even... wonder?"

He shakes his head. My unease deepens.

"Dean, when I told you I didn't want children, you agreed with me. You said it was fine."

"It was."

"But what did *you* want?"

"I wanted what you wanted. I understood."

"But even when we were dating..." A simmer of tension rises in my chest. "When we fell in love, you didn't... didn't ever think of us having children?"

"Why would I when you closed that door?"

"You never wanted to open it? Never pictured yourself as a father or me as..."

My voice fades. We look at each other for a long moment. Something is off. I don't know what it is. Dean has always moved forward in life, always made things happen. So why hasn't he ever imagined our marriage as... as *more*?

"Liv." He slides his warm hand beneath my chin and lifts my face to look at him. "Not having children doesn't make us any less married. Any less in love. It doesn't make us any less a family."

"It doesn't make us more either, does it?"

He drops his hand to his side and steps back. "I didn't think either of us needed more."

"Not more *than* each other," I say. "More *with* each other."

"I have more *with you* than I ever thought I would," he replies, his voice tense. "But if our marriage is suddenly not enough for you, then a baby sure as hell isn't going to solve anything."

"Why do you keep implying I'm missing something?" My spine prickles with irritation. "That I mentioned a baby because I need something to do, or because our marriage isn't enough? Why can't it be because we're strong and happy together?"

"It can, but not now, Liv. Regardless of what you decide, I told you it's a bad time."

"Do you think there will ever be a good time?" I ask.

Dean sighs and drags a hand down his face. "I don't want to have this conversation here," he says.

"You don't want to have this conversation at all."

It's a sharp retort that should bring me some satisfaction, but instead I just feel hollow. Because I know I'm right.

We're avoiding each other. There's tension. It's lousy. Part of me wishes I hadn't even opened this particular door. Why would I want to change anything about our marriage?

There was a time when I never thought I'd have the life I do now. Never thought I'd be safe or have a home. I certainly never thought I'd fall in love.

But all of that happened because I met Dean. He's the one who turned my whole world right side up, who transformed all my warped ideas about relationships. Who proved that white knights really do exist. Who discovered alongside me that we are so much better together than alone. So why is the mere idea of a baby causing a rift between us?

I have no answer to that question. And I'm not sure I want one.

Tonight Dean is going to the banquet with Kelsey. She shows up looking classically sexy in a black sheath dress and a long strand of pearls. She wears almost no makeup except for bright red lipstick, which—combined with her disdainful expression—makes her look like Greta Garbo or Marlene Dietrich. With blue-streaked hair.

"What're you going to do?" she asks me while we wait for Dean to finish getting ready. "Pop popcorn and watch movies? Drink wine? Can I stay with you instead?"

I kind of wish she would—even though I wouldn't tell her everything that's been going on, I'd like her no-nonsense company.

Dean emerges from the bedroom, still knotting his tie. He looks incredible, masculine and handsome with his hair combed away from his forehead and his navy suit pressed to perfection.

"Wow," Kelsey remarks in admiration, glancing from him to me. "Maybe *he* should stay just so you can have the fun of taking that suit off him."

Dean and I both laugh, but the sound is forced and rusty. Kelsey gets it immediately because she frowns and looks at both of us again. I suspect my husband will be subjected to the third degree en route to the banquet.

I give him the obligatory kiss, hug Kelsey and tell her to behave. They head off. I'm somewhat relieved to be alone because at least now I don't have to pretend.

I take Kelsey's advice and eat some popcorn while watching an action movie, then part of a romantic comedy. But I'm soon bored, so I turn off the TV and page through a magazine. Then I wander over to check my email at my laptop by the window.

After surfing a few book-related websites, I'm bored again and restless and wishing Dean were here and everything was like it was before the idea of a baby made it all so messy.

I type a few words into a search engine. A massive list of results appears—live porn, amateur videos, free porn, fetish movies, hardcore videos, bondage, girls with glasses... girls with glasses?

Out of curiosity, I click that link. Sure enough, a screen of clips appears of half-naked girls with glasses. At least they're honest about their advertising.

They're in various stages of apparent arousal and intercourse. I don't know whether to be intrigued or not. I've seen porn videos, of course, but not such a proliferation or such a niche market.

I click on a clip. There's a guy between the spread legs of a girl wearing glasses. He's rubbing his erection, teasing the head around the folds of her sex, slipping partway into her opening before pulling back again.

I've always liked it when Dean does that to me.

I switch to another clip. An older man is actively pumping into another girl, but his belly is fat and jiggling, which grosses me out. A third clip has a woman looking astonishingly uninterested while giving a blow job. I close the window. I find another clip of a decent-looking man and a girl wearing horn-rimmed glasses.

She's on her hands and knees, and he's gripping her ass as he thrusts into her from behind. The camera angle isn't ridiculously close, but it's close enough that I can see his cock moving in and out of her. It's smooth and slick.

His fingers dig into her flesh. He's pumping hard enough that her whole body is rocking with the motion, her large breasts swaying beneath her, her mouth open on a moan.

I squeeze my thighs together a little. I'm wearing yoga pants, and they're getting warm. Not to mention that I'm frustrated over not having had sex with Dean in a while.

The man in the video shifts his position, planting his foot on the bed to enhance the depth of his thrusts.

Dean does that too. It works.

My breathing increases. The girl is moaning in a long, steady stream. She's also sweating. Her hair is long, longer than mine, and sticking to her back in damp strands. The man slaps her bottom a few times, causing her to shriek and her skin to redden. She has a great ass, round and smooth and tight.

I feel perverted, but I'm getting achy in a good way. A way that I can't deny. I make sure the curtains are drawn before I pull my pants off and kick them beneath the desk. I'm too embarrassed to actually touch myself while staring at a hardcore video clip, but I don't stop watching.

The sounds of the man's hips slapping against the woman emerge from the speaker. She grabs the headboard and starts to push against him. It's graphic and raw. They're moaning and panting. Then he lets out a grunt and pulls his cock from her, rubbing the shaft between her ass cheeks as he spurts over her back.

I love it when Dean does that to me.

My heart is pulsing fast. I press my thighs together again and feel the burgeoning throb. I shut the laptop and move to the sofa, pulling my underpants down my legs and tossing them aside.

I'm wearing a T-shirt, but I'm in a hurry now and I reach beneath it to shove my bra up so I can play with my breasts. I rub them hard, tweak the nipples, and feel sensation uncoiling through my belly. I spread my legs and thrust a hand between them, unsurprised but still embarrassed by how wet I am.

At least my perversion is a secret one.

I close my eyes and imagine Dean and I in the same position—him thrusting into me from behind while I grip the headboard and rock back against him.

It takes almost no time at all. I know exactly how to touch myself and where. And with images of Dean clutching my hips, pumping in and out of me before he comes all over my bottom…

Oh… oh!

Vibrations flood me, causing my breath to stop and my whole body to tremble. I massage myself more urgently, aching to feel every last shudder through my veins. I squeeze my eyes shut tighter, watching Dean reach beneath me to finger my sex as I stay there on my hands and knees, rocking against his hand, begging…

Another series of trembles courses through me before the sensations slow. I tug my hand from between my thighs and lie there panting as the delicious images fade.

"Liv."

My eyes fly open. I stare at Dean, who's standing by the door, his suit jacket tossed over his arm and his keys in his hand. For a heart-stopping second, I expect to see Kelsey right behind him, but the door is closed. He's alone.

And I'm... like this.

Shit.

I scramble up from the sofa and try to yank my T-shirt down over my hips, but it's too short. I'm naked from the waist down, and a fiery blush shoots across my skin. I fumble around trying to find my pants, underwear... anything to cover myself... finally I grab the quilt from the back of the sofa and wrap it around my waist.

I tuck one corner in to secure it, then use both hands to push my tangled hair back. I attempt a bright smile, which I'm quite certain is a miserable failure.

"I... I wasn't expecting you until about midnight," I remark.

"It's almost one."

"Oh. I... uh, I lost track of time."

"I can see that."

My blush grows so hot I feel like I've been set aflame. It should be silly to be so embarrassed. Dean's watched me masturbate before—hell, he's told me numerous times to do it in front of him—but this is different.

This is weird.

My bra is still hitched up over my breasts. I cross my arms and try to casually tug it down again.

"How... how was the banquet?" I can't stop blushing. I must look like a tomato.

He tosses his jacket over a chair. "Long and boring, but the food was okay. Chocolate mousse for dessert."

"How'd Kelsey do?"

"She rose to the occasion and charmed all the right people."

"Think it'll help with her proposal?"

"Probably."

For a minute, we just stand there staring at each other. I can tell he wants to say something, but I don't know what.

I'd feel better if he'd just come over and kiss me and make some wicked comment about how I occupy myself when I'm alone. Then I'd feel a *lot* better if he'd tug the stupid quilt off me and slip his hand between my legs...

"Well." He rubs the back of his neck. "I'm beat. I'm going to take a shower and go to bed."

He goes into the bedroom. I sink onto the sofa and press my hands against my hot cheeks. My eyes sting with tears of embarrassment and anger, but this time I don't let them fall.

Instead I just sit there and try to breathe. My disappointment in my husband is so sharp I can taste it, bitter and cold.

"Was it porn?" he asks the next morning.

"Yes."

It was also you. A month ago, I would have told him everything.

We don't say anything else about the episode. I'm no longer embarrassed.

Now I'm just sad.

CHAPTER SIX

AUGUST 28

"Liv, check this out."

Allie pokes her head in the door of the bookstore. I push a few books back onto the shelf and follow her outside to admire the rainbow window display she's constructed.

"Looks great." It does, too—all colorful with big, cotton clouds and silver streamers of rain.

"Good." Allie pushes her glasses up as we head back inside. "Hopefully it'll get some people in for the book signing. This local gal writes novels that all have themes about color. She's coming Saturday afternoon, so we'll see if that helps traffic on the weekend. We could sure use it."

"Business isn't so great, huh?" I ask.

"No. And they're raising the rent on this building at the beginning of the year, so…" Her voice trails off and she shrugs. "We'll see what happens."

"Hey, how was your date?" I ask, in an effort to divert the topic from her dwindling business. "Didn't you go out with Brent again last weekend?"

"It was great." Her cheeks get a little pink. "Brent is nice and cute and a great kisser."

"Can't go wrong with any of those qualities."

"You got that right."

We both look up when the bell over the door rings. A plump, blond woman strides toward us, a sheaf of flyers in the crook of her arm.

"Morning, ladies," she says. "I'm Natalie Bergman from Epicurean, the kitchen and cookware store over on Larkspur."

"Oh, I love that place," Allie says. "I got a bunch of stainless steel pots from you guys and some great napkin rings."

Natalie beams. "Glad to hear it. You might be interested in this, then." She waves a flyer at both of us. "We still have a few spots open for a cooking class that starts next week. I was wondering if I could put a flyer in your window."

"Sure. Leave a few on our counter, too."

Natalie stacks up the flyers and hands one to me to tape in the window. "It'll be a great course, held over in the Epicurean kitchen classroom. Tuition includes all supplies and food."

I skim the flyer. *French Cuisine Classics! Learn the techniques of French cooking in this sixteen-week intensive course. All levels welcome. Tuesdays 7:00-9:00 p.m.*

"I have the registration forms too." Natalie digs into her

bag and produces another stack of papers. "If either one of you wants to take one."

"I will." I'm almost surprised when the words come out.

Natalie hands me the form. "You'll love the course, really."

After she leaves, Allie asks, "You're going to do it?"

"I don't know. Are you?"

"Nah." Her red curls flop as she shakes her head. "I'm not much for cooking."

"Neither am I."

I guess that's the point, though. If you don't know something, you find out about it. And if you can't do something, you learn how. Especially if it's something that intimidates or scares you.

Dean isn't home when I return to our apartment, but his briefcase is by the door. I remember that he was going to play football this evening, so I leave the flyer on the front table next to a pile of mail and put a frozen lasagna in the microwave.

I head out to tend to my balcony garden. A few blooms still flourish in the late summer sun, but the plants are starting to wither a bit. I clip off dead flowers, sweep up the leaves, and water the plants.

Dean comes back, dirty but cheerful because his team won the game. I'm glad when he comes over to kiss me—even with things all weird and tense between us, he still kisses me often and strokes my hair, and I still rub his lower back in passing and hug him around the waist. While we try to pretend everything is okay.

He heads off for a quick shower before dinner while I set the table.

"How was your day?" he asks, pulling a clean T-shirt over his head as he comes out of the bedroom.

"Good. Worked at the bookstore for a few hours." My stomach twists suddenly as I take the flyer from the front table. "A woman from a cookware store dropped this off. She asked if we could put it in the window."

Dean glances at the paper. "Classic French cuisine?"

"I… I was thinking of registering for it." My heart thumps against my ribs.

"That's a great idea," Dean says.

"It is?"

"Sure." He drops the flyer back onto the table. "Don't you think so?"

"Well, yeah. Lord knows I'm a lousy cook."

"So you'll learn to be a good one."

"It's once a week for an entire semester," I say.

"Sounds like you'll learn a lot, then."

"It's expensive."

"Doesn't matter."

I drum my fingers on the table. "So it's okay if I register?"

"Of course it's okay." Dean looks at me with a hint of puzzlement. "You don't need my permission to take a class, Liv. If you want to register, go ahead. I think it's a great idea."

I turn and head back into the kitchen. I wonder if I was secretly hoping he might talk me out of it, but now a spark of excitement lights inside me.

I could actually learn how to cook. The pressing need for that particular skill hits home when I take the burned, gummy-looking lasagna out of the microwave.

Surely I can do better than *this*.

Dean pauses in the kitchen doorway, shuffling through the pile of mail.

"Anything good?" I push a knife through the pasta.

He doesn't respond. I glance at him. Concern gleams in his expression as his eyes meet mine.

"Dean?"

He moves closer to me and puts an envelope on the counter. My heart stutters. I recognize the looped handwriting, even though I haven't seen it in ages.

I pick up the envelope and peer at the smudged post-mark. Austin, Texas. That means nothing. She could have been passing through, probably en route to Mexico.

I'm surprised she remembered our address. I'm surprised she even *has* our address.

Dean settles his hand against the nape of my neck. "You want to open it?" he asks.

"Not really."

We stand there for a few minutes. Unease simmers in my belly. Finally I rip open the flap, my fingers shaking. I unfold the single sheet of paper, and position it so Dean can read it too.

> *Liv,*
> *Stella tells me you're still married. I moved to Florida last year and am now traveling through the south. I could use the money you promised, so please send a cashier's check care of the address below.*

I let the letter fall to the counter and try to think. It's

been, what… three years? I'd been married to Dean for just a few months. We were living in Los Angeles—his last fellowship position before starting at King's University.

Through some convoluted communication with my aunt Stella, I found out my mother was living less than an hour away in Riverside. I wrote and told her Dean and I were going to be passing through (which we weren't), and that I'd like to see her. I didn't expect her to respond. The following week we drove out.

It'd been a brief visit—an hour, tops. Dean was outwardly polite and inwardly seething. My mother was indifferent toward him and hostile toward me. I tried to be composed and did not succeed.

"Guess she doesn't have my email address," I say.

Dean pulls me closer, spreading his hand over the side of my head. He doesn't say anything. He doesn't have to. He knows what it's like, how knotted everything gets inside me. My memories of my father are faded almost to nonexistence, and I had a twisted relationship with my mother.

When I had a relationship with her at all.

All the old emotions roil up into my chest—anger, fear, sadness, inadequacy. I've learned to control them over the years, but they swarm up again the minute she makes contact.

Dean wraps his arms around me and shifts so our bodies are pressed together. It feels good, the muscular length of him against me, his arms tight around my back. I rest my cheek against his chest and breathe.

He's so solid, so secure. He's been the one constant in my life, the one person who hasn't abandoned me or given up on me. The one person who would tell me not to give up on myself.

I move away from him first, pressing my lips to the side of his neck. I'm no longer hungry for dinner—least of all micro-waved lasagna—and Dean says he had a late lunch anyway, so we both settle in for the evening.

He goes into his office to work, and I change into my nightgown, curl under an old quilt, and find an *I Love Lucy* marathon to watch.

Lucy Ricardo. She would've been a good mother. Nutty, but good. Probably a heck of a lot of fun, too.

The candy factory episode is half over when Dean emerges. He sits beside me on the sofa, and we shift around a little until I'm lying with my head in his lap. He strokes his hand over my hair, then underneath the quilt and around to my breasts.

It's been two weeks now—longer than we've ever gone without some form of intimacy—and my whole body floods with relief and arousal. For a few minutes, Dean rubs my breasts through the cotton of my nightgown. I squirm as my nipples harden, and then he starts to roll them between his fingers. Heat tingles across my skin.

Dean strokes the curve of my hip, gathers the material of my nightgown in his fist, and drags it up to my waist. I can feel him getting hard, and I rub my cheek against his crotch. Urgency spools through my lower body, sparked by my increasing pulse.

I shift again until I'm lying face-up with my head still in his lap, and he's looking down at me with a hot gaze that makes my blood shimmer. I squeeze my thighs together because the delicious throb is starting. Dean pushes the quilt aside and pulls my nightgown up farther so my breasts are exposed.

His breath escapes in a rush as he palms the full globes. I shiver.

"So damn beautiful," he mutters.

It's an incredibly erotic feeling, lying there with my head in his lap and my nightgown bunched up, naked except for my white cotton panties. He starts stroking me again, sliding his hand to rub my breasts, my nipples, and back down over my belly to the edge of my panties. He slips his fingers teasingly beneath the elastic.

"You want to come, beauty?" he whispers.

The husky note in his voice fires my excitement. In response, I writhe against his hand. I'm still squeezing my thighs together because the throb is building, but Dean urges my legs apart.

He pushes his hand beneath my panties, fingers toying through the damp curls, until he reaches the place where my arousal is centered. Then he splays his hand over my folds, sliding one finger easily into me while his thumb circles my clit.

It's not enough. I buck my hips, trying to thrust myself harder against his hand. A smile tugs at his mouth. He slides his arm beneath my shoulders, his other hand coming around to pluck at my nipples. Fire streams through my veins.

I press my face into Dean's shirt and moan. My skin is hot, flushed. His breath echoes through his chest. I feel my arousal coiling tighter, and even though I crave that explosive release, I love this moment of being close to my husband again, hearing the pound of his heart against my ear, the heat of his body flowing into mine.

He grips me harder just before the tension breaks, as if

he knows I can't prevent it any longer. His hands and fingers work harder—in me, over me, on me—and then the sensations rocket through me, causing me to choke out his name as I clench my thighs around his hand and ride the exquisite wave.

He holds on to me, easing the last tingles from my body, and then I go limp and just breathe against him while he strokes my damp belly.

After a few minutes, he tugs my nightgown back over my hips. I can still feel his erection and think I should do something about it, but he doesn't seem to expect anything in return, and anyway I'm drained from all the tension of the past weeks and now this.

So I'm grateful when he pulls the quilt back over me and lies down behind me, wrapping one arm around my waist. There's not a heck of a lot of room on the sofa for both of us, but it's a warm, cozy cocoon, and I fall asleep with the movement of his breathing against my back.

I go to the bank the next day and get a cashier's check. I consider writing a return letter to my mother, but I can't think of anything to say. I put the check in an envelope and seal it, then scribble the address and drop it in the mailbox on the way home.

It's unsettled me, the unexpected contact. I try not to think of my mother often, even though she's still there like a shadow.

I don't have many pictures of her or good memories either, but the letter ignites flashes of our life together—the hot, vinyl interior of our old car, the floorboards littered with crumpled potato-chip packages and candy wrappers.

The stares of other kids as I walked into what felt like the hundredth classroom. Sitting cross-legged on a beach boardwalk as my mother arranged her bracelets and necklaces for sale. The sound of her moans coming from a stranger's bedroom.

There's now a perpetual tight knot in my chest. I try to ignore it, try not to think about the fact that it's tangled up with all the other confusion that has risen to the surface in the past few weeks.

After Dean leaves the following morning, I clean the living room and do a load of laundry before heading out. On my way to the Historical Museum, I stop to get a coffee at a place on Ruby Street.

"Mrs. West?"

I'm not accustomed to being called that, so at first I don't respond.

"Mrs. West?"

I turn. Behind me is the blond grad student I'd met outside Dean's office—Marcy… no, Maggie. She's looking at me a trifle uncertainly, her pretty face bare of makeup, her hair pulled back into a messy bun. A heavy-looking backpack is slung over her shoulder.

"Maggie Hamilton," she says. "We met last week. I'm one of Professor West's students."

"Yes, of course. How are you?"

"Busy." She rolls her eyes and sighs. "Grad school is not for the faint of heart."

"No, I imagine it's not."

"Everyone tells me I should be glad I'm working with Professor West, though." Maggie holds up a finger to indicate that I should wait while she places her coffee order. Then she turns back to me. "You know, because he's so brilliant, and it'll be great to have his name behind my work."

"I'll tell him you said that." I step back to add cream to my coffee. "Good luck to you."

"Thanks." She grabs two coffees from the server and puts them into a paper-cup carrier along with a few sugar packets.

"I'm meeting with him right now," she continues before I can leave. "Thought I'd bring him a coffee too. We're supposed to tackle my thesis topic again, so I figure a little buttering-up can't hurt." She gives me a half-grin. "But don't tell him I said *that*."

I shake my head and say nothing. Words jam up into my throat. I move to get some napkins while she waves and pushes the door open with her shoulder, balancing the coffee tray in one hand. I watch as she heads for a blue hatchback parked at the curb.

I'm not jealous—Dean has taught and advised plenty of pretty grads and undergrads, and I've never once had reason to be concerned. And nothing about Maggie Hamilton should make me apprehensive, except that she's a young woman bringing my husband a coffee.

Which is exactly what makes the knot in my chest tighten.

As I walk down the street, I try to push Maggie Hamilton out of my thoughts, but she's there and Dean's there and they're sitting in his office drinking coffee that she brought him and discussing her paper about medieval gynecology or whatever.

When I get to the museum, I hate that I'm giving in to a worry that shouldn't even exist, but I call Dean on his cell phone and ask if he wants to meet for lunch.

"Sure, but it'll have to be quick. I have a one o'clock departmental meeting before my Crusades seminar."

The dullness of his afternoon schedule is oddly reassuring. I work at the Historical Museum for a few hours, typing up a new brochure and showing a group of kindergarteners around. Then I head over to campus.

We get sandwiches from one of the university eateries and sit on a bench in the quad. It's a hot, end-of-summer day—bright sun, boats dotting the lake, blue sky. Students walk along the paths cutting through the grass, their backpacks hitched over their shoulders and their strides purposeful.

"I saw one of your grad students at Java Works this morning," I remark. "Maggie Hamilton."

"She told me." He pulls a sandwich from the bag and hands it to me. "She's not one of the better students. Far from it, unfortunately."

"How did she get into the grad program, then?"

"Her father is a big donor to the university," Dean says. "The chairperson of the history department, Jeffrey Butler, was also the medieval history professor at the time. He accepted Maggie's admission, but only worked with her for a year before he retired."

"That's why you ended up with her?"

He nods. "She took a year off, then reentered this summer. She thinks she's entitled to be in the program."

"Did you approve her thesis topic?"

"Not yet. She doesn't get that she needs to review the existing research before coming up with her own original question. She's got a lot of work to do."

This, too, is oddly reassuring, though I don't want to examine the reasons why. We eat in silence for a while, sharing a bag of pretzels and watching the passersby.

"How did you know you wanted to study medieval history?" I ask. I know he had a childhood love for the King Arthur tales, but I've never known how he got on that career path later in life.

"Junior year abroad," Dean replies. "I went to Italy and Spain. Worked on an archeological dig. One of the professors liked the work I was doing on material culture and suggested a research project combining that with architectural analyses. I thought it was fascinating."

"Fascinating?"

"Yeah." He shrugs. "Studying relics of times past, figuring out what people did, who they were. You're reconstructing the memory of a society, changing and revising it when you discover something new. It's important."

"Aside from King Arthur, why medieval history?"

"It's when a lot of modern institutions started. Important works of literature, printing press, religion. The bridge between the ancient and the modern worlds."

I pick the crust off my sandwich and toss it to a nearby bird. "I was a library sciences and lit major because I like to read."

He chuckles. "I didn't apply to grad school thinking I'd change the face of medieval scholarship, Liv. Some things you learn as you're doing them."

Like parenting, I think, except people like my mother don't learn anything.

I rub my chest, the knot still tight in the middle of my breastbone. Dean shifts to look at me.

"And?" he asks.

"Oh, hell. Maybe you're right. Maybe I'm thinking about a baby because I have nothing else to do. And what if we did have children and I turn out to be like my mother?"

He puts his hand on my back. "You're nothing like your mother."

"God knows I did everything I could to prove that to myself," I say.

"So why are you worried about being like her?"

"Because what if everything I've done in my life is to prove that I'm not? I finished high school, graduated from college, met and married you, tried to find a stable job, a career of some sort... all to convince myself I'm different from her."

"Liv, you *are* different from her. You have nothing to prove to anyone, least of all yourself. You never have."

"But I still haven't *done* anything, Dean. I went to college thinking I'd start a career, do something important, but instead..."

"Instead you married me." Tension threads his voice.

"I married you because I love you. I wouldn't change that for the world. But what if I hadn't? Would I have made something of myself or would I still be working at Jitter Beans? Or would I have headed off to some other city just like her?"

"What's the point of wondering that, Liv? None of that happened. And you know I'll support you in whatever you want to do."

I toss the rest of my sandwich to the birds. Dean's hand slips away from me. The ache in my chest expands.

He picks up our empty wrappers and throws them in a garbage can. He stands there for a minute, the afternoon sun glowing off his hair, his expression both pensive and remote.

I love him to my bones, but suddenly I'm wondering what I might have been without him.

CHAPTER SEVEN

*E*ven in the early part of our relationship, Dean didn't give up on me. He could have—and I don't think I would have blamed him if he had—but he didn't. He didn't give up on the idea of us. And his persistence made me believe in *us* too.

A few days after the museum lecture and our first date, he came into Jitter Beans and asked me to his place for dinner. I agreed, trying to suppress my nervousness. I was finally seeing a handsome, kind man whose smile made my pulse race. It was exactly the kind of *normal* I had been craving for years.

"It's me, Liv."

Just the sound of Dean's voice through the apartment intercom sent a tingle over my skin.

It's me.

Is it really you?

"I'll be right down," I called into the speaker.

I grabbed my coat and did a quick check of my reflection in the mirror. I was pleased by the flush of expectation coloring my cheeks and the sparkle in my eyes. I looked happy.

I *was* happy. I'd never had this kind of anticipation for a man. Despite my earlier anxiety, it felt good, like champagne bubbles zinging through my veins.

"Hi." Dean was waiting in the foyer, a smile creasing his face.

My heart gave a leap at the sight of him. He wore jeans and a button-down shirt open at the collar to reveal the column of his throat. For an instant, I wondered what it would feel like to press my lips against his taut skin.

"Hi," I replied somewhat breathlessly. I extended the potted plant I'd brought him. "It's called a peace lily. It has white flowers that bloom in the spring."

"This is for me?" He took the plant with a bemused look as we walked out to the car.

"Yeah. It's really easy to care for. Just water it regularly, about once a week, and make sure it gets some sunlight. The leaves will start to droop if it needs water."

"I'll just call you if I need plant advice." He shifted the pot to one arm and opened the passenger side door for me. "Thanks. No one's ever given me a plant before."

He set the plant on the floor of the backseat and got behind the wheel, then drove to a colonial-style building located on the west side of town. I followed him into his apartment on the third floor. Despite the ideal location, the furnishings were utilitarian and spare with a chipped Formica table, plastic chairs, and a plaid sofa.

I approached a wall of large windows that overlooked a quiet, tree-lined park. The evening light spilled over the expanse of grass and illuminated a playground in the distance.

"Nice place," I remarked.

"Comes with the job. Should I put the plant by the windows?"

"Sure, but it shouldn't get too much sunlight." I took the plant from him and set it on the table. "Are you going to decorate at all?"

"Hadn't intended to, no." He pulled the cork on a bottle of wine and poured two glasses.

"You should. Hang some pictures, get some curtains, a few more plants. Maybe a couple of throw rugs."

"I don't need that kind of stuff," Dean said. "I'll only be here until the end of spring semester."

A strange feeling uncurled in my chest at the reminder that his stay in Madison was temporary. He seemed to realize it too, because a faint consternation darkened his expression.

"So how do you like Madison?" I asked in an effort to dispel the sudden strain.

"It's great. Lots to do, good students." He handed me a glass, then slid his gaze over me. "And there's this really pretty girl I like."

Pleasure heated me from the inside out. I was wearing a loose black skirt and a scoop-necked white T-shirt that was apparently flattering, given the way Dean's eyes lingered on the swells of my breasts. My nipples budded in response, and I knew he'd be able to see the hard peaks through the thin cotton of my shirt and bra.

Our gazes met again with a spark. I turned away from him.

"How did you get the UW position?" I asked, going for a curious-and-friendly tone.

"Usual application procedure. I didn't work at all last year, so I wasn't sure they'd make an offer, but they did."

"Why didn't you work?"

"I was writing a book, and my grandfather was sick, so…" His voice trailed off, and he shrugged. "Because of that gap, I want to take a few more postdoc positions before settling into something permanent. Good diversification too."

"Spoken like a true professor." I curled up on the sofa and took a sip of the wine, which was probably a fancy, expensive vintage—not that I could tell the difference. "And where do you want to end up?"

"With whoever makes the right offer," Dean said.

"What's the right offer?"

"A university with plenty of funding, tenure, research opportunities. Either a place that already has a solid Medieval Studies program, or an institution that wants to create one. There've been a few openings in recent months, but none I was interested in."

"So you're still waiting for the right one to come along?"

"The right one is always worth waiting for." He winked at me.

My face heated with a flush of pleasure. Dean settled on the other end of the sofa, the lines of his body relaxed.

I let my gaze sweep over him, appreciating the way his shirt stretched over his muscular chest, the jeans molding to his long legs. As much as I liked the way he looked in his tailored suits and ties, I loved the way casual clothes fit him to perfection, loved the rumpled look of his hair and stubbled jaw.

"What about you, Olivia Winter?" he asked. "What are you going to do with your life?"

"I don't know yet," I answered honestly. "I'm hoping for library work or maybe something with a publishing company."

"And where do you want to end up?" Dean asked.

"Wherever I feel at home." The confession slipped from my mouth before I realized it was out. I ducked my head to take a sip of wine, embarrassed by the Pollyanna nature of the remark. "So, uh, what's for dinner?"

I felt his gaze on me, intent and curious, then he unfolded himself from the sofa and stood. "Baked eel, pickled cabbage, and parsnip pie. Recipes from a medieval cookbook."

"Oh." I tried not to look disconcerted.

He chuckled. "I'm kidding. We're having manicotti, green salad, and focaccia bread."

"That sounds much more appetizing." I followed him into the kitchen as he took a pan of bubbling pasta and cheese out of the oven. "Did you make it?"

"No, sorry. Ordered it from a restaurant downtown. I can't seduce you with my cooking."

"You don't need cooking to seduce me," I said without thinking.

Wow. Where did that come from?

Dean flashed me his gorgeous, hint-of-wicked grin. "I'll keep that in mind."

After he showed me where the utensils were, I set the table in the dining room while he finished getting the food together. I moved an open shoebox from the table to the windowsill, noticing that it was half full of various types and lengths of string.

I picked one up. It was a worn piece of white string, the frayed ends tied together in a knot. Why would anyone have a shoebox filled with loops of string?

Dean came in with the plates and put them on the table.

"What's this for?" I asked, holding up the string.

"String figures."

"What?"

He took the string from me and looped the ends around his middle fingers, then did some quick maneuvers with his other fingers, tucking them under the loops and pulling the string taut. He extended his hands to reveal a pattern of three triangles between two parallel lines.

"It's like the game cat's cradle," he explained. "You make figures and patterns with a loop of string."

"Oh," I said. "That's…" …*about the dorkiest thing I have ever heard.*

It also made me like him even more.

"… interesting," I finished. "Where did you learn to do that?"

He shrugged. "Practiced a lot when I was a kid."

"Kind of a different hobby," I remarked.

"Yeah." He unhooked the string from his fingers. "Spent a lot of time in my room. String figures and the knights of the Round Table."

"You were into medieval history even as a kid?"

He nodded. "The King Arthur tales anyway. Excalibur, Mordred, the Holy Grail, all that stuff. Guess that planted the seed."

I had the sudden sense he'd just revealed more about himself in those few lines than anything else he'd told me so far.

"Did you have a favorite knight?" I asked.

He gave me a wry smile. "Galahad, of course. Proclaimed the greatest knight ever." He tossed the string back into the box. "I'll show you how to do string figures one day."

"Can't wait."

He chuckled at my less-than-enthused tone, then went to retrieve the food before we sat down. My nervousness eased a little now that I had a bit of insight into his childhood. Still a polar opposite to mine, though. At least he'd had a room to call his own.

Over dinner our conversation flowed comfortably—I told him about the classes I was taking, he talked about his research, we discussed the different things to do in Madison and Chicago.

We went back to the sofa for coffee and chocolate cake. As Dean put a cup on the table in front of me, he reached out to push a stray lock of hair behind my ear. His fingers brushed my cheek, and a tingle skimmed through me.

My reaction to him was both exciting and unnerving. String figures aside, he was experienced in ways that were foreign to me, his confidence born of an assurance I couldn't imagine and didn't know if I could handle.

And still, I wanted to try.

"So." I pleated the folds of my skirt. "You don't have a girlfriend?"

"Yeah, I have a girlfriend," Dean said. "She's just out of town right now."

He grinned when he caught the look on my face. "Liv, of course I don't have a girlfriend. And I'm very glad I don't because otherwise I wouldn't be here with you."

"Oh." A blush warmed my cheeks. "That's nice. Thanks."

He still looked amused. "You're welcome."

I gathered my courage and pressed forward. Better to know now what I was getting into. "But I'm sure you've had a lot of girlfriends, right?"

"I've had girlfriends, sure."

I certainly didn't expect a different answer, but my heart still shrank a little at his admission. "Any serious ones?"

"Depends on what you mean by serious." He sat across from me. A shuttered darkness concealed his eyes. "There was a woman in grad school. Helen. She was a close friend of my sister's. Still is. She also became close to my mother. They stay in touch."

"Was that how you met her?" I asked. "Because she was a friend of your sister's?"

"I'd known Helen for a couple of years through my sister. Then we both ended up at Harvard for grad school. She studied art history."

"How long were you together?"

"About three years."

"Why did you break up?"

"Different goals." A tense undercurrent threaded his voice. "Among other things."

I wondered how two PhDs—in history and art history, no less—could have different goals. "And she lives in California now?"

"She took a job at Stanford while she was still finishing her dissertation. Not far from where my parents and sister still live." He reached out to refill our coffee cups. "Anyway, I don't want to talk about them right now."

"What do you want to talk about?" I asked.

"You."

My stomach tightened. I tried to smile.

"Not much to talk about there," I said.

"Not true." He leaned his elbows on his knees and studied me, those penetrating eyes seeming to look right into my soul. "What's your key, Olivia?"

"My key?"

"An old friend once told me that everyone has a key to unlocking their secrets. What's yours?"

"Um… I'm pretty sure I don't have a key."

"I'm pretty sure you do."

"Well, if everyone has one," I said, "what's yours?"

"Ah." A twinkle flashed in his eyes. "You have to discover that yourself."

"Then you have to do the same with me."

"Challenge accepted."

My anxiety ratcheted up a few notches at the idea that he would probe for information about me. I was well-protected with several layers of scar tissue, but that night of the museum lecture I'd realized how difficult it would be for me to withstand Professor Dean West. And now I wasn't entirely sure I wanted to.

"String figures and medieval knights," I said softly.

He lifted an eyebrow in question.

"The keys to unlocking you." My heart beat faster as something indefinable crossed his expression.

I knew I was right. I just didn't know how those keys worked.

We looked at each other for a minute across the expanse of the sofa. I trailed my gaze to his mouth, remembering the warm touch of his lips against mine, the gentle way he held my face. Never had I been kissed with such heat and thoroughness. I wanted him to kiss me like that again.

Dean moved closer to me, lifting a hand to my hair with a restraint that gave me the chance to retreat if I chose to. I didn't move. The air simmered with heat as he tugged at my ponytail and released it from the band. My hair sifted over my shoulders, and he speared his fingers into the strands, combing out the tangles. A breath caught in my throat.

"I wanted to touch you the minute I saw you," he said, his gaze on my lips.

"I… I wanted that too," I whispered.

He rested his hand against the side of my face and leaned in to kiss me. The touch of his mouth sent a wave of heat into my blood. I grasped the front of his shirt and melted into the kiss, opening my mouth under his and letting him inside. Hot and damp, our tongues slid together, his breath warm and chocolaty.

A moan escaped me, urgent and filled with growing need. Tentatively, I forced my fists to unclench from his shirt and spread over the expanse of his chest. His hard muscles shifted beneath my hands as I slowly traced the lines up the length of his torso. He was all heat and lean, tensile strength, coiled with a power that I instinctively knew was both safe and protective.

He moved over me, his arms bracing on the sofa cushion beneath me as he angled his mouth more firmly over mine. Arousal flared in my belly as I felt the muscular weight of him moving on top of me, my breasts pressing to his chest. My nipples tightened, a response that jolted a shock of pleasure to my core.

Dean's kiss grew harder, more possessive. Trembles vibrated

through me. I sank against the sofa and gripped his back. After a moment of hesitation, my heart pounding, I slipped my hands beneath his shirt and over his naked skin. His smooth muscles flexed and pulled beneath my palms. He stroked his tongue over my lower lip. My sex throbbed.

"Ah, Liv…" His voice was hoarse as he eased back to look at me. He trailed his hand over the side of my neck down to my chest.

I drew in a breath when he cupped my breast, brushing his thumb over my hard nipple. Even through the cotton of my shirt and bra, I could feel the warmth of his hand. He shifted on top of me, nudging his knee between my legs. My skirt slid up my thighs.

I was falling, sinking into a whirlpool of sensations. Everything about him filled me—his fresh, clean scent, the taste of his chocolate-laced breath, the touch of his hands and scrape of his whiskers.

My mind fogged with pleasure and swirls of color that concealed any darkness. I arched my hips, seeking relief from the ache pulsing in my sex. He smoothed his hand up my bare leg, stroking the tender flesh of my inner thigh before brushing the cotton of my panties.

I moaned, pushing upward, heat spooling through me. His mouth came down on mine again the same instant he increased the pressure of his finger, sliding it against the damp crevice of my sex.

I gripped the sides of his head suddenly and wrenched away. I stared at him, our breathing hard. His eyes were hot with lust for *me*. Twin currents of energy—fear and desire— lanced into my heart. My face flamed.

"Olivia?" Dean cupped my cheek. Beneath the lust, confusion sparked in his expression. "What's wrong?"

"I… I'm sorry," I gasped, burning with shame and unfulfilled need.

Dean levered himself off me, his shoulders cording with tension. "No, it's me. I went too fast."

"No, it's not that. I…" *God in heaven.* Words stuck in my throat. Explanations tangled in my brain.

Dean tugged my skirt back down my legs and sat up. He dragged his hands over his face and through his hair, expelling his breath on a heavy sigh.

I stared at him, wanting to touch the strong lines of his profile, smooth my hand over his neck. I fought the ache threatening to break open my chest.

"Dean." My voice was thin and ragged.

He held up a hand. "Just… give me a minute, Liv."

Silence filled the space between us, broken only by the sound of our breathing. He pushed to his feet and went into the bathroom.

Embarrassed and not wanting to prolong the awkwardness for either of us, I slipped on my shoes, grabbed my bag, and hurried out the door. The street was bordered by several other apartment buildings, so there were at least three bus stops.

Cold air whipped against my face. Buttoning my jacket, I walked a few blocks to a stop farther away and prayed a bus would arrive soon.

"Liv!"

I tensed as Dean hurried toward me, his jaw tight with frustration. His jacket was open, his hair messy. He came to a stop and glowered at me.

"Where are you going?"

"Home." I hunched into my jacket against the chill.

Dean swore, pulling a hand down his face again before he visibly tried to regain control of his emotions. "If you want to go home, I'll take you."

"I do want to go home."

"Then come on." He turned and stalked toward the apartment building.

I shoved my hands into my pockets and followed him to the underground parking garage. Tears stung my eyes. I badly wanted to explain, but I didn't know where to start. And Dean's irritation felt like a forbidding wall I couldn't breach.

He yanked open the door for me, then went around to the driver's seat. Tense silence filled the air as he drove down University Avenue, his hands gripping the wheel. I thought he'd drop me off and leave, but he got out of the car to walk me to the front door.

I stopped on the doorstep and turned, keeping my gaze on the column of his throat. "I'm sorry."

He let out a breath and lifted a hand to touch me, then dropped it to his side. "You don't need to apologize. It's my fault."

"I'm not... I mean, I don't want you to think I'm playing games," I said.

The idea that he might think that of me was laughable. I was incapable of playing games with men. I didn't know any of the rules.

"No," he said. "I don't."

I fumbled to fit my key in the lock, my eyes stinging again. Dean waited until I was safely inside, but didn't respond to my mumbled good-night. Still, I felt his gaze on me through the glass door before I turned to walk up the stairs to my apartment.

Old memories and nightmares blistered my sleep that night until finally I got up and spent hours staring blindly at the TV. A black, empty pit cracked open inside me. At dawn, I hauled myself over to my computer and opened my email to find a message from him.

Liv, I'm so damn sorry. Can I see you again?

No. That was all I needed to say. I would never hear from him again.

N-o… My hands trembled on the keyboard. *No, you can't, Dean. You can't see me again, and I shouldn't want to see you…*

I stared at the message, trashed it, and wrote: *You can come over tonight.*

I hit the send button before I could think anymore. I sat there with my heart pounding until his response came four minutes later. *I'll be there at seven.*

I dressed and went to morning classes, worked an afternoon shift at Jitter Beans, then tried to study at the library before going home. I showered and changed into loose black pants and a T-shirt.

After clipping my hair back into a ponytail, I paced the living room until the bell rang five minutes before seven. I buzzed Dean in and left my apartment door partway open.

"Liv?" He knocked and pushed it open the rest of the way.

"Hi." I ran my shaking hands over my thighs, unable to

stop myself from drinking in the arresting sight of him in jeans and a rugby shirt that looked thick and soft. His hair was rumpled in the way I was beginning to love, the length brushing the top of his collar and curling over his ears.

He shut the door and shucked off his jacket, not looking anywhere but at me.

"Liv, I'm sorry," he said.

I shook my head. "It wasn't your fault."

"Yes, it was." His eyes flashed with self-directed irritation. "I went too fast, and I scared you. I didn't mean to."

Oh, Sir Galahad…

My throat constricted. "I wasn't… I don't want you to think…"

I didn't even know what to say, much less how to say it. As much as I had thought about being with a man like Dean West, I didn't know if I could ever actually *do* it.

And I didn't understand why he would even want me to.

Dean was successful, authoritative, experienced, sophisticated, assured.

I was not.

"Look, I…" He rubbed a hand over the back of his neck, slanting his gaze away from me. "I haven't been with a woman in a while, Liv."

"You haven't?"

"Since before my grandfather got sick. I had to deal with him and his illness, and between that and my book it didn't leave room for anything else. Or the desire, really."

"Oh."

"I'm telling you because you're the first woman in a long time whom I like," he said. "And I didn't mean to act like a horny teenager on his first date, but I did and I'm sorry. I do have more control than that and can move more slowly."

I almost smiled. Well, that was something. A sexually experienced professor who had been abstinent for a while, and now wanted... me. It would have been funny if it weren't another glaring reason why we couldn't possibly work.

Or could we?

A whisper in my mind, faint as the last ring of an echo.

I stared at Dean, the fathomless depths of his brown eyes, the lock of hair brushing his forehead. I remembered when he had pulled me close to him, and we fit together like the pieces of a puzzle.

I looked at his mouth and recalled how it had settled seamlessly against my lips. How his body had locked to mine, my curves yielding to the hard planes of his chest.

Maybe we could fit in other ways too, convex and concave, angles and hollows. His confidence might bolster my own. Certainly he could show me what true pleasure felt like. And I...

I'd have loved to believe I was a fair lady to his knight, but from what I could remember of the King Arthur tales, none of the women met with a desirable end.

No, I was just Olivia Winter. Still trying to find my way through. A woman who knew very well that knights didn't exist but held out hope that good men outnumbered the bad. A woman who still believed in leaps of faith, as long as you trusted your instincts.

I gestured toward the sofa. Dean and I sat down next to each other. Anxiety clenched my stomach as I struggled for a way to tell him the truth.

"I'm sorry I freaked out last night," I finally said. "It really wasn't you."

"What was it, then?" Dean asked.

"I…" *Just say it.*

A crease formed between his eyebrows. "Liv, I shouldn't have—"

"Dean, I'm a virgin."

He blinked. "What?"

My heart felt like it was about to claw out of my chest.

"I… I'm a virgin," I repeated. "I… I've never had intercourse before."

"Oh." Comprehension dawned in his expression. "So that's why you…"

"I just… I don't want you to think it was anything you did," I said. "It wasn't. Everything we did… I liked it. I wanted it."

I wanted you.

"It's weird, I know," I continued. Sweat collected at the base of my throat. "I'm twenty-four."

"It's not weird," Dean said.

Oh, with me, it definitely is.

"Well." I let out a shaky breath. "I wanted you to know. When I… when I asked you about your girlfriends, I didn't tell you that I haven't had a serious boyfriend. Ever. I've dated some, but mostly I've just kept to myself."

He frowned, as if he were trying to figure out what I wasn't saying. I avoided looking into his eyes, tracing my gaze over his shoulders and arms. My pulse tripped at the way he sat—the wide masculine stance of his feet on the carpet, his hands linked loosely between his knees.

"I'm not frigid or anything," I added quickly. "I mean, I have a collection of erotica and I... I touch myself... oh, God."

My face flared with embarrassment. *What the hell am I doing?* I pressed my hands to my cheeks and closed my eyes.

Dean moved close enough that I could smell his delicious mixture of soap and autumn air, and then he closed his hands around my wrists and pulled them away from my face.

I forced my eyes open, my throat aching. Tension still lined his features, as if he knew there was more, but warmth and affection filled his expression. That alone eased some of my rampant fear.

"Olivia." He skimmed his fingers across my hot cheek. "I want you. I won't hide that. I can't. But that's not the only reason I asked you out."

"Why did you, then?"

"Because you... you're different." He rubbed a lock of my hair between his thumb and forefinger. "I've spent most of my life trying too damn hard to prove myself to other people. To surpass their expectations. Or trying to fix things when I failed. But that only meant driving myself harder to succeed."

Something inside me loosened at his confession. I knew all about presenting a very specific version of yourself to others. No matter how heart-wrenchingly difficult it was.

"I don't feel like I have to try so hard with you," Dean said.

"So you're saying I'm easy?" I lifted an eyebrow skeptically.

A smile tugged at his mouth. "I mean you're easy to be with. I need to prove myself to you, but in a good way. Because I want to, not because I have to."

He suddenly looked embarrassed and let go of me. He paced to the windows, his hands shoved into his pockets.

"I don't think turtles have very interesting lives."

North's voice, wry and gravelly, echoed at the back of my mind. Some of my anxiety eased.

Dean was no reclusive turtle. That much was certain. He had an innate self-assurance, a way of moving through the world that I wished I could cultivate. And he was sexually confident, even I could see that, experienced in how to please a woman. He would know exactly what to do.

The question was—did I want him to do it to me?

The answer was—

I gazed at the expanse of Dean's back, the way he stood with his feet apart, as if he were rooted to the ground. Solid. Secure.

"What about those string figures, professor?" I asked.

"What about them?"

"You said you'd show me how to do them." I paused. "I'll bet you carry a piece of string around, don't you?"

He turned to face me, his eyes sparking with amusement. He dug into the pocket of his jeans and produced a loop of string. With a few maneuvers, he hooked it around his fingers into a familiar pattern and approached me.

"Do you know cat's cradle?" he asked.

"Believe it or not, I do." I pinched the X-shaped pattern, pulled it around to the middle, and fastened the string around my fingers.

Dean took the string from the top, looped it to form another pattern, then held out his hands and let me make the next move.

CHAPTER EIGHT

*D*ean came into Jitter Beans often over the next couple of weeks. Every time I saw him, my pulse sped up and bright, happy sparks flew through me. We had dinner, met between classes for lunch or coffee, took walks in the Arboretum.

He didn't kiss me again in those early days, though he touched me often. Gentle touches—pushing a lock of hair away from my cheek, holding my hand, cupping the back of my neck. The brush of his fingers filled me with a pleasant heat.

The more time I spent with Dean, the more I liked and trusted him. And it wasn't long before he proved that he was meant to be my hero alone.

"Bears," he said one afternoon as we walked up State Street after my shift at Jitter Beans.

"No way." I poked him in the side. "Definitely the Packers. I'd be a terrible Wisconsinite if I weren't a Packer Backer."

He scoffed. "Then you must love dancing the polka."

"Why would I love dancing the polka?"

"It's the Wisconsin state dance. Since you're such a loyal Wisconsinite and all."

I poked him in the side again, harder this time, which made him laugh and reach out to tweak my nose. I decided not to be annoyed since it was so darned cute the way his eyes crinkled at the corners when he laughed.

"How do you even know the Wisconsin state dance if you're from California?" I asked. "Oh, I forgot. You're kind of a geek."

He flashed me a smile. "Got a problem with that?"

"I have a problem with the fact that you prefer the Bears," I said. "*Star Wars* or *Star Trek?*"

"*Trek.*"

"We are so incompatible," I moaned. "Star *Wars.*"

"Lucas jumped the shark with *Episode One*," Dean said. "*Star Trek* has always had a universal message about justice and a utopian society."

"*Star Wars* is about the battle between good and evil. What's more universal than that?"

"*Star Trek* had alien babes in bikinis."

"You don't remember Princess Leia's bikini?"

"Oh, yeah." He got a glazed, faraway look in his eyes. "Good point."

"I rest my case. Ben and Jerry's or Häagen-Dazs?"

"Both."

"Me too. Except for Chunky Monkey, which is gross."

"Ah." Dean gave a sigh of relief. "We have common ground. Tolstoy or Dostoevsky?"

I rolled my eyes. "Whatever, professor."

Dean winked at me. I smiled back, enjoying the lovely heart flutters spreading warmth through my veins.

He opened the passenger side door for me, then went around to get behind the wheel of his car.

"How was work?" he asked as he headed toward Dayton Street.

I told him about an espresso maker mishap and a couple of irrelevant stories about the customers. We took the elevator to my apartment, which he hadn't been in since the night of my confession two weeks ago.

"Nice place, by the way," he remarked as we went inside. "I didn't notice before. How long have you lived here?"

"Since July." The rent on the shoebox-sized apartment was more than I could comfortably pay, but it was close to downtown, the university, and Jitter Beans. I'd spent a lot of time at garage and rummage sales looking for inexpensive furnishings, and I was pleased with the way my decorating had turned out.

I'd found some mismatched round tables that I refinished a light honey color and placed alongside my curved sofa. Floating shelves held my books, prints of English gardens lined the walls, and I'd placed lamps strategically to light the corners. Sheer, sage-green curtains softened the utilitarian blinds, and my indoor garden of fifteen plants sat on a multi-tiered stand beneath the window.

Dean touched one of the plants. "You really have a green thumb. What kind are these?"

"Mostly flowers, but there's a spider ivy on the bottom

tier," I said. "Geraniums, begonias, pentas. I bought a yellow amaryllis last week. I haven't named it yet."

"Named it?"

Embarrassment heated my cheeks. "I name all my plants. Svengali, Mrs. Danvers, Cruella de Vil, the White Witch."

He turned to look at me. "You name your plants after villains?"

"Just a silly thing. A way of turning something bad into something good." I went toward the kitchen. "Can I get you a soda?"

"Just water, thanks."

I poured him a glass and returned to the living room. He'd wandered over to examine the books on the shelves. I flushed at the thought that I had some spicy erotica titles tucked in among the textbooks. If he saw them, however, he gave no indication. Or he didn't mind.

Instead he picked up the small, framed picture of North that I kept on the lower shelf. Nervousness rolled through me suddenly. I'd never talked about North with anyone, not because I didn't want to but because I'd never had anyone to talk about him *with*.

I'd taken the picture outside North's workshop and made a bunch of silly faces until he'd finally smiled. His grin showed through his bushy beard, the little braid tied with a red ribbon visible on the right side, and his leathery features squinted against the sun. His long, graying hair was pulled back into a ponytail.

"Your dad?" Dean asked.

"No." I put the glass on the coffee table and wiped my hands on my skirt. "Just a good friend from California. Not that kind of friend," I added when he glanced at me with a hint of a scowl. "The kind of friend who helps you remember which way is up. And who reminds you that sometimes that's the only direction you can go."

Dean looked at me, still holding the photo. "You're lucky to have a friend like that."

"North was... special."

"North?"

"Short for Northern Star Richmond."

"Seriously?"

I smiled. "His parents were hippies."

Dean put the photo back on the shelf. "So you used to live in California?"

"I traveled there a few times with my mother, then I went back before I started at community college. Lived on a commune."

"A commune?"

"They're called other things now. Intentional communities. Cooperative living. But, yeah, it was near Santa Cruz. Twelve Oaks. My mother and I lived there when I was thirteen, then I went back by myself a few years later. I thought I'd just visit for a week or so, but I stayed for a year. North was the guy who ran the place."

I realized I was opening the door to questions I didn't want to answer. I gestured to the sofa. "So make yourself at home. I'm just going to take a quick shower and change."

"Take your time."

He settled on the sofa and picked up a coffee-table book about the history of literature. I went into my bedroom and closed the door. As I stripped out of my clothes, my heart pounded harder. I was acutely aware that a thin wall separated me from Dean.

Was he remembering that night in his apartment? Was he thinking about kissing me again? Was he thinking about me undressing?

My blood warmed at the speculation. I pushed my underwear off and stood there naked for a moment, staring at my reflection in the mirror on the opposite wall. I didn't often look at myself naked. My legs were short but well shaped, and I had a curvy, full-breasted body that I was still, at twenty-four, trying to feel comfortable in.

I slid my hands down my waist, which tapered to round hips and my not-quite-flat belly. I tried to imagine Dean's hands on me, his long fingers sliding across my hipbones and down between my legs.

I shivered and turned away from the mirror. My cheeks warmed. I pulled on a thick robe and ducked into the bathroom. After turning on the shower, I stood under the hot spray and wondered what it would feel like to breach the distance between my imagination and reality.

My very vivid imagination. My very mundane reality.

I wanted to live in the space where the two met. I imagined it as a place of sunlight and green trees where a man and I wanted each other with crackling desire and our bodies fell into pleasure.

I closed my eyes and let the water stream over my face. What if Dean was thinking about me in the shower? What if he was imagining what I looked like naked and wet? I trembled at the thought, almost feeling the heat of his gaze.

A bolt of arousal went through me. I grabbed the soap

and lathered up, drawing in a sharp breath when my palms glided over my hard nipples. Pleasure zinged along my nerves. He was *there*. Sitting so close…

I rubbed soapy froth over my belly. The bubbles slipped from my skin. Hot water pounded on my neck and shoulders. I grasped the shower bar and rubbed the soap between my legs, unable to resist pressing a finger into my cleft. A shudder rocked me. *Oh…*

Was Dean imagining this right now? Was he thinking about me rubbing soap over my body? Was he picturing me playing with myself, sliding my forefinger over the folds of my sex, pressing my hand against my clit?

I could *see* him standing there, all hot and aroused while he watched me. I could see the burn in his eyes, the flush of his cheekbones, the heaviness of his cock against his trousers.

I pressed one hand to the tiled wall and lowered my head against the spray. I worked my fingers faster, harder, my blood swelling with urgency. His fingers would be adept, expert, his touch precise.

He would know when to slide a finger into me, when to roll his thumb around my clit. He would suck my nipples at the same time, intensifying my arousal, his breath hot.

Oh, I wanted it, wanted to know what it was like, wanted his hands and mouth on me. I saw him clutching my hips, lifting me, pushing his cock between my legs, his eyes filled with desire. I saw myself, pink-flushed and panting, writhing against him, water beading on my breasts, my hair plastered in wet tendrils to my skin.

I imagined what it would feel like, him filling me with one deep thrust as I gripped his shoulders and begged for more. My nerves flared with sparks. I would tighten my inner flesh around his thick shaft, feel his groan rumble against my neck as he pushed inside me again and again, driving us both to the edge of bliss.

He'd talk dirty too, his voice rough in my ear, his fingers digging into my hips. *"Open your pussy for me, Liv... I want to fuck you deep... so deep you'll still feel it tomorrow... make you come until you scream... ah, you're tight... so damn good..."*

He would thrust slowly at first, then harder, an intense, thorough fucking that would shake my body and wrench his name from my throat as I arched my hips and creamed all over his cock...

A gasp escaped me as I came, clenching my thighs around my rapid fingers, vibrations rolling through me. I shuddered and inhaled a gulp of hot, steam-laced air as the sensations peaked and ebbed. Breathing hard, I absorbed the final quivers as the water began to cool.

I turned the faucet off and stepped out, pressing a towel against my face as my heartbeat slowed. I had no idea how long I'd been in the shower, but likely it was far too long for a "quick shower." I dried off, shrugged into my robe, and darted back into the bedroom.

Soon, I silently promised myself as I dressed in jeans and a sweatshirt. Soon I would close the distance between us again. I knew it would be so much better than anything I could imagine.

And I could imagine quite a bit.

After brushing my hair, I went back into the living room. Dean was still sitting on the sofa, working a loop of string into patterns between his palms.

"Sorry," I said, my voice breathless. "Uh, the shower felt too… good, I guess."

"No problem. Game doesn't start until six." He unlaced the string from his fingers and looked at me.

I knew my face was still flushed from my little erotic interlude, and I had the sudden fear he knew exactly what I'd been doing.

Not fear. *Hope.*

The realization struck me.

I *hoped* he knew what I'd been doing. The idea that he'd been sitting here, imagining me in the shower the way I'd imagined him watching me… my breath caught.

Dean's cell phone rang, breaking apart my thoughts. He sighed as he pulled it from his pocket. "Sorry, Liv."

"Go ahead."

His expression tensed as he looked at the caller ID. "Paige? What… no, I didn't tell her I'd do anything… if he doesn't get his shit together…"

My stomach knotted. I suspected he was talking about his brother. Paige must be his sister.

"You're damn right he won't," Dean snapped into the phone.

Uneasy at overhearing a private conversation, I went into the kitchen and turned the water faucet on full blast to drown out Dean's voice. After a few minutes, he came in, his expression set with frustration. I tightened my hands on a dishtowel.

"Is everything okay?" I asked.

"Depends on what you mean by okay." He tossed his phone on the counter. "My brother has been a troublemaker his whole life. I wouldn't give a shit if it didn't cause problems for everyone else." His mouth twisted. "It's kind of fucked-up."

Oh, Dean. I know all about fucked-up.

It should have made me wary, this revelation of a bitter family relationship in which he was tangled. Instead I wanted only to erase that pained look on his face, ease the furrows lining his forehead.

I stepped closer to him. I pressed my forefinger between his eyes, smoothing away the deep crease. His breath hitched, his gaze searching mine.

I was becoming accustomed to seeing Dean look at me with affection and heat. I was not accustomed to this look of aggravation, the sense that he *needed* something from me.

What? What could I give him?

I certainly wasn't the kind of woman who could comfort a man with her body. Or with her cooking. Or even with any good suggestions on how to deal with his family.

I tilted my head to the kitchen table. "Sit down."

"Shouldn't we get going?"

"In a minute. First sit down."

He sat. I stood behind him and took his earlobes between my thumbs and forefingers, then rubbed them gently.

"Uh…," he said.

"It's an ear massage. Excellent way to reduce stress and release endorphins. Just relax."

He didn't obey the command right away, given the tightness of his neck muscles. I stroked his earlobes, then pressed along the outer edge of his ears all the way to the top. I massaged the whorls and behind his ears along his skull. After a few minutes, the tension in his shoulders eased.

"That feels really good," he remarked.

"You sound surprised."

"Where'd you learn to do that?"

"There was a woman at Twelve Oaks who was into ear reflexology," I explained.

Dean closed his eyes while I started the massage process again, rubbing his earlobes, the exterior, then moving to the back of his neck. I looked down at his hair and thought about pressing my lips to the top of his head.

I kneaded the muscles of his shoulders. Warmth flowed from his skin up the length of my arms.

"Ear reflexology is a whole practice," I said in an attempt to redirect my thoughts. "Different points on the ears relate to different parts of the body, that kind of thing. I don't know much about it, except that it feels good. Sometimes that's enough."

"Sometimes that's everything."

Crowds of people clad in red UW jackets and sweatshirts streamed toward the football stadium. A layer of clouds further darkened the evening sky, and a brisk chill swept across our faces as we walked alongside Dayton Street.

I nudged Dean's arm. "You forgot your gloves."

"It's okay."

I took my hand out of my pocket and wrapped it around his so his fingers wouldn't get cold. He closed his hand around mine.

We followed the swarm of red toward the stadium, where a log-jam of people crowded one of the arched entrances. Dean paused to dig two tickets out of his pocket, then eased me ahead of him as we kept walking.

Voices and laughter rose like flocks of birds, a palpable excitement in the air. I circled around a group of college boys and joined the slow lines moving into the stadium.

I turned back to Dean, only to find a group of people had gotten between us. I knew he wasn't far behind, so I stepped out of the line and craned my neck around to look for him. I took a few more steps away toward the stadium, and then I was between the wall and the crowd.

A sudden unease raced through me. I didn't like the feeling of being trapped. I started to push back into the line, but two big, young men moved in front of me.

The backs of their red sweatshirts filled my vision. Their laughter rang in my ears. The smell of beer and brats assaulted my nose.

Panic hit hard and fast. I froze. My chest tightened, and my heartbeat raced. Sweat broke out on my forehead. I tried to draw in a breath, but the air was stale and hot from all the bodies, and it stuck in my throat like a stone.

The boys were turned away from me, oblivious to my presence, their voices eager as they discussed the upcoming game. Black spots swam in my vision. My skin prickled with cold. Part of me knew what I needed to do to calm down, but I couldn't do it.

Fear paralyzed my brain. The crowd surged. The bigger guy bumped against me. My stomach roiled with nausea.

"Liv, sorry, I thought you…" Dean pushed past the frat boys. "Liv?" He stopped and grabbed my arm. "What's wrong?"

I was shaking too hard to respond. He pulled me away from the wall, away from the boys. I stumbled. My legs weakened as dizziness swamped me.

Dean slid his hand beneath my elbow and guided me to a bench, the crowd still swarming in a sea of red.

"P-panic attack," I whispered. "Need... need to... b-breathe..."

A woman's voice penetrated the ringing in my ears. I forced air into my lungs and looked up, her face a blur, her words sounding very far away.

"... all right... need help... ?"

I clenched my fingers around Dean's arm and shook my head. He settled his other hand on my back as he declined the woman's offer of assistance. She moved away. I pulled in another breath. My chest ached.

"Liv, look at me." His voice was calm, steady.

I tried, wanting to anchor myself, but I couldn't focus on his face, couldn't suppress the urge to run. I lowered my head. The world spun. I tightened my fingers on Dean's arm, overwhelmed by the horrible feeling that I was about to lose my grip on reality.

"Talk... talk to me," I gasped. "C-count."

"Take a deep breath in. Nice and slow." He sat beside me on the bench. He pulled my scarf away from my throat, the rush of air a welcome relief on my hot skin. "One. Two. Three."

I managed to pull a breath into my lungs. A new, different fear arose that Dean's proximity would intensify my panic, but instead the pressure of his hand and the rumble of his voice loosened the constriction in my chest.

"Again," he ordered, tilting my chin toward him. "Another breath on the count of three, okay?"

I stared at his serious expression, his unwavering gaze, and nodded. He counted. I inhaled. Again and again until the tension began to seep away with every exhale. My heartbeat steadied. I kept my hand curled around Dean's arm, finding comfort in the solid feel of his muscles beneath his sweatshirt.

He counted. I breathed. Over and over until air filled my chest without hurting, and the sharp pain in my throat dissipated.

When I finally felt more in control, I swiped at my damp forehead and rested my elbows on my knees. My heartbeat still pounded in my head, but it no longer felt as if it was about to burst.

I stared at the ground. Embarrassment, shame, began to fill the empty space inside me.

"Drink some water, Liv."

I accepted the bottle Dean extended and took a small sip. Slowly the world around me came into focus again. A few people still milled around, but the last of the crowd was disappearing through the entrance. A raucous cheer came from inside the stadium like steam billowing from an enormous pot.

I clenched my fists to hide the lingering trembles. I couldn't look at Dean.

"Better?" he asked.

I nodded. "S-sorry." I rubbed a hand over my face and looked toward the stadium. "The game's about to start."

"I don't care about the game. Can you walk home or should I call us a cab?"

"I want to walk." Grateful that he no longer expected us to go to the game, I stood on shaky legs. "But you don't have to…"

"Come on." He slipped his hand beneath my elbow again as we headed back toward Dayton Street. I kept my scarf loose and unfastened the ties of my sweatshirt to feel the cold air. Exhaustion swamped me.

We walked the length of Dayton Street in silence. The movement felt good, dispelling the threads of anxiety and tension. I shoved my hands into my pockets and hunched my shoulders as we rounded Marion Street to my apartment building.

"You don't have to come up," I said, the words sticking in my throat as I fumbled to find my key.

"I need to know you're okay."

I let him follow me inside and up the elevator. Once in the safety of my apartment, I sank into a chair and rested my head against the back.

Tears stung my eyes. I tried not to think. I heard Dean rustling around, and then the scent of peppermint tea filled my nose.

"Found it in the kitchen," he said, placing a cup on the table beside me.

I sat up slowly, too exhausted to hide my dismay. "I'm… I'm so sorry."

"I'm not a fan of peppermint tea, but you don't need to apologize for it."

I managed to crack a smile and looked up. He stood right in front of me, not too close, his hands loose on his hips. Despite the wry tone of his voice, his eyes were dark with concern.

My heart hurt with a different kind of ache. The threat of a panic attack always hovered at the edges of my consciousness, but I hadn't experienced one in over three years. The fact that I just had reminded me with the force of a blow of my damaged psyche. And the fact that Dean had witnessed it…

God in heaven.

"I'm... they don't happen often," I finally stammered. "I... I almost forgot how to deal with them."

"How long have you had them?" he asked.

"They started when I was eighteen. I went to a therapist and learned behavioral and breathing techniques, but even then they didn't happen often. I know the triggers, so I've managed to avoid situations that might cause them."

Dean frowned. "Crowds?"

"Sometimes," I said vaguely. "I haven't... haven't been around people much in the past few years."

I couldn't get into this. Not now. Maybe not ever.

I put a hand over my eyes. "I'm sorry, Dean. I'm exhausted."

I couldn't muster the courage to ask, but I wished he would stay. Though I'd never panicked before without the specific trigger of feeling trapped, the threat of another attack was still there. As much as I didn't want Dean to witness my panic again, I was more scared of being alone.

"I hate to leave you, Liv."

I lowered my hand to look at him. The tender concern in his expression eased my anxiety. "I'm really not a total basket case."

"I know. How about I sleep on the sofa tonight?"

"You wouldn't mind?"

"I want to." He drew a few strands of my hair between his fingers, looking as if he were studying them in the light.

Relieved and glad to have something to do besides sit there trembling, I went into my bedroom to get him a clean towel and washcloth. I found an unopened toothbrush in the bathroom cabinet and a fresh bar of soap, which I put on top of the folded towel.

"I keep extra quilts in here." I took a few magazines and books off the storage chest that served as a coffee table. "Hold on, I'll get you a pillow too."

Apparently sensing my surge of jittery energy, Dean stayed out of the way while I bustled around getting a quilt spread out and the pillows fluffed.

"Here's a clock if you want to keep it beside the sofa." I put a battery-powered digital clock on a small table. "Do you want the remote control too?"

"Liv." Dean put a gentle hand on my shoulder. Affection and something else, something more somber, filled his eyes. "Everything's fine."

"Okay." I ran my damp palms over my thighs. "Sorry... sorry again for..."

Shit. My throat jammed up.

"Stop apologizing, Liv. Go get some sleep."

Rather than try and speak, I just nodded and went into my room. I slipped into a T-shirt and pajama bottoms and managed to brush my teeth and hair before falling into bed. The one blessing of a panic attack, if one could call it a *blessing*, was that I always slept hard for a few hours afterward. It was one of the few times I was able to sleep well.

I woke to the reddish glow of my clock. One thirty-two. Pushing aside the covers, I went into the kitchen for a glass of water. The living room curtains were partly open, allowing a thin stream of moonlight to illuminate Dean stretched out on the sofa. Clutching the glass, I moved closer to look at him.

It should have been strange to me that his presence was a comfort rather than cause for apprehension, but it felt entirely... normal.

I put the glass down, then sat on a chair by the sofa and looked at him. He seemed younger in sleep, the lines of his face eased, his closed eyes concealing the flashes of darkness whose source I still didn't know.

I could almost see him as he might have been as a boy—full of youthful energy and confidence, knowing he would blaze a trail through the world, surrounded by people who admired him.

A band tightened around my heart. How different from my own wariness, my inability to envision my own future beyond the tangled, dark forest of my childhood where an oppressive queen ruled.

Dean opened his eyes. We looked at each other for a moment before he pushed up to sitting. He dragged a hand through his hair, over his rough jaw.

"Hi," he said, his voice hoarse with sleep.

"Hi. Thanks for staying."

I couldn't believe how comforting it was to have him here, how grateful I was to wake up and not be alone. Even when I was at Twelve Oaks… I'd never felt so warmed by the presence of another person.

I have been so fucking lonely.

My throat tightened.

"You okay?" Dean asked.

"Can I get you anything?" I whispered. "Something to drink?"

He shook his head. Moonlight slanted through the curtains, a stripe of it cutting across the shadows on his face.

I owed him an explanation. I knew that.

I took a breath. "Dean, I'm… I need to tell you some things about me."

Faint wariness flashed in his eyes. "Okay."

"When I said I traveled a lot as a kid, it was because of my mother," I explained, resisting the memories pushing at the back of my head. "Crystal. She was very self-centered. Controlling. She'd been a spoiled, coddled child… actually had a successful career as a child model for a couple of years and was in a national commercial.

"But the career offers waned when *her* mother got a reputation for being unreasonable and demanding, a typical stage mother. No one wanted to work with Crystal anymore. She was in some beauty pageants and talent shows, but then she got pregnant with me when she was seventeen. Changed her whole life. She never stopped resenting me for that."

I reached for my water and took a sip. "Her parents disowned her because of the pregnancy. She had to drop out of high school and move in with my father. They never got along. They fought a lot about money… or lack thereof. They broke up when I was seven.

"I found out later that my father was having an affair." The word lodged in my throat. "He was going to leave my mother to be with the other woman. My aunt Stella, my father's sister, once told me he'd still wanted to have a relationship with me, you know, still be my father. But my mother said she'd never let him near me again.

"So she packed up her car and we took off. She was restless, always wanting to be somewhere else, always wanting to find the attention she'd had as a child. We moved a lot. I lost track of the number of cities and towns we stayed in."

"How long did you and your mother live like that?" Dean asked.

"Until I was thirteen. I finally told my mother I was going to live with Aunt Stella up in Pepin County. I wanted to have a normal life. My mother and I had a huge fight about it.

"We were in Dubuque. I woke up one morning and she was gone. She'd taken the car, most of our stuff. I had just enough money for a bus ride to Madison, where I called Stella to come and pick me up. I didn't hear from my mother for years."

"You lived with your aunt after that?"

"Yes. Through high school."

"When did you see your mother again?"

An ache crawled over my heart. "When she came to visit right before my senior year. She wanted me to come with her again, but I refused. She'll never forgive me for leaving her."

And in some ways, I would never forgive myself.

"Did you ever see your dad again?" Dean asked.

"No. I guess Aunt Stella heard from him a few times when he was looking for me, but she didn't often know where we were either so she couldn't tell him anything. Then when I was eleven, we got word that he'd died."

"How did your mother manage to support you?"

"She hooked up with a lot of men," I said. An unwelcome barrage of male faces and voices went through my brain. "That was how she found places to stay. She'd convince a guy to let us live with him for a while with the understanding that she'd share his bed. Most of the time, she waited until they agreed… or sometimes after she'd moved in… before telling them she had a daughter."

"What the—"

"She told me to hide a lot," I explained. "To wait in the

car while she spent a few hours at a bar. Sometimes she left me at a public library, then came back to get me after she'd found a guy. Sometimes she made an effort to earn money by selling jewelry that she made, but I think she found it easier to rely on men to support her."

I stared at my hands clutched around the glass of water.

"She was quite beautiful," I said. "That was part of the reason she never had trouble finding a man. She had long blond hair and green eyes. A great figure. And she was confident as a woman, secure in her sexuality. Even if she wasn't looking for someone, men were attracted to her. The problem was that it was rarely the right kind of man."

My voice faded. There had been good men in the six years we were on the road. A karate instructor who gave me forms lessons and talked to me about things like respect, focus, and self-discipline. An insurance salesman who built model airplanes as a hobby. A camera-shop owner who taught me the basics of photo composition.

An MIT-graduate-turned-hippie named Northern Star who convinced me I was worth something.

I pushed the thought of him aside. That one hurt too much.

"Through men and sex, my mother found the attention she'd lost when she was younger," I said. "It seemed so... easy for her."

"But it was horrible for you."

"I hated every minute of it," I admitted. "When she left me alone, I was so scared she'd never come back. And I couldn't stand having to live with men I didn't know, sleeping on dirty sofas or on the floor. I'd often hear my mother having sex in the next room. A few times I walked in on her and some strange man. It doesn't take a genius to understand why I'm still a virgin at twenty-four."

Finally I looked up at Dean. He was watching me, wary, tense, as if steeling himself against what I hadn't yet confessed.

"I was... I'd always tried hard to be invisible so no one would notice me," I said. "And for a while it worked. My mother was so stunning, so forceful, that no one paid attention to her quiet, mousy daughter. I'd also learned there was safety in hiding, that if people didn't know you were there, they couldn't bother you. That was exactly how I wanted it."

I drew in a breath. "But my luck ran out when... when one of the men messed with me." I spoke in a hard rush, desperate to finally get it out. "Another one tried a year later, but I got away from him in time."

Dean swore—a violent, cutting sound—and shoved to his feet.

"The guy was... he masturbated in front of me," I said, bile rising in my chest as the memory stabbed the back of my head. "First when I was asleep. I was nine. I woke up once in the middle of the night and saw him standing beside my bed. I didn't know at the time what he was doing, but I knew it was wrong. I... I didn't know what to do, so I pretended I was still asleep."

"Jesus, Liv."

"My mother... she knew about it." I could hardly speak past the tightness in my throat. "I saw the door open one night, Dean. There was... there was no lock on the door, and

I *saw her* look in when he was doing it. I thought for sure she would stop him, that she'd protect me, that she'd do something, but…"

"She didn't?" His voice was strangled.

I shook my head, the harshness of the betrayal splitting open inside me. "I watched her close the door. I didn't move. Couldn't. She'd left me alone with the sick bastard."

"Liv, I—"

I held up my hand. "She wouldn't listen when I told her we had to leave. All I could do was avoid the guy as much as possible and pray he didn't do anything else. Then one day he brought me a cake for my tenth birthday. Told me he'd only let me have a piece if I touched his penis. He took it out and started to… and before I could get away from him, my mother walked in."

"What… what did she do?"

Old, raw anger and fear pierced my heart. My vision blurred.

"She blamed me for exciting him," I confessed. "Said if I'd been wearing a looser T-shirt, he wouldn't have been tempted." I hugged my arms around myself. "It wasn't the last time I'd hear some version of that accusation."

"What the hell, Liv?" Rage flared through Dean, his fists clenching. "What kind of mother says that to her daughter?"

"She had problems of her own." Sensing his anger about to explode, I rose to approach him. "I've tried to accept that, but it takes work. A couple of weeks later, we finally left the guy's house. I'd never been so thankful to move. God knows what else he would have done."

Dean swore again and pressed his palms to his eyes. "I'm

so fucking sorry, Liv. I suspected something had happened to you, but I hoped to hell I was wrong."

Oh, there's more.

I couldn't tell him all of it, though. Not now. Too soon.

"Is that the cause of your panic attacks?" he asked.

"Some, yes," I admitted. "I've been through a lot of therapy. Learned how to deal with it. But I want you to know before…" *…this goes any farther.*

He lowered his hands to look at me. "Before what?"

"I don't… I don't expect you to stick around and try to deal with my issues." My chest hurt as I forced the words out.

Dean looked at me for a minute before he cupped my face in his warm hands.

"I meant what I said the other night, Liv," he told me. "If you don't want to do anything, we won't. If you want to go slow, we'll go slow. If you want to end this right now, I'll walk away from you. It'll kill me to do it, but if you want me to, I will."

The choice is yours, Liv.

He didn't have to say it. His gift of a *choice* was a balm to my cracked heart.

"I don't want you to walk away," I said.

"Good." The lines between his eyes eased with relief.

I gripped his wrists, a knot of fear binding my throat. "But you… you might want to go," I warned.

Darkness flashed in his expression. "Why?"

My eyes stung. I swallowed hard.

"Here be monsters," I whispered.

A heartbeat of silence, brewing with danger, filled the space between us. Then Dean tightened his hold on me and, with his thumbs, brushed away the tears that spilled down my cheeks.

"Liv," he said, his voice rough with tenderness, "you don't have to be afraid."

"Why not?"

"Because I'll slay monsters for you."

CHAPTER NINE

$\mathcal{S}$eptember eased into October of our first year together. Burnished leaves flared from the trees and began to fall in a blazing carpet of yellow and red. A pleasant chill bit through the air. Classes continued, the rhythm of the semester settling into a soothing march.

Being with Dean was so easy that my fear began to subside. If anyone could slay monsters, he could—though I would never ask that of him. I did know he was the one with whom I could discover all the hot, sexy things I'd imagined but never done.

I knew he was waiting for me to let him know when I wanted more, that I had to be the one to make the next move. I knew he would wait for as long as it took.

It didn't take long. I thought about him a *lot*. My dreams

burned with memories of his lips crushing mine, his hand sliding up my naked thigh, my breasts pressed against his chest. I woke breathless and throbbing, often rubbing myself to orgasm before I even got out of bed.

A week after my confession, I invited him over to watch a movie. Which I asked him to pick. Which was my mistake.

"Oh, Lord." I dumped a pot of fresh-popped corn into a bowl and rolled my eyes. "Is that another key to unlocking you, then? Obscure foreign movies?"

He looked offended. "This is not an obscure movie. It's a classic Tarkovsky film about a fifteenth-century Russian icon painter."

"Oh, well in that case…"

"Give it a chance, would you?" He put the disc in the machine and hit the play button before settling back on the sofa.

I'd give it a chance because he looked astonishingly sexy sprawled out over my sofa, one arm slung over the back so that the material of his T-shirt stretched across his broad chest. His hair was all disheveled, his jaw coated with the stubble that I'd come to expect on casual evenings and weekends.

As long as I could sneak glances at him from the other side of the sofa, we could have been watching a movie about the bubonic plague, for all I cared.

I handed him the bowl of buttered popcorn and sat down, tucking my legs underneath my skirt. The movie started with a man getting entangled in the ropes of a hot-air balloon, which then caught a gust of wind and carried him through the sky.

After that somewhat promising start, there was drama about people seeking shelter in a barn to escape a rainstorm, then a philosophical discussion between two monks about grief and knowledge.

Fifteen minutes in, I took the popcorn bowl back and ate a few handfuls. Twenty minutes in, I yawned. Thirty minutes in, I felt Dean glance at me.

"No?" he asked.

I snored.

"Ah, Olivia." He sighed and reached for the remote control. "You're breaking my heart."

"My being bored by a movie about a *Russian icon painter* is enough to break your heart?" I said in disbelief. "What happens when I tell you that medieval history puts me into a coma?"

"Quick!" Dean clutched his chest. "Administer mouth-to-mouth resuscitation."

I giggled. He straightened and winked at me before turning off the TV.

"Okay, then," he said. "A Russian icon painter doesn't do it for you. What does?"

"This really handsome medieval history professor." My breath escaped me with the blunt confession.

Our gazes collided across the expanse of the sofa. A current of electricity crackled between us. We hadn't kissed since that night in his apartment. I knew we both wanted to. I also knew I had to be the one to initiate it.

I pushed the popcorn bowl aside and got to my knees. My pulse intensified as I moved across the sofa and knelt by his side. A slight tension rippled through him. I put out a hand and placed it on his warm chest. His heart pounded.

"What does the R stand for?" he asked.

"The R?"

"Olivia R. Winter. Rachel?"

"Rose."

"Olivia Rose Winter." His voice wrapped around my name, deep and caressing. "Pretty."

"Thanks." I tilted my head to study him. "Have you ever dated a student before?"

"You're not my student, but no. Never."

"So why me?"

"Couldn't stay away from you." He lifted a hand to cover mine where it rested on his chest. "Didn't want to."

"I'm not…" I swallowed to ease the dryness of my throat. "I'm not like other girls."

"I know."

"And you're okay with that?"

"More than okay."

I wondered why, but couldn't bring myself to ask for fear he might expect more of my own revelations. I was twenty-four, and I had yet to explore my own sexuality deeply and thoroughly. I'd wanted to for years, but was thwarted by so many things—fear, danger, shame, inhibitions.

None of which I experienced with Dean.

I knew I could be unreservedly passionate with him. He'd take me places I'd only dreamed about and keep me safe the entire time. Even when I'd confessed about the scars knitting through my soul, he had not retreated.

Just the opposite, in fact. He'd drawn his sword in readiness to protect me.

I curled my fingers against his chest. "I'll need to go slow."

"I can go slow."

"It might be too slow for you."

Dean looked at me for a long minute, a shallow crease between his eyebrows, as if he were trying to figure me out.

"I like downhill skiing," he finally said.

I blinked. "Okay."

"I like speedboats and bungee jumping." He leaned forward and put his hand beneath my chin. "I also like hiking, rock climbing, and fishing."

"That's... um, very diverse of you."

A smile tugged at his mouth. "My point is that fast is fun. It's exciting, an adrenaline charge. But slow is no less satisfying. In fact, it can be even more of a rush to work and savor every step rather than fixate on getting to the end."

"Well." I exhaled a long breath, my skin tingling at the idea of savoring every step. "That's good to know."

"I'll wait." He lowered his hand from my chin and sat back. "Until you're ready for me."

"And you won't..."

"I won't pressure you."

"I know." I stared at the half-circle of tanned skin above the collar of his T-shirt. "I meant, there's a lot of *other* stuff besides intercourse that I'd like to do with you first, but I'd hate for you to think I'm..."

"Playing games?"

"Or being a tease." I forced my gaze back to his.

Pain and anger flashed in his eyes, emotions I'd seen that night I told him about my childhood.

"I don't think that of you," he said. "I won't."

"Okay." My heartbeat sped up a little. "So we can fool around but take it slow and see where it leads us?"

"We can do that, beauty."

Beauty.

I smiled, pleasure diminishing my unease like sunlight on shadows. I turned my hand where it rested on his chest so our palms met. His strong fingers closed around mine.

"Can I tell you something?" I asked after a few minutes.

"Sure."

"Remember when I told you I..." My belly tightened. "Uh, when I told you I'm not frigid?"

"Actually, you didn't have to tell me that." Amusement creased his eyes. "I already knew."

I blushed. "Well, I have a lot of fantasies."

"About what?" His heartbeat increased beneath our entwined hands.

"Lately... you."

"Me."

I nodded.

"And what kind of fantasies do you have about me?" His voice was getting husky.

"Pretty explicit ones." My blood grew hot as I remembered my fantasy from that very morning of me wrapping my legs around his hips as he drove into me hard enough to make my body tremble.

Definitely wasn't ready to confess that one yet.

"I've done a lot more in my fantasies than I have in reality," I admitted.

He didn't ask why. He waited for more.

"But my fantasies have always been about anonymous encounters," I continued. "Never about a man I know. Until you."

He leaned closer to me, his eyes brewing with heat, but

he didn't touch me beyond the clasp of my hand against his chest.

"And what do we do in these fantasies of yours, Olivia Rose?" he asked.

I swept my gaze to the line of his mouth, my pulse spiking at the memory of his lips crushing mine. "Lots of kissing and touching."

"Nice."

"Oh, it's nice." I brushed my thumb against the secret notch beneath his lower lip.

Though Dean's eyes fairly smoldered, he didn't move to kiss me. The last remnants of my unease slipped away as I closed the distance between us and pressed my mouth to his. His lips were so warm and firm that I melted at the sensation of them moving against mine.

I curled my fingers into the material of his T-shirt, flicking my tongue out to probe at the seam of his lips. My pulse leapt when he opened his mouth to let me inside, then I put my hands on either side of his face and deepened the kiss.

A lovely haze descended over me. He tasted like butter, his breath hot against my lips. My heartbeat continued to throb, every beat pulsing heat through my veins. After a long moment of kissing, I paused to stare into his lust-filled eyes.

"Don't you want to touch me?" I whispered.

"More than I want to breathe."

"I promise I won't freak out this time."

He exhaled hard. "I promise I won't act like an ass if you do."

"You didn't. I'm just not used to this." I tightened my hand over his. "But I really liked the way you touched me."

"One day I'm going to touch you in a thousand different

ways and show you how to touch me." Dean slid his hand around the back of my neck. "But right now we're just going to make out."

He pulled me closer, easing back so I could stretch out on top of him. I loved the coiled strength of his body beneath mine, the way our chests pressed together and our breath moved in tandem. He drew my head to his and kissed me, the pressure slow and exquisitely easy.

The man knew how to kiss. He rubbed his lower lip against mine, slid his mouth down to nibble at my neck, flicked his tongue out to lick the corners of my lips. His hands spread over the back of my head, angling our mouths together. My eyes drifted closed.

Heat and pleasure billowed through me. I sank into the sensations, unafraid, tunneling my hands into his hair to hold him against me. Our kisses went from soft and gentle to open-mouthed and hot, then back to soft and gentle again. I lost track of time as my heart beat in time to the instinctive rhythm of our kissing, the gentle easing in and pulling back, like waves rippling the glass-smooth surface of a lake.

Dean pressed his mouth to my cheek, trailing a path to my ear where his breath tickled the strands of hair against my neck. He lifted his head to look at me, his eyes filled with both desire and affection, and stroked his hands down to rub my back.

"Okay?" he asked.

"Okay," I breathed.

His fingers flexed against my waist as our lips met again. I closed my teeth gently over his lower lip, eliciting a groan from deep in his throat. Emboldened, I spread my hands over his chest. The heat of his body burned through his shirt and up my arms. His heartbeat pounded against my palm.

Through the cloud of passion, I was dimly aware of his erection pressing against my leg, and my own body softened in response. A coil of urgency tightened through me, but even then I knew we wouldn't go any farther than this heart-melting, delicious kissing.

And we didn't. I don't know how long it lasted, but somehow it felt as if we had never been apart. We broke the rhythm at the same time, both lifting our heads to stare at each other.

The sight of him—his hot, dark eyes, sharp features flushed with heat, rumpled hair—warmed my blood all over again. He pushed his hands through my hair, easing the loose strands away from my face.

Then he pressed the back of my head gently, urging me to rest against his chest. He brushed his lips across my forehead. I relaxed on top of him, listening to the steady sound of his heartbeat.

He stroked his palms up and down my back as our breathing slowed. Lulled by the sensations, I drifted into a smooth, deep sleep, one unbroken by sharp-edged dreams.

And when dawn appeared through a crack in the sky, I woke with a feeling of safety I had never before known.

We'd changed positions on the sofa during the night, and now the length of Dean's body pressed against my back. His chest moved steadily in the rhythm of sleep. His breath warmed my skin. One of his arms was flung around my waist, and his hand curled loosely around my wrist.

A wave of pleasure surged beneath my heart. I lay still for a long moment, folded into the arms of this warm, strong man who was willing to bear the weight of my confessions. A man who admired my resolve and still wanted to protect me. A man who saw beauty in me.

Behind me, he shifted, his stubble scraping my neck, his voice a whisper. The crack in the sky opened wider, filling with light the color of apricots.

PART II

CHAPTER TEN

OLIVIA

SEPTEMBER 4

There are nine of us in the cooking class, each standing behind a long wooden table with a small range and oven at each station, and a sink in between. The classroom is at the back of Epicurean, a gourmet kitchen cookware and cutlery store, and a wall of windows looks out onto the floor—gleaming stainless steel pans, racks of dishes, colorful ovenware, tablecloths, and linen napkins.

I open my satchel and remove my notebook, then check

to make sure I brought at least three pens. You know, a backup in case one runs out of ink and a spare in case my station neighbor needs a loan.

I tighten my hair in its ponytail, then line up my notepad and pen beside the range just as my cell phone rings.

"Are you still at the library?" Dean asks.

"My cooking class starts at seven. I told you yesterday."

"Oh. Sorry, I forgot."

Irritation prickles my skin. "Yeah, well, there's a chicken pot-pie warm in the oven for you."

I snap the phone shut with an audible click, which catches the attention of the woman at the station beside me. She gives me a sympathetic smile.

"It started out as a frozen pot-pie," I say, dropping the phone back into my bag. "Obviously the reason I'm here."

"Welcome, everyone." A blond-haired man wearing a white chef's jacket steps up to the instructor's station at the front of the room. "I'm Chef Tyler Wilkes, owner and executive chef of the restaurant Julienne over in Forest Grove. Natalie invited me to teach this class for the next few months, and I hope I can help you learn some exciting new cooking techniques."

At this point, I'd be happy to learn any cooking technique, whether or not it's exciting.

Chef Tyler Wilkes drones on about a bunch of his accomplishments—four-star this, five-star that, an award here, another award there—then he wants us to introduce ourselves and tell everyone our reasons for taking his class.

Charlotte Dillard, my station neighbor, just returned from a culinary tour of France and is anxious to recreate some of the dishes she enjoyed. Laura Gomez has had a lifelong love of food and is considering leaving her insurance job to pursue cooking as a career. George Hayes, the one man in the group, recently retired and is finally getting around to trying new things. Susan Chapman wants to learn more about preparing local and organic ingredients to provide healthy, delicious meals for her family.

My introduction couldn't be more straightforward.

"I'm Olivia West. Everyone calls me Liv. I'm taking the class because I can't cook."

Tyler Wilkes smiles at me from behind his station. Even though I'm in the third row, I'm a little dazzled by the effect of brightness.

He's cute, I think in the abstract way I think puppies and stuffed animals are cute.

"Why don't you think you can cook, Liv?" he asks.

"Uh… I don't think I can't. I know I can't."

"Why?" he persists.

I have no idea what he's talking about. The rest of the class is looking at me, as if expecting some grand philosophical answer like, "Well, I wasn't really nourished as a child, so I never understood what…"

Oh, shit.

My fingers curl on the edges of the counter. For a second, I feel blindsided.

"Liv?" Tyler Wilkes presses.

"Er, I guess… I mean, I've never done much of it. Cooking, that is. In my life." My face is starting to get hot.

Tyler Wilkes smiles again and moves on to talking about what to expect from this class (good cooking techniques, the basics of classic French cuisine, learning to cook individual dishes, then the grand finale of preparing an entire menu), then he reviews all the implements at our stations.

I'm half-listening, taking notes mechanically. My mind fills with unwanted memories of my culinary past—greasy, fast-food hamburgers; dinners of saltines and fried eggs, scrounging in a stranger's pantry for a can of beans.

Suddenly I want Dean so badly my chest aches. I want to feel his arms tight around me; I want to press my face against his neck.

I force my attention back to the front of the room. Tyler Wilkes is demonstrating, with lightning-fast speed, how to chop carrots, celery, and onions for something called a *mire-poix*, a word he writes on the whiteboard behind him.

Then he tells us all to get started. I grab a carrot, and the sound of knives thwacking against wood fills the room as we all start chopping. Tyler Wilkes walks around observing everyone's "knife technique."

I concentrate, slicing the carrot down the middle, then into neat little cubes. Tyler Wilkes pauses beside my station neighbor Charlotte and praises the speed and evenness of her carrot dicing.

"Thank you, Chef," she replies, glowing.

"How are you doing, Liv?" He stops in front of my station.

"All right... uh, Chef." That sounds weird.

"Tyler," he says, a smile in his voice.

I glance at him. He's not much taller than I am, not much older, and he has a pleasant, open face and bright blue eyes.

He watches my chopping for a minute. "Too tight."

"Excuse me?"

"You're holding the knife too tightly. These three fingers should be loose around the handle."

He reaches out and puts his hand over mine to ease my fingers from the handle. I jerk away so fast the knife clatters to the cutting board.

"S-sorry." I wipe my palms on my apron. A blush crawls over my neck.

Tyler holds up his hands and steps back.

"Relax," he says, nodding toward the knife.

I don't relax at all, but I manage to get my *mirepoix* completed to Tyler's satisfaction, though he gives me a lecture about the value of uniform dicing. Then he sends us all off with our *mirepoix* in take-out containers, a packet of information about knife techniques, and instructions to practice.

When I get home, Dean is watching the news, his long body stretched out on the sofa and his feet on the coffee table. Relief almost makes my knees weak. I drop my satchel and container on the kitchen table, then cross to him.

I burrow beside him. He settles his arm heavily around my shoulders, pulling me closer. He presses his lips against my hair.

"You smell like an onion," he remarks.

"I chopped two of them. I mean, I *diced* them."

"Nice. Makes me want onion rings."

"Maybe I'll make you some before this class is over."

"That's my girl." He glances at me. "How'd it go?"

"Okay, I guess. Makes me realize how much I don't know about cooking."

"So that's why you're taking the class, right?"

I nod, thinking of my fellow students and their reasons for wanting to learn how to cook. I think of Tyler Wilkes, who has already accomplished so much.

How? Why? What gave him a dream to pursue? And why

do some people—like my mother, who had such a promising start—end up with nothing?

Still troubled, I move away from Dean and go to take a shower and change into my nightgown. I crawl into bed and try to lose myself in a novel, but the words swim in front of my eyes.

The bedroom door opens. Dean approaches me and brushes his hand over my hair. Some of my unease dissipates. He *knows*.

I grasp the front of his shirt. "Give me a kiss, professor."

He slides his hand around to the back of my neck and lowers his head. His mouth meets mine in the warm, seamless way that has always soothed my prickly emotions.

A ripple of need courses between us. I shift as he puts his hands on either side of my face to angle his lips more securely against mine. Our tongues touch, and I feel the pulse of urgency flare to life in his blood.

He moves away from me and starts to unfasten his shirt. My heartrate increases as I watch him push it off his muscular chest and shoulders. He lowers his hands to the button-fly of his jeans where there is already a tantalizing swell.

He pushes his jeans halfway down his hips. I stare at the line of hair arrowing from his flat belly beneath the waistband of his boxers. He climbs onto the bed. Anticipation billows through me. My book falls to the floor.

I rise onto my knees to meet him and slip my hands into the open waistband of his jeans. His skin is warm. Just brushing my fingers against his smooth erection sends a heated charge through my veins.

He grabs a fistful of my nightgown. "Take this off."

I can't help smiling. Sometimes he loves the way I look in the long, snow-white gown (I suspect it makes him think of something a medieval virginal maid would wear, though Professor West would never admit to having such a fantasy). Other times he complains that the voluminous material just gets in the way.

I'm happy to shuck the thing off, since I'm starting to get hot. I drop it onto the floor beside the bed and press my body full against his. He lowers his head to kiss me as his palms come up to massage my breasts. He has an expert touch, his thumbs circling my stiff nipples as his fingers slide into the crevices beneath the heavy globes.

Sparks shoot through my body, down to my sex. I moan against his mouth and struggle to shove his jeans the rest of the way off. He helps, and then we're both naked and his cock is pushing against my belly as his hand slips between my thighs.

The simmer of tension becomes a full boil. I start to squirm against his hand, and then I'm not thinking about anything else but his touch and the anticipation of his hardness filling me.

I grasp his shaft and stroke it, thrilled by the pulsing sensation beneath my palm, by his groan of pleasure. He thrusts into my fist. I slide my thumb over the hard knob of his cock and sense his own coiled desire unleashing. At this rate, we could both come by stroking alone, but then Dean eases me onto my back and plants both hands on either side of my head.

I know what he wants, and I'm glad. I love the missionary position. I love watching Dean's face as he fucks me, the shifting muscles beneath his taut skin. And I love watching my own body roll beneath his, my breasts jostling in rhythm to his thrusts.

His eyes are dark, almost black. His breath is hot against my neck. After putting on a condom, he pushes his knee between my thighs.

"Open for me, Liv."

I spread my legs wider, feeling the head of his cock nudge at me. Trembling, I draw in a sharp breath and clutch his shoulders. He moves his hand between us and positions himself, then thrusts hard. I cry out, aware of some unidentifiable emotion coursing through me alongside the mounting urgency.

Dean pushes his hands beneath my damp thighs, spreading me farther apart as his pumping grows deeper, stronger. It's delicious, this heavy stroking, the fullness firing my blood. I shift and writhe, matching his thrusts as best I can as the pleasure becomes all-consuming.

Sweat trickles down my neck, between my breasts. This is exactly what I need, this feeling of being taken, overwhelmed by the crackling heat of our union. I lift my legs, my knees hugging Dean's hips, and sink into the sensations.

The tension mounts to breaking point. Stars explode. I cry out again, digging my fingernails into his back when rapture spills through my veins. Before the vibrations slow, I grip his biceps.

"Harder," I whisper, wanting this to go on forever. "Fuck me harder…"

He plunges deep, so deep my body jerks with the impact, and then he slides out and does it again. I can hardly believe it, but I'm still convulsing around him, and then his mouth descends on mine—open, wet, hot. I grip him tighter as he crests the wave and comes down the other side.

When he slows to a stop, he eases aside and takes me with

him so I'm half-lying on top of him. I press my hand against his chest and feel the strong rhythm of his heartbeat.

We're quiet for a while. The tightness in my body has loosened, but I can still feel the rustle of disquiet, the anxiety evoked by shadows of the past.

I swipe at my damp forehead and tuck myself closer to Dean. "I didn't even ask you about your day."

He wraps a lock of my hair around his finger. "University business as usual."

"The semester's going well?"

"So far, so good. Got a journal article to edit about food served at Anglo-Saxon feasts."

"Like baked eel and parsnip pie?"

He gives me a puzzled look. I smile.

"Remember that first time I went to your place for dinner?" I ask. "You told me we were having medieval food, and for a second I might have believed you. But you'd really gotten take-out manicotti from an Italian restaurant."

"I did?"

"You don't remember?"

"I just remember trying not to stare at you too much."

"I liked it when you stared at me." I rub my cheek against his shoulder. "I still do."

"Even though I offered you take-out manicotti on our second date?"

"Best manicotti I've ever had." I think about all the food-related things Tyler Wilkes talked about earlier this evening. "You know, by the end of this cooking class, I'm supposed to be able to make an entire menu of French cuisine classics."

"You will." Dean pats my hip. "Learning anything is a

process, right? Julia Child wasn't born knowing how to make *coq au vin*."

I give a muffled laugh. "I don't even know what that is."

"Chicken cooked in red wine. You've never had *coq au vin*?"

I shake my head.

"That French restaurant over on Dandelion must have it on their menu," Dean says. "I'll take you there for dinner this weekend. Get you inspired."

"Thanks, but I'm working nights at the bookstore both Friday and Saturday."

He frowns. "Nights?"

"Allie's going to keep the store open until midnight on weekends," I explain. "She wants to catch some of the post-movie and theater traffic."

"You're going to be there until midnight?" Dean shakes his head. "No way."

Now I frown. "What do you mean, no way? Allie will be there too."

"It's not safe."

"It's the middle of downtown! Plenty of people are out on Friday and Saturday nights."

"I don't like it, Liv."

"I can't let Allie work alone, Dean." I try to keep my tone reasonable. "But she will if she has to because she's already advertised the extended hours. And I'm her only employee. Her boyfriend is going to help sometimes, but he works at a hotel and can't be there every weekend. Plus this is one of the reasons Allie hired me."

"Why didn't you tell me about this earlier?" Dean asks shortly.

"I didn't think it was a big deal."

"I wouldn't have let you take the job if I'd known."

I stare at him. "You wouldn't have *let me*?"

He sighs. "I didn't mean—"

"Yeah, I know what you meant." Irritation laces my spine, and I pull away from him. "You make the decisions, right? I'm just supposed to go along with them."

"That's not true, Liv, and you know it."

"Do you not remember telling me you'll support me in whatever I want to do?"

"Of course I remember."

"Well, I *want* to do this," I persist. "I have a schedule that I intend to honor. Look, I don't like it when you work late or when you travel, but I don't complain about it or try to stop you."

His mouth tightens, but he can't refute my statement. "Will there be a security guard?"

"Allie can hardly afford to pay me, Dean. She certainly can't afford a security guard." I force down my annoyance and reach across to put my hand on his chest. "There are at least four restaurants on the same street, a movie theater at the end of the block, and that incense shop that must be open until one. It's safe."

He's still frowning. I curl my fingers against his chest. All we need is another thing to be frustrated with each other about.

"Allie needs the extra help, and I like her a lot," I say. "I really want this job."

He lets out his breath in a hard rush. "All right, but keep your cell phone with you."

My shoulders stiffen. "I wasn't asking your permission."

"Good, because I wasn't giving it."

The air between us vibrates with unpleasant tension. I grab my robe and go into the living room, thinking my own company is now preferable to his.

Kelsey knows things are still strained between Dean and me. On Sunday night, she comes over to keep me company after Dean goes off to play football with some friends.

"You want to talk about it?" She settles beside me on the sofa and holds out a bowl of popcorn.

I take the bowl and glance sideways at her. "Did he tell you anything?"

"Night of the banquet, he said you guys were having a rough patch." She pours a glass of wine and takes a sip. "That's what he said. Rough patch. Like he was talking about stubble he forgot to shave."

I smile, but my heart shrinks a little. Even though Dean would have to be an idiot not to realize we're disconnected, it hurts to know he's told Kelsey while he and I still haven't worked through anything.

Kelsey pours a second glass of wine and pushes it my way. I look glumly at the popcorn and pick a few kernels, thinking back to how this marital discord all started.

"When Dean and I were dating, I told him I didn't want to have children," I finally confess.

"Oh." Kelsey arches a brow. She doesn't seem surprised. "Why not?"

"I had a tough childhood," I tell her. "My mother was totally self-centered and lousy at parenting. I've never been all that confident I could do any better."

"And Dean knows that?"

"Yeah. He was okay with it, too. Not having children."

"So what's the problem?"

"Well, recently I was… I started thinking about it. Thinking maybe I *could* do better than my mother."

"Seems natural enough," Kelsey remarks. "I guess most women think about motherhood at some point. But that's the reason you and Dean are going through a rough patch?"

"Partly," I admit. "Just the idea made things… messy."

And even though Dean and I haven't discussed it in a while, the issue is still there, hanging over us like a shadow.

"He doesn't even want to consider it right now," I say.

"For what it's worth, I think a lot of men are reluctant to have a baby at first."

"It's not just that." I crumble a popcorn kernel between my fingers. "Dean's spent the last five years thinking I didn't want children. *I've* spent the last five years thinking that too. I didn't expect him to jump right on board the baby train just because I *might* have changed my mind."

"So what is it, then?"

It's that I'm uncertain about my own husband's faith in me. In us.

"Dean and I have always…" My breath hitches a little. "We've always been able to talk about stuff, no matter how awful. We've gotten through it together. But this… I mean, it's a totally natural topic for a married couple, but with us… I don't know. It's like the very idea created all kinds of tension and doubt. Like something is…"

Wrong.

I can't even say it. I can't pinpoint the source of my unease. It's more than Dean's reluctance to have a baby, more than my own fears of inadequacy, but I have no idea what.

I shake my head and reach for the remote control. "Never mind. We'll work it out. Did I tell you my cooking class started last Tuesday?"

Kelsey looks as if she wants to say more, but she accepts my dismissal and sits back to watch the movie she brought.

When Dean comes home, his clothes are stained with mud, he's got a bruise on his cheek, and he smells like cold and wind.

I like the grubby athletic look on him, and since Kelsey is gone, I decide to follow him into the shower. Certainly not the first time I've done this after he returns home sweaty and adrenaline-charged.

I go through the bedroom to the closed bathroom door. I hear the shower running, and my heart speeds up at the thought of water and soap sluicing down his naked body.

It'll be okay, I tell myself. *We love each other. We'll work it out.*

But the door is locked.

CHAPTER ELEVEN

September 18

I'm learning a new language that includes words like *braising*, *sautéing*, and *flambéing*. Chef Tyler Wilkes discusses different ways to cook vegetables, stocks, and cuts of meat, the best uses of herbs, and the best utensils for various dishes. Today we're making hollandaise sauce and learning how to poach eggs.

I smack yet another egg against the rim of the bowl and break the shell. Holding my breath, I pull the shell open and watch the egg slide out—a gloppy mess of whites and a broken yolk. Plus bits of shell.

Shit.

I glance at Charlotte's station. Her egg is sitting all bright and shiny in the bowl, waiting to be poached, and her hollandaise sauce smells heavenly.

Double shit.

"You okay, Liv?"

I glance up at Tyler, who has stopped on the other side of my station. I wipe my hands on my apron and sigh.

"Yeah. Just can't crack an egg to save my life." I gesture to the trash bin, which holds the evidence of at least four decimated eggs.

"It's okay," Tyler says. "There are plenty of eggs in the world."

"Doesn't make it less of a waste," I mutter.

"Look." He comes around the counter to stand beside me and picks up an egg. "Don't crack it against the bowl. Tap it on the counter until there's a small dent, then hold it like this and press your thumbs in to pull the sides apart."

He demonstrates and drops a perfectly formed egg into the bowl. Then he nods at me. "Your turn."

If it was frustrating before, it's even more so now with Tyler watching me. I break another egg too hard and poke my thumb right into the yolk.

"This is stupid," I mutter, dropping the egg into the trash. "Can I make scrambled eggs instead?"

"Poached eggs with hollandaise sauce. You can do this, Liv." He picks up another egg and puts it in my hand. "Tap it."

I tap the egg against the counter until it's dented. Tyler moves closer to me and reaches out, as if he's going to put his hands over mine. Then he pauses and glances at me.

"Okay?" he asks.

Don't be an idiot, Liv.

"Yeah. Sure."

His hands settle around mine, his thumbs pressing against my thumbs.

"Slowly," he says.

He pushes his thumbs and guides my hands to pull the crack apart. The shell breaks open gently, the whites and yolk slipping out fully formed into another bowl. No bits of shell follow.

"There." Tyler steps back with a grin. "Save that one for poaching. Remember how to separate the eggs for the sauce?"

He continues to watch me as I break another egg and try to separate the yolk from the whites. Although he makes me a little nervous, I appreciate him letting me do the actual work. After a few attempts, I have four yolks in a bowl, and Tyler guides me through the sauce-making process again so the eggs don't scramble and the emulsion doesn't break.

"Okay, you're ready to poach now," he says, gesturing for me to pick up the egg in the bowl. "Keep the water just below a simmer."

I lower the heat on the stove, swirl the water around with a spoon the way Tyler showed us, then hold the egg over the pot. I look at him.

"What do you think?" he asks.

"I think it's ready."

"Be gentle. Slide it in slowly."

I slip the egg into the pot. We both peer into the bubbling mixture of vinegar and water as I use a spoon to push the whites over the yolk.

"It's coming apart." I point to the strings of white breaking off the egg.

"No, it's fine. Just trim those after you take it out. Time it carefully, decide how firm you want the yolk. Don't forget to use a slotted spoon." He nods. "Looks good, Liv."

It's a little ridiculous how pleased I am at the compliment.

"Poached eggs with hollandaise sauce." I set the plate in front of Dean and watch as he examines my offering.

In the four days since learning this recipe at cooking class, I've tried to make it twice at home. This is my third attempt. The sauce is too thin and grainy, but I hope Dean doesn't notice.

"Looks good," he remarks.

"Supposedly a French classic. Took me forever to learn how to crack an egg."

He takes a bite. I chew my thumbnail.

"How is it?" I ask. I'd tasted it myself (*Taste your food* being one of Chef Tyler Wilkes's oft-repeated mantras), and thought it was okay, but this is the first time Dean is sampling anything I've made. Actually, it's the first real dish I've cooked for him.

He coughs and reaches for his coffee. "Good. Uh… salty and… lemony."

"I added more lemon juice and cream to try and fix the sauce, then salted it again at the end." I pick up my spoon and try it. My tongue twinges with the bite of excess salt and sour lemon. "Damn. I shouldn't have done that. Sorry."

"It's okay. It's good, Liv." Dean gamely picks up his spoon again, and I love him for it, but I reach out to take the plate away.

"I'll try again another time. Toast and cereal coming up."

I turn away from him and scrape the eggs into the trash.

"You can wait for a soufflé, but a soufflé can never wait for you." Tyler whips up eggs and cream in a bowl, his whisk increasing in speed until I expect to see sparks fly. "You must carefully control every element of its preparation."

My classmates and I watch him and take notes at the same time, a process we've gotten used to in the past few weeks. While I can't imagine any scenario in which I would actually want to serve a soufflé, I'm willing to give it a try in class.

We start our own preparations, but I soon fall behind my classmates because I get shell in my egg whites.

Beside me, Charlotte whisks her whites to perfection and soon has her ramekin buttered and ready to put in the oven. I glance at the clock and hurry a little, adding hot milk and tempering the yolks. By the time I get my filled ramekin into the oven, I'm at least twenty minutes behind everyone else.

One by one, decent soufflés emerge from the ovens— Charlotte's is the most perfect, high and rounded. I wait for my timer to go off, resisting the urge to peek in the oven. When the timer dings, I take out what appears to be a pancake rather than a fluffy soufflé.

"Everyone gather round, and let's take a look at Liv's soufflé," Tyler calls.

Great.

My classmates come over to gawk at my dish, and I swear Laura even clucks her tongue in sympathy.

"What might have caused Liv's soufflé to fall?" Tyler asks.

"Something made the air bubbles pop," George replies. "Liv, did you open the oven while it was cooking?"

I feel like I've been accused of stealing a cookie from the cookie jar. "Uh, no."

Everyone else chimes in.

"Maybe her oven temperature wasn't stable."

"Her egg whites weren't whisked properly."

"Maybe she got some yolk into the whites."

"Mmm." Tyler peers at my soufflé. "I'd venture to guess that last idea is probably the right one. A tiny bit of fat from the yolk can destabilize the protein of the whites."

"I'll remember that for next time," I assure him. "No eggs-tra yolk in the whites."

My classmates all chuckle appreciatively, and Charlotte pats my shoulder as they head back to their stations. Tyler's still looking at my soufflé, and then he gives a little shrug.

"Soufflés can still taste good if they fall," he says. "They're just missing the wow factor."

"Isn't taste more important than wowing?" I ask.

"Yes, but everyone likes being wowed now and then." He pauses and reaches for two forks. "It's like getting a present in a grocery bag or one wrapped in nice paper and ribbons. Same present, but the one with the ribbons is a lot more enjoyable. And you know that the person who gave it to you put time, effort, and thought into making you happy."

That makes a striking degree of sense.

"Cooking's the same way," Tyler says. "Please the one you're serving by making it right."

He holds out a fork. We scoop up bites of my soufflé and try it. It's heavy, but it tastes okay.

"Not bad, eh, Chef?" I ask.

"If it was a chocolate soufflé, you could serve it and call it a molten cake," he says. "Not bad, Liv."

I can't help smiling. He takes another bite and nods.

"Soon," Tyler continues, "I want you to make another soufflé because you need to know how it feels to make one that both tastes good and rises." He points his fork at me. "And before this class is over, you're going to know you *can* cook."

I'm still not sure about that, but I appreciate his faith in me and confidence in himself. I wrap up the rest of the soufflé and start cleaning my station.

My classmates leave as I'm finishing, then Tyler approaches and offers to walk me to my car. Since it's past nine, and Epicurean is closed, I agree.

"Hope I didn't embarrass you with the soufflé," he remarks. "I just think we can learn from each other."

"You didn't embarrass me." I glance at him. "But you don't seem like you need to learn anything more about cooking."

He shrugs. "I don't think you ever stop learning. No matter what you do."

Sounds like something Professor West would say.

"How'd you get started being a chef?" I ask.

"My parents owned a restaurant in Ohio, so I grew up in a kitchen. Except theirs was a diner, and my dad said he wanted me to do better than that. So I went to culinary school to learn more about fine dining, then opened a place in Cleveland before moving to Forest Grove."

"Why did you move to Forest Grove?"

"Followed a girl." He shoots me a half-abashed smile. "Didn't work out."

"Well, you ended up with a successful restaurant."

"True. Ever been to Julienne?"

I shake my head. "Was that the girl's name?"

He gives a shout of laughter. "Her name was Emily. You remember we learned julienning that first week? It's a style of cutting food into thin strips. Also called matchsticks."

"Oh, yeah. Hey, you should call your next restaurant Chop. Then you could start a series of others—Mince, Dice, Cut, Slice."

"Actually…" He chuckles. "Not a horrible idea. Want to be a partner?"

"Nah. I like to eat too much to want to know all that goes on behind the scenes."

"You should come over to Julienne sometime and check it out," he says. "I'll make you all my specialties. Filet mignon or seared tuna, roasted scallops, strawberry tart. You'll enjoy it."

"I will. I'm sure my husband would too."

I don't know why I said that. I wear a wedding ring, which I'm sure Tyler has seen considering the number of times he's looked at my hands while I've chopped and diced and whisked.

We stop beside my car. He smiles again. In the light of the streetlamps, his smile is still gleaming white. He's close enough that I can smell the scents of parmesan and chives clinging to his chef's jacket.

"How long have you been married?" he asks.

"Three years." I open the trunk so we can put my stuff inside. "Together five."

"Hmm." He puts my container-encased soufflé in the trunk. "Guess it worked out for you, huh?"

"I guess so."

I guess so? What the hell kind of answer is that?

I toss my satchel into the backseat. "Well, yeah. Of course it worked out. We're very happy."

"Good for you." He slams the trunk and rests his hands on top of it as he looks at me. "Not many people are happily married these days."

"Dean and I are."

Why do I sound defensive?

I open the driver's side door. "Thanks for walking me out here, Tyler. See you next week."

"Sure, Liv. Bye."

When I glance in the rearview mirror as I drive away, I see him standing there watching me.

Thoughts of my childhood appear to me in flashes, like cards shuffling. I try not to dwell on it, especially memories of my mother. Tonight, though, I have a dream about a boy I once knew.

My mother and I spent the summer in a beachside community in North Carolina. She'd hooked up with a man she met at a gas station and was supposedly cleaning his house in exchange for room and board.

This time, at least, we had our "own" place, since the guy let us stay in a room above his garage. It was small and hot, but there was a kitchenette with a fridge, and if you craned your neck while looking out the window you could see a pale strip of ocean in the distance.

The man—whose name I can't remember—had a son a

few months older than I. Trevor Hart. We'd have been in the same class if school were in session, but since it was summer we had nothing to do. He was a skinny, towheaded kid with bright blue eyes, freckles, and an utter determination to be my friend.

By the time I was nine, I'd learned to keep my distance from people, learned not to make friends too fast because chances were we'd be moving again soon.

But Trevor and his boundless enthusiasm were hard to resist. Plus I had no one except my mother, and when I was with her it was all about what she wanted, what she needed, what she had to do.

To get away from that for a while, I warily started hanging out with Trevor. The second week we were there, he hauled one of his old bikes from a shed and asked me to ride with him to the beach.

"I don't know how to ride a bike," I said, eyeing the rusted two-wheeler dubiously.

"Oh." He scratched his head. "Guess you'd better learn."

Every day for a week, that kid held the bike while I tottered to and fro, trying to learn how to balance. Every time I fell, he picked up the bike and asked if I was okay. Every time I pedaled, he cheered.

And when I finally managed to bike the length of an entire street, he ran alongside me the whole way, yelling, "You got it, Liv! You're riding a bike! You're doing it!"

We were inseparable for the rest of the summer. We spent most of our time biking to the beach where we played putt-putt, ate ice cream, and swam in the ocean.

Trevor Hart had plans. He wanted to be a firefighter, a

paleontologist, a police officer, a construction worker, a deliveryman. He wanted to parachute jump, go to India, fly a plane, swim with sharks, climb Mount Everest.

He was the first person who asked me what I wanted to be when I grew up.

"I don't know," I answered truthfully.

"You gotta be something," he said, licking up a drop of melting ice cream from his cone. "What about a skydiver?"

"I don't think I'd like that."

"I saw this program about a circus college where people go to learn trapezing and tightrope-walking and stuff. You could do that."

I was pretty sure I couldn't, but I loved that he thought I could.

"Maybe I could be a clown," I suggested. That actually sounded kind of fun.

"Yeah!" His eyes lit with enthusiasm. "That'd be totally awesome. You could have pink hair and drive one of those tiny cars. You'd be great at that."

"You think?" I smiled, pleased. "Thanks."

"You gotta tell me when the shows are, though," he said, "cuz you never know, I might be at Everest base camp or something."

I'd little doubt he would be.

"Come on." He tossed his cone wrapper into a trashcan and headed back to our bikes. "Let's go to the fun house on the boardwalk and you can practice."

My mother and I had left town at the end of August, just as Trevor was getting ready to go back to school. We said we'd write to each other, and for a few months after that, I did. But of course my mother and I were always moving, so soon any return letters Trevor sent got lost somewhere on the road behind us.

The dream I have now about Trevor Hart is a collage of moments—his gap-toothed grin, his cheering me on, his belief in my future.

And when I wake, I wonder whatever became of the boy who'd been my best friend for just one summer. As I lie there staring at the pattern of sunlight on the ceiling, I think Trevor might have grown into the type of man Tyler Wilkes is.

The thought makes me surprisingly happy.

CHAPTER TWELVE

OCTOBER 5

"Any conclusions?" Kelsey pulls her sunglasses from her bag and slips them on as we walk down Avalon Street.

I don't bother pretending I don't know what she's talking about. "No. Still in a rough patch. I didn't handle the whole thing very well."

"How's Dean?"

"Okay. Busy. At least he's got important stuff to do."

I kick at a loose stone. I'm glum. Things with Dean and I aren't bad, but they're not great either. He's busy with work, I stay occupied with the Historical Museum, the bookstore, and cooking class. We have sex every now and then, but still not nearly as often as we used to.

"And how's the cooking class?" Kelsey asks.

"Fine. I'm not all that great at it, but I guess it's fun."

"Good Lord." Kelsey stops in the middle of the sidewalk. "What kind of Debbie Downer are you becoming?"

I blink. "What?"

"Are you listening to yourself?" Her voice takes on a whiney note. "*I'm not good at it, I don't do anything important, I fucked it up.* What's up with that? So things with you and Dean are kind of crappy right now. Doesn't mean you're allowed to walk around flogging yourself."

I can only stand there staring at her. Kelsey takes off her sunglasses and looks hard at me.

"If you're letting Dean's reluctance about a baby do this to you—" she spreads her arms out as if to encompass all my self-criticism, "—then what happens if you actually have a baby, Liv? Is that what you want to teach a kid? When the chips are down, you blame yourself and moan about how lousy you are at everything?"

Good God. She's right. Not only do I dislike where things stand with me and Dean, I'm also not all that nuts about myself right now.

"Well?" Kelsey demands. "Is that what you want?"

"No. No way." I frown back at her.

I'm not like this. It's true I'm still searching for something, but God knows I've fought my way through pitch darkness before. I know I have the strength to somehow untangle this mess with my husband.

Dean and I both do.

"So?" Kelsey waves her arms around again. "What're you going to do?"

"I don't know yet," I admit, but there's a very real, determined tone in my voice. "I'll think of something."

She steps back and nods. "Well. I guess that's a start." She pokes me in the chest with her forefinger. "And I never want to hear this whiney, I'm-a-piece-of-shit crap from you ever again."

"Yes, ma'am. I love you."

She sniffs and puts her sunglasses back on. "Don't you dare hug me here in the middle of the sidewalk. Come on. You're buying me a milkshake."

As we continue walking, I can't resist slinging an arm around her shoulders and giving her a quick squeeze. She mutters under her breath, but returns the gesture before we enter an ice-cream parlor.

After some debating, we agree that we each need our own milkshake, so we place the order then sit at a table by the window. She entertains me by grousing about her fellow professors and grad students, I tell her she needs to get laid, and she agrees heartily while we survey Avalon Street looking for a potential candidate.

"Hey, you and Professor Marvel be nice to each other." Kelsey squeezes my shoulder as we part ways outside the ice-cream parlor. "And you be nice to yourself, okay?"

"Promise." I subject her to another hug before we head in opposite directions.

I don't feel like cooking anything tonight, so I stop at a deli on Ruby Street to pick up one of our routine meals of roasted chicken, green beans, and pasta salad. Because it's still light out, I take a shortcut through the parking lots behind the buildings.

The instant I turn the corner, I sense someone behind me. My heartrate kicks into high gear, and I struggle to pull in a breath. I quicken my pace.

"Mrs. West?" a woman's voice calls.

I stop and turn. A young woman approaches me, a backpack slung over one shoulder. I take another deep breath and will my pulse to stop pounding. As the woman nears, her features and her curly blond hair sharpen into clarity.

Crap. I force a smile.

"Hi, Maggie."

"Mrs. West." Maggie stops in front of me, her own breathing fast. She glances behind me, a quick, furtive look. "Sorry, I saw you heading this way."

"No problem."

"Is… uh, is Professor West with you?"

"No." Unease suddenly rises in my chest. "Are you supposed to meet with him or something?"

"No." She shifts her weight to her left foot, her eyes darting from the lot to me and back again. "Just wondering."

"Is everything okay?" I ask.

She stares past me again. Her lower lip trembles. Tears flood her eyes.

Oh, no.

"What's wrong?" I put down my bag and move closer to her, my unease deepening. I know this has to do with my husband.

"He won't approve my thesis proposal." Maggie swipes the back of her hand across her eyes. "I told him my dad will freak out if I don't get it approved this semester because he's expecting me to apply to law school in the spring."

"Law school?"

"My dad's a partner in a law firm and wants me to follow in his footsteps." She fumbles in her backpack for a tissue. "I have to get a master's degree to get into law school because my undergrad grades were lousy. So my father agreed to let me major in history because I promised it would take only two years.

"I should be finished already, but I took a year off after Professor Butler retired then when I reentered the program, I had to switch to Professor West. Now *he's* being a total hard-ass."

She wipes her eyes. "My dad threatened to cut me off if I don't finish by the end of the year since I've already been in grad school for three years already. But I can't even get started until Professor West approves my thesis proposal!"

I have no idea what to say. None of this is my business. I don't have the right to defend Dean because I don't know why he won't approve her proposal. I do know that he has a good reason for his decision, but it's not my place to explain that to Maggie Hamilton.

"Do you want to go to law school?" I finally ask.

She heaves a sigh. "I don't know. But my dad's funding my education and made it clear that's what he wants. And he'll have a job waiting for me in his firm, so you know, how can you turn that down? And if I *did* turn it down, he'd cut me off right *now*, so… whatever."

Though I find it difficult to sympathize with a girl who has obviously had a great deal handed to her on a silver platter, I do feel sorry that she's so upset.

"That sounds unfair," I say, well aware of the hollow tone to my words.

"Yeah, well." Maggie swipes at her eyes again and hitches her backpack over her shoulder. "I'm going to visit my parents next week, and I want to tell my dad everything's on schedule. Maybe… maybe you could talk to Professor West for me?"

"No, I'm sorry. I can't."

"Please, Mrs. West? I could really use some support, you know, girl to girl?"

"I'm sorry," I repeat, more firmly this time. "I don't interfere with my husband's work. It wouldn't be right for me to talk to him about a proposal I don't know anything about."

Fresh tears spill down her freckled cheeks. "Maybe if you explained about my dad and the—"

"Maggie, really. I can't help you. But my husband is a reasonable man who has always been willing to work out solutions with students. I'm sure if you talk to him, he'll—"

"He'll tell me to review the damned research, like he always does, except there's so much of it and I don't know Italian well enough to read all the papers he's given me. And he totally doesn't get that I also have to start studying for the LSAT."

"It sounds like you're trying to do too much."

"I don't have a choice, Mrs. West! I could have started writing in the summer if Professor West had just signed the proposal. Please, will you talk to him?"

"I'm sorry."

Her mouth hardens into a line. She dashes a hand across her eyes and tries to suppress a hiccupping sob.

"Maggie, if you'd tell my husband what you told me…"

"I *have* told him. He just cares about his star students like Sam and Jessica."

"He cares about all his students."

"Yeah, right." Her voice is bitter. "Maybe he cares about some of them *too* much."

The edge to her remark slices into me. I take a step back, my hip hitting the fender of the car behind me. "What?"

She hitches her backpack over her shoulder. "Sure your husband is willing to work with students, Mrs. West. Especially female students, just like his predecessor. Maybe he's being such a hard-ass with me because he expects more than a thesis proposal."

She spins on her heel and stalks back to the street. Part of my brain screams at me to follow her and demand an explanation, but I can only stand there staring after her. I can't even form a coherent thought.

Was she… is she talking about… did I understand that… ??

My breathing is getting too fast again. I press a hand to my chest and count in my head as I draw in a breath and let it out slowly. Again. After a few minutes, my heartbeat settles but my mind is spinning.

I pick up my grocery bag and walk home. When I open the front door, I hear the sound of the shower running. I unpack the groceries and go into the bedroom. Dean left his muddy football clothes on the floor. I dump them into the laundry hamper and stare at the bathroom.

There's a knot in my stomach. I swallow hard and go to ease open the bathroom door a little more. Fragrant steam billows through the room, fogging the mirror and the shower door. Behind the glass, I see the outline of Dean's strong body, and my heart pounds.

Another step. I stop. His hands move as he soaps his chest, and I imagine wet lather slipping over his slick muscles, tracing all the ridges with my fingers… then his hand slides down to his groin. My gaze follows.

Even through the fogged glass, I can see that he's hard. Unexpected lust jolts me at the evidence of his readiness. Before I can back away, he curves his hand around his cock and starts stroking.

My knees weaken. I grab the towel rack. I've seen him masturbate, of course, but never like this, never without him knowing I was there. His movements are easy and fluid, his body rocking slightly as he thrusts into the vise of his fist.

I suck in a breath, part of me thinking I should leave him in privacy and the other part mesmerized by the sight of such an intimate act. He presses one hand against the tile wall while the other works his erection faster. Heat blossoms through my entire body. I press my legs together as I start to throb in response.

How often does he do this?

What, or rather *who*, is he thinking about?

The thought dampens my own arousal a little. I continue to stare at him, at the length of his cock, the rapidly increasing movements of his hand. His head falls back, the hot water pounding across his skin as his body jerks with release. His rough groan filters into the steam. I wish I could feel its low vibrations against my skin.

He's still pressing his hand against the wall, his head lowered against the spray, his chest heaving.

I back out of the bathroom, close the door, and return to the living room. I'm breathing fast as I pace, my mind filling with images that both arouse and dismay me—Dean thinking about another woman naked, fantasizing about fucking her... his grad student with her pretty smile and toned body.

The bedroom door clicks open. My breath catches in my

throat. He's only wearing a pair of boxers, his skin still damp, his arms raised as he scrubs at his wet hair with a towel. When he lowers it, he sees me standing there.

My mouth is dry, though I don't know if it's from fear or my own thwarted lust. Unfortunately I suspect it's the former.

Dean loops the towel around the back of his neck. "You okay?"

I twist my hands together. "I don't... no. Not really."

He waits. He knows I'll tell him eventually, but it takes a minute to drum up my courage.

"Do you... uh, do that often?" I gesture to the bedroom.

He flushes a little. "Not often, no. Not if you're here."

"So why now?"

"I didn't know you were home."

I cross my arms. My nipples are still hard. I have to know. "Were you thinking about her?"

"Who?"

"Your grad student." I can't bring myself to say her name.

Dean frowns. "My grad... Jessica?"

"No." I try to keep my voice even. "Maggie."

"Maggie?" He looks stunned. "You thought I was thinking about her?"

"Were you?"

"Of course not. Why would you think that?"

"I saw her today. In the parking lot behind the deli."

He doesn't say anything, again waiting for more.

"She's... uh, the first time I met her, I suspected she had a thing for you."

"How do you know?"

"I can tell. I'm not blind." Neither is Maggie Hamilton. Or any other woman when it comes to Professor Dean West.

"Liv." He pulls the towel from his neck and tosses it onto the sofa. "I'd be lying if I said sometimes other women… even grad students… haven't come on to me. But do you think I respond? Do you think I'd ever let them cross the line? Do you think *I'd* ever do that?"

I don't like the turn of this conversation, as if I'm at fault for having doubts. In the deepest part of my heart, I know he's honorable and loyal to the core.

At the same time, there's a lot I don't know right now. And every day I have the disquieting sense that the pool of "don't knows" is growing larger.

"Maggie Hamilton implied that you've made a move on her," I tell him.

Dean stares at me. "What?"

"That's what she said." I swallow past the lump in my throat, the resurgence of unease. "She's upset that you won't approve her… her thesis proposal, and then she said maybe you're expecting more from her."

"What the fuck…" Dean paces away from me, his shoulders stiffening. "I won't approve her thesis because her research and methodology are incomplete! I told her that. I told *you* that. I won't put my name behind a student who produces lousy work. And she won't take my suggestions or find another topic, so we're at a deadlock."

"Why hasn't she changed advisors?"

"Because she claims it would set her back too far since she already started with the previous professor, and then she took a year off. She still thinks she can earn her master's by the end of the year, even though she hasn't started writing her thesis. Much less done any useful research. I've been telling her that since last summer."

He swears and paces again, running a hand through his hair. I tighten my arms around myself, feeling the thump of my heartbeat. I could care less about Maggie Hamilton's poor research abilities.

"Why... why would she imply you treat the female students inappropriately?" I ask.

"I don't know! I haven't even talked to her in a..." He stops suddenly. Tension rolls through his body as he turns back to face me. Darkness suffuses his eyes.

I take a step back. My throat aches.

"Liv."

I can't look at him.

"Liv." His voice roughens. "Do you *believe* her?"

No. *No!*

The denial boils inside me. But it is not powerful enough to dissolve the hard-edged fear that has prodded at me for weeks now. I clench my hands into fists, digging my fingernails into my palms hard enough to hurt.

"I don't... I don't know what to believe anymore," I whisper. I realize that is the unvarnished truth. A wave of dizziness washes over me.

"Liv... Jesus, Liv..." The words crack as Dean backs away, pale beneath his tan. "No, for the love of God. You think I would do that to you, to us, after... why the fuck would you... *no.*"

"I'm sorry, Dean! I feel... for weeks now, I've felt like you're keeping something from me, but I have no idea what it is, so when she said—"

"You thought that was it?"

"I'm just… things have been so messy between us, and then she… why would she say that?"

"No." His voice is forceful now, lined with steel. "No, Olivia. I have never made a pass at another woman since the day I met you. Since long *before* I met you. If you can't believe that, then I don't know what the fuck we're even doing anymore."

He turns and leaves. A second later, the bedroom door slams shut. I sink into a chair and bury my face in my hands.

Is it true? Have I stopped trusting my own husband?

If so, where in the love of God does that leave us?

CHAPTER THIRTEEN

OCTOBER 9

"*R*ock the blade, Liv." Tyler Wilkes pauses beside my station.

"Sounds like the name of a chef's concert series." I shoot him a grin. "Rock the Blade, fronted by Chef Tyler Wilkes on the sauté pan."

"Funny. Now pay attention to what you're doing."

I turn back to chopping chives. The voices of my fellow students and their occasional laughter rises around me and Tyler. Oil sizzles in pans, blades thwack against cutting boards, oven doors open and close.

It's all become pleasant and very welcome over the past

weeks, a familiar cadence that soothes all my tangled, barbed-wire thoughts.

"Careful." Tyler steps closer. "Move it backward to get ready for the next stroke."

He puts his hand over mine on the knife handle, then takes my other hand and places it against the top of the blade. He's done this often since that first time when I kind of freaked out. Now I'm used to his hands-on guidance, and I appreciate it because he shows me exactly how to do it right.

"This stabilizes the cutting board," he explains. "Now rock the blade up and down without moving the tip. Keep it in the same position, and let the knife do the work."

He guides my hands into the rhythm. It's easy and satisfying to feel the sharp blade chopping the chives into uniform pieces.

Tyler steps back to watch me. "Good. Got all your *mise en place*?"

"Yes, Chef."

"Remember the chicken breast won't take long to cook. Give it a good sear, then finish it in the oven."

"Got it."

He watches me chopping herbs for a couple more minutes before he nods with approval. "Nice work, Liv. Told you I'd make a chef out of you yet."

He winks and smiles, which makes a pleasant warmth glow through me. Even at almost thirty years of age, I apparently still have the urge to earn the teacher's approval.

At the end of class, we sample our own dishes and everyone else's. My chicken turned out dry and, according to Tyler, under-seasoned, but overall it's not a bad dish. At least it's edible.

"How do you feel?" Tyler stops by my station again when we're cleaning up and getting ready to leave.

"How do I feel?" I have no idea what he's talking about.

"Yeah. About your cooking skills. You were pretty shaky about your abilities at first. Since it's been a few weeks now, I was wondering how you feel. Are you enjoying yourself?"

Hmm.

"I don't know if *enjoy* is the right word," I admit. "I mean, it's frustrating when I can't even crack an egg properly. But that soufflé did taste good, right? And I'm learning a lot."

"Are you practicing at home?"

"Sometimes," I say, then add, "though honestly, it's so much easier to pick up a roasted chicken on the way home."

"Not nearly as good, though," Tyler says, "for your taste-buds or your soul."

"I don't think cooking is the best thing for my soul right now." I'm surprised that I admitted such a thing, but Tyler only tilts his head and looks at me consideringly.

"What is, then?" he asks.

Fixing my marriage.

I shrug and scrub at the spotless counter. The insane thing is, I want to say the words aloud. I want to tell him that things are tough right now, that my marriage is rocky, that I'm doubting both my husband and myself.

And that it hurts.

I lift my head to look at him. He's watching me with curiosity in his blue eyes. His blond hair flops over his forehead. I find myself staring at his mouth, then jerk my gaze back down to the counter.

"Friends?" he asks.

I swallow. The air feels different, charged with something I'm not used to, something not right, something I should reject.

"They're good for one's soul," Tyler says.

"Yes," I agree. "And maybe food?"

He grins. "Any time you want, Julienne is open. I'll cook you a meal that'll make your soul sparkle again."

That, I think, is a meal I'd love to eat.

Today's Saturday. Dean wakes me up early and tells me to get dressed for a hike. It's been ages since we've gone hiking at dawn, and I struggle with the urge to burrow back under the covers.

"Come on, beauty. Let's talk."

I push the comforter aside and peer at him. He looks serious, but not angry. Given our recent discord, the thought of spending a couple of hours hiking with him is appealing. So lured by the hope that we will find our way back to each other, I haul myself out of bed to dress and eat a quick breakfast.

We put on jackets over our jeans and sweatshirts, hitch on our backpacks, and head out to hike one of our favorite trails that crests along the edge of the mountain and overlooks the lake.

"I sent you an email with my flight information for the conference next weekend," Dean says.

"Is your paper ready?"

"Finished it last night."

"How long will you be gone?"

"Four nights. I'll drive to the airport and leave my car in the lot."

I follow behind him, stepping where he steps. Some leaves still cling precariously to the tree branches. Below the rocky ridge, the lake shimmers and undulates with a light wind. We pass a couple of other hikers, but the trail is mostly ours.

By mutual agreement, we stop at the top of an outcropping of rocks and find a place to sit. We eat granola bars and drink water, enjoying the quiet and the bird's-eye view of the lake and town.

"Since the day we met, I haven't wanted anyone but you," Dean says.

My heart jumps a little.

"Never looked at another woman," he continues. "Never thought about one. It's always been you, Olivia."

My white knight. I reach over to squeeze his hand.

"I know."

I've always known. I've always believed in him. That belief has been shaken in recent weeks, but my heart still knows the truth. I just have to remember to listen.

We fall silent. A breeze rustles through the leaves, and a bird hops along the path in front of us.

"You remember I told you about Helen?" Dean asks.

I turn to look at him. His gaze is on the lake, but something tense emanates from him. My stomach tightens.

"The woman you were with in grad school?" I ask.

"She wanted to get married."

"That's not surprising."

"We figured we'd finish our dissertations, find jobs. Get settled first."

"Makes sense."

He stares at his water bottle, rolling it between his palms.

"So we… well, a few times we were kind of careless with birth control."

The knot in my stomach worsens. I don't respond.

"She got pregnant."

Jesus. Where is he going with this?

"And she… uh, she got rid of it," he continues. "She was stressed out over her dissertation, working two jobs, both of us still teaching and taking classes… she thought it was a mistake."

"*She* thought all that?"

"I didn't… I mean, we'd talked about having kids some-day, but after we were married. So yeah, she was right. It wasn't… it was a lousy time. I didn't argue. Hell, I drove her to the fucking clinic."

I don't know what to say. I hadn't known this before. Is this why he'd never questioned my own lack of desire to have children?

"So you… you regretted it?" I ask.

"I don't know. I think so. It didn't even seem real at the time. I was… what, twenty-two? We didn't even talk about it much. Then a year later, Helen was still working on her disser-tation when she got the Stanford job. I'd done my coursework, so I went with her. She said she'd work while I finished my research. We were out there for two months before she said she wanted a baby."

"Oh."

"I don't know what it was. I figured it was guilt, sorrow, family pressure… maybe a combination of all three." He pauses and shrugs. "Helen was close to my mother and sister. I told you that."

"Did they know about the abortion?"

He shakes his head. I see it then, an old, familiar guilt that has never fully gone away.

"Helen made me promise not to tell anyone, not that I would have," he says. "She started her job, then I got word I'd been awarded a fellowship to study in Madrid for a year. When Helen heard about it, she flipped out. Said she'd never have taken the Stanford job if she knew I'd leave in six months, that she did it because of my parents. Then she told me she was pregnant again."

"But you—"

"She'd stopped taking the pill. Didn't tell me. I shouldn't have relied on her to deal with birth control. But I did, and that's what happened."

"But you weren't married. I mean, I thought your plan was marriage, then kids."

"It was."

"So what…" It hits me then, like a blow to the gut. "You married her, didn't you?"

He nods, his jaw tightening. "There was a lot of pressure from our parents. I wanted to do the right thing. Thought it would work, that everyone would be glad. That it'd all *fit*, you know?"

My chest burns, and I have to remind myself to breathe. Part of me understands this about Dean—his intense urge to fix things, to prove himself a success, even at the expense of his own happiness.

Another larger part of me can't process the magnitude of this revelation.

"Why… why didn't you tell me?" My voice is tight, strained.

"Because I still don't think of it as a real marriage."

"What the hell does that mean?"

"Helen and I had gone through grad school together, we had similar career goals, on paper we were a perfect match. But it didn't happen the way it was supposed to. It was like the plan went totally off course."

"What happened to the baby?"

"Helen lost it at thirteen weeks. She'd told a lot of people early on. She was excited. Then when she had the miscarriage, we had to tell all those same people about it. That was rough."

"Then what happened?" I ask, not at all certain I want to know.

"She got pregnant again four months later. Second time, she told only my parents and hers, but she lost that one at nine weeks. Third time—"

"*Third* time?"

He nods. "Didn't tell anyone until she was into her second trimester, but then, fifteen weeks in… ah hell, Liv, it was all so shitty."

"Oh, Dean." Some of the wind goes out of me at the thought of another woman, of *Dean*, contending with three miscarriages.

"Yeah, well, that was it."

"What do you mean—that was it?"

"Everything unraveled after that. She was devastated, I was convinced it all had something to do with the abortion and I blamed myself for not having stopped it… and soon neither of us could figure out why we'd gotten married in the first place."

He shakes his head. "Helen's parents blamed me, said I

should be the one working, that I was putting her under too much stress. They were right. I wasn't doing *enough*. But I didn't know what enough was.

"Even though Helen and I both had normal genetic test results, I didn't want to try again, thought it was too much. Helen had this idea that we needed to be a perfect couple, we had to have a baby, but we couldn't agree on anything. Fought all the time. Finally she filed for divorce. I didn't contest it."

I sit there for a long time, processing what he's just revealed.

My stomach twists sharply. Dean knows everything about me, even the black, raw parts. I'd thought I knew everything about him but ever since I brought up the idea of a baby, I've sensed I was missing something. Now I know my instincts were right.

I haven't known my husband completely.

Tears sting my eyes. I blink them away.

"It was tough on Helen," Dean continues. "Tougher than I can imagine. And I couldn't be… what she wanted. I didn't even know what that was. I tried… we went to counseling, I tried to get her to take a year off, offered to put my research on hold until we figured it out. All we ended up doing was fighting about work, about trying again, what our marriage should be, what it *wasn't*…"

"Why didn't your parents ever say anything?" I ask, even though I know the answer, know that this miserable failure of a marriage was just one other thing the West family would cover up with layers of brittleness and suppressed anger.

"My family doesn't talk about the shitty stuff, Liv."

My heart lurches. I push to my feet, an ache filling me. "And neither do you."

"What?"

I whirl to face him. A riot of emotions spins in my head. "You're still doing it! You spent so many years trying to fix your family, to be the hero, while all these secrets festered and none of you would acknowledge them."

I struggle to take a breath, feel my heart beating too fast. "And you told me before we got married that you didn't want to do that anymore. You didn't want to try and prove yourself to them, you wanted your life to be about what you wanted..."

And you wanted me.

"But you did exactly what they did, Dean." The tears spill over, unchecked, my spine stiffening. "Exactly what you said you *didn't* want to do anymore. You buried a secret and refused to talk about it. Even with me, after all we went through. It's the same damn pattern!"

He just stares at me. He knows I'm right.

"I understood why you did it before." I pace a few steps, struggling to keep my breathing under control. "I got it, all right? I knew because I'd done the exact same thing, hid a secret so it wouldn't shatter the illusion of who I was *supposed* to be. But now? Why in the love of God would you do this *now*? And to me?"

"I want to fix whatever the hell is going wrong with us, Liv." He crumples the water bottle between his hands. "The whole mess with Helen... I couldn't imagine having kids after that, so when you told me *you* didn't want any, I... I just wanted to forget the whole damn thing."

"You can't forget something so horrible, Dean." A knot fills my throat, prickles of ice erupting on my skin. "You can only use it to make you stronger."

He stares at the ground, his fingers tight around the crushed bottle. "It was really fucking ugly, Liv. I don't want that to happen to us."

"Why would you think that? I'm not Helen!"

"I know!" He looks up at me. "I feel things for you that I never felt for her, which is why I can't stand the thought of you going through what she did."

"Telling me about it isn't the same as me going through it."

His jaw tenses. "You'd have been hurt anyway."

"I'm hurt now! I'm more hurt and upset that you *didn't* tell me than I'd have been if you had! God, Dean, I'm not a fragile wallflower who can't handle anything. Don't you know that by now? This is exactly what we went through when you tried to keep me from your family."

"Right," he snaps. "And look what happened to us then."

I stare at him, my heart cracking at the bitter memory. My breath saws through the air. My pulse races.

"Liv." Dean drops the water bottle and stands. The tension dissipates from his features and concern floods in. He grasps my shoulders. "Breathe, Liv."

"I'm not..."

"Breathe!"

"I'm not panicking!" I shove away from him and stalk toward a grove of trees.

I pull air into my lungs and exhale slowly, aware of Dean hovering behind me, always there, always ready to anchor me to the ground.

Except this time, he's the one who pulled it out from underneath me.

I press my hands to my eyes and struggle for control.

"Liv, please." He sounds desperate. "It was... everything changed, you know? All for the worse. I don't want us to change."

Neither do I.

But I can't bring myself to say it because beneath that wish is the hot, jagged knowledge that we already have changed.

I turn to grab my backpack. Dean closes his hand on my arm. I shake my head. He releases me and turns to pick up the water bottle and his backpack.

I head back down the trail, my chest tight with anger and hurt. He falls into step beside me.

"Liv, I'm sorry."

"Why didn't you *tell* me?"

"I didn't want you to... you know..."

I glance at him. "What?"

He's looking off to the side, down toward the lake. A faint color crests his cheekbones. "I didn't want you to think less of me."

I stop in my tracks and turn to face him. "You thought I'd think *less* of you because you had a bad marriage? Because you... your wife lost three pregnancies?"

"No. Not because you're the type of person who'd think like that but because you're not."

"I don't understand."

"You're good, Liv." He grips my hands, holding them both tight. "You've always been good. You've never made shitty decisions that hurt the people you love, that veer your entire life off course, that you'll regret forever. You've never disappointed anyone, never failed."

"Dean, that's not true!" My vision blurs, all the old emotions swamping me. "I left my mother when I was thirteen, I refused to go with her again when she came back, I never told anyone about what happened to me, for months I wanted to hide from everything and everyone—"

Anger clenches his jaw. "But you didn't. You never needed to prove yourself to anyone except yourself. You did all those things to survive."

His hands tighten on mine, his voice intense. "You're so damn strong, Liv, and you don't even realize it. I'm the one who's always had to show people I'm successful, an achiever, the best at everything I did. I'm the one who's always been a goddamn egotist. A groveler. And you... you're the first person who's ever... Christ, Liv, sometimes the way you look at me makes me feel like I can hang the fucking moon."

"Because I've always believed you can."

"I know! I've never had to prove myself to you. And if I'd told you about the shit-storm of my marriage... ah, hell, Liv. I couldn't stand the thought that you'd look at me any differently."

"I..." My throat is aching. "I don't know why you thought I would."

"I'm sorry." He lets go of me and drags a hand through his hair, letting out a heavy sigh. "Please believe that, if nothing else. I want... I thought if I told you, if you understood about the whole pregnancy thing... I don't know. I want us to be okay again."

My heart breaks a little more. Once upon a time I would never have imagined we could be anything *but* okay.

We don't speak the entire way back. When we reach the place where we started, Dean pulls me to him and tucks me underneath his arm.

I move closer to him, but there's a gap between us, my shoulder pressing into the wrong place, my body no longer fitting quite so perfectly into the space against his side.

CHAPTER FOURTEEN

OCTOBER 16

*H*e was married before. My husband was married before.

He was my first in so many ways—my first lover, my first *love*, my first confidante, my first and only hero—but he knew a lot of women before me and had had a lot of experience. And while that knowledge has needled me every now and then, I've always been secure in the fact that I am his first and only wife.

But, as it turns out, I'm not.

I'm not who I thought I was. I don't even know how to process that. I can't make any sense of it.

And I have no idea what to do with this new information

about the Former Wife, so I'm trying very hard not to think about it. Not to think about her or what the hell happens next. Both Dean and I know how buried secrets can poison you, which is just one of the things that makes it so hard to accept that *he hadn't told me.*

Suppressing a surge of pain, I put a mixing bowl on the counter of my cooking station and yank open the cutlery drawer.

"You can do it, Liv," Tyler insists. He's standing beside me, looking neat and professional in his chef's jacket.

I glower at him. I feel like I'm in detention. Everyone else in class is steaming fish *en papillote*, but Tyler has instructed me—and me alone—to make a soufflé.

Yeah.

I'm still struggling with the knotted idea of Dean's *first* marriage, still trying not to think about it while unable to make it go away, and now Tyler is singling me out to do something I really don't want to do.

"But why?" I sound a little whiney. I've made three soufflés in the past six weeks and they've all been disastrous.

Tyler is firm—and oblivious to my inner turmoil. "I told you why. You need to know what it feels like to make a proper soufflé."

"Tyler, I'm sure I can live quite happily without experiencing that thrilling emotion."

"Maybe so. But I still want you to try."

I mutter and grumble to make a point. I really want to wrap fish up in cute little paper bags, but because I am still a dutiful student who always does what the teacher asks, I get out a carton of eggs.

After another couple of seconds, I turn off my internal

complainer and focus on the task. I complete the *mise en place*, measuring out the ingredients, grating the parmesan cheese, separating the eggs.

On a whim, I also chop scallions, cheddar cheese, and a few strips of cooked bacon. I mix butter and flour for the sauce, then whisk in hot milk and seasonings.

Once I get going, I lose track of time. Around me, the sounds of cooking rise in a pleasing symphony—chopping, sizzling, stirring. I beat the egg whites, slowly folding them into the sauce and rotating with the grated cheese. I pour the mixture into the ramekin.

My oven beeps to indicate the preheating is complete. I carefully slide the dish inside, then close the door and turn on the interior light so I can watch it cook. I alternate between cleaning my station and peering through the glass.

After my station is clean, I twist a dishtowel anxiously and crouch in front of the oven. The darned thing actually looks good. It's rising.

Don't fall. Don't fall.

As I wait for the endless last five minutes of baking time, I realize Tyler hasn't stopped by my station at all to check on my progress. I stand to look for him. He's making his rounds to all the other stations, pointing out this and that.

He catches my eye. I feel like holding up my hands in a "Dude, what's the deal?" gesture—after all, he made me attempt the soufflé again—but then he winks.

The timer dings. I almost hold my breath as I grab two oven mitts and open the door.

Oh my God.

It looks incredible. Puffy and golden-brown, my soufflé

rises dramatically over the rim of the dish a good three inches, like a movie star preening for the camera. It's at least doubled in volume. The heavenly aromas of cheese, bacon, and scallions drift to me in a wave of heat.

"Tyler." My voice comes out a squeak. My heart pounds as I carefully transfer the dish to the counter. "Tyler!"

Now it's a shriek because, Good Lord, the man has *got* to see this before it starts to collapse.

My fellow students all turn, and Tyler hurries to my station. The rest of the class follows.

Even though my pulse is racing, I don't say anything. That goddamn perfect soufflé speaks for itself.

"Wow." Charlotte sounds appropriately awed, and the others all murmur in impressed agreement.

I look at Tyler. He's grinning like I just won a Michelin star.

"Not bad, eh, Chef?" I ask, unable to stop smiling.

"Not bad at all, Liv." He's looking at me rather than the soufflé.

"Did you put bacon in it?" George asks, sniffing the air around my station. "It smells wonderful."

"Yes, I added bacon, scallions, and cheddar."

"Why'd you do that?" Tyler asks.

"Just thought it would taste good."

He nods with approval, then passes out forks to all of us. "You do the honors first, Liv."

A twinge of nervousness goes through me, but really, how can something so beautiful taste bad? I dig my fork in, relieved that the inside is creamy but not runny. I take a bite and my mouth fills with the fluffy, delicate flavors of cheese and egg accompanied by the smoky tang of bacon.

I stare at Tyler.

"Well?" he asks.

"It's good." I wipe a crumb from my lower lip. "I think…
I think it's really good."

He pushes his fork into the crust. One bite, and he doesn't
say anything. Then he takes a second bite. A heart-stopping
instant later, his eyes warm and a smile spreads across his
face.

"Excellent, Liv. Fluffy, cooked perfectly. Love the bacon."
He puts his fork down and steps aside to let the others try it.

My fellow students *ooh* and *ahh* with appreciation as
they taste the soufflé, with most of them going back for seconds. There's nothing left of it by the time they've finished.
They all congratulate and praise me before returning to their
stations.

"You did it, Liv." Tyler puts his hand on my arm and
squeezes. He looks incredibly proud. "You made the perfect
soufflé. How do you feel?"

I don't even think I can describe how I feel, which is a
little embarrassing because, well, I made a soufflé. I didn't save
the world. Still…

"I feel pretty amazing," I admit.

"Told you. And you did it all by yourself."

"Is that why you didn't come to my station at all tonight?"

"Yes, it is. You can cook, Liv. And well. You just needed
the confidence to know you can do it."

He gives me a little salute and returns to his instructor's
station. I finish cleaning up and drive home.

"I did it." I drop my satchel on the table. "I made the
perfect soufflé."

"Did you bring it home?" Dean peers at me from behind the newspaper.

"No, we ate it all. That's how good it was. It was fluffy, creamy, airy, tangy…"

"Hmm. Sounds like you."

I flop down beside him on the sofa. "Really, I've never made anything like that before. I had no idea making a soufflé could be so rewarding. I added my own twist to the recipe, bacon and scallions…"

The paper rustles as he turns a page. I nudge him with my elbow.

"Dean, are you listening?"

"Yeah. Bacon. I'm getting hungry. Let's order bacon burgers from Abernathy's."

Inspired by the idea, he pushes off the sofa and goes to the phone. I scowl at his back. Okay, so soufflés aren't exactly on Professor Dean West's radar, but a little enthusiasm would have been nice.

Not that I ever express much interest in Ottoman architecture or medieval apocalyptic imagery.

I go to shower and change, and by the time I'm done the food order has arrived. After we eat, Dean goes into his office while I do a little cleaning and fill the coffeepot so he won't have to bother in the morning.

After watching a police drama on TV, I head to the bedroom and stop by his office. The light is on, and he's at his desk going through some papers.

"Is that your conference presentation?" I ask, nodding at the stack in front of him.

"Abstracts for one of the seminars." He organizes them into

a pile and puts them in his open briefcase. "My flight leaves at six on Saturday morning."

I realize I'm almost looking forward to his absence for a few days. I need the time to be alone and try to untangle all my snarled thoughts and emotions.

"Dean, what happened with that grad student?" I hover by the door. "Maggie Hamilton?"

His jaw tightens. "She went out of town a few weeks ago. Haven't talked to her, but she's sent a couple of emails about her proposal."

"Have you approved it yet?"

"No. I told her we'd discuss it when she returns. Given recent circumstances, I'm going to tell her she needs to change advisors."

"I'm sorry… about all that."

He shakes his head. "She was totally out of line. In more ways than one. I won't work with her anymore."

That, at least, is a relief.

I approach Dean and step between his chair and the desk. He pushes the chair back a little to make room so I can curl into his lap. He's only wearing a pair of pajama bottoms, and his chest is warm and muscular.

He folds his arms around me and presses a kiss to my temple. At times like this I never want to leave the comforting, protective circle he's always wrapped me in. I tuck my head beneath his chin, and we sit for several long minutes. He smells like soap and toothpaste. I listen to his heartbeat, feel the movement of his breath.

He pats my hip. "I should finish up here, beauty."

"Okay." I kiss his neck and ease away.

I'm still awake when he comes into the bedroom almost an hour later. He climbs into bed beside me, but makes no move for anything sexual.

I turn to look at him, sliding my hands beneath my head. "What did she study?"

"Who?"

"Helen."

"I told you. Art history."

"But what field?"

"Nineteenth-century European. Classicism, realism, impressionism. She did her dissertation on the Pre-Raphaelites."

Something clicks in my brain from a long-ago art history class. "Weren't the Pre-Raphaelites influenced by medieval art?"

"Late fourteenth century, before Raphael." He glances at me. "Why?"

"It's just kind of… uncanny, you and she. Your fields of study. Should have been a perfect match."

"All we had were similarities in our research. Everything else was very imperfect. Hell, it was downright defective."

"Was she good at her work?"

"She got hired at Stanford, so yeah. She was good." A slightly irritated tone colors his voice. "Why are you asking?"

"I'm curious. Even though it ended badly, she was a big part of your life."

"Not anymore."

"When was the last time you talked to her?"

"Years."

"Does she still teach at Stanford?"

"Yes." He sighs and switches off the bedside light. "I really don't want to talk about her."

Apprehension spreads through me. A million questions crowd my head, have been piling up ever since he told me about his first wife.

His *first* wife. The word still stings like a thistle. That makes me his second wife.

What was she like? Did he make her laugh? What kind of movies did they watch? How was the sex? What did they do? Where did they travel? Did he know how she liked her coffee? Could she cook?

I want answers to everything, not because I care about Helen but because it has so much to do with Dean. Because it's all such a part of him, his history, his life.

I put my hand on his shoulder. "Dean, I—"

He turns away toward the opposite wall. "Liv, I thought we were done with this."

A bubble of anger bursts inside my head.

"You're never *done with* a rough past, Dean," I say, pushing to sit up. "You think you can just tell me about it and it'll go away? That you make this big revelation and suddenly everything is back to normal with us?"

His back muscles tense. He doesn't respond.

"We need to go to counseling again, Dean," I say.

"I'm not discussing my first marriage with a damned counselor."

My first marriage.

Even he still thinks of it as his first. When we got married, when we said, *"I do... ,"* he'd done it all before. And I had no idea.

A wave of exhaustion slams against me. I roll over and stare at the ceiling. I don't even have the wherewithal to battle all the old emotions that I hate—fear, inadequacy, anxiety. Loneliness.

Everything that I'd felt before I met Dean. Everything I thought we'd replaced with love and trust. I can feel it all breaking through again now, and I don't know what to do.

CHAPTER FIFTEEN

OCTOBER 19

I make a trip out of town this afternoon. We have a new exhibition opening at the museum, and we've ordered the signage and wall-text from a printer in downtown Forest Grove.

I volunteered to pick up the completed order. I tried to tell myself I was being helpful, that the trip had nothing to do with the fact that Tyler Wilkes's restaurant is four blocks from the print shop.

After picking up the order, I store the materials in the trunk of my car. Then I walk that four blocks to Julienne. It's a chilly, sunny afternoon, dried leaves brushing the sidewalks, people heading in and out of the cafés and shops.

I'm nervous, unable to shake the feeling that I'm doing something wrong. I stop outside Julienne and pull my cell phone from my satchel.

"Dean?"

"Hey. Where are you?"

"Forest Grove. I had to pick up some signs for a new exhibit."

"Oh." There's some rustling of papers on the other end. "Careful you don't hit rush hour."

"I will… um, that's why I'm calling. I'll probably be late."

"Yeah, me too. Ton of work to do, then a football game."

"Okay. I'll see you this evening, then."

"Drive safe."

I snap the phone shut and shove it back into my satchel. I stare at the calligraphic writing on the window of the restaurant. Then I turn and start walking away.

"Liv?"

Shit.

I turn. Tyler is standing at the open door, looking at me quizzically. He's wearing his chef's jacket. He gives me a tentative smile.

"Thought that was you. What are you doing here?"

"I was… I had to run an errand at a print shop down the street."

He holds the door open. "Come on in. I hope you weren't going to leave without stopping by."

I make a show of pushing back my coat cuff to look at my watch. "Actually, it's getting late and—"

"Come on." He pushes the door open farther. "We close from three to five to prep for dinner, so I can show you around."

"I don't want to interrupt your work."

"You won't." He tilts his head toward the inside. "I did say you could stop by anytime."

Something knots in my stomach, but I walk past him into the restaurant. The interior is elegant, quiet, with perhaps forty linen-draped tables and booths, soft lighting, leather seats. Muted paintings line the walls beneath ivory-colored crown molding. A few servers walk around setting the tables.

"It's beautiful," I say truthfully.

Tyler smiles. "Thanks. I like it. Come on back to the kitchen."

The hum of voices and clank of pots and pans rises as we walk to the back of the restaurant. Several chefs bustle around, checking simmering pots, peeling potatoes, scaling various cuts of fish. They give me nods of greeting when Tyler introduces me, then return to their tasks.

"We change the menu according to what's available or in season," Tyler explains. "Tonight we've added king salmon and grass-fed beef tenderloin."

He hands me a menu. The food is impressive and mouth-watering, including seared scallops, wild mushroom salad, slow-roasted veal, and fresh apple tart.

"Sounds delicious." I put the menu on the counter. "I'll have to come here with Dean sometime."

Saying my husband's name aloud eases a little of my tension. Tyler studies me for a moment, then nods to a table near the kitchen.

"Sit down. You can sample some of what we're serving."

"I really can't..."

"Come on, Liv. Aren't you hungry?"

Well, yes, I'm hungry. I didn't eat lunch, and it's four in

the afternoon, and I likely have a dinner of microwaved pizza in my near future.

I take off my coat and look at my watch again. "I can't stay long."

"It won't take long." He moves to pull out a chair at the table, then stops. "Wait a sec. I have another idea."

He disappears into a backroom and returns with a chef's jacket. He holds it out to me.

"What's that for?" I ask.

"Come on. I'll show you how we make a few things."

"Tyler, you don't have to—"

Instead of arguing with me, he goes behind me and puts the jacket around my shoulders. "We'll make the salmon so I can show you how to fillet it."

He returns to the kitchen. I watch him for a second, then push my arms into the jacket sleeves and button it up. The name *Julienne* is embroidered on the lapel. I fish in my pocket for a rubber band and fasten my hair into a ponytail, then go to wash my hands.

This is fine. I'm not going to sit there while he cooks for me. I'm going to watch what he does and learn something. Exactly like in class, just a different venue. Totally fine.

I go to where Tyler is standing. There's a whole salmon lying on the counter in front of him, and he patiently explains all the different parts, then demonstrates how to scale and cut a perfect fillet. His movements are so fluid it's like he's cutting through butter.

"Your turn." He flips the salmon over and hands me the knife.

"I'll destroy it."

"Liv, stop thinking that everything you try will end up a disaster," Tyler says. "Don't saw at it. Keep the blade tipped toward the backbone."

I have no idea how much a salmon like this costs, but I don't want to be the reason Tyler's unable to serve it. Nervous again, I make the first cut near the tail.

"Don't go through the backbone. Tilt the blade." He puts his hand on mine to guide it. His handling of the knife is far more confident than mine, and we slice the second smooth fillet from the fish. It's a good feeling.

Tyler shows me how to remove the bones, then preps the fillet for sautéing with braised lentils. Another chef is working on a mustard, crème-fraiche sauce, and Tyler sends me over to him. Although the other chef is working fast, he doesn't seem bothered by having to stop and explain the technique to me.

When I return to Tyler, he shows me how to season and sear scallops.

"The less you mess with food, the better it is," he says, stepping aside and nodding for me to put the scallops in the hot pan. "Don't put too many in, and don't move them around until they're ready to be turned."

He doesn't coach me when to flip them, but I'm very aware of him watching as I slide a spatula under the scallops. To my relief, they're a lovely golden brown. I know from class that it's easy to overcook scallops, so I take them from the pan about thirty seconds before I think they're completely cooked.

Tyler hands me a clean dish and we plate the scallops with celery-root puree, fava beans, and arugula.

"Now go and eat," he says, nodding to the table. "Scallops can't wait or they get rubbery."

By now my stomach is growling, so I sit down and eat. The scallops are excellent, crispy on the outside, soft and creamy on the inside. I finish them all just as Tyler brings me the perfectly cooked salmon and braised lentils, which are melt-in-your-mouth delicious.

He pulls out the chair across from me and sits.

"Not bad, Chef," I remark, which of course is a vast understatement.

His grin tells me he knows that. "Glad you like it."

I wipe my mouth with a napkin. "Your dad must be really proud of you."

"He would be." A shadow crosses his face. "He died a few years ago."

"I'm sorry."

He shrugs. "I finally convinced my mom to sell the diner after he died. She's living down in Florida now near my sister. I see them a couple of times a year. I'm thinking of opening a place down there someday."

He looks at my empty plate and stands. "Hold on. One more thing I want you to try."

A few minutes later, he returns with a warm, flourless chocolate torte adorned with raspberries and homemade coffee-bean ice cream.

"The ice cream is my favorite," he says. "When it comes down to the basics, I'll always pick good ice cream over anything else."

He watches me as I eat the torte. I'm very conscious of his gaze.

"Tyler, this was amazing." I lick the crumbs from my fork. "You didn't have to take the time to show me so much, but I'm glad you did."

"So am I. And I offered, remember? I was thinking we should come here as a class one afternoon. Like a field trip. So everyone can see how a restaurant kitchen runs."

I look at him for a minute. His face is flushed from the heat of the stove, and his blond hair is ruffled. A few strands stick to his forehead. There's a smear of chocolate on the front of his chef's jacket.

Cute, indeed.

I pull on my coat and stand. "Thanks again. I won't tell Charlotte I was here, though, because she'll get jealous."

"Charlotte doesn't have a reason to be jealous." He pauses. "Does she?"

"No." I duck my head. "Of course not. I'll, uh, see you in class."

He walks me to the door. Before I leave, he puts a hand on my shoulder.

"Hey."

I stop.

"Did it make your soul sparkle again?" he asks.

For some insane reason, my throat closes over. I can't speak past the constriction. Instead I just nod and pull away from him. He lets me go.

"See you in class, Liv."

I hurry outside and walk back to my car. It's not until I take off my coat before getting into the driver's seat that I realize I'm still wearing the chef's jacket. I pull it off and stuff it underneath the seat, then head home.

I smell like olive oil, salmon, dill, chocolate. I need a shower.

My chest is tight, even though I did nothing wrong.

Did I?

At home, I drop all my things on the counter beside Dean's keys and briefcase. The shower is running. I remember the time I'd tried to join him in the shower and encountered a locked door.

Now my chest is so tight it hurts.

I go into the bedroom. The bathroom door is open.

I fumble with the hem of my T-shirt and start to take it off, then stop. Instead I reach underneath it, unhook my bra, and toss it aside. I take off my skirt but leave my panties on.

Before I can think too much, I enter the bathroom. Steam coats the air, blurring the mirror and the shower door. The outline of Dean's body is behind the glass, his arms raised to scrub his hair.

He turns at the sound of me opening the shower door. Water cascades down his chest. My eyes follow the rivulets down to his groin. He's already half-erect. That alone makes my heart throb. I wonder again what he's been thinking about, standing here naked with hot water pounding over his skin.

I'm your wife, Dean.

I don't know if the reminder is meant for me or him. Water splashes through the open door onto me, dampening my T-shirt.

Dean's gaze goes to my breasts. My nipples harden and tent the soft cotton. My belly starts to swirl with desire, and I reach up to rub my palm across my breasts.

Dean places one hand flat against the door and pushes it fully open.

"Get in here," he orders.

The gruff tone of his voice pulses through me. I step inside. The water drenches me in seconds, plastering my shirt to my skin and outlining every curve. Dean closes the door hard enough to rattle the glass on its hinges, then he turns and hauls me against him.

I move my hand down to brush against his cock. "What were you thinking about?"

"You."

"Really?"

"Porn."

"No way."

"No." He slides his hand around the back of my neck and pulls me to him. "You. Really. Naked and moaning and creaming all over my prick."

A shiver rocks me. The hard edge to his voice floods me with arousal.

His mouth crashes against mine, and lust surges like an ocean swell. I can feel the adrenaline from the football game still racing through him, the heat of his skin beneath the water.

He lifts his head. "You taste good."

"I had... I had some chocolate."

"Nice."

Yeah. It was nice.

I suddenly want it rough.

Dean's cock pushes hard against my belly, fully erect now, but when I slip my hand down to grasp him, his fingers curl around my wrist.

He twists my arm behind my back. His breath is hot against my lips. "Don't move."

I don't. Except that my chest is heaving as I watch him pull back to cup my breasts, flicking the tips through the wet cotton, running his long fingers beneath them.

He turns me around so my back is to his chest, locking one arm securely around my waist. He slides his other hand over my hip and peels the shirt up to expose my white panties.

"Are you hot under here?" His fingers tangle in the elastic waistband before he pushes them halfway down my thighs.

"God, yes."

I shudder, wanting to both part my legs and press them together to soothe the growing ache. Dean pushes the panties off me, then slips his fingers between my thighs and starts working me in exactly the way he knows I like, his forefinger trailing up one side and circling my clit before stroking down the other side.

In no time, I'm writhing against his hand, and moans echo off the shower stall. I'm hoping the hot water holds out because the whole thing feels so good—the steaming, pounding water, Dean's exploring touch, his other arm tight around my waist. The T-shirt clings to me like a second skin, and I'm aroused by the sight of my full breasts draped in the wet cloth, my nipples hard as cherries.

Three more hard strokes from Dean, and I come with the force of an exploding star, quaking and tightening my legs around his hand. His chest heaves against my back, and then we're tumbling out of the shower, dripping wet and not stopping for towels on the way to the bedroom.

My breasts crush against his chest as we fall onto the bed, our mouths seeking, tongues tangling. Water spills from our skin, evaporating in the carnal heat. He lifts away, his eyes hot as he stares at the shirt still plastered to my body. He pushes it up farther to expose my breasts, splaying his big hands over them, squeezing them together.

I spread my legs, my knees hugging his hips. My desire sparks all over again when his erection presses against my inner thigh. I can feel the urgency uncoiling through him. Above me, he's all heated, damp skin and smoky eyes and I know he wants it, wants me…

I twist around, bucking him away, and get on my hands and knees. I push my ass toward him. "Do it like this."

My voice is low and strained. This position has always been explosive for both of us, though I've never quite gotten used to the way it makes me feel exposed and vulnerable. But right now, I want it, want the reminder of Dean's possession and my own compliance.

Renewed arousal clenches my belly. He grabs a condom from the nightstand and rolls it on. He settles his hands on my waist, pulling me into position, and then his cock nudges at my opening. Sweat trickles between my breasts. I squeeze my eyes shut.

"Hard," I whisper.

He tightens his hands on my hips before he slides into me with one powerful thrust. I gasp, jerking forward, wincing at the sensation of utter fullness. Dean pulls me against him and thrusts again. My nerves are on fire. I fumble for a pillow and bury my face in it, emptying my mind of all thought as he starts to pump.

"Push back." His voice roughens with the command. "Fuck yourself on me."

I shudder and drive my hips backward, matching his

rhythm. My world distills to pure sensation—my husband's hands gripping my body, his cock sliding in and out of me, his breath hot against my back. Tendrils of wet hair cling to my face.

My ass slaps against his flat stomach, the smack of flesh on flesh echoing in my head. The wet cotton shirt abrades my nipples and sends heat sparking over my skin. Dean's thrusts are forceful, his groans rumbling above me.

Air scorches my lungs. He slams into me all the way, jarring me to the core, pleasure mixing with an edge of pain. My pulse pounds. I'm quaking with urgency, and he knows it because he slips a hand beneath me and splays his fingers over my aching clit.

"Tell me what you want, Liv."

"Oh…" I twist my hips, trying to rub myself against his hand, feeling that explosion of bliss so close. "I want to come again… please, let me…"

He takes his hand away, sliding it up to my breasts beneath the T-shirt. I cry out with frustration and reach between my legs. Dean grabs my wrist and pins my hand to the bed, plunging so far inside me that my whole body shakes with the impact.

"Don't touch yourself," he says hoarsely. "You'll come just from taking me deep."

Heat floods me. My thighs tremble. I shove back in desperation, craving release. My mind fills with images of me on my hands and knees, Dean all fiery and tense behind me, his muscles corded with exertion, his chest damp with sweat. His thick, veined cock sinking into my body.

"Work for it," he orders. "You look so fucking hot… show me you want it… harder… ah, that's it…"

I brace my hand on the headboard and writhe shamelessly against him, pumping myself onto his shaft and urging us both toward ecstasy. My breasts sway beneath me, cries of pleasure tearing from my throat. Pressure coils around my nerves.

"Dean!" The pillow muffles my scream as I convulse around him, my inner flesh tightening. He shoves hard once more before withdrawing. A second later, he rubs his cock into the crevice of my ass. His groan shakes the air as he comes long and hard over my lower back.

Gasping, I sink onto my stomach. Dean pulls away and rolls onto the bed beside me.

We lie there wet, panting, and sweaty. Shudders continue to tremble in my blood, those tiny aftershocks of lingering pleasure.

I shift, turning onto my side. Dean is watching me, wariness dissolving the satiation in his eyes.

Jesus. Does he suspect something? Why should he? And what is there to suspect anyway? I haven't done anything wrong.

Have I?

No, dammit, I haven't. He's the one who lied about his previous marriage. I haven't lied about anything.

I sit up to pull off the T-shirt, which is no longer wet and sexy but cold and clammy. I grab my bathrobe and wrap it around me. I don't look at him as I make an intricate knot in the belt of the robe.

"You okay?" He's still watching me.

I don't know how to answer that question.

"Second time I've caught you thinking about me in the shower," I remark, forcing lightness into my tone. "I should walk in on you more often, if your fantasies lead to this."

Though I'd intended it as a teasing comment, darkness flashes across Dean's face. The first time I'd walked in on him, my fears had provoked ugly accusations and doubt.

He pushes off the bed. Tension ripples in the air between us.

"I need to finish packing." He pulls on his boxers and goes into the living room.

I take a few breaths to calm my still-racing heart. I'm tired and confused and in no mood to go after him and dredge up all our problems. I need to figure things out myself first, which I hope I can do while Dean is at the conference.

My throat constricts. I suddenly can't wait for him to leave.

After Dean heads to the airport, I spend the morning alone in the apartment. The strain of recent weeks is gone in his absence, and I let myself enjoy the peace and quiet.

I have a cup of coffee, read a magazine, do some laundry, clean out my closet, watch a gardening show. In the afternoon I spend a few hours at the Historical Museum, and since I'm off work at the bookstore this weekend, Kelsey calls to invite me to a Mexican restaurant for dinner.

"Is it still the baby thing?" Kelsey sits back and sips her gigantic margarita. When I don't respond, she glances at me. "Or is something else wrong?"

"No." I duck my head and take a long sip of my own, less-gigantic margarita. The *baby thing* has been overwhelmed by the *former wife thing*.

"We'll work it out," I say vaguely. "It just takes time."

I won't tell Kelsey what Dean told me—it's his story to

tell, after all—but she's savvy enough to read between the lines. She piles a chip with guacamole and crunches into it.

"Whatever the deal is, Liv, the man loves you to his bones," she says. "Even I can see that, and I'm about as romantic as a tree branch."

"Liv?"

Kelsey and I both look up to see Tyler Wilkes approaching our table.

"Tyler." I smile. It's the first time I've seen him without his chef's jacket on. He's wearing tan trousers and a well-fitted, button-down shirt the same shade of blue as his eyes. He looks good.

He stops beside our table and there's a moment of awkwardness as we try to figure out how to greet each other. Finally he puts an arm around my shoulders and we exchange a brief hug. I catch a whiff of his aftershave before I pull away and introduce Kelsey.

"Tyler is my cooking instructor," I say, then launch into a list of Tyler's many accomplishments, which I'm surprised I even remember.

"Impressive." Kelsey purses her lips around her straw for another dose of margarita. She glances from Tyler to me.

"I expect Liv is going to be the most improved student by the end of the year," Tyler says. "She's a hard worker and she has great potential. And she makes a mean soufflé."

I flush and roll my eyes, even though the compliment secretly pleases me.

"So, what are you doing here?" I wave my hand at the restaurant, which is a nice place but certainly no fine-dining establishment.

"Just met a friend for dinner," Tyler says. "The chile relleno here is the best for miles."

I glance behind him, wondering if the "friend" is female. And then wondering why I care.

"Don't you live in Forest Grove?" I ask.

"No, I've got a place over in Rainwood. About the same distance from here to Forest Grove."

"Can you stay?" I gesture to the chair beside me. "We're just getting ready to order."

"No, I gotta get back to Julienne. I like to be there on weekends. Remember you've still got a standing invitation. Next time I won't even put you to work." He nods at Kelsey. "Nice meeting you."

"Yeah. You too."

"Bye, Liv. Good to see you."

"You too, Tyler."

I watch him go. I don't really care that Kelsey is looking at me like she's trying very, very hard not to interrogate me.

I *haven't* done anything wrong. And Tyler's compliments and admiration make me feel good. Frankly it's nice to feel that way these days.

Our food arrives, and I ask Kelsey about her work as we eat. Ranting about her fellow professors is enough to keep her off the subject of Tyler, and by the time she drops me off at home she seems to have forgotten about him.

I don't forget about him, though.

I lie in the big, empty bed and think about him and all his accomplishments and the easygoing way he has with people. I think about his vast knowledge of food, how he can debone a chicken within minutes, how he knows the exact temperature to cook a scallop, and how he can identify every cut of beef. He even knows how to make a perfect risotto.

I roll over and stare at the other side of the bed. Tyler is like Dean in some ways. Both of them possess an encyclopedic knowledge of their fields. Both are accomplished, dedicated, wholly passionate about their work. Both excel at what they do.

I press my hand against Dean's cold pillow, then fumble for the phone on the nightstand. "Dean?"

"Hey, beauty. Did you get my voicemail?"

"Yes. I…" I curl my fingers into the pillow. "Just wanted to talk to you."

"How was your day?"

"Fine. I had dinner with Kelsey. She says hi. She wants you to bring her back some peach preserves."

"Do you want anything?"

"I want you to come home."

"Four days only. I love you. I'll call you tomorrow night."

"I love you too."

He's already hung up, so I don't know if he heard me. I drop the phone back onto the cradle and close my eyes.

If Dean had been sleeping beside me, I don't know if I would have dreamed about Tyler Wilkes. I'll never know. But I dream about him now—a dream that's slow and easy and sweaty.

I dream about his body, compact and firm with a light mat of blond hair scattered over his chest. I dream about the way his mouth would feel against the bare skin of my shoulder, my throat, my breasts. I dream about his weight on top of me, how we'd fit together, how it would feel to wrap my legs around his hips. I imagine his skin smells like fresh herbs and citrus, that his hair feels thick and smooth like straw.

When I wake, I'm damp with perspiration, and my blood throbs a restless beat. I shift around, resisting the urge to press my fingers between my thighs, to rub the ache away.

I roll to my side, breathing hard, wincing as my sex pulses with the movement.

This is not what I expected. Not what I want.

I haven't felt so shaken, so uncertain, in years. Since before I met Dean. I thought the whole reason I started considering the idea of having children was because I've put my past behind me, I love my husband, we're settled in Mirror Lake, my life has become what I always wanted but never had before—secure, happy, safe…

So what the hell am I doing having an erotic dream about another man?

And what the fuck else has my husband not told me?

The anger I've been suppressing breaks loose like a swarm of bees.

I press my hands to my eyes. My heart is beating too fast. I force my mind back to our conversation, everything Dean said about his relationship with Helen. His first wife.

"I shouldn't have relied on her to deal with birth control. But I did, and that's what happened."

All thoughts of Tyler Wilkes dissolve into the pool of dread spreading through my entire being.

I climb out of bed, pushing the covers aside. I yank open the drawer of Dean's nightstand and look at the box of condoms inside. There's another one in the bathroom. And a third in the drawer of a table beside the sofa. I've known for years where Dean keeps the condoms, but now it's like I'm finding them for the first time.

Is that why Dean always used condoms with me, even when I tried birth control pills? Was it because of Helen's betrayal? Did he think I'd do the same thing?

The thought makes me cold. Doubts flood me again—Dean's reluctance to talk about a baby, Maggie Hamilton's ugly insinuations, the secrets Dean and I both harbored so that we wouldn't ruin the illusion of who we were supposed to be.

He was always the successful overachiever. I was always the good girl. God forbid anything should destroy the images we fought so hard to maintain.

I go into Dean's office and sit at the swivel chair in front of his desk. I look at all his papers, flip through legal pads covered in his scrawled handwriting, page through books marked with Post-Its.

I turn on his computer. The desktop appears as a grid of PDF files, documents, images. I open a few of them. An article about the San Clemente church in Rome, another about "architectural polychromy." A draft of Dean's paper for an archeology journal. Pictures of medieval cathedrals, town plans, archeological sites.

I open a web browser and look at his browsing history of news and sports websites, email, conference information.

I click on Dean's university email. The password is saved, so I log on. There are messages about classes and papers, the conference, airline and hotel confirmations. Halfway down the message list, I see the name that makes my breath stop.

Helen Morgan.

With a shaking hand, I click on the message to open it.

TO: Dr. Dean West, King's University
FR: Dr. Helen Morgan, Stanford University
SU: Conference

Dean,

I wanted to let you know that I'm submitting a paper for inclusion in your Words and Images conference. The topic is about the Pre-Raphaelite use of medieval icons. I've been working with several medievalists recently, and the conference would be a way for me to expand my research into more interdisciplinary areas.

Since I do not want to miss a professional opportunity, I thought I would let you know (as a courtesy) of my intentions.

Sincerely,
Helen

There's a reply from Dean.

Thanks for letting me know. Best of luck.
Dean

I stare at the message. My heart freezes.
My husband lied to me again.

CHAPTER SIXTEEN

OCTOBER 23

*O*ver the next couple of days, I refuse to curl up and hide. Even though my chest is tight with dismay, I get through my hours at the bookstore and Historical Museum, then attend cooking class on Tuesday evening.

I can hardly look at Tyler. I think of my sex dream every time I catch sight of his blue eyes and blond hair. Every time he flashes me a smile, which I do not return.

When he reaches over my cutting board to point out my uneven dicing of a pepper, I stare at his hand and remember imagining how it would feel on my skin.

Class seems to last forever, and I quickly clean my station and pack up my things when it's over.

"Everything okay, Liv?" Tyler stops in front of me, a crease of concern between his eyebrows.

"Fine." I shove my notebook into my satchel. "Why?"

"You seem a little stressed out tonight, not really focused. I didn't make things weird for you with your friend, did I?"

"What… oh, Kelsey. No. Not at all. I'm just… no. Everything is fine."

I stare at his throat. I'd dreamed about flicking my tongue into the hollow just above his collarbone. Dreamed about him pressing his hand to the back of my neck, exactly the way Dean does.

Jesus. I'm a fucking mess.

Tears sting my eyes. I duck my head and grab my satchel. "See you next week."

"Hey, Liv."

I stop, but don't turn to look at him. He grasps my wrist, turns my palm up, and presses a piece of paper into it. I glance down.

"My phone number," he says, his voice low enough so the others don't overhear. "Don't mean to be presumptuous, but call if you want to talk or anything. You know, as friends."

"Yeah. Sure. Thanks."

I make it out to my car before the tears start falling, scraping my throat. I manage to compose myself and leave the parking lot before my fellow students or Tyler come out.

Out of sheer exhaustion and the need for escape, I sleep through the night—a bleak, dreamless sleep.

The next morning, I dress in warm clothes, then take a walk along one of the mountain trails. A touch of winter is in the air, the trees shedding their red-and-gold leaves, geese hovering around the lake. After a couple of hours, I return home to wait for Dean.

I finally hear his key in the lock at around three. He comes in all rumpled and travel-weary, wraps his arms around me for a tight hug, then goes off to shower and change.

"Kelsey's preserves." He puts a few jars of peach preserves on the counter. "And some for you. Great on toast."

"How was the conference?"

"Good. I'm starting up a project with three European students on medieval guildhalls and public architecture." He goes into the kitchen and grabs an orange, telling me all the details of the project and the archeology it will involve.

I know the routine. And I know enough not to confront him right when he gets home. So I wait a few hours while he unpacks and winds down, checks his email, organizes his notes and books.

It's almost dinner before he realizes I've barely said a word since he came home. I place an order for Chinese take-out. Dean stretches out on the sofa.

"You have your cooking class last night?" He reaches for the remote control and glances at me. "How was it?"

"Fine."

"What did you make?"

Chicken? Fish? "Veal. Veal scaloppini."

"How did it turn out?"

"Okay. A little dry. But good, I guess."

He continues looking at me. "So what's wrong?"

I take a deep breath. "You told me you hadn't spoken to her in years."

"Who…"

"Helen."

"I haven't."

"Then why did I find a message from her in your email?"

He frowns. "What were you doing checking my email?"

"Trying to find out what else you might be keeping from me," I snap, refusing to feel guilty for having spied on him. "I specifically asked you when you'd last talked to Helen and you said *years*, then I found an email from her about your conference. When were you planning on telling me about *that*?"

"Liv, there's nothing to tell."

"She said she's planning to attend your conference next year, Dean, which means she'll be in Mirror Lake. You didn't think that was worth telling me? And why did you lie about having contact with her?"

"I didn't lie. You asked me when I last *talked* to her, and it's true that it's been years since I have."

"Don't be an ass." My fists clench, old insecurities and anger boiling into my chest. "You knew exactly what I meant."

"Liv, it's just an academic conference." Irritation hardens his features. "You read the email, obviously… all Helen said was that she was submitting a proposal."

"Did it even occur to you to tell me?"

"Why would you care who's attending a Medieval Studies conference?"

My heart shrivels a little at the implication that I have no interest in his work. And at the knowledge that I have done nothing to actually express interest.

"I care if it's your ex-wife, Dean."

He sighs. "Look, I didn't think it was a big deal, okay? Do I want to see Helen again? No. Do I give a damn if she presents a paper at the conference? No. She's a scholar. She has a right to her career. She'll attend the conference and leave, just like everyone else."

He turns away to toss the remote onto the coffee table, his jaw set, as if that's the end of the conversation. I walk to the table beside the sofa and open the drawer. My hand trembles as I take out the condom package and hold it up.

"What about these?" I ask.

"Condoms?"

"Helen was the reason you've been using condoms all this time," I say.

Dean shakes his head. "Now what are you talking about?"

"She lied to you about birth control. That was how she got pregnant. And you told me you shouldn't have trusted her." I throw the box at him. It hits him square in the chest. "Did you not trust me either?"

"Liv, what—"

"You were the one who told me to stop taking the pill, told me you'd just use condoms."

"I told you to stop taking the pill because it made you sick. Not because I didn't trust you to take it."

"What about the patch? Shots? You didn't want me to use those either."

"Because they're also hormonal—"

"No, because you didn't want me to be the one in control of it. Because of *her*."

"Liv, for Christ's sake, I'd never think that of you."

"Then why? What man *likes* using a condom, Dean? For

three *years*? There are a zillion other options out there, and you didn't want me to use any of them!"

It occurs to me that it took me this long to even question his decision. I don't know if that's a measure of my own stupidity or of the simple fact that I've just never had reason to question him about anything.

He doesn't look guilty or ashamed. More than anything, he just looks baffled.

"Liv, the condoms have nothing to do with Helen."

"Don't they?" My tears spill over. "You don't want a baby with me because of what happened with Helen, right? Why else would you have wanted to wear condoms for so long?"

"Because you told me years ago that you didn't want children!" Frustration edges his voice. He stands and approaches me. "I'm not... Liv, yes, Helen tricked me into a pregnancy that I didn't want. But never once have I thought you'd do the same thing. Why would I have when you said you'd never wanted children anyway? Not to mention that I've always trusted you a hell of a lot more than I ever trusted her."

"But not enough to tell me you were *married* before."

"Liv—"

I hold up both hands. "I don't want this anymore, Dean."

"What?"

"This." I gesture to the air between us and wipe my wet face and runny nose with my sleeve. "This crap that's going on. I hate it. We had it good, didn't we? Then I mention a baby and suddenly everything goes to hell. What the fuck happened? Don't married people talk about babies and families? Why does everyone else manage to do it without all... *this*?"

"I don't know."

The fact that he just admitted that is enough to make my throat close. Professor West knows everything. Doesn't he?

"Why didn't you tell me earlier about Helen?" I ask.

"Because it was shitty. I didn't want you to know about it."

"You didn't think I could handle it."

"No. I wanted to protect you."

"So you lied."

"I didn't lie."

"By omission, yes, you did."

For God's sake. Our marriage is not supposed to have *lies*. My stomach roils with a surge of nausea.

"I told you everything, Dean," I whisper, "because I *knew* you could handle it. I knew you were strong enough to work through anything with me."

"Fuck, Liv." He scrubs his hands over his face, tension cording his forearms. "I know."

"But this whole time… did you think I wouldn't do the same for you?"

"No, of course not. I just didn't want you to."

"I'm your wife! I want to know everything about you. I thought I did."

"Liv…"

"Did you think I'd never find out the truth about Helen?" I pace a few steps away from him, my heart clenching. "Did you think you could keep it a secret forever? Especially when I brought up having children?"

"I don't know what I thought." He sits on the sofa and leans his elbows on his knees. He stares at the floor. "I wanted *you*, Liv. That was all I wanted. And I thought… I thought I was all you wanted."

I swipe at my tears again. "You were."

"You said you never wanted kids, and that was fine with me," he says. "You're right. We had it good. So good that I didn't think we needed anything else."

We had it good. We both used the past tense without realizing it.

"I've given you all I have," I say, my throat closing over the words. "All I am. You know that. Why didn't you do the same for me?"

"I did. The disaster with Helen was... it's not important. Not to us."

"How can you say that when it affected your response to having a baby with me?"

"What do you want me to do now, Liv?" Frustration steels his voice as he lifts his head to look at me. "Whatever it is, I'll do it. I'm sorry I didn't tell you. It was in the past, and I didn't want you to have to deal with another shitty thing. That was it. It had nothing to do with us."

"Everything about you has to do with us."

"I can't change it, Liv! What do you want me to do?"

"I don't know." My voice cracks.

We stare at each other. I see with sudden, sharp clarity exactly what our marriage has been. Dean has been in control of all the barbed-wire things that could hurt me. And I have been willing to let him be my shield, to keep the bad stuff away.

Except now the bad stuff is like quicksand beneath my feet, pulling me under, and my husband can't rescue me from it.

The buzzer sounds, breaking the tight, strained air.

I go downstairs to collect the take-out order, but neither of us is hungry. I leave the containers on the table and go into the bedroom, closing the door. For a while, there is silence from the living room and then the sounds of a football game on TV.

Dean is gone by the time I haul myself out of bed the next morning after a sleepless night. I know he's just gone to work, but for the first time ever I wonder what would happen if he didn't come home.

CHAPTER SEVENTEEN

OCTOBER 30

"*E*xcellent, Liv." Tyler takes another bite of my filet and nods with approval. "Very well-seasoned, perfect sear on the meat. The sauce is the right consistency. Maybe just a bit more tarragon, but overall delicious. Great job."

Pleasure flows like light through me, dispelling the anxiety and dismay that have permeated the last week. I smile and cut off a slice of beef with my fork. He's right. It's crusty on the outside, tender and juicy on the inside with a nice tang of chives.

Tyler grins and gives me a pat on the shoulder. "See? You can do more than you think you can. That soufflé was your turning point. I'm really proud of you. And you should be proud of yourself."

"I am." It's true. Two months ago, I never would have believed myself capable of turning out a delicious meal of porcini-encrusted filet mignon accompanied by fresh herb butter.

Next to me, my station neighbor Charlotte gives me the thumbs-up sign. I smile back at her and pack up the rest of the meal before starting to clean my station.

"Hey, Liv, could you stay after class for a few minutes?" Tyler asks. "There's something I want to ask you."

I ignore a twinge of unease. "Sure."

My station is spotless by the time everyone else has left and the kitchen store, Epicurean, has closed. I hitch my satchel over my shoulder and approach Tyler at his station. The top few buttons on his chef's jacket are unbuttoned, revealing the hollow of his throat and a half-circle of skin down to the top of a T-shirt beneath.

I pull my gaze from his throat to his face, forcing my voice to sound casual and breezy. "So, what's up, Chef?"

"A TV crew is coming to film a segment at Julienne in December," he says, gathering up his things and turning off the lights. "They're doing a documentary about chefs who use local and organic ingredients. So for the segment about me, they want to mention the cooking class and interview a couple of my students. I was wondering if you'd be interested in participating."

"Me? Really?"

"Really." He holds the front door open for me. "You've improved a lot, Liv, and I think they'd have some interesting questions for you. Plus, you're articulate and... uh, well... they want people who'll look good on camera."

That comment should deepen my unease, but instead I'm pleased. "You think I'd look good on camera?"

"Well, yeah." In the dim parking lot, a flush colors his face. "You look good… you know, all the time, so you'd look great on camera."

We pass his car and he stops to put his stuff in the trunk. After feeling so lousy for so long, I'm now intensely warmed by his compliments.

"Thanks."

"So you'll do it?" he asks as we continue to my car.

"Sure. Sounds like fun." I open the passenger side door of my car and place my satchel and containers on the seat. "Will they want me to say nice things about you, though?"

"Wouldn't hurt." There's a smile in his voice. "The question is, do you *have* nice things to say about me?"

I turn. He's standing right behind me, too close, resting one arm against the car roof. Even in the light of the streetlamps, his eyes are very, very blue. I'm trapped between him and the open door of the car, but I don't feel threatened. Just warm, almost sheltered.

"I have a lot of nice things to say about you," I admit.

I am acutely aware that things are getting dangerous. That I should get in the car now and drive away.

But I don't.

"Yeah? Like what?" He doesn't move closer to me. He also doesn't move back. He studies me, his gaze flickering down to my mouth and back up to my eyes.

"You're a great teacher," I say. "An amazing chef. You're patient, confident, supportive. And you help your students believe in themselves."

He looks at me for a moment, then shakes his head. "Wow. Tell that to the producer, and I might end up with my own show."

"You deserve one." I mean that, too.

"Thanks." He moves a little closer.

I don't back away, not that I could have even if I wanted to. Which I don't. He puts one hand on the car door behind me and lowers his head.

I stiffen when his mouth touches mine. Confusion rises in me, warring with curiosity.

And interest. Yes.

His lips are gentle but unfamiliar, fumbling for a second before settling against mine. For a moment, he doesn't move and we stand there with nothing but our lips touching feather-light. Then he shifts, and the pressure increases.

I jerk away. The back of my head hits the edge of the car door.

Tyler stops and straightens, his gaze searching mine. I pull in a breath and just stare at him. He slides his hand to the back of my head and massages the place where I'd bumped it. His fingers are warm and strong. Pleasure unknots my tension, smoothes down my spine. Then he lowers his head again.

This time, I meet him halfway. Our lips touch, still soft. Because he is not much taller than I am, we fit together easily and without strain. Warmth begins to ease through my blood, washing away my lingering fear. He moves his lips lightly against mine, unthreatening, almost comforting. He tastes like chives and tarragon.

It's nice. Very nice.

He slides his hands down to my hips and curls his fingers

into the material of my skirt. After a moment's hesitation, I rest my hands on his waist. I can feel the heat of his skin even through his chef's jacket. So close to me, his body feels the way I'd imagined it—firm and solid.

My fingers tremble. Desire flickers low in my belly. The scents of the kitchen cling to him—melting butter, the fragrance of chopped herbs, sweet onions, ripe peppers, olive oil. It's potent, delicious, sparking a hunger for more than just food.

Tyler doesn't try to push things too fast, too far. He doesn't press his body against mine or try to touch me beyond grasping my hips. His kiss is sweet, almost tender, and the sensation of it lights something within me that I thought had gone out.

I swallow hard, my hands tightening on his waist as I part my lips tentatively. His fingers flex in reaction as our tongues touch. It's smooth and easy... too easy.

My heart pounds. He makes a noise in the back of his throat. Within seconds, our lips are pressing harder together, tongues tangling in an effortless rhythm.

A rhythm that makes me want him.

The realization hits me hard, cracking through the haze of lust. I freeze. My hands drop away from him.

He lifts his head and stares at me, his breath hard against my lips. He looks almost as shocked as I feel—not because the kiss happened, but because of how it felt.

I manage to get my hand up between us to ease him away. He steps back, rubbing a hand across his mouth.

"Liv." His eyes fill with consternation. "I'm sorry. I—"

"No." I can hardly get the word out. "Don't apologize. It wasn't your fault."

"It's just that... I mean, that first day of class, the way you were standing there... kind of forlorn and uncertain, and so damn pretty... I wanted to... I wanted to rescue you, you know?"

My throat closes over. Only one man in the world has ever rescued me.

"Stop, Tyler. Please."

I want to say *I'm married*, but that would be unfair. He knows it, and I sure as hell know it, and yet we met each other in a kiss that was far easier than it should have been.

I reach out to put my hand on his chest, but stop before I touch him.

"I'd better go," I say.

Tyler backs away while I close the passenger door and go around to the driver's seat.

"Are you... uh, will you come back to class?" he asks.

I hesitate, but nod. "Yes. We'll just... let's forget this ever happened."

"I'm sorry," he repeats. "I don't usually... I mean, I never..."

"Tyler." My hand shakes as I start the car. "It's okay. I'm not upset with you."

But there are no words to describe how I feel about myself right now.

"That looks good, Liv." Samantha Davis, the curator of the Historical Museum, stops beside the display case where I'm arranging a collection of pioneer cooking equipment.

I dust off my hands and step back. "Once they get the glass back on, I'll put up the wall text."

"Great." Samantha tilts her head and looks at me. "You

know, we really have appreciated all the work you've been doing for us. Would you be interested in helping out with the Historical Society's holiday festival? It's more hours, but there are a few perks. Volunteers get tickets to some of the shows at the Performing Arts Center, and we have a fun party at Langdon House on Christmas Eve."

"Sure. Sounds like fun."

Samantha smiles. "I'll tell Felicia to call you to set up a schedule."

She heads back to her office, and I fuss with the display for a few more minutes.

"Liv."

Dean's voice startles me. I turn to find him standing by the door, dressed in a suit and tie, his hands shoved into the pockets of his trousers.

"Dean. Hi." My palms start to sweat. I rub my hands down the front of my thighs and approach him. "What are you doing here?"

"Came to take you to lunch, if you're free."

"Um, sure. I just… I just need to finish up here and grab my stuff."

"Okay. I'll wait."

I try to quell the nerves jumping around in my stomach as I put a few things away and retrieve my satchel from behind the volunteers' desk.

It's been two days since Tyler and I kissed each other in the parking lot, and I haven't seen Dean much at all. He's gone to work before I wake up, and we spend our evenings in separate rooms of the apartment.

Which, although that's been par for the course lately, is

now something of a relief since it's allowed me to avoid the massive question of *what the hell do I do now?*

As Dean and I walk out into the bright fall sunshine, the movement of his body so familiar next to mine, I know I can't avoid that question much longer.

"How were morning classes?" I ask.

"Good. Busy with grading midterms."

"Midterms are over already?" I shuffle my feet to make the leaves crackle beneath my shoes. "Next thing you know, it'll be Christmas."

"Yeah." He glances at me. "You want to go anywhere?"

"Not really. Why?"

"I was thinking we could take a trip somewhere for a week or two. Hawaii, Florida. Someplace warm."

I'm a little surprised by this. Dean has always liked a cold, snowy Christmas.

"Uh, any particular reason?" I ask.

"Maybe it would help to get away for a while," he says.

It's the first time he's acknowledged that we need actual *help*. Only he has no idea that I've made things even worse.

I mutter something noncommittal as we head into a café for lunch. Our conversation is casual and impersonal—work, students, local happenings. I tell him about the Historical Society's holiday festival, and he tells me about the progress of the book he's writing on medieval architecture. We discuss the weather.

Yeah. The weather.

After lunch, we walk back outside and stand on the sidewalk.

"Want a ride home?" Dean asks.

"No, I'm going back to the museum. I'll walk."

"Okay." He glances at his watch. "So I'll see you tonight."

"Sure. Any ideas for dinner?"

"Make something from your class, if you have time," he suggests. "Sounds like it's going well for you."

I wouldn't say that, exactly. "I can make parmesan chicken."

"Great." He hesitates, then leans forward to brush his lips across mine. "See you later."

I watch him go. He's never hesitated before kissing me. Ever.

I work at the museum for a few more hours, then stop at the grocery store on the way home for the chicken ingredients. It's an easy recipe, one of the first dishes Tyler taught us to make, and by the time Dean comes home the kitchen smells good and the chicken is almost done.

Our dinner conversation is almost a repeat of our lunch conversation, except that Dean compliments my cooking. Then he goes into his office while I clean the dishes and muster up the courage to do what I know I have to. The longer I wait, the harder it will be.

Maybe I shouldn't tell him at all. A vindictive part of me wants to keep it a secret, the way he kept his first marriage from me. But I can't do that.

For years, Dean has been my best friend, my confidante, the love of my life. We've fought for each other. My demons have cowered in the face of his strength. My secrets have always been safe with him.

Except this one is different.

I stand in the kitchen for a while, my heart pounding with nervousness. I try not to think about Tyler Wilkes, but of course that's impossible because he's the reason I have to make this confession in the first place.

And yet this is not about him at all. This is about me and my husband.

I shove thoughts of Tyler away and approach Dean's office. My hand shakes as I knock on the closed door.

"Come in."

I push the door open. Raw fear tightens my stomach. He's sitting at his desk, his shirtsleeves rolled up to the elbows, papers and a thick book spread out in front of him. My eyes move almost involuntarily to the spot beside his computer where he has always kept a framed photo of me.

The photo is still there. Faint relief curls around my heart.

He looks up, his expression one of distracted concentration. It's a look I'm not all that familiar with since I don't often interrupt him when he's working.

I swallow hard and run my hands over my arms.

"Dean." My voice comes out tight, strained.

He frowns and swivels in his chair so that he's facing me. My heart feels like it's about to claw out of my chest.

"I... I need to tell you something," I say.

He doesn't speak, but his frown deepens. I want to sit because my legs are starting to shake, but there's only one chair in the room and he's in it. And I do not want to prolong this by suggesting we move to the living room.

So I grasp the doorjamb with one hand to steady myself. "I've always told you the truth, right?"

He nods. I take a breath and keep going.

"And... I guess it's obvious that you and I have had some trouble lately."

Nothing. His expression doesn't change.

"I was... remember when you said you wondered if I was

thinking about a baby because I had nothing to do?" I ask. "I was mad at first, but it was a fair question. I think that's why I enrolled in the cooking class. I wanted to do something fun, something different." I swallow again to ease my parched throat. "And it's been… well, I'm enjoying it. Learning a lot. But…"

I should have rehearsed this. I have no idea how to say it.

"But?" he asks.

"The instructor… I told you about him. Tyler Wilkes." I stare over his head at the bookshelf on the opposite wall. I'd suspected I might be crying by this point, but my eyes are dry. "The other night, he was walking me to my car and we were talking, and then kind of suddenly he… he kissed me. Or I kissed him. Well. We sort of… kissed each other."

My stomach tightens to the point of pain. I grip the doorjamb harder and force myself to look at Dean. He hasn't moved, but he's gone pale beneath his tan and a vein is throbbing in his temple.

Bad sign. But it's done.

"You kissed him," he finally says.

"Yes."

"Your cooking teacher."

"Yes."

He stares at me in disbelief. The heavy sound of my pulse pounds in my ears.

"Was it good?" His question slices the air, sharp as a blade.

"What?"

"Was it good?" he repeats. "Did you like it?"

"Dean—"

"No, really, Liv. What kind of kisser is your *cooking teacher*?"

His voice drips with derision, and I'm struck with an irrational urge to defend Tyler.

Instead, I look my husband in the eye. "Are you sure you want me to answer that?"

He swears and stands so quickly that the chair skids backward and hits the bookshelf. I take a step away. Anger flares in Dean's eyes, sparking the air, tightening his muscles.

"How did it happen?" he demands. "Has he made a move on you before?"

"No." *Not really.* "No. It was... Christ, Dean, things have been so lousy with us and he was... I don't know. He was a friend, I guess. And after you and I had that big fight, he walked me to my car after class and... I don't know. It just happened."

"Did he force you?" Fury edges the question.

"No." My face burns with embarrassment and old shame. I pull in a breath and repeat the stark admission. "No. It was mutual."

He starts to pace, the lines of his body stiff with tension, his hands flexing. It's a tight, contained anger that I've never seen before, and it makes my nervousness spike again. I have no idea where to go from here.

Dean stops. "Why?"

"Why what?"

"I know why he kissed you. Why did you kiss him?"

"Because I... I guess I just wanted to."

"And did you want him to fuck you?"

My embarrassment flares hotter as I remember the dream I had about Tyler. "It wasn't... no. Dean, it was a kiss. Nothing more."

"Did he touch you?"

"No."

"Does he know you're married?"

"Yes." The hostility of his questions, as if he's trying to bully something more out of me, incites my own anger. "I didn't have to tell you, Dean. You'd never have known if I hadn't."

"So why did you? To piss me off?"

"Because I wanted to be honest with you," I retort. "Which is more than I can say for you."

"What the hell does that mean?"

"You kept a previous marriage a secret from me for *five years*," I say, and now the tears start to blur my vision like a flash flood. "Not once, apparently, did you think you should be honest with me about everything. Not once did you trust me enough to tell me the truth."

"I told you it wasn't because I didn't trust you!" Dean pivots and stalks toward me. "And don't turn this back on me."

"You won't even talk to me about Helen!"

"What the fuck does that have to do with you kissing another man?"

"I might not have if you hadn't lied to me," I snap. "Yeah, I kissed Tyler. I kissed another man because my own husband has been acting like a fucking *ass* about the idea of having a baby with me and because he's a coward who suddenly divulges the fact that I'm his *second* goddamn wife. You're lucky I haven't walked out on you."

"Am I?" His expression darkens like a thundercloud. "And where the fuck would you go, Liv? Do you want to know what would happen to you if you left?"

He crosses the room in three strides and stops in front of me, his anger so palpable, so harsh, that I have to force myself not to move away even though I'm shaking hard and tears are rolling down my cheeks.

"I'll tell you what would happen." He lowers his head to look at me, his eyes pitch-black. "You'd end up like your mother, Liv. You'd find a beat-up sedan and leave town, you'd pick up odd jobs wherever you could, you might even end up—"

A sharp, loud crack splits the air as my open palm hits his cheek. He doesn't flinch, but it's a hard enough slap to stop his tirade.

We stare at each other. A red imprint spreads across his jaw. I swipe at my face with my sleeve and gulp in air.

The room spins around me, my whole world tilting off axis, everything I've known and believed in for five years suddenly in brutal doubt.

Dean steps back, his chest heaving, his expression a mask of fury. He pushes past me. A few seconds later, the front door slams shut.

I slide to the floor and sob until I can hardly breathe.

CHAPTER EIGHTEEN

NOVEMBER 2

*W*e can barely look at each other. Neither of us has apologized for what we did, what we said. Neither of us has tried to make amends. It's a shattering hurt—his comparing me to my mother, my betrayal with another man.

After a day of tension thick enough to crack, I pack a bag and put it in the trunk of my car. I drive to the university and go into the history department. Dean is not in his office, and the administrative assistant tells me he's in the middle of an introductory course lecture.

The doors of the lecture hall are closed, but Dean's deep voice echoes through. I slip inside. It's dim, the only light coming from the podium at the front and the huge images of illuminated manuscripts glowing on a screen.

It's one of those big rooms with auditorium seating, and it's nearly full of students. I slide into an empty seat in the back row. I haven't sat in a lecture hall for ages.

Dean is at the front of the room, a pointer in hand, exuding professorial authority in his tailored suit and tie. He gestures at the intricate scrollwork on the edge of one of the manuscript pages, his voice warm with enthusiasm as he talks about marginalia, the burnishing of gold foil, the richness of detail.

My heart tightens. I've attended his lectures in the past, but I don't often see him in his role as a prominent professor.

In fact, rather than express interest in his classes on medieval manuscripts, I'm more likely to yawn when he starts talking about the Book of Hours.

Not exactly supportive, that.

I glance at the students. The majority of them are listening intently, their attention shifting between Dean, the slides, and their notes. He pauses a few times to ask them questions, to engage their opinions and ideas. A discussion ensues about the way wealthy people commissioned manuscripts and instructed the artists to include a donor portrait somewhere on the page.

Pride nudges at me. My husband's easy authority, his engaging approach, and his depth of knowledge are captivating.

Okay, so medieval history is still a little dorky. But when brought to life by Professor Dean West, it breathes and glows with color.

"All right, everyone, that's it for today." Dean glances at the clock and puts down his pointer. "Remember your bibliographies are due on Friday. Review session for the essays is tomorrow, so bring any final questions."

Noise and voices fill the hall as the students gather their things and shove books into their backpacks. A line of students forms in front of Dean's podium, and he patiently answers one question after another.

I wait until all the students have filed from the room, leaving a hush in the air. Alone now, Dean turns off the podium light and collects his notes and papers.

I stand. My chair squeaks as the seat flips back into place. Dean looks up and watches me walk down to him.

"Great lecture," I remark.

"What are you doing here?" He puts a stack of folders into his briefcase.

"I called Aunt Stella this morning. I thought I'd visit her for a few days."

He stops. "Why?"

"Well." I shove my hands into my coat pockets and clear my throat. "I think… you know… it's tough right now, and we could use some time apart."

Irritation flashes in his eyes. "How do you think time apart is going to help?"

"I don't know that it will," I admit. "But being together is pretty lousy these days, don't you think?"

Dean snaps his briefcase closed. "How long will you be gone?"

"A few days. I already asked Allie for the weekend off. I was thinking of coming back on Tuesday."

"I don't like the idea of you driving all that way alone."

"I'll be fine. I'll call you along the way." I pause. "Okay?"

He doesn't look as if it's the least bit okay, but he gives a short nod. "Do what you want, Liv."

I struggle against a wave of annoyance. "What I *want* is for us to figure this out. And maybe one of us can come up with a way to do that if we're apart."

The door slams open. Dean and I turn to see a young man hurrying down the steps.

"Sorry, Professor West, I forgot to ask you about a source for my paper." He dumps his backpack on the table and digs through the pile of books and papers inside.

I step back, my gaze on Dean. I want to tell him I love him. He looks as if he wants to say more too, but instead turns his attention to the student.

I leave. Fifteen minutes later, I'm on the highway heading toward Aunt Stella's. I don't really want to visit her, but frankly I have nowhere else to go.

That's a very sobering thought.

It was a long time before I first took Dean to meet Aunt Stella. In late October of my first year with him, Stella called to ask me if I could come back to Castleford to help with a church rummage sale one weekend.

I had work and a bunch of studying to do, but I agreed to help her because Aunt Stella and her husband Henry had given me a place to stay after I left my mother. No matter what else happened, I would remember that.

So I got someone to cover my shifts at Jitter Beans and planned to leave early Saturday morning.

Dean offered to come with me that weekend, but I declined. I wasn't ready for him to meet Aunt Stella yet. I didn't want to share him with anyone.

"Be careful on the road," he said as he put my travel bag in the trunk of my car. "And call me when you get in. Got your cell charged?"

I nodded. Part of me was a little insulted by his fussing— I'd been on my own for years and done just fine, thanks—but a larger part of me was warmed by it.

It was nice to have someone be concerned about me. It was nice to have *him* be concerned about me.

He slammed the trunk and turned to fold me into his arms. "I'll miss you, beauty."

"I'll miss you too." I realized it would be the first weekend we had spent apart in the past month and a half. I hugged him around the waist, loving the feeling of his tall, strong body against mine, the scent of his soap and shaving cream. "I'll be back tomorrow night."

He grasped the lapels of my coat, pulling me closer, and lowered his head to kiss me. So warm and delicious. He gave my ponytail a light tug. "See you soon."

"See you," I echoed.

I got into my car while he stood on the sidewalk watching me, his hands in the pockets of his coat and his scarf loose around his neck. A breeze ruffled his thick hair. Looking at him, I had a sudden rush of longing. I didn't want to leave him, not even for two days.

That scared me a little. We'd been together less than two months, hadn't even talked much about our relationship, and already I didn't want to be apart from him? Even after I'd spent so many years alone?

Dean lifted his hand as I started the ignition. I gave him a little wave and headed off for the almost four-hour drive, deciding I could use the weekend to try and gain some perspective.

I got on the Beltline and headed north, following the highway into farmland surrounded by tilled fields and trees stripped bare of reddish-gold leaves.

Aunt Stella and Henry lived not far from the Minnesota border in a small town where older houses clustered around the downtown area and newer ranch homes spread along the outskirts. Their house was within walking distance of Main Street, a stretch of road lined with a few shops and restaurants.

I'd lived in Castleford for a little over five years and left the minute I turned eighteen. Few things in the town had changed over the years.

When I arrived that afternoon, Stella had a lunch of baked ham and potato salad ready. She'd been older than my father by eleven years, and she rarely spoke of him or their parents. Her skin was weathered, her faded blond hair cropped close to her head, her mouth set in a perpetual slash.

She had always treated me with distant courtesy, though if she resented being saddled with her brother's daughter, she never showed it. When I first came to live with her when I was thirteen, Stella laid out her expectations of me with the precision of a general planning a military strategy.

I would go to school, do my share of chores and housework, behave well, earn good grades, attend church and related functions, and contribute to the household with income from a part-time job. I would not smoke, drink, sleep around, or miss curfew. If I caused a hint of trouble, Stella and Henry would reconsider their decision to let me stay.

I gave them no reason to reconsider anything. I could not have met their expectations more perfectly if I'd written them myself.

"Classes are going well?" Stella asked me, as she forked a slice of ham onto my plate.

I nodded and told her about the courses I was taking, what it was like living in Madison, my job at Jitter Beans. Henry came in halfway through lunch, on a break from his work as an electrician, and gave me a nod of greeting.

Even though I'd lived with them for almost five years, Henry and I never had much of a relationship. He was a short, sinewy man who liked working outdoors, drinking beer, and hunting. He had grudgingly agreed to let me stay when I first came to Castleford, but made it clear he wanted little to do with me.

I was glad about that. Henry ignored me, I avoided him, and it was one less thing for me to deal with.

"Rummage sale starts right after services tomorrow morning," Stella told me as she began washing dishes. "This afternoon we need to collect donations, then go to the church to help set things up."

"Just let me know when we need to leave." I brought my travel bag upstairs and into my old bedroom at the back of the house. I sat on the bed and called Dean on my cell phone.

"What're you doing?" I asked, after assuring him I'd arrived safely.

"Just got back from the gym," he said. "You?"

"I'm on rummage sale duty this afternoon." I thought about telling him I wished he was here, but decided against it.

"So what are you doing tonight?" I asked.

"Thinking about you."

"Oh, please."

"I've been wanting you to hear you say that."

I giggled. "Well, it's true you're not all that easy to resist, professor."

"I'm trying very hard not to be."

I flopped back on the bed and looked at the ceiling, the phone still pressed to my ear. I knew he wanted me. I knew one day he'd have me. I just didn't know why he'd chosen to wait for me.

"Hey, Dean?"

"Hey, Liv."

"Why are you waiting for me?" I asked.

"Because you're worth it."

"You don't know that."

"Yes, I do."

"How?"

"I've been around. I know when something's good."

My throat tightened a little. "What if you're wrong?"

"I'm not wrong."

A knock came at the door, followed by Aunt Stella's voice. I sat up.

"I have to go," I told Dean. "Call me tonight?"

"I will."

I ended the call and hurried to join Stella. We drove around town picking up promised donations for the rummage sale, then went to the church's fellowship hall where volunteers were setting up tables. We were given a lecture about the organization of the goods, and then Stella went to sort clothing while I hauled boxes in from the foyer.

I didn't mind being among Stella's friends—they were mostly older women whose children now had children, and I only remembered them from church and occasional town functions. They knew me as Stella's nice, quiet niece, and they were all pleased to hear about my move to Madison and enrollment at the UW.

I spent the afternoon sorting books, toys, glasses, and dishes while the other volunteers put price stickers on everything and fussed about the best placement for certain items. We took breaks for coffee and cookies, commented on the usefulness or quality of cookware, dresses, and handbags.

It was an agreeable and satisfying way to spend the afternoon—helping out these ladies who believed in their church and community and who had always been kind to me.

Stella and I ate leftover ham for dinner, then I excused myself to go and study. I took a quick shower and changed into comfortable clothes before sitting at the narrow desk in my bedroom.

I was tired from the physical work, but forced myself to read a few chapters of a geography textbook and type up a rough outline for a paper about library collection development.

I was starting to read another article for a political science essay when my cell phone rang. I pressed the button to accept the call.

"How have the processes of democracy and federalism affected political modernization in Russia?" I asked.

"Well, if a nation is trying to establish simultaneous democratic and federal structures, it has to build a system of regional support," Dean said. "That would be difficult in Russia because of its constitutional nature, and there would be a lot of conflict over government policies. And often the benefits of federalism to democracy aren't apparent until years later."

"Thank you."

"You're welcome. Why didn't you walk away?"

"What?"

"The day we met," he said. "Why didn't you walk away from me after I gave you your stuff back?"

A sudden memory of that day rolled over me—how I'd wanted to feel his hand close around my arm, the hot pull of attraction I'd felt toward him, the way he'd looked standing on the sidewalk with the sun glinting off his hair.

"I don't know," I said.

"You do know. Why?"

Because I've been around in a different way and finally I know when something—when someone—is good. Finally I trust myself.

"Because I didn't want to walk away from you." I folded and unfolded the corner of a notebook. "Because you were handsome and nice and I wanted... more."

"So did I."

"Did you look for me?" I asked.

"Almost."

"Almost?"

"I resisted because of the professor-student thing. But when I saw you in Jitter Beans, I knew I was done."

I smiled. "Done? Or were you just getting started?"

"Yeah. That."

"So was I." *In more ways than you even know.* I paused. "Have you started thinking about me yet?"

"Uh huh. What're you wearing?"

I chuckled, even as heat bloomed in my chest. "Isn't that a long-distance cliché?"

"Yes, but I still want to know."

I glanced down. "Pajama bottoms and a tank top."

"Color?"

"Navy blue pants. Pink tank top."

"Is it tight?"

"Sort of." Just the sound of his voice made my nipples tent the cotton material. "What about you?"

"Boxers and a T-shirt."

"Is it tight?"

"My boxers are."

"Oh." The heat intensified as I imagined him stretched out on his bed, one arm behind his head, his T-shirt riding up to expose the flat, hard planes of his abdomen. A bulge pressing against the front of his boxers.

"Are you wearing a bra?" he asked.

"No. And my nipples are hard."

His groan made me smile.

"Are your boxers even tighter now?" I asked.

"No, because I just took my cock out."

A bolt of arousal shot through me so fast I sucked in a breath. "Oh."

He gave a muffled laugh. "You have no idea what those little *ohs* do to me."

"So tell me." Emboldened, I pushed away from the desk and went to lock the door, then lay down on the bed.

With the distance of miles between us, I didn't have to worry about losing my nerve in the midst of the crackling heat Dean roused. As much as I craved his touch, his kisses, it would take a little more time before my tension fully waned with the hot physical stuff.

But just the sound of his voice, rumbling low in my ear… and my lingering inhibitions melted away like ice on heated glass.

"Every time your breath catches in your throat, I get hard," Dean said. "Makes me want to know what kind of sounds you'll make when I'm buried deep inside you."

When. Not *if.*

I pressed my legs together as explicit images flashed in my mind.

"It's going to be good," I whispered, trailing my hand over the hem of my tank top.

"It's going to be fucking explosive." His voice lowered to a rough growl.

I shivered and eased my tank top up a few inches. My skin was hot under the glide of my fingertips.

"What're you doing now?" Dean asked.

"Tracing my belly button."

His chuckle settled in my blood. "I'm way ahead of you."

"What are you doing?" I asked, my heart beginning to throb a heavy, slow beat.

"Stroking my cock."

"Are you completely hard?"

"As a rock."

"Oh." I closed my eyes and imagined him lying there with his hand wrapped around his erection and his body tensing with lust. I drew my hand up higher beneath my shirt, remembering his touch on my skin.

"Are you on the bed?" he asked.

"Yes."

"Naked?"

"No."

"Pull your shirt up."

A shudder rippled through me as I eased the hem of my shirt up over my bare breasts, a rush of cool air tickling the tight crests.

"Rub them," he said. "Pinch your nipples."

I cupped one breast in my hand and squeezed the nipple lightly between my thumb and forefinger. A shock of pleasure traveled clear down to my sex.

"Are you still stroking yourself?" I whispered, my mind awash with images of him stretched out on the bed, massaging his cock while thinking about me.

"Yes." His breath escaped on a hiss. "I'm so hard it hurts."

"Are you close?"

"I could come any second, but I won't. You need to tell me more first."

I pressed my breasts together and squirmed, heat sliding through my veins.

"What do you want to know?" I asked.

"How wet are you?"

"I'm…"

"Touch yourself and tell me."

I couldn't help the flush sweeping me from head to toe. My heart pounded hard. I wiggled my pants down until the elastic was around my thighs, then curled my fingers against my sex.

"How wet are you?" he repeated.

I dipped into my cleft, trailing my finger down one side and up the other, then circling my clit. The light contact blazed across my nerves.

"Very wet," I breathed. "I wish you could touch me."

He groaned. "Tell me what you look like."

I shifted up onto one elbow. "I'm... my shirt is up around my breasts, and my nipples are so hard... and my pants are down around my thighs, so I can't really spread my legs too wide..."

"Oh, fuck, Liv. Keep going."

I swallowed hard. Sweat broke out on my forehead as I swept a hand over my belly again. "But I can edge my fingers far enough in to tickle my clit..."

"Do it now."

I did, unable to prevent a moan when I pressed the pulsing knot. "God, Dean, I'm so turned on..."

"Bring yourself off. Tell me how you do it."

"I... I like to put two fingers on either side... like that... and keep the heel of my hand against my clit... then push a finger slowly inside..."

"You're tight, aren't you?" His voice was raw. "I'm going to slide into you like a glove."

My breath stopped at the idea of him filling me, stretching me. I squeezed my inner flesh around my finger, wishing it was his big, thick length. My clit throbbed against my hand. The sound of our breathing, heavy and hot, filled my head.

"What do you want, Liv?" he whispered, low and guttural.

"I want..." I arched my body, loving the taut anticipation, the promise of release. I pushed my finger farther into my channel and moaned. "I want to come."

"Tell me what else you want."

"Oh..." I pushed my hips up farther and pressed my hand against my clit. My blood streamed like melted honey through my veins. Fantasies flooded my mind—everything I'd imagined and dreamed about since meeting him.

"I want you to touch me," I gasped, working my hand faster between my legs. "I want you to lick my breasts and rub my clit. I want to watch you stroke yourself. I want to feel you, hard and throbbing, and I want you to thrust deep inside me and make me come all over your cock... oh!"

An explosion of shudders rained through me at the same instant Dean's rough grunt echoed in my head. I bit my lip to prevent myself from crying out, even as the vibrations peaked with a hard surge.

Panting, I fell backward onto the pillows, running a hand over my half-naked body. "I'm... wow."

His chuckle rumbled in my ear. "You are wow, indeed."

I sucked in a breath and closed my eyes. "Did you come hard?"

"Christ, Liv. Fucking rocket."

I shuddered as the picture flashed before me—him all sweaty and breathing hard, still sliding his fist loosely over his damp shaft, trails of semen pooling on his stomach.

"One day will you do that while I watch?" I asked.

"The second you ask, I'll have my cock in hand."

"The *second* I ask?"

"The nanosecond you ask. In fact, you don't even need to ask. Just bat your eyelashes at me, and I'll take my prick out."

I giggled. "Better make sure we're not in public, then."

"I'll make sure."

We both fell silent as our breathing finally slowed. I rolled onto my side, pushing my hair away from my face, the phone still close to my ear.

"Hey," I whispered. "Thanks."

"For what?"

"Waiting for me."

"Waiting has never been so hot." He paused. "Thanks for trusting me."

"I'll see you tomorrow?"

"I'll be waiting."

CHAPTER NINETEEN

November 6

"How was it?" Dean looks at me from over the top of the sports magazine he's reading.

I drop my travel bag on the floor and shrug out of my coat. "Fine. Aunt Stella says hello. She sent you a pound cake."

I pull the brick-hard cake from my bag and put it on the counter, then go into the bedroom to shower and change. My few days with Stella and Henry provided no sudden insights into how to save my relationship with Dean, but the brief separation from him did make it a little easier to breathe.

I helped Stella around the house and in the garden, ate at the town's diner, went to the farmer's market and a couple of garage sales. The weather was unseasonably mild, so I took a few long walks and drove into the countryside. I even baked an apple pie, which actually turned out pretty good.

It was a simple few days, and I'm glad I went—even if the big, ugly questions loomed up again the moment I stepped into the apartment. Even if Dean and I still don't know how to tackle them.

He gets up from the sofa and looks at his watch. "I'm meeting someone for lunch, then I have lectures, office hours, and a late seminar."

"Who are you meeting for lunch?"

"A guy who's thinking of applying to the doctoral program. Why?"

"Just wondering."

It's back again—this tight, persistent tension in my chest. Did I want to know if he was meeting Maggie Hamilton? Would I care if he was?

No. And no.

Maggie Hamilton is no threat to our marriage. Neither is Tyler Wilkes. The danger lies solely between me and my husband.

Dean changes into a suit and tie and heads out after giving me a perfunctory kiss on the cheek. After he leaves, I spend the afternoon doing laundry and cleaning, mostly to occupy my time.

It's Tuesday. I don't know what to do. I don't want to miss cooking class, but... yeah. Not the most favorable of circumstances.

Dean's not home from work by six-thirty, so I finally decide to attend class. I should set things straight with Tyler anyway. I'm the first one there, which is good, and I walk to the instructor's station.

Tyler glances up and gives me an uneasy smile. "Hi, Liv. I… uh, I wasn't sure you'd show up."

"Why?"

"You know, because of what happened."

"I told you I'd come back," I remind him. "Did you think I'd be too ashamed and change my mind?"

"Well, no." He scratches his head. "Um, just that it'd be like this. You know, awkward. I'm really sorry. It was a mistake. I never meant for that to happen."

I sigh. "Look, never mind. I just wanted to tell you I'm not mad. I don't blame you. And you're right, it was a mistake. We're both just going to forget it now, okay?"

"Yeah, okay. Sure." He looks a little disappointed, but makes no further remark.

I head to my station to get organized for the evening. The other students file in, and we exchange greetings and small talk until the clock strikes seven.

Tyler calls for our attention and discusses the various cuts of pork, then demonstrates how to butterfly the tenderloin and prepare it with roasted apples and onions.

We watch attentively and take notes, then start on our own preparations when he's finished. I put out my bowls and wash the apples. Just as I'm taking the knife from a drawer, I look up to see Dean walk into the room.

I drop the knife with a clatter. My heart hammers.

This can't be good.

Dean catches my eye. He looks handsome as the devil—his navy suit impeccable, without a single crease, his tie perfectly knotted, his dark hair brushed away from his forehead. Aside from his five o'clock shadow, you'd never know he just spent an entire afternoon in meetings and teaching classes on Gothic architecture.

He comes toward me, his long stride and air of confident authority drawing the attention of the other students. "Hello, Liv."

"Dean." I wipe my clammy hands on my apron. "What are you doing here?"

He scans the room, his eyes growing cold.

Shit.

Tyler is looking at us from his station. After a heartbeat, he approaches.

"Can I help you, sir?" he asks Dean politely.

"Dean West." Dislike and intimidation radiate from Dean. He sizes Tyler up in one glance and clearly finds him lacking. "Olivia's husband."

"Oh." A crimson flush crawls up Tyler's neck to his cheeks. He's sweating a little from standing over a hot stove, and he wipes his forehead with his sleeve before responding. "Uh, good to meet you. I'm Tyler Wilkes. Liv is… um, she's doing great."

"So I've heard."

I wince. "Dean, what are you doing here?"

"Thought I'd sit in on class, see how things go."

"I'm not sure that's—" Tyler begins.

"You don't mind." Dean looks Tyler hard in the eye. "Do you?"

Embarrassment heats my face. Dean is taller than Tyler, and he's looking down at the poor guy as if daring him to say yes, he does mind. Tyler swallows. A bead of sweat drips down his temple.

"Dean, that's really not—" I begin.

"I'll sit over there." Dean nods toward several chairs placed against the wall. "Go on with your lesson, Chef Wilkes."

"Er... okay." After hesitating, Tyler steps back and glances at me. I try to give him a reassuring smile, which I'm certain comes out more like a grimace.

The other students return to their preparations, their initial curiosity waning as they learn who Dean is and the apparently uninteresting reason for his visit. He sits down, his arms crossed and his gaze level on me.

Focus, Liv.

I turn back to my work. My hands are shaking, but after a few minutes I calm down and get my ingredients in order.

I know Dean will not cause a scene. He's here to stake some sort of manly claim, to intimidate Tyler, but he'll be civilized about it.

Sort of.

I slice several apples and onions, retrieve olive oil and mustard from the pantry, get the pans heating. I even start to feel a twinge of pride at the knowledge that Dean is watching me, especially after his nasty remark that I could end up like my mother, who had no viable skills of her own.

Now I know how to prep a kitchen, how to season and cook different cuts of meat, how to make stock. I know about fresh herbs, sauces, acidity, various salts, and flavor profiles. I know how to cut vegetables and the best purposes for different knives, pans, and pots. Hell, I even know how to carve a whole chicken.

Hah. Take that, Mr. Medieval History Professor.

The pork tenderloin is thick and need to be cut, so I take out the slicing knife with a flourish.

"How's it going, Liv?"

Tyler stops uncertainly in front of me. It would seem strange to the other students if he ignored me, so I know he's here for appearances rather than any real interest in how I'm doing. In fact, he looks as if he'd rather be anywhere but at my station.

"Uh, just fine, thanks." I give him a weak smile and turn my attention back to the pork.

"Your pan is too hot." Tyler comes around to lower the heat under my skillet. "And your butter is going to burn if you don't add oil to it."

"Right. Sorry." I flip the meat over and start to saw it in half, which I know is the wrong technique but I'm getting nervous again. I can feel Dean's hostile stare burning into Tyler.

"Wait." Tyler steps closer. "Let the knife do the work, Liv. When you're doing a butterfly cut, keep the knife parallel to the cutting board."

He reaches out to put his hand over mine on the knife handle. I jerk away. My breath catches in my throat. Tyler drops his hand to his side and steps back.

"Well, you remember how I did it, right?" he asks.

"Yeah. Sure."

"Okay. Stay focused."

He moves on to Charlotte's station. I wipe my hand on my apron and grasp the knife. A sudden flash of that night, that kiss, makes my chest tighten with dismay.

I don't know why I kissed Tyler. I've never wanted to look at another man since I met Dean. And not only did I let myself kiss Tyler, I actually liked it.

I glance at Dean. He's watching me, his arms still crossed, his expression unreadable.

I don't know if he's forgiven me. I don't know if I've forgiven him. I certainly haven't forgiven myself.

I slice into the tenderloin. Suddenly a searing pain flares through my entire hand and up my arm. I let out a sharp cry and drop the knife. Dean is beside me in less than a second, reaching out to grab my wrist.

"Liv?" Tyler hurries toward me.

"Back off." Dean growls the order at him. Tyler skids to a halt.

"Oh, Jesus, Liv." Charlotte stares at my hand. "Someone call 911!"

I start to protest that it's not that bad, but then I look down and see what appears to be a river of blood pooling onto the cutting board, over the knife and the raw meat.

My blood.

Dizziness swamps me. I sway against Dean. He grabs a dishtowel and wraps it around my hand, then guides me to a chair. The other students huddle around, buzzing with concern. Dean presses the towel tight against my hand to stem the flow of blood.

"Everyone, step back, please," Tyler calls. "The medics are on their way."

The crowd eases away to give me room to breathe. My head spins, the pain starting to throb. There's blood on my apron.

Within minutes, two paramedics arrive, and then I lose track of what happens—tightness on my hand, a blood pressure cuff, lots of questions. Someone puts my legs up on a chair.

Dean moves back to let the paramedics work, but keeps his hand tight on my shoulder as he confers with them. I hear the words *blood loss*, *deep cut*, and *nerve damage*, all of which seize my chest with fear.

"Dean?" My own voice sounds very far away.

"Right here." He lowers his head close to my ear. "Hang in there, beauty."

The paramedics bandage the wound and suggest I go to the ER. I don't want to go to the ER.

Dean hauls me up against him. His arm around my shoulders might be the only thing keeping me upright.

"Come on," he says. "I'm taking you."

There's a lot more talking, voices rising with concern, and next thing I know I'm in the backseat of Dean's car with Charlotte by my side. Dean drives to the nearest hospital and stops at the emergency entrance. After a brief discussion, Charlotte goes to park his car in the regular lot while Dean and I go inside.

In the ER, he leaves me briefly to fill out the paperwork before I'm led to an examination area. A doctor and nurse ask more questions, all of which Dean answers, and then they unwrap the wound and clean it with a stinging solution that makes me yelp.

I stare at the cut, which looks huge and gaping red. "What... what about nerve damage? The medics said..."

"We'll check for that, Mrs. West."

After an injection of anesthetic, the doctor sutures the

wound, then asks me to move my hand in various positions, hold a pen, flex my fingers this way and that. He bandages my hand again with gauze and tape and writes up a prescription for pain medication.

Dean talks with the doctor for a few minutes, but by now I'm so drained I don't bother to listen. If it's good news, I'll know soon enough. If it's bad news, I don't want to know yet.

George has brought my satchel to the hospital, and he and Charlotte are in the waiting room when we finally emerge. Dean gives them the update, assuring them I'll be fine, and thanks them for accompanying us.

"Did someone turn off my stove?" I ask George. It seems like an important question to ask.

"I did," he says. "We got your station cleaned and sanitized, too. Everyone will be glad to know you're okay."

Finally Dean and I head home. In blessed silence. I stare out the dark window, seeing both our reflections in the glass.

He has to help me undress since I can't use my left hand. I feel sort of silly just standing there while he pulls off my apron, still caked with dried blood, and unfastens my skirt and blouse. His movements are gentle but impersonal, and once I'm in my nightgown I sink onto the sofa with a sigh of exhaustion.

Dean rests his hands on his hips, his eyebrows drawn together. "Need anything?"

"No."

"Do you want a cup of tea?"

"No." My eyes are getting heavy. "But thanks."

I don't remember anything after that. I wake when a gray, wet light filters through the curtains. Rain splashes against the windowsills, patters onto the roof.

Sometime during the night, Dean put my quilt over me. I burrow back under its familiar warmth and watch raindrops race each other down the window.

"How do you feel?" Dean's voice is soft.

I look to where he's sitting in the overstuffed chair next to the sofa. He's still wearing his trousers and shirt from last night, only now both are abominably wrinkled. I push myself onto one elbow, then wince as pain spirals up my arm.

"I don't know," I say. "Okay, I guess."

"Do you want a pain pill?" he asks.

"Yes, please."

Dean brings me a glass of water and the medication, then crouches beside the sofa. He reaches out to push my hair away from my face, tucking it behind my ears. I look at him, the angles of his face that I know so well, the shape of his mouth and thick-lashed eyes.

"Did you sit there all night?" I ask.

"Yeah. Why?"

"You smell really bad."

He grins and pushes up to standing. "You'll be okay if I take a shower?"

"Please do."

While he's gone, I head into the guest bathroom to pee. I manage to wash my good hand and splash water on my face. I look wretched, pale and gaunt with bruised circles ringing my eyes and my hair a tangled mess.

Good thing I don't plan to go anywhere or see anyone for days. Maybe ever again.

Feeling incredibly sorry for myself, I head back to the living room, pausing once to breathe through a wave of dizziness.

When Dean emerges from the shower—freshly shaved, dressed in worn jeans and a clean white T-shirt—I'm curled back up on the sofa.

"What did the doctor say?" I finally ask. "About permanent damage?"

"Your mobility is good, but because of the depth of the cut, you might have some numbness in your fingers for a while. They'll be able to tell more when the wound heals." He pauses. "Do you remember what happened?"

"Not really. The knife just slipped, I guess. I still have trouble remembering how to hold the damn things properly."

I flex the fingers of my right hand. Dean returns to the chair beside the sofa. He's close enough that I can smell the soap-and-shampoo scent of him. I could use a shower too, but I don't want to move.

We're quiet for a few minutes before he says, "It's my fault."

"It's not your fault."

"I shouldn't have barged into your class like that." He drags a hand through his hair, self-directed anger flashing in his eyes. "It upset you, threw off your concentration."

That's true, but I don't bother acknowledging it. We've punished each other enough.

I reach out and put my good hand on his knee. "Forget it, Dean. We both made mistakes."

"Did I scare him, do you think?"

I manage a hoarse laugh. "Yes. You definitely did."

"Good." He puts his large hand over mine, his fingers tightening. "I'm sorry."

"I'm sorry too."

Silence falls. I turn my palm upward so we can lock our

fingers together. As I watch the rain spilling down the window, I realize nothing between me and Dean will ever be the same again.

A strange calm settles in my heart. Maybe Dean needs to see me as more than his ever-faithful wife and the girl he needs to protect. And maybe I need to see him as more than my unwavering husband and the man who effortlessly takes care of everything.

Maybe this was meant to happen, this discovery of cracks where now a different, new light can shine through.

PART III

CHAPTER TWENTY

DEAN

She didn't turn away. She could have—she had the perfect reason to—but she didn't.

Instead she looked right at me when I crouched beside her and touched the sleeve of her gray sweatshirt. Instead she brushed the dirt from her hands and told me she was okay. Instead she asked me about medieval knights while I stood between her and the busy street and tried not to stare at her curved body.

Instead she stepped toward me. I had the strange thought that she wanted to come even closer.

NOVEMBER 20

I run outside a lot these days. Usually when the weather gets cold, I work out at the gym, play basketball, or run the indoor track at the university. Not this year. First thing in the morning, I put in five or six miles through town.

Liv is still asleep when I leave. She sleeps hard. She has ever since we got married. Before that, she slept restlessly, tossing and turning, waking often. Now my getting up, shuffling around the bedroom, turning on the bathroom light—none of it stirs her. The smell of coffee, though, that gets her going.

I press a kiss to her hair before I leave. I love her hair—thick, straight, shiny. I could spend hours nuzzling her hair, touching it. A sweet scent drifts from her, vanilla and something fruity. Peaches maybe. She always smells good.

She doesn't move. I pull on my running shoes and head out the front door.

Mirror Lake is still, silent, only a few lights shining. My shoes slam against the road as I pick up the pace. Down Emerald Street, a path along the lake, back up into a residential neighborhood of refurbished old houses.

Thoughts that crowd my head all day, when I can't shove them aside, whip away the faster I run.

Run. Run. Don't think. Don't imagine. Don't remember.

Cold air hits me, the sharp sting of wind. Ice in my lungs. The grayness of dawn. My mind empties. For an hour, there's only muscles burning, chest expanding, blood pumping. Into town again, past shops, restaurants, the movie theater.

It's a good run, almost seven miles. I walk the final blocks home. A bakery on Avalon Street is just opening its doors. I stop to buy a bag of muffins.

The lights are still off in the apartment when I get home. I shower and dress in trousers, shirt, and tie before going to make coffee.

The pot's almost full when Liv emerges, pushing her hair away from her face. She's bundled in a robe that has enough padding to keep her warm in an avalanche.

She gives me a sleepy half-smile and pulls out a chair at the table. I add cream and sugar to a cup of coffee and hand it to her.

"Thanks." She takes a sip and sighs with bliss. The breathy sound makes my cock twitch.

I turn away from her to pour myself a cup of coffee. We haven't had sex in weeks, since before she kissed that bastard. Neither of us has mentioned it. I assume she hasn't been interested, especially after the accident.

Her left hand rests on the table. The doctor removed the stitches yesterday, and now a scar mars the skin of her palm. I can't stand that she got hurt so badly. That it was my fault.

My throat constricts. I fight down a wave of anger.

"Working at the bookstore today?" I ask.

"No, but I have a shift at the Historical Museum," Liv says. "We're putting together a quilt exhibition along with things like spinning wheels and looms. Oh, you know that old Victorian house over on Tulip Street, the Langdon House? The Historical Society decorates it every Christmas as part of the holiday festival and tour. Trees, lights, ornaments, the works. Samantha asked me to help with that this year too."

I glance at her, my anger draining at the pride in her brown eyes. Since we moved to Mirror Lake, Liv has struggled to find a place for herself, and now she seems to have found it. She loves working at the Historical Museum and the bookstore, and with her newfound interest in cooking...

Shit.

I slide a hand to the back of Liv's neck and bend to kiss her. She makes a little noise of surprised pleasure and opens her mouth to let me in. I tighten my grip on her neck. She gets it, and leans in for a harder kiss.

Her lips are full, soft. One of the first things I noticed about her as she stood in front of me on the busy sidewalk. Probably one of the first things other men—

Stop.

I straighten and run my hand through Liv's hair. My heartbeat's kicked up a notch. I sit at the table and open the paper. Swallow some coffee, eat a muffin. Chew, swallow. Swallow, chew.

Don't think about him.

Him and her.

I push the paper aside and stand. She looks up.

"I need to head out early," I say. "I'll see you this evening. Call if you need me."

She smiles. "I always need you."

For now, her words are enough. Enough to diminish the fire of jealousy I can't put out. But I have no idea what'll make it flare again.

Work is a predictable routine, though I'm edgy about my grad students these days after Liv told me about Maggie Hamilton's insinuations. I haven't seen Maggie since she left town a few weeks ago.

When she gets back, I'll tell her to find another advisor or change majors altogether. She should never have been accepted into the program to begin with, so I don't feel bad about dismissing her.

Today I give a morning lecture, teach a grad seminar, and hold office hours. A few students trickle in—one complaining about her essay grade, another asking if he can revise his paper, a third with some genuinely interesting questions about music and liturgy.

With ten minutes to go, a sharp knock sounds on the door. Kelsey walks in, dressed in a tailored suit and heels, the blue streak in her frosted blond hair almost glowing.

Kelsey. Sharp, feisty, brilliant. Too blunt for her own good, but that's one of the reasons I like her. Impossible to bullshit Kelsey. And you know you're never getting any bullshit from her.

"What're you doing here?" I ask.

She frowns and flops into a chair, peering at me through her rimless glasses. "We have a lunch date. You forgot?"

I look at my desk calendar. "Yeah. Guess I did. Sorry."

"Well, now you're paying."

"Deal." I stand and shrug into my suit jacket. "Where are we going?"

"Somewhere off-campus so I can bitch about my research team without worrying that someone's going to overhear." She looks me over. "And since you're paying, somewhere expensive."

We end up at a ridiculous French place with low lights and linen tablecloths. The hushed atmosphere doesn't stop Kelsey from launching into a tirade about the ineptitude of her team, the lazy grad students, and the lack of proper equipment.

She exhausts herself before the entrees arrive, then spears a fork into her salmon and gives me a penetrating look.

I know what's coming.

"You and Liv worked out your troubles, huh?" she says. "That's what she told me, anyway."

"So why are you asking me?" I have no idea how much Liv told Kelsey about what happened. I do know Liv, though, and she wouldn't spill all the sordid details, not even to Kelsey. She's too private.

But I also know Liv needed someone to talk to during the whole fucked-up mess. And since I wasn't around, she'd naturally go to Kelsey.

"You're the one who first told me you and she were in a rough patch," Kelsey reminds me. "Was it all because Liv started thinking about having kids?"

Was that all? I don't even know.

I do know that when Liv told me early on she didn't want children, I was relieved. I like kids, but after everything that went down with Helen—not to mention my doubts about being a decent father—I was fine with the idea of just me and Liv. More than fine. It was what I wanted.

"It's natural, you know," Kelsey tells me. "That Liv would change her mind. Biological clock and all."

My insides tighten. "Yeah."

"She seemed upset that you weren't on board."

"There was nothing to be on board about," I snap. "Liv didn't even know if she wanted kids. She still doesn't. And what business is this of yours anyway?"

Kelsey doesn't flinch at the snarl in my voice. "It's my business because you two have always been the most freakishly happy couple I've ever known. And God knows, if you two can't make it, what hope do the rest of us have?"

Great. No pressure there.

"It's fine," I lie. "We worked it out."

"Why don't you want a baby?" she asks.

A black fear rises in my chest, swamp-like, dragging bitter memories along with it. I grab my water and take a gulp, shake my head.

"Leave it, Kelsey."

She understands the hard, "back off" tone and shrugs. We eat in silence for a couple of minutes. All the troubles of recent months, not to mention this new crap with Maggie Hamilton, roil inside me.

I can't tell Kelsey any of it. She doesn't know about Helen either because Kelsey and I lost touch when we were in grad school. I'd been too mired in a shitty marriage and excessive work to maintain contact with my old friends.

And I'm too fucking embarrassed to tell Kelsey about Maggie's lies. What if Kelsey wondered about them the way Liv did?

Christ. All I need is the *two* most important women in my life doubting me.

"Okay, I'll back off." Kelsey looks at her plate and uses her fork to make a little design with her carrots. "Just… you know, I love you two assholes and want you to be happy. So I'm here if either of you needs me."

Two specks of color appear on her cheeks. I can't help a faint smile.

"Thanks."

She frowns. "But don't tell anyone I said shit like that. I've got a reputation to maintain."

"Don't worry. I'll tell everyone what a hard-ass you are."

"I'd better be, considering the amount of time I spend on the elliptical machine."

"I'm making chicken piccata," Liv calls from the kitchen. "Does it smell good?"

"Smells great." It does too—lemons, capers, and garlic.

I drop my briefcase by the front door and go in to find her looking adorable, if frazzled, in gray sweatpants and a flower-print apron with her hair trapped in a high ponytail. Her face is flushed from the heat of the stove. She turns her cheek to me for an obligatory kiss, then waves me out of the kitchen.

"Go, go. Fifteen minutes. I need to get everything timed right."

I change into flannel pajama bottoms and a T-shirt, then stretch out on the sofa to watch the news. Pot lids bang in the kitchen. Water runs. The oven door slams shut. Liv curses.

"Need any help?" I ask.

"No thanks. Just a few more minutes."

Although I love that she's been trying so hard to learn to cook, I still hate that she took that class. If she hadn't, she'd never have met that goddamn chef, they'd never have kissed, and we wouldn't have had the fight that nearly killed us.

But she did. And they did. And we did.

Fuck.

I scrub a hand down my face and try to focus on the TV.

"Ready!" Liv calls.

I go to the table, where she's put out two plates of chicken, potatoes, and green beans. "Looks amazing."

"I hope it's good." She waves me to sit before taking her place. "So tell me about your day."

First I try the chicken, which is juicy and tasty with a bite of pepper. "This is delicious."

"Really?" She gives me a smile so bright my heart clenches. "You like it? I added more lemon than the recipe called for, but I thought it'd add a nice kick. And I put in a few flakes of cayenne."

"You're becoming a great cook, Liv."

Still smiling, she digs into her own meal and asks again about my day. I give her an overview and tell her about lunch with Kelsey—and what Kelsey said.

"She thinks we're freakishly happy?" Liv repeats.

"That's what she said."

She pokes at the remains of her chicken and glances at me. "What do you think?"

I don't know how to answer that, so I play dumb. "About what?"

"Are we freakishly happy?"

Irritation pulls at me. She knows the answer, so why is she putting me on the spot? How the fuck can a couple be *freakishly happy* if the wife kisses another man? How can they be happy at all?

A swarm of anger fills my chest. I smother it with effort.

"If we were, we'd live in a circus," I say, fighting to keep my voice even. "And no one on the outside looking in knows the full truth."

It's not what she wanted to hear. I can see the disappointment in her eyes, the slight hunch of her shoulders.

What the hell was I supposed to say? *"Yeah, sure, we're freakishly happy."*

Then she'd be mad because I was lying.

Fix this, West. Make it okay for her.

I go around to her side of the table and grasp her shoulders, pulling her up and against me. She settles easily into my arms like she always has, her hands sliding around my waist, her breasts pressing against my chest. She gives a little sigh of contentment that makes me want to both hold her forever and tear her clothes off right there.

Now I suppress the urge to do the latter. I tighten my arms around her.

"No," I murmur against her hair which now smells like chicken piccata. "We are not freakishly happy. We are not freakishly anything. We're two people who love each other. We had a tough time. We worked it out because we want to be together. Because we can't imagine being with anyone else. Because we don't want to be."

She slips her fingers inside the waistband of my pants to stroke my lower back. Blood starts to pool in my groin, my prick pushing against her belly. She looks up at me, then reaches one hand down to palm my crotch. Although uncertainty flickers in her eyes, her tone is light.

"You want to hold that thought until I clean the kitchen?" she asks.

"Yeah." I pull in a breath. "Sure."

I close my eyes for a second, conjuring images of medieval saints and monastic architecture to will my erection away. Once I can move again, I help Liv clear the table before she gestures me out of the kitchen.

I go into my office and work on a paper about the Romanesque architecture of the Speyer Cathedral. Focusing on work has always been an easy out, a way to stop thinking about things I don't want to think about. Years of study have taught me how to close off everything except triple-aisled basilicas and octagonal domes.

Liv would call that ability a "dorky professor thing." I call it a survival technique.

Tonight, it's nearly ten when I finally look up from the computer. The sound of the TV buzzes from the living room. I'd half-expected Liv to come find me, but she rarely comes into my office when I'm working.

I shove away from the desk and go into the living room. She's lying on the sofa… asleep. She looks younger when she's asleep and you can't see the hint of shadows in her eyes. But I know they're there.

Her ponytail is askew, fanning strands of long hair over the sofa cushion. I look at her face, her parted lips, the arch of her throat. Her breasts move with each breath. My prick hardens again. Her T-shirt has ridden up to expose the skin of her torso, pale and smooth.

I shift and wince as my erection grows thick against my thigh. I grab it and squeeze, feeling that familiar pull in my groin.

I tug a quilt over Liv, turn off the TV, and return to the bedroom. Close the door.

I stretch out on the bed and rub my dick through my pajama pants. Can't help hoping Liv wakes up and comes into the bedroom. I want her mouth on mine, want to curl my fingers in her hair while she wraps her hand around my cock... Christ.

The images flash through my brain as I tug my erection out and start to stroke it. Urgency tightens my nerves. All I have to do is think of her—full, round tits bouncing in time to my thrusts, her lips parted and face flushed, the grip of her pussy around my shaft.

Pressure builds. I work my cock faster, driving myself toward release. My heart pounds. I imagine pressing my hands to Liv's damp thighs, spreading her wider, sinking into her tight, wet heat.

I can hear her moaning my name, begging, pulling her legs up so she can feel every thrust, so she can take me deep. *"Dean, fuck me harder... yes, just like that... oh, God... I'm going to come... I feel it... oh!"*

I tighten my hand on my shaft and rub my thumb over the head. My spine tenses as the pressure snaps. I groan, semen spurting over my stomach as I imagine shooting deep inside Liv while she squirms beneath me and strains toward another orgasm.

I fucking love watching her come. Her whole body shakes, she wraps her legs around me, and digs her fingers into my back. Her throaty, little cries fire my blood all over again.

My wife.

I stroke my cock until the final pulses ebb. My breath is ragged. I grab a few tissues and wipe the dampness off, then stare at the ceiling.

Not long ago I'd have thought nothing of waking Liv up by rubbing her breasts or kissing her. She'd open her eyes and fall right into me, her mouth seeking mine. Instead, she's asleep in the other room and I'm in here jacking off.

The last of the pleasure fades. Guilt pushes its way back in.

I should have told her years ago about my first marriage. Of course I know that. Numerous times I almost did. Then she'd turn her warm, brown gaze on me, her "You're my hero" look that broke my heart in two, and the confession disintegrated in my throat.

What if I told her and that look changed? What if she wondered how much I was to blame for the disastrous marriage? What if she questioned my ability to deal with conflict? To solve problems? To *fix* things?

What if she thought I was weak, hadn't treated Helen right, hadn't done as much as I could have? What if she wondered what was wrong with me?

The questions knotted my brain until I'd finally shoved it all down and told myself to forget it. To focus on Liv, make our relationship a haven of warmth and safety. To love and protect her. To keep anything from hurting her more than she already had been.

That was all I wanted. It's all I still want.

But I'm failing. I have no fucking idea how to fix what's gone wrong in our marriage. I have no idea if my wife will ever again look at me the way she used to.

CHAPTER TWENTY-ONE

Dean

November 21

"*This one is Cruella de Vil. The Queen of Hearts. Poison Ivy. Maleficent.*"

That was when I knew I could fall hard for her, this girl with the long, dark hair who named her houseplants after villains.

The girl who tried to make something good out of something wicked. Who made me want to know her as much as I just *wanted* her.

I watch Liv as she plucks dried leaves from the hibiscus

beside the window and checks the soil. She hasn't named her plants since we got married. I haven't realized that before. Now she says, "My amaryllis needs water," or "My violets bloomed."

Liv goes into the kitchen and returns with a small watering can. She waters all the plants, then opens the curtain to let in the first rays of sun.

"What happened to Cruella de Vil?" I ask.

"Cruella de Vil?"

"You haven't named your plants since we got married."

"Oh." She looks faintly surprised by the comment. "No, I guess I haven't."

"Why not?"

Liv shrugs and tips the watering can over the last plant.

"After we got married, I didn't need to make something good anymore," she says, heading back to the kitchen. "I'd already found it."

I drop the newspaper onto the coffee table. Try to stifle the bitter shame and guilt.

"I'm working at the bookstore until six." Liv pauses in the kitchen doorway. "Do you want me to pick up anything for dinner?"

"No. I can grab something on the way home."

Liv nods and goes into the bedroom. I wait for her to finish getting ready before going in after her.

She looks pretty and autumn-like in a russet wool skirt and blue sweater with little pearl buttons marching up the front. As I watch her brush her hair, I have a sudden image of unfastening those dainty buttons one by one to expose the creamy swells of her breasts. I want her to look at me with heat brewing in those brown eyes. I want to taste her.

"I'll see you tonight, then." Liv drops the brush back onto the dresser and peers at herself in the mirror.

My heart is beating too fast. *Tonight* sounds like an eternity.

"You have time for coffee later?" I ask.

"Sure. My shift at the Historical Museum ends at twelve-thirty, but I have to be at the bookstore by two."

"I'll meet you downtown, then."

As she passes me in the doorway, I grab her around the waist and pull her against me. I lower my head to kiss her hard. A gasp stops in her throat. My blood heats. I increase the pressure of my mouth until she opens for me. Her body arches, her hand spreading over my chest.

You're mine, Liv. Remember that.

Before jealousy can burn me again, I ease away from her and rub my thumb over her lips. "I'll call you around one."

"Okay. Love you." She slides her hand against my chest again before she leaves. A few seconds later, the front door closes.

I go take a cold shower and change into a suit and tie, then head to the university. The town's awake, people easing into their days. Students traipse across the frost layering the quad, huddled into coats and hats, grasping paper cups of coffee.

I stop at the main office of the history department. Exchange a greeting with Grace, the administrative assistant, and a few comments about the weather. After collecting the papers and mail from my box, I head to my office.

Halfway down the hall, I see Maggie Hamilton coming toward me. Tension and anger fill my veins. We both stop.

"Professor West." She gives me an uncertain smile. "I was just coming to see if you were in your office."

For a second, I don't know what to do. I don't want her in my office. I also don't want to do this in the corridor.

I step toward my office and push on the door, wedging it wide open. "Come in."

She follows me in. I move behind the desk to put it between us. I remain standing and cross my arms. My spine is stiff enough to break.

"I heard you approached my wife recently." I dig my fingers into my biceps. Try to keep my voice low. "That was entirely inappropriate."

She nods, looking contrite. "I know. I was just... desperate, you know? Nothing I do seems to be good enough for you."

"No excuse. I could write a letter to Dr. Hunter as department chairperson about this, but I won't as long as you change advisors."

Maggie stares at me. "I can't change advisors. You know that. It'll delay my degree even more."

"You should have thought of that before you..." ...*lied about my integrity.*

I have a sick feeling that will open another can of worms, so I leave it alone. And all I need is to remember that my wife didn't know whether or not to believe those implications.

My chest tightens.

"... before you chose your topic," I finish. "It's no secret how you got into the program, Maggie. If I'd been the Medieval Studies professor at the time, I'd never have approved your admission."

Angry tears spring to her eyes. "Look, I know I wasn't the best student, okay? But I'm here because I have to get good grades and a master's so I can get into law school. If I don't,

I'm totally screwed. I'm going to stay with my parents so I can—"

I hold up a hand to stop her. "Go talk to the registrar about changing advisors. That's all I can tell you."

There's a movement at the open door behind her, and one of the other grad students peers in.

"Jessica." Relief eases my tension. "Come in."

"I don't want to interrupt." Jessica glances warily from Maggie to me.

"It's okay." I give Maggie a pointed look. "We're done."

Maggie swipes at her eyes, glowers at Jessica, then stalks out of the office. An awkward hush descends. I move a few books off the desk so Jessica can put her backpack down.

"Sorry about that." I wait for her to take a seat before I sit down in my office chair.

"Sorry you got stuck with her," Jessica replies wryly as she unzips her backpack. "I know she's under pressure from her father, but… well, anyway, I wanted to check in with you about my paper before Thanksgiving break."

"Sure. What've you got?"

She pulls out some notes, and we spend the next hour discussing Foucault, dedicatory prologues of medieval illuminations, and cosmic imagery. It's a welcome respite, and by the time Jessica leaves, my jagged thoughts have eased.

I get to work for the rest of the day. Organize notes, give a lecture on medieval monasteries, and head a grad seminar on visual culture. There's a Medieval Studies meeting in late morning, then a few of the other professors and I go to lunch.

After we're done eating meatball subs and discussing a course on Latin paleography, I step outside and call Liv on her cell.

"Hi." She sounds breathless. "Are you at work?"

"Just finished lunch at the Boxcar. Where are you?"

"Deli down the street," she says.

"I'll come and meet you."

I shut my phone and head to the intersection of Avalon and Poppy Streets. The Italian deli is crowded with lunch customers, so I wait outside.

Through the window, Liv is giving her order to the young guy behind the counter. He says something that makes her smile. He smiles in return, then gestures with his hands. She laughs.

Jealousy floods me fast and hard. I know that kid. His dad owns the deli. He's friendly to everyone. And I fucking hate that just the sight of Liv smiling at him makes me feel like... like *this*.

I stalk away from the window and wait at the curb. My blood is hot with anger at myself for not trusting her, at her for not trusting me.

It's a knife-like stab, the memory of Liv's hesitation when I asked if she believed Maggie's lies. Five years ago, when Liv and I first met, she'd never have thought I was capable of wrongdoing. Never. She wouldn't have given me a chance if she had.

Liv steps out of the deli with a paper bag in one hand. She gives me a little wave as she crosses the sidewalk. She tucks herself against me for a hug and kisses my chin. Some of my anger drains.

"How was your morning?" Liv asks.

"Good. Busy."

"I picked up our Thanksgiving turkey before my shift at the museum. Anything else you want for dinner?"

"Whatever you make will be great." I pull her closer. "Let's get a coffee, and I'll walk you to the bookstore. My next class doesn't start until three."

She slides her arm around my waist as we walk. I wish it were enough to make everything okay.

⌒⌒

"This is it!" Liv circles the entire Douglas fir and reaches out to skim her hand over one of the branches. "Nice and fluffy. There's this space back here, but we can turn that toward the wall. What do you think?"

"Looks great."

"Good." She beams at me. She's all bundled into her winter coat with her cheeks red from the cold. "Let's get it, then. I'm going to buy some holly and mistletoe too. You get them to wrap the tree up, okay?"

"Yes, ma'am."

She trundles off to the shack to pay, and I flag down a guy to wrap the tree in netting. We haul it out to the car and get it secured on the roof before Liv comes out with a bag containing enough holly to fill our living room and a bunch of pine boughs tucked under her arm. She has always insisted in getting our Christmas tree the weekend after Thanksgiving, as if she's trying to extend the holiday season as long as possible.

"I'll make us some hot chocolate when we get home," she says after unloading her bounty into the backseat.

At home, we drag the tree into the foyer and up the stairs. Liv disappears into the kitchen to make the hot chocolate while I set up the tree in its usual spot beside the window.

"Perfect! I love it." Liv hands me a mug of chocolate and puts another one on a table. "Let's get the lights up. I already checked them, and they all work."

I watch her as she puts on a CD of Christmas carols and unwraps the lights. There's a pretty glow about her, a sense of anticipation that she always gets around the holidays as she decorates and plans, making Christmas into a freaking magical winter wonderland.

The way she's always made it for me. The way she never had it as a kid.

That's the thing about Liv. She's pure. Despite experiences that could have irrevocably fucked her up, turned her into someone hard and jaded, she's still wholesome. She has a wary edge, a guard against the world, but it never affects her core of innocence.

I love that about her. When she looked at me over the counter at Jitter Beans, her brown eyes glowing with sincerity ("*Room for cream in your coffee, sir?*"), I felt like my heart was about to pound out of my chest.

She might as well have said, "*Room for me in your life, sir? Room for me in your bed?*"

Yes. And hell, yes.

Sure there was some Neanderthal instinct. Not just for sex, though that was powerful. There was also an urge to make her mine, to claim her so she'd never belong to another man. So she'd never want another man.

Which is just one reason her thing with that cook is still messing with my head.

What the fuck did I do wrong? How did I fail?

It was more than not having told her about my first

marriage. It had to be more than that. If that was it, then maybe I shouldn't have told her at all because I can't for the life of me figure out how to fix any of this.

"Can you get the top branches, Dean?"

I set down my mug and go to help her hang the lights. We decorate the tree together with shiny glass balls and ornaments Liv has collected over the years. She tells me where to hang the mistletoe and spreads the holly over the fireplace mantel, then digs around for the stockings.

I sit on the sofa and watch her for a few more minutes. When the decorations are finished, glittery and sparkling, I crook a finger at Liv.

"Come here."

She sits beside me and folds her body against mine, her hand sliding over my thigh. I tangle my fingers in her hair and pull her head up to mine for a kiss. She tastes like chocolate, her breathy sigh warm against my mouth before she eases back to look at me.

I know that look in her eyes. It's a look that makes my blood heat.

"It's been too long," she says.

I take her wrist. "You feel okay?"

"Fine. My hand doesn't hurt at all anymore. I just... you know. I miss you."

Ah, hell.

I tuck my fingers beneath the waistband of her jeans. "How about I just make you feel good?"

"You always make me feel good. But I want *you*, Dean." She shifts around until she's facing me and straddling my lap, a position that makes me burn. "Badly."

"Liv."

"Come on." She rocks her hips. "Fuck me."

Christ. Raw words from her pretty mouth, and I'm hard in an instant.

She starts working the buttons on my jeans. Her nipples tent her sweater, and her breathing is getting faster. Just watching her get turned on makes me hotter.

By the time she has my prick in her hand, I know I'm done for. She moves off my lap and kneels on the sofa beside me.

"It's always so good with you." She swipes her tongue across the head of my cock. "Especially when it's been a long time."

A bolt of shame, embarrassment, hits me hard. It's been a long time because I fucked up. I let my screwed-up relationship with Helen dictate how I treated the love of my life.

I kept a big secret from Liv because I wanted to protect her. I only ended up hurting her, driving her to kiss another man. If things hadn't blown up when they did, who knows what else might have happened...

A growl starts low in my chest. Possession and lust flood me. I grab Liv's hair and yank her up to me, kissing her hard enough to make her gasp in surprise. Although some part of me is aware enough to be mindful, I'm none too gentle as I slide off the sofa and bring us both to the floor.

Not only does Liv not care, she wraps her arms and legs around me like tentacles and opens her mouth under mine. My prick pulses hard against her thigh. She twists her hips.

"Take off my jeans," she says, reaching for the hem of her sweater. She pulls it over her head, and my heart kicks into high gear at the sight of her breasts straining against her bra.

She unwraps her legs from my waist and rises onto her

elbows to watch as I yank her jeans off. I press my hand between her thighs. Heat burns through her panties. She spreads her legs, watching me. As much as I want to rip her underwear off and sink into her, I want even more to make her beg. I slip a finger beneath the elastic of her panties and tease her cleft.

A visible shudder ripples through her. I nod toward her bra. "Now you take that off."

She flicks at the clasp, and the white straps falls off her shoulders. Jesus. Every time I see her naked breasts, I can't wait to touch them, pinch her nipples, feel them pressing against my chest. Can't wait to watch them bounce in time with my thrusts.

I stop, my breath hard. Liv stares at me, then reaches for the drawer of the table beside the sofa. She grabs the package of condoms inside, rips one open, and moves back toward me. Her face is all flushed with heat, her hair spilling around her shoulders as she rolls the condom onto my erection.

"Dean." Her voice is strained.

"Tell me."

"I want you." She lies back and stretches her arms over her head in a pose that's sexy as hell.

"Say it." I pull her panties down her legs.

"Fuck me." She hooks her feet around the small of my back. "Please."

I move between her thighs. Our prolonged abstinence makes the flame of pleasure stronger. I sink my cock into her, all thought dissolving into pure urgency as her hot tightness grips me. She shifts, opens wider, grabs the sides of my head and pulls me down closer.

Her tongue pushes into my mouth as I thrust into her. Need boils through me. She hugs my hips with her thighs and bucks upward. It won't last long, not for her or me.

I brace my hands on either side of her head and pump harder. My head spins with the sensation of her clenching around my shaft. My whole body tightens with pleasure.

"Oh, Dean." Her fingernails rake my back. *"Dean."*

I slide a hand down her stomach, through her damp curls to her clit. Liv moans, her fingers digging in harder as I start to rub. Her body tenses, her breath catching hard in her throat, and then she sinks her teeth into my shoulder and comes hard and fast.

Her flesh vibrates around my shaft, milking an explosive orgasm from me that I can't contain. Coming with her is like nothing I've ever felt, a deep pumping and release that shatters us both.

I manage to roll to the side, taking her with me and pulling her on top. Her naked body goes limp against mine, her chest heaving. I push her hair away from her face, stroke my fingers through the long tangles.

"So good," she whispers, pressing a kiss to my throat. "It's always so good with you."

She never answered my question. When she confessed she'd kissed that bastard, I asked her if it was *good.*

Why the hell did I ask that? Why was that my first question? *"Are you sure you want me to answer that?"* she'd replied.

Fuck no. But her non-answer made it worse.

Liv lifts her head to look at me. Her eyes darken.

"What is it?" she asks, but then comprehension and guilt pass across her face. She knows exactly what I'm thinking. She pulls away and reaches for her bra. "It's never going to go away, is it?"

I push to standing and go into the bathroom to get rid of the condom. My heart's pounding, but no longer from lust. The physical satisfaction disappears like smoke. I return to the living room and put on my boxers.

"You didn't answer my question," I say. Jealousy tightens my chest. "Was it good with him?"

Liv stops in the motion of pulling her sweater on, then slowly pokes her head through. She drags her fingers into her hair and twists it into a ponytail.

I can't stand it. Can't fucking stand the thought of another man getting close enough to touch her. To *kiss* her.

My fists clench.

Liv rummages in a drawer and finds a rubber band. She's stalling.

"Liv."

She snaps the band around her hair. "Why do you want to know?"

Good question. Because I like torture?

"Answer me." My fingers dig into my palms.

"Yes." She fumbles with the cuffs of her sweater. "It was a decent kiss. It meant nothing, but it was fine. Nice." Sadness and remorse flash in her brown eyes. "Is that what you wanted to hear? Does that make it better?"

There's no answer to that.

I turn away—away from the Christmas tree, the holly on the mantel, the mistletoe tied with a red ribbon. Away from Liv.

CHAPTER TWENTY-TWO

DEAN

NOVEMBER 28

*S*now falls outside my office window. The history and art history departments are housed in a classical old building, and I'm fortunate to have an office that overlooks the lake. The light snow gathers onshore and caps the mountains.

I finish filing some papers and collect a few books to return to the library. I have a lecture in an hour, then a meeting about the conference we're hosting. So far we have an impressive roster of attendees, including several scholars from Germany, Italy, and Spain. And possibly my ex-wife.

I don't want to see Helen again, not even at a conference, but it's been... what? Almost fifteen years? We made some bad mistakes, had some rough times. At least we ended it before we managed to bring any kids into the world and risk screwing them up through our own horrible marriage.

I stop that thought before it goes any farther. I don't want to think about it, to relive any part of it. Don't want the guilt to stain my current life more than it already has.

I get through the lecture and meeting, then grab a duffle bag from my office and head to the campus gym. After changing clothes, I run the indoor track, forcing the thoughts to disappear into the pounding of my heart.

Still it's not enough and I lift weights until my muscles burn, then work the rowing machine as the light outside the windows fades.

"Good Lord. Take a break, why don't you?" Kelsey strides into the gym, a duffle over her shoulder and her coat dusted with snow. "How long have you been here?"

I stop rowing and grab a towel to wipe the sweat off. My blood hammers, my muscles ache. "Don't know. What time is it?"

"Almost six. I stopped by your office to see if you wanted to play racquetball, but you were already gone."

"Yeah. I should get home. Liv's probably trying to cook lasagna or something." I swipe down the machine and loop the towel around the back of my neck.

I don't like the way Kelsey is looking at me. Too sharp, too penetrating.

"Racquetball tomorrow, okay?" I say. At least if we're playing racquetball, she can't interrogate me. "I'll meet you here."

"Sure."

To my irritation, she falls into step beside me as I head to the locker room.

"You and Liv want to catch a movie or something this weekend?" she asks.

"I don't know what she has planned, but I'll check."

"There's also the holiday art fair," Kelsey suggests, "if you can stand Christmas wreaths and wooden Santas and enough goodwill to make you want to throw up."

That makes me grin. "Sounds great."

"Okay, then." She stops before the door of the women's locker room. "Racquetball tomorrow at four?"

"Be ready to get creamed."

"You know I don't mind being creamed by you, Dean." With a wink, she heads into the locker room and lets the door swing shut behind her.

I head toward the men's locker room. At least my relationship with Kelsey is the same. If I'd ever tell anyone what Liv and I went through, what we're still going through, it would be Kelsey. The fact that I won't underscores just how shitty it all is.

I shower and dress, then drive home. By now, I've come to expect the smells of cooking drifting from the kitchen, but there's nothing except the scents of pine and holly.

Liv's curled on the sofa watching the news. She turns to watch me enter.

I drop my duffle and briefcase on the table. "Hey. How was your day?"

"Okay."

Her eyes are all puffy. She's been crying.

Shit.

I sit beside her and pull her against me, brushing my mouth across her temple.

"Sorry," I mutter.

She lets out a shaky sigh. "Me too. How are we going to fix this?"

The only thing I can think of is that I need to get the hell over it, but I don't know how. All I know is that I drove her toward another man and... anger floods my throat.

"Will you come with me to counseling again?" Liv asks.

I want to say yes. I should say yes.

But I can't stand the idea of a counselor gnawing at my problems. Expecting me to talk about more than I want to. Making Liv go through it all again. Telling me this is all my fucking fault.

"Maybe," I finally say.

I pick up Liv's hand and rub my fingers across the scar on her palm. Guilt punches me in the stomach. If I hadn't stalked into her cooking class like a barbarian out for revenge, she wouldn't have lost her concentration, wouldn't have sliced her hand open with a knife.

Thank God there was no permanent damage, but she'll always have the scar.

I need to stop punishing her. As much as I hate the thought of her kissing another man, this whole mess *has* been my fault.

I want to protect Liv from everything, but I can't protect her from the truth. No matter how ugly it is. I know that now. I just need to remember it.

I run a hand down Liv's back. "Hey, Kelsey wants to catch

a movie or something this weekend. She also mentioned the holiday art fair."

"The art fair's this weekend?" Liv's eyes light up. "I love the art fair. I've been wanting a new wreath for the front door. Oh, maybe we can meet Kelsey for breakfast first. The tearoom down on Poppy Street has a Saturday special with free cinnamon lattes. I'll send Kels an email to set it up."

She scrambles off the sofa and heads for her laptop. Her excitement eases some of my apprehension. For now.

Matilda's Teapot is a nightmare of chintz tablecloths, china cups, frilly curtains and at least five tables filled with pink-cheeked grandmas. A plump woman in a floral dress and lace apron—quite possibly Matilda herself—guides us to a table.

As we sit down on the curved Victorian-style chairs, Kelsey shoots me a look. I shrug in defense and tilt my head toward Liv to indicate this was her idea.

"I heard they're closing this place soon because the owner is retiring and there's no one to take over," Liv says. "It's a shame because it's such an institution."

Kelsey rolls her eyes and opens the pink menu. "Do they have steak and eggs here?"

"Try the crepes," Liv suggests. "With homemade berry preserves. They're delicious."

"I need something more substantial if I'm going to wade through piles of cheesy reindeer ornaments," Kelsey says.

Liv looks a little crestfallen. "I thought you wanted to go to the art fair. Dean said you were the one who suggested it."

Kelsey has the grace to appear contrite. "I know, I know. You're right, it'll be fun. They always have someone selling great fudge."

The waitress brings our free lattes—both Kelsey and I also ask for black coffee—and we place our orders. Crepes for Liv, eggs and toast for me, quiche for Kelsey. Liv orders a side of scones and cream and a selection of tea.

I look at her. She's leaning across the table, telling Kelsey about the holiday exhibition at the Historical Museum. The sight of her hits me in the chest. So pretty with her long hair and bright eyes. And so pure and damaged at the same time, like a priceless vase threaded with cracks.

No wonder I couldn't stay away from her. No wonder I wanted to be her hero. No wonder another guy—

"Dean?" Liv nudges me with her elbow. She and Kelsey are looking at me expectantly.

"Sorry." I swallow some coffee, fighting the anger. "What?"

"Kelsey has tickets to Handel's *Messiah* next weekend," Liv says. "Do you want to go?"

"Yeah, sure."

Kelsey frowns. "Why are you so spacey these days? Liv, did he tell you I beat him at racquetball twice this week? Mr. Competitive hardly tried to get off an offensive shot."

Liv shoots me a glance. "He has a lot on his mind with the conference next year and his book."

Kelsey's frown deepens as she looks from Liv to me. I smother a rush of shame and turn to my food. Liv and Kelsey chatter on all through breakfast before I pay the bill and we head to the art fair.

Every year it's held in a huge room at the convention

center, with tables of arts and crafts for sale. The place smells like pine and cinnamon. Christmas music wafts from overhead speakers. We leave our coats in the coatroom and wait in a short line to buy tickets.

"I want to look at the wreaths first." Liv grabs a basket at the entrance and heads into the crowd.

Kelsey and I follow. She tucks her arm through mine. "It's still the baby thing, isn't it?"

I haven't even thought about the *baby thing* in weeks. "No."

She doesn't look as if she believes me. I watch Liv as she examines a table filled with Christmas wreaths. Her hair is pulled back in a messy knot, her cheeks flushed from the outside cold and inside warmth. She's talking with one of the vendors, gesturing to a wreath, smelling some sort of flower.

"She'd be an amazing mother," Kelsey remarks.

"Yeah."

I feel her looking at me. "And you would be an amazing father."

I don't reply. She pulls me to a halt and turns to face me.

"You would, Dean," she insists. "I know it."

"No one knows that."

"Liv does. She wouldn't have thought about children if she didn't know that about you."

That has never occurred to me before.

"What do you think of this one?" Liv comes toward us, holding up a wreath about the size of a tire. "It's made of noble fir, cedar, juniper, and I just love these little frosted pinecones."

"Looks great," I say.

Liv beams. "She'll throw in a snowman ornament and a garland too. I'll pay now and she'll hold it for us to pick up later."

She heads back to the wreath table. Kelsey and I look around at some of the other arts and crafts, and before we've gone halfway through the room Kelsey has a basket full of star-shaped glass ornaments, Christmas cards, handmade earrings, nutcracker stocking holders, and scented candles.

"For gifts," she tells me defensively when she catches me grinning.

"Uh huh."

"Come on, I'm hungry. That quiche wasn't enough for me." Kelsey hooks her basket over her arm. "Let's find the fudge. Where's Liv?"

We wind through the crowd to the section where vendors sell gourmet food items and gift baskets. I catch sight of Liv and point her out to Kelsey. We head toward her.

Then I stop.

He's there. The chef who taught Liv's cooking class. The man who kissed her.

He's standing behind a vendor's table. And he's looking at my wife. Liv is a short distance away, her expression guarded but polite as she *talks* to him.

Rage boils so fast, so hard, that it propels me forward. I shove Kelsey aside and plow through the crowd to get to Liv. The other guy jerks his gaze to me, alarmed.

"Dean!" Sensing danger, Liv whirls around before I reach her. Her eyes widen. She holds out a hand to prevent me from crashing over the table and strangling the chef.

Which I'm this close to doing.

"Dean." Liv spreads her hands across my chest and tries to push me away from the table. "It's okay. Dean, it's nothing."

The chef—whatever the hell his name is—stares at me, his face white. Good. Let the little bastard be scared.

"What were you saying to him?" I'm half-aware that people are glancing in our direction, but I don't care.

"Nothing. Just hello. He's selling spice mixes." Her fingers tighten on my shirt. "Dean, *please*."

"Really... really, man, it was nothing," the chef stammers.

I point a finger at him. "Stay the fuck away from her."

Another hand closes on my arm. Kelsey. She yanks hard enough to catch me off-guard. "Come on, Rambo. Take a seat."

She manages to pull me to an eating area and shoves me onto a bench. Liv stays where she is, watching me warily. The crowd resumes its normal movement.

Kelsey bends to look me in the eye. She looks pissed. "What the hell was that?"

I pull in a breath, my anger still hot. "She kissed him."

"What?" Kelsey steps back, blinking in confusion.

"That asshole was her cooking teacher. He walked her to her car one night and kissed her. She kissed back."

Kelsey shakes her head. "I don't get it. *Liv* kissed him?"

"That's what I said."

"But why..." She glances back at Liv in disbelief. "You're kidding me."

"I'm not. Ask her. Then ask her if it was good."

"Oh, Dean."

"Fuck, Kelsey." I drag a hand down my face. "I can't get rid of it."

She doesn't say anything. I'm grateful. There's nothing she can say that would make it any easier.

"Dean?" Liv's voice is tentative as she appears behind

Kelsey. She glances from me to Kelsey and back again. "Please don't be mad."

I exhale hard. "I'm not mad."

"You look mad."

"I'm not mad at *you*."

She doesn't seem convinced. I'm not either.

"Okay." Kelsey takes Liv's arm and backs her up a few steps. "Dean, Liv and I are going to finish looking around. You stay here and chill out. We'll come back when we're ready to leave."

I watch them disappear into the crowd. Liv turns once to look at me, and then she's gone. I wait all of ten seconds before I leave the center and walk back out into the cold.

CHAPTER TWENTY-THREE

OLIVIA

*D*ean is still not home when I get back to our apartment this evening. He called Kelsey earlier to tell her he'd left the art fair, but he didn't answer his cell when I tried to call him. I spent the rest of the afternoon working mindlessly at the bookstore. My stomach is a knot of anger and regret.

I stare at the Christmas tree in the corner, the twinkling lights reflected in the windows. I think of the first Christmas Dean and I spent together, four months after we first met. A fairy tale—dark woods, tangled vines, handsome princes and all.

I press my hands to my eyes and try to breathe. I don't know how we will ever fix this. *If* we ever will.

At eight, I change into my nightgown and crawl into bed, staring at the pattern of light and shadows on the ceiling.

Dean is the only man I've ever wanted. The only man I've allowed into my body, into my heart. The love of my life, who taught me more about happiness and pleasure than anyone else ever has.

So I don't understand why I felt the way I did for Tyler Wilkes. I don't understand why it was easy to kiss him, why I gave in to the pull of attraction. Had I wanted Dean to find out?

The thought stops my breath.

Dean has never been threatened before. He's never had reason to be. I have always been the starry-eyed girl who melted at his touch. I let him into places even I didn't want to go.

He knows he has all of me. And yet when he told me about his first marriage, I discovered I hadn't had all of him.

When I kissed Tyler, had I wanted to shift the balance between me and Dean? Warn my husband that I could keep part of myself separate from him too?

Except that I didn't. I could never have kept that kiss a secret from Dean, no matter what he kept secret from me. Even now, he has all of me.

I hear Dean close the front door and toss his keys onto the counter. Then he appears at the bedroom door. He looks windswept, his cheeks ruddy from the cold, his hair messy, as if he's been running.

The sight of him—this man I still love with everything I am—makes my whole body ache with longing and sorrow.

Tension falls like a curtain. We stare at each other. When

he moves closer, I can see the anger edging his muscles, the planes of his face.

He stops by the bed. His hand drops to the button of his jeans.

"Don't say no," he says. His voice is rough.

I can't tell if it's an order or a request. I don't care. I shake my head.

I won't say no. I don't want to say no.

He works the buttons of his shirt and yanks it off his shoulders, then unfastens his jeans. His erection is already pushing against the fly, and arousal curls through my despair at the sight of the long, thick length.

He grabs a fistful of the comforter and pulls it away from me, his dark gaze skimming my body beneath my nightgown. Aside from a pair of cotton panties, I'm naked underneath the thin cotton, and his scrutiny alone makes my nipples peak. I suppress the sudden urge to cross my arms, to hide.

He kneels beside me on the bed and runs his hand over the front of my body, his fingers sliding beneath my breasts and tracing a path to my belly. Although his touch is achingly familiar, the intensity of his expression, the edge of lingering anger, creates a flare of both apprehension and excitement in me. My heart pounds, my blood heating.

Curving his hand around the back of my neck, he pulls me forward, his mouth locking against mine. His kiss is hard and insistent. He smells like night, like the wind. He thrusts his tongue past my lips, a deep invasion that incites a spear of lust.

I grasp his arms, urging him closer, wanting his weight on top of me. He straddles my hips, his erection pressing against my belly.

"Did he get this close to you?" His question is an accusation.

I should say no. *No.* The word screams inside my head.

Instead, I look up at him and whisper, "What would you do if he did?"

A firestorm of anger flares behind his eyes. I suck in a breath as a riotous combination of arousal and anxiety rises in me. Dean lowers his face so close to mine I can feel his breath on my cheek.

"I'd fucking kill him," he mutters.

He yanks my nightgown up and presses his hand between my legs, one finger probing beneath the elastic of my panties into the cleft of my sex. I gasp, bucking my hips upward, seeking his entry.

He whispers something low against my mouth, then captures my lower lip between his teeth and bites. A twinge of pain spurs my arousal higher.

I pull away from him and stare into his eyes. "You never thought I could be attracted to another man, did you?"

"Goddammit, Liv."

"You thought I'd always be the good girl who couldn't possibly—"

His lips bruise mine with the ferocity of a kiss, forcing me open, pressing me down. I dig my fingers into his arms and wrench my mouth from his. Our breath mingles hot and heavy between us. My blood throbs. His eyes are almost black. Something feral flares in his expression, a sense of possession I've never seen before.

You are mine, Olivia. Mine.

He doesn't have to say it. Even through the storm of emotions, the heat swamping us both, I still know the truth.

Yes. Yours. Always.

His mouth crashes against mine again, and I open for him, melting, gasping under the delicious onslaught. He grabs a fistful of my hair and angles my head to deepen the kiss. My hands find his jeans—unfastened, but still on—and I shove at the waistband, writhing beneath the increasing pressure of his fingers between my legs.

"Dean. Take them off."

He shifts to rid himself of his jeans and boxers, and then he moves naked over me, all hot, tense muscles and damp skin. He pushes my nightgown up past my waist, rips the panties off my legs, and spreads my thighs. His first hard thrust jars my entire body, filling me with sweet, aching pressure. I close my thighs around his hips and scrape his back with my fingernails.

Wild urgency spirals through me. Sweat pools on my throat, drops rolling down between my breasts. Dean pauses for a second to tug my nightgown over my head, and then he groans low in his throat at the sight of my bare breasts.

That reaction alone almost makes me come, but I don't want it to be over, not yet, don't want this exquisite pounding rhythm to end.

I don't want him to let me go.

I close my eyes and wrap my arms around his back, moan as he pushes deeper, faster. He grips my hair again and tugs hard enough to make me open my eyes on a gasp.

"Look at me." His order is low, rigid.

I stare at him, his face glistening with sweat, the burn of his eyes. I'm aroused by his anger, by his unyielding control.

It's both an apology and a punishment, this frantic,

desperate fucking. My breasts jostle against him, his chest hairs abrading my nipples. Tension builds tight and fast, the pressure almost unbearable.

I thrust up against him, sink my teeth into his shoulder, taste the salt of his skin. Tears spill from the corners of my eyes.

He shoves his hands beneath me, grips my bottom to haul me closer. His breath is harsh, hot against my throat, his groans vibrating into my blood.

I open my mouth to draw in a lungful of air. My veins sear with heat. Pleas fall from my lips in an endless stream.

"Dean... oh, God... harder, please... make me come... please, *please*..."

I writhe beneath him, shifting and pushing and rubbing. Aching. He eases back far enough to edge a hand between us and splays his fingers over my clit. One touch and I fly apart with a broken cry, convulsing around his hardness, digging my fingers into his shoulders.

As shudders rack my body, he thrusts deep again and comes inside me. My name wrenches from his throat on a growl of pleasure.

He collapses on top of me, his weight delicious against my sweaty skin, his chest heaving. I press my face against his shoulder, my cheeks still wet with tears. He puts his hand on my neck and turns my head for another hard, possessive kiss.

I'm trembling, gasping. He eases to the side, slides a hand down to my sex again and rubs, as if he knows I'm not finished, that I need more. His fingers are so adept, so familiar, that I come again within seconds, sobbing his name, clutching at him.

He wraps one arm tight around me, stroking the sensations from me until I start to calm. My heart slows, the pulsing ebbs.

We're silent for several long minutes. Breathing. I can't look at him. I'm sore everywhere, inside and out.

He moves away from me, and then we're no longer touching.

"Christ, Liv," he whispers. "What the hell are we doing to each other?"

I don't know. I don't know. I don't know.

I press my hands against my eyes to try and stem the tears that will not stop. After a few minutes, he gets off the bed and goes into the bathroom.

I lower my hands and stare at the ceiling through blurry eyes. Moonlight eases past the curtains, painting the ceiling with a broken pattern.

We can't do this anymore. Can't keep hurting each other. Our marriage has always been an island, a safe place where sea-dragons and monstrous creatures can't reach us. Now we're letting them in, gnashing teeth and all, and we are failing to protect each other.

I wipe my eyes, climb out of bed, and dress in jeans and a sweatshirt. The sound of the shower comes from the bathroom.

Trying not to think, not to feel anything, I take a duffle bag from the back of the closet and throw in a few changes of clothes and underwear. I open the bathroom door, refusing to look toward the shower where I know I'll see Dean's body outlined against the fogged glass. I toss a few other toiletries into the duffle and hurry to the kitchen.

Halfway out the door, I remember that my car is very low

on gas. The shower is still running when I toss my key-ring on the counter, grab Dean's car keys, and leave our apartment.

Thank God there is a light on in Kelsey's house. I tried to call her on my cell phone first, but her machine picked up. I didn't think I could explain without bursting into tears again, so I just drove over. I grab my bag and head up the steps to her tidy bungalow nestled on a quiet street called Mousehole Lane.

Shivering, I ring the bell and wait. She pulls open the door.

"Liv? What are you doing here?"

"Sorry, Kels, I tried to call." Part of me notices that she's wearing some expensive silk pants and a flowy tunic kind of thing.

She looks at my duffle bag and frowns. I don't have to say anything else. At least, not now. She knows.

"Get in here." She gestures me into the foyer.

I drop my bag on the floor and unbutton my coat, then stop. I sniff. "Is that *incense*?"

To my shock—and unexpected but welcome amusement—Kelsey actually flushes a little. I peer around her shoulder at the living room, where the lights are low and several sticks of incense glow in a special holder. Classical music drifts from the speakers. Then I see a guy sitting on the sofa with a glass of wine in his hand.

I duck back into the foyer and whisper, "Oh shit, Kelsey, I'm sorry. You're on a date."

She waves her hand in dismissal. "Never mind. He's been after me for months. He can wait a little longer."

"I'm not going to ruin your evening." I reach for the door handle, but she snaps the lock shut and gives me a stern look.

"No, you are not," she replies, then grabs my arm and marches me into the kitchen. "But you are going to tell me what the hell happened. Wait here."

She shoves me onto a barstool at the counter and disappears into the living room. The front door closes. When she returns, she's carrying two glasses of wine.

"What about your date?" I ask.

"I sent him home. I'll deal with him later." She deposits a glass of wine in front of me. "Now talk."

I can't talk because the tears are choking my throat again. I swallow some wine. "You first. Who is he? Why didn't you tell me you had a date tonight?"

"His name is Adam, he's an engineer at SciTech, and we met when I went over to talk to them about a new computer modeling program. He's totally not my type, but like I said, the guy's persistent so finally I agreed to give him a chance. And he did bring good wine."

She takes a sip and nods in approval.

"Why is he not your type?" I ask.

"Oh, you know." She waves a hand like she's swatting at a fly. "Conservative, conventional. But this is not about—"

She stops as a loud banging rattles the front door.

"And here comes the Incredible Hunk." Kelsey rolls her eyes and indicates I should stay seated as she slides off the stool. "He sounds pissed."

Although I feel like a coward for letting her contend with

Dean alone, I know she can handle him better than I can right now. His angry voice comes through the door, which I assume Kelsey has wisely not opened with the expectation that he would crash through.

My cell phone rings. I don't answer it. The front door bangs again, hard enough to shake the hinges. I gather a breath and go to the foyer, where Kelsey is standing with one hand on the doorknob and the other on her hip.

"Let him in, Kelsey, or your neighbors are going to call the police."

"I'm not letting him in." She holds out her hand. "Give me your cell."

I pull my phone from my pocket and give it to her. She dials a number and waits, tapping her foot impatiently. The thumping on the door stops.

"Dean, shut the fuck up, okay?" Kelsey snaps into the phone. "I'm not letting you in. Liv is here, she's safe, and you both need to cool down before you talk. Got it? So quit banging on my goddamn door like you're storming a castle. Go home, take a cold shower, have a drink, and call Liv tomorrow."

I can hear Dean's angry voice through the phone, but can't make out what he's saying.

Kelsey gives a long-suffering sigh. "Dean, I'm not unlocking the door. Liv doesn't want to talk to you right now. And if you don't leave her alone, I'll call the cops. Don't think I won't. How do you think the university will react when they hear that distinguished Professor West was arrested for acting like an ass?"

He's still yelling at her, but Kelsey ends the call and hands me the phone. "Keep it off. Let him yell at voicemail."

She puts a hand on my shoulder and steers me back to the kitchen. We both wait a few minutes, but there's no more noise. Kelsey pushes my wineglass back in front of me as we sit down at the counter again.

"God, now we all need a drink," she mutters, downing half her wine in one swallow. "How'd he know you were here?"

"Probably an educated guess when he realized I'd taken his car."

"Okay. So talk to me, Liv." Kelsey stares at me from behind her glasses, as if knowing I have no defense against her penetrating blue gaze.

Which I absolutely do not.

With a groan, I cross my arms on the counter and thunk my head against them. "Oh, Kelsey, I fucked things up bad."

Admitting it to her makes my tears swell like a tidal wave. All the pain and anger of the past few weeks boils up inside me. I start sobbing so hard that I can't hear what Kelsey is saying, but she stays beside me, stroking my back and letting me cry.

When the tears finally ease a little, I lift my head and swipe at my eyes.

Kelsey hands me a tissue. "Don't get snot on my counter."

"Sorry." I scrub at my cheeks and blow my nose.

Kelsey props her chin on her hand. "So you kissed another man."

"Yeah. Big mistake, obviously."

"Dean said you liked it."

I look at her. "He told you that?"

"You're surprised? You told *him* that, apparently."

I groan and bury my face in my hands. "You know how bad things were, Kelsey. I was… I don't know. The whole thing was so screwed up, and then with the pregnancy scare… Dean's the only one I ever wanted, and then we had this big fight… and Tyler was just *there*. He was nice and he liked me and it was so simple compared to the mess going on with Dean."

I gulp down another wave of sobs.

"He's cute, too," Kelsey says.

"What?"

"Tyler. The chef." Kelsey takes another sip of wine. "Not all hunky and masculine like Dean, but adorable. Can't say I blame you for wanting to kiss him."

"Kelsey, you're not helping."

"I'm not trying to. I'm telling you the truth." She sets her glass down and looks at me. "So you told Dean, and he's still pissed."

I nod and rub my finger over a line in the granite countertop. I can't tell Kelsey anything else. Not about how Dean is the only person who has made me feel safe, protected, and unconditionally loved… until now.

I can't tell her that our recent troubles have tilted my entire world off its axis. I can't tell her that for the past four months, I've been terrified. That I haven't been so scared in years.

"Why did you leave him?" Kelsey asks. "What did he say?"

"He won't let it go," I admit. "You saw how he acted at the art fair, like he was ready to beat Tyler into the floor. He's still so mad. And I don't know what to do to make it go away."

"So he's not so much upset about the actual kiss as the fact that you liked it," Kelsey says. "Well, he's a guy. You're his woman. I can see how that'd be a hard blow to his ego. I'm sure he's entirely forgotten that he's capable of being attracted to other women."

"I don't think he's forgotten that. He just wouldn't act on it."

Kelsey leans her head on her hand and narrows her gaze. "Look, Liv, you made a mistake. You admitted it. You're sorry. You've tried to make it right. And frankly, I think you've done all you can."

"You do?"

"Yeah. The ball's in his court." She pours more wine into her glass. "Dean is older and more experienced than you. A *lot* more experienced. He's known other women. He knows you. He just hasn't grasped yet that you needed to feel something for another guy to realize just how much you love *him*."

I stare at the light reflecting off the wineglass.

"I don't think he'll ever understand that," I say. "I barely understand it myself."

"Look. Dean's had a lot of girlfriends. A lot of experience with women. He's been loved, he's loved them. He's been hurt, he's hurt them. He had all the highs and lows before he met you. So since meeting you, he's never looked back. He never had to. He knew you were the one for him, and that was it."

Kelsey swivels around to face me.

"You, on the other hand," she says, "were totally thrown off by Dean's reluctance about a baby."

Not to mention his revelation about his ex-wife. I don't know if he would ever tell Kelsey about that. I certainly won't.

"It's no surprise you started doubting both Dean and your marriage," she continues. "It's no surprise you started wondering what it might have been like with another man."

"I didn't wonder..." My heart plummets. "Oh, hell."

Kelsey's mouth curves in triumph. "It's okay, Liv. Dean's

never had to wonder about other women because he went through it all before he met you. You didn't. And this whole recent fuck-up just meant you had to figure out *now* what Dean already knows."

"God, Kelsey." I rest my head in my hands. "Why aren't you a psychologist?"

"Because my friends are the only people I give a damn about."

She collects our glasses and heads to the sink. I'm quiet for a minute as I try to process everything she's said.

"Will you please explain all that to Dean?" I ask.

"Hah." Kelsey rolls her eyes again. "He's a man. He'll give me a blank stare, tell me I'm full of shit, then go off to pummel a punching bag."

"So what am I supposed to do?"

She squeezes my shoulder. "Don't worry. He'll get it sooner or later."

I'm not so sure of that. Fatigue settles hard in my bones.

"Is it okay if I stay here awhile?" I ask. "Just a day or... a year or so."

She smiles. "You know you can stay as long as you need to. I even have a quilt you can use."

She brushes her hand over my very tangled hair. "It'll be okay, Liv. And you know I love Dean, but this mess is his fault too. You've done what you can, and if your husband doesn't get his shit together fast, I'm coming down on him like an anvil."

❦

The following day there's one message on my phone from Dean. His voice is tense. *"Liv, this is between us, not Kelsey. You tell me when you want to talk."*

I don't call him back right away because I don't yet know what to say, but I listen to the message three times. Dean probably doesn't even realize how those two sentences encompass so much.

Everything we've ever been through has only been between us. And once again, Dean is giving *me* the choice of determining what happens next.

After having breakfast with Kelsey, who thankfully does not mention Dean, I head to the bookstore for the Sunday morning shift. Allie is busy planning a kids' holiday and cookie-decorating party.

"I thought we could also have some craft stations where kids can make menorahs and Christmas ornaments and stuff," she says as she peers at the computer. "Then we'll have story-time, of course, and I'll put up a display of holiday books. Think you can advertise this at the Historical Museum? Like if you get some school tour groups?"

"Sure. I'll print out flyers and bring them with me tomorrow."

Allie glances at me as I straighten the boxed calendars in front of the counter. "You okay?"

"Fine. Why?"

"You look kind of tired."

"Oh, just holiday stress or whatever." I wave my hand dismissively.

"Sure that's all it is?" Her eyes narrow behind her purple-framed glasses.

"Yeah." Her scrutiny makes me uneasy. "Why?"

"I was wondering if you're… you know." Her voice lowers to a loud whisper. "Preggers."

Shock bolts through me so fast I grab the edge of the counter to steady myself. "What?"

"Well, remember we were talking about having kids?" Allie says. "And I've seen you looking at the pregnancy books. I figured you and Professor Hottie were trying to get pregnant." She tosses me a grin. "God knows I'd be trying three times a day if he were involved."

There's a lump in my throat. I can't even respond. Dean and I haven't talked about the idea of a baby for weeks. The topic has disappeared into the mess of everything else.

"No," I finally manage. "I'm not pregnant."

"Oh." Allie stares at me. "Oh shit, Liv, did I put my foot in it? You're not having fertility issues, are you? Because my sister had to take these shots for a while, but you know, now she has *three* kids and they drive her crazy but they're all adorable and perfect and she and her husband are happier than ever."

I laugh, even as tears sting my eyes suddenly. I go around the counter and give Allie a big hug, which she returns with a hint of puzzlement.

"What's this for?" she asks.

"I don't know. I'm just really glad you're my friend."

She smiles, pleased. "Thanks. You're pretty great too. Now get back to work before I ask you to the prom."

"Hey, speaking of dating, how's it going with Brent?" I ask.

"Really well," Allie says. "He even invited me to visit his parents on Christmas Day. They live down in Rainwood, so we're going to see my dad in the morning and Brent's parents in the afternoon."

"Where does your dad live?"

"Here in town. He's got a place on the other side of the lake. He's a nutjob but I love him. He's the one who convinced me to open a bookstore. He's all about following your bliss and voodoo stuff like that."

"What would you have done if you hadn't opened the bookstore?" I ask.

"I dunno. I was an art major in college. Again not because it was the practical thing to do, but because my dad convinced me I should do what I wanted to do."

"I didn't know you were an artist."

"I'm not. Catastrophic failures at several art shows convinced me of that." She gives me a rueful look. "Hence the bookstore. Which now isn't doing so great either."

"You'll think of a way to turn things around," I say. "You just need a different angle."

Allie shrugs and turns back to the computer. "Yeah, well, if you fall seven times, you get up eight, right?"

Right.

I head out around noon and walk to where I parked Dean's car at the curb. Sunlight glints off the shallow piles of snow lining Emerald Street, and the sky arches clear and blue overhead. As I wait for the engine to warm up, I finally work up the courage to call him.

"What do you want me to do, Liv?" he asks.

My heart pounds. "I think we should go to counseling again."

His breath escapes on a hiss, but he says, "Fine."

I blink. "Fine?"

"Yeah, I'll go with you, if that's what it takes."

The tension in my shoulders eases. I know Dean hates counseling, finds it uncomfortable and awkward. He doesn't like the personal questions, the expectation that he's supposed to rehash everything about his life—stuff he's long done with. But he's gone before for my sake, and the fact that he just agreed now gives me a surge of hope.

"Okay," I say. "I'll call Dr. Anderson and ask if she can refer me to someone in the area."

"Okay." He pauses. "I want to see you."

"I want to see you too, but I think we both need a few days apart."

The air on the other end of the phone vibrates with irritation. "What did Kelsey say to you?"

"What do you mean?"

"Did she tell you not to see me?"

"Kelsey doesn't tell me what to do, Dean. I can make my own decisions about us."

"I know she told you something. What was it?"

His irritation bites at my own nerves. "We figured out that between this mess about a baby and your revelation about an ex-wife, it's no surprise I wondered what things would be like with another man."

His curse is so sharp that my stomach roils.

"You told her about Helen?" he snaps.

"Of course not." I know I should stop, that this is unfair, that this will only hurt us more, but I'm suddenly flooded with images of Dean and another woman.

"No one ever talks about Helen, do they?" I ask acidly. "Not even you."

"Goddammit, Liv."

I take a breath and try to fight the churning emotions. I can't stop the painful thoughts still whipping around my mind like a tornado.

I gave you everything I am. Why couldn't you do the same for me?

"I'll call you later this week." It's all I can manage to say before ending the call. I shove my phone into my satchel and head back to Kelsey's house.

She comes home shortly before dinner after having stopped in at her office, ranting about some grad student who is doing a poor job with his computer modeling.

She changes into a caftan, then pours herself a glass of wine. After she's done fixing a plate of chips and salsa, she sits at the counter and gives me one of her laser-beam stares.

"You talk to Professor Marvel today?" she asks.

"Yeah. We agreed not to see each other for a few days."

She barks out a laugh. "You mean you told him you didn't want to see him for a few days and he got all hot under the collar again."

I groan and press my fingers against my temples. She pats my shoulder.

"He's a guy, Liv," she reminds me. "One who is very accustomed to getting what he wants."

I know that all too well. I reach over to help myself to one of her chips.

"Hey, Kelsey?"

"Yeah?"

"Did you ever do anything with Dean?"

She glances at me. "Would it bug you if I did?"

I've never thought about it before, but I don't have to. I don't like to think about Dean with his many former women—and I really hate even the idea of his ex-wife—but Kelsey is different.

She's my best friend too, and she's gold throughout even if she can flatten you with her stare alone. If I weren't around, I'd want Dean to be with her.

"No," I say. "I'm just curious."

"No." Kelsey piles a chip with salsa and pops it into her mouth. "Dean and I have never done anything."

"Not even in college?" I ask.

"I was into girls in college."

This is news to me. "Really?"

"Yeah. Call it my experimental phase. Lasted two years."

"So what… uh, what made you go back to guys?"

"Oh, a couple of studs my senior year, then a long-term boyfriend in grad school." Kelsey flips her hair away from her face and reaches for her wineglass. "Great guy, smart as hell. Great sex too. Made me realize I preferred hard muscles and harder dicks."

"What happened to him?"

"He wanted to get married, which obviously wasn't my thing. Plus I got a job offer and we went our separate ways."

She shakes her head. "Nah, Liv. Dean's one helluva package, but we'd never screw up our friendship. And we'd be lousy together anyway. Always snarking at each other and fighting like dogs over who gets to be on top."

It's true Dean and I haven't had that problem before now. We just took turns.

I reach for another chip, then drop it. I sigh and climb off the barstool.

"Hey." Kelsey nudges me with her elbow. A crease forms between her eyebrows. "You guys will get through this."

Two weeks ago, I would have agreed. Now I no longer know what to believe.

CHAPTER TWENTY-FOUR

Dean

December 7

Five days without Liv pass like a black cloud. Kelsey called once to tell me Liv was fine, but that I needed to "get my shit together and fast." I hung up on her.

I fucking hate the empty apartment. I hate seeing all the cheery Christmas decorations that remind me of Liv. I work late, go home and crash, then leave again at six. I've gotten through the days on mindless autopilot—running, coffee, lectures and seminars, grant proposals, workouts.

I don't think about how I've managed to fuck everything up. I don't think about the fact that Liv hasn't told me when she'll come home. *If* she'll come home.

After I'm done with classes and meetings, I head to the gym and take out my frustration on the heavy bag. On day six of Liv being gone, I'm punching the bag so hard my knuckles and arms ache. Within minutes, I've worked up a sweat.

"Whoa, slugger." Kelsey stops beside me in a tank top and workout pants, a towel thrown over her shoulder.

"Get out of my way." I drive my fist into the bag.

"Nope. We need to talk."

I slam the bag harder. "I don't want to talk."

"Too bad."

Jab, cross, jab, cross.

"Dean."

I take a breath and step back. "Not in the mood, Kelsey."

"You never will be if you keep this up." She moves in front of the bag to stop me from throwing another punch at it. "Come on. Let's hit the treadmill."

"I hate the treadmill."

"I know, but it's either that or I'll drag you out for coffee and you'll have to look at me while I interrogate you. Which is the worse evil?"

The woman has a point.

I grab her towel and swipe my face, then head to the row of treadmills by the window.

"Liv said it was a mistake," Kelsey says as she starts the treadmill beside mine.

"Really? Imagine that."

"She's upset that you're not letting it go."

"You think I fucking can?" I hit the button to make the treadmill go faster. "Would you be able to?"

"She's not the only one at fault, Dean."

"Oh, for Christ's sake…" I shut the treadmill off, not wanting to hear what I already know.

I stalk toward the men's locker room. She follows.

"Back off, Kelsey."

"No."

I shove the door open. She bangs through it after me. A few half-dressed men by their lockers stare at her. One whistles.

"Hey, lady, this is the men's locker room," one of them snaps.

"Shut up, asshole. You've got nothing I haven't seen." Kelsey stares him up and down. "And I mean nothing."

The others laugh. I go to my locker around the corner, where at least there's no one else around. Kelsey follows. She's like a freaking parasite.

I spin the combination on my locker and wrench it open. "My marriage isn't your business."

"You and Liv are my business because you're my best friends." Kelsey steps around to face me. Her mouth is set, her eyes hard with determination. "I know how much she loves you. She wouldn't have started thinking about a baby otherwise. And if you keep punishing her for one mistake, you're not only going to make her miserable, you might wreck your whole marriage."

"You think I don't know that?" Anger flares through me, hot and fast. I slam a fist against the locker. "You think I don't want to forget it, to pretend it never happened? I need a god-damn steak knife to carve the image out of my head. That bastard kissed my wife and she… she fucking *liked* it."

I'm breathing hard. My heart pumps, my blood burns. Kelsey stares at me, her eyes unblinking behind her glasses.

Before I can react, she grabs the front of my sweaty T-shirt and pushes me back against the locker. Then she presses her mouth hard against mine.

What the—

Her lips pry mine open and her tongue pushes inside. She digs her fingers into my shoulders. She slides her body against mine.

Soft. She's soft. Thin and wiry, but soft with nice breasts… and Jesus, her nipples are hard and poking against my chest. My cock twitches, swells. She presses closer. She runs her hands across my abdomen, down to my waist, then around to grip my ass.

Before I can think, I grab her hips and haul her toward me. A moan escapes her throat. I clasp the back of her neck, angle her head to a better position, and kiss her deep.

She tastes sweet, like apples and sugar. My blood simmers. Her tongue sweeps across my teeth, her breath hot.

I put my other hand on the small of her back and shove my hips against her, forcing her to feel the full length of my erection. She started it, so now she'll get all of it.

She's not shocked. I should have known she wouldn't be. Instead she grinds against me and licks my lips and splays her legs over mine. If we weren't in a men's locker room, I wouldn't be surprised if she started stripping.

I wouldn't be surprised if I let her.

Kelsey thrusts her hands into my hair, then pulls her mouth away from mine and steps back.

We stare at each other, chests heaving. She looks as stunned as I feel. She swipes a hand across her lips.

"So, uh… sorry," she mutters.

"What the hell was that?" My head is spinning. I stare at her mouth, reddened from the pressure of mine.

Kelsey pulls in a breath. "Was it good?"

"What?"

"Was that a good kiss?"

"You know it was, but what—"

"Do you get it, Dean?" Kelsey asks. "You can *like* kissing another person. It's normal. Hell, it's human. Just because you're married doesn't mean you shut off a natural, biological reaction."

"You kissed me to make a point?"

"I made it, didn't I?" She steps forward and puts her hand on my chest. Something softens in her sharp eyes. "Look, Dean. Liv may have thought a ten-second kiss was nice, but she loves the hell out of you. That's why she told you, because she doesn't want to have any secrets from you. She loves you that much, enough to confess a huge mistake. But you keep punishing her for it, and you're going to drive her away. Do you get it?"

Her speech ricochets through my brain. *She loves you that much… you're going to drive her away…*

If six days without Liv makes me feel like this, I can't imagine what—

"Yeah." I force my fists to unclench. "I get it."

"So she kissed another guy." A slight smile curves Kelsey's lips. "You kissed another woman. Call it even."

"Am I supposed to tell her about this?"

"I'll talk to her." Kelsey turns and starts to leave. Then she stops and looks back at me. "For the record, Dean, I didn't kiss you just to make a point."

"Then why?"

"I always suspected it'd be good with you," she replies. "Thanks for proving me right."

Then with a wink, she strides through the locker room and out the door.

Fuck.

Women make me crazy.

I grab a clean shirt and jeans from my locker and head for the shower.

It's snowing when I leave the gym. I toss my duffle in the trunk of Liv's car and climb into the driver's seat. I turn on the ignition, then reach down for the lever to push the seat back again. My fingers brush against some cloth.

I pick up whatever it is and pull it out from under the seat. A crumpled shirt? I unfold it. For a second, I can't process what I'm looking at. I shake out the material. A surge of red-hot anger floods me.

It's a white chef's jacket. Hidden under the seat of my wife's car.

CHAPTER TWENTY-FIVE

OLIVIA

I'm fixing myself a plate of spaghetti when a loud knock comes at the door. I glance at the clock. Six p.m. Kelsey isn't home yet, though she told me this morning she was going to the gym and then to run some errands after work.

I wipe my hands on a towel and go into the foyer. My heart thumps when I peer through the peephole and see Dean standing on the doorstep.

"Let me in, Olivia." He sounds as if he's trying to control his tone of voice.

Better to deal with this alone than when Kelsey is here. I unlock the deadbolt and open the door. Nervousness floods me at the sight of him—the scowl on his face, the flop of hair over his forehead, the corded muscles of his neck.

What...

"Is Kelsey here?" he asks.

"No."

"Good." He pushes past me, slamming the door behind him before stalking into the living room. The controlled anger radiating from him unnerves me. I know he's mad, but the past few days should have given him time to calm down.

"Dean?"

He turns and tosses a bundle of white material at me. I hadn't even realized it was clenched in his fist. I catch it.

My heart plummets. The word *Julienne* embroidered on the front sears into me, the lingering smells of dill and chocolate clogging my throat. I drop the chef's jacket at my feet.

"What the fuck, Liv?" Dean spreads his hands, his eyes flashing. "What was that doing in your car? Under the seat?"

My stomach pitches, as if I'm standing on the edge of a huge, black abyss. As if I'm about to fall, knowing the descent will be endless.

"What haven't you told me?" His voice is tight enough to break.

"I... I went to..."

"Is that *his*?" he snaps.

"No. I mean, yes, but... God, Dean." I cover my face with my hands, unable to look at him. I know I can give him nothing but the truth. "I was... I was in Forest Grove one afternoon, picking up some signs for the museum, and I stopped at his restaurant. He showed me around the kitchen, and then he gave me a cooking lesson."

I feel like I've just said *"... and then he gave me an orgasm."*

I force myself to lower my hands. Dean hasn't moved, his gaze dark, his chest heaving with the force of his contained anger.

Guilt splits my heart in half.

"It was nothing," I say, but the words come out weak, as if I'm trying to convince myself as much as him. "I'm sorry."

He just stares at me, his hands on his hips. "I remember that day."

"What?"

"When you came back from Forest Grove. You got into the shower with me. Tasted like chocolate. Then you wanted me to fuck you rough."

Heat and embarrassment fill my throat. "Dean..."

"What, Liv? Am I wrong?"

I shake my head. He's not wrong. That is exactly what happened. Exactly what I'd wanted.

"You know..." I swallow hard. "You know you're the only person I'd ever ask for anything like that."

"I knew that once. Before you spent the afternoon with another man, then came home and asked me to fuck you."

"For the love of God, Dean. I cooked! I didn't engage in foreplay."

His mouth compresses. "Didn't you?"

I can't even respond. He knows better than anyone that foreplay doesn't have to involve touching. He's the one who taught me that.

A sudden sense of foreboding fills me, the precipice beginning to crumble beneath my feet.

Dean is silent for a long minute. The air between us stretches thin.

"All right, Liv." He drags a hand through his hair, his breath expelling in a hard rush. "You can come home. I'll move out for a while."

I stare at him. "Wait... what?"

Some of the anger drains from him, but his jaw is tight with tension as he meets my eyes.

"Whatever I'm not giving you is fucking us up," he says. "If we're apart, maybe I can figure out what the hell it is."

My stomach rolls with queasiness.

"We're... separating?" I have to shove the word past the bile rising in my throat. Separating? *Us?* "Are you punishing me? Is that what this is about?"

"Why did you leave the other night?" he asks. "Were you punishing me for not telling you about Helen?"

Was I?

"What about counseling?" I ask.

"Would you have told a counselor about this?" He shoves the chef's jacket with his foot.

I have no idea. The self-admission makes me sick.

Dean's eyes harden. "We need to stop lying to each other before spilling our guts out to a goddamn counselor."

"Why do you think separating will help anything?" My fingernails dig into my palms.

"You said it last month. Being together is lousy right now."

"But we can't work anything out if we're not together," I say. "I'm not... I won't come home unless you're there."

Dean looks at me, his expression unreadable. Then he closes the distance between us. The familiar scent of him, soap and maleness and winter air, floods my senses in a wave. For a second, I think he's going to touch me, but his hands stay shoved into his pockets. His eyes are shuttered.

"I don't want to punish you, Liv. But you were right to leave. We need to be apart."

I feel so brittle, so icy, that I can't even let the tears fall. I watch through black-edged vision as Dean steps back, his gaze still on me. Then he turns to leave.

The front door clicks shut with a hollow echo. I can only stand there staring at the empty space my husband's departure has left.

A torrent of memories chokes me. Before Dean, I was so alone, tight like a piece of paper crushed into a ball. With him, my entire being smoothed out, all the secrets cocooned in the pleats of my soul finally opening.

Now I can feel myself crumpling again. Shutting down.

The nausea surges. I make it to the bathroom before I throw up.

Christmas is less than two weeks away. I don't return home. I can't stand the thought of being there without Dean.

I send him an email telling him I'll stay with Kelsey and that he doesn't have to leave the apartment. He responds with a short "okay" and tells me he's had snow tires put on my car and will leave it at Kelsey's the following day.

A week passes, slow and sluggish. My heart aches. I try and ignore it by getting out as much as possible—the Historical Society is putting on holiday tours, so I help out with preparations and decorating. I volunteer at the library and have lunch with Allie a few times at Matilda's Teapot, which is planning to close for good in February.

Dean and I don't contact each other. Kelsey says she's seen him at the university gym several times, but he doesn't say much to her and declines her offers of racquetball. For once, she hasn't pushed him to tell her anything else.

She also told me about their kiss, which was one of the few things in the past two weeks that has made me laugh. I could only imagine Dean's shocked reaction.

I work every day at the Happy Booker, but don't put all my hours on my time card because I don't want Allie to think she has to pay me when I'm mostly trying to keep myself busy. During the day, interacting with people and working, I'm able to keep my emotions in check.

But lying in bed alone at night, my mind floods with thoughts and memories of Dean. Several times I find myself reaching for my cell phone, my finger poised over the speed-dial to call him. Somehow I manage to stop myself, even though I want nothing more than to hear his deep voice.

I miss him, of course. I want things to be the way they once were, when we couldn't wait to touch each other, when our kisses were so warm and easy, when he'd press his mouth to my temple and pull me into the place by his side where I fit perfectly.

I dream about us too, those hot, sexy dreams I used to have after I'd first met him. Except this time I know the breathless truth of those fantasies—I know exactly how his hands feel on my breasts, the taste of his skin, the way his cock pulses heavy and smooth in my palm. I know how our bodies arch together, how his fingers dig into my hips, how his breath heats my neck and his chest rubs against mine.

I wake in the predawn hours, restless and throbbing, and press my fingers between my legs to bring myself to a sharp, hard orgasm. Just as I used to do early on, before the days when I would roll over in bed and encounter his warm, muscular body.

Then I would slide my hand over his chest and down to his half-erect cock, stroke him into full readiness before he was even fully awake. Then I'd move my leg over his thighs to straddle him and ease his shaft into me with one slow glide.

Then I would thrust up and down, arching my body, squeezing and pressing his cock, until his groan broke through the air and his hands clutched my bottom and we both spiraled over the edge in a collision of bliss.

I want him so badly I ache. And worse, I have no idea what will happen now. I don't know if he's going to call me, if I should call him, if he thinks we're done for good. I don't know how either of us plans to spend Christmas.

"You want to come with me to visit my mother for Christmas?" Kelsey asks one morning at breakfast as she peers at me over her coffee cup.

I must look awful for her to be gazing at me with such sympathy.

"No, thanks."

"She'll go all Russian Betty Crocker on you and spoil you rotten with her *blinchiki* or tea cookies or whatever," Kelsey cajoles.

I smile. "No, really, but thanks."

"What's Professor Marvel doing?"

"I don't know." I wonder if Dean will visit his parents in California, but I doubt he'd go with this mess still piled up between us. God knows he'd never explain any of it to his family.

After Kelsey heads off to work, I clean the house and do a load of laundry. I have a day off from both the museum and the bookstore, which means hours of blankness stretch out in front of me.

I drive downtown and park the car. I cast a glance at our apartment as I walk along the snow-encrusted sidewalks bordering Avalon Street. The curtains of our living room are pulled shut, no light shining behind them. The plants on the balcony are withered and frozen, ice piling over the potted soil.

I see Dean as he's entering a coffeehouse on the corner. My heart jolts at the sight of his tall, familiar figure clad in a black peacoat, his hair ruffled by the cold wind, a scarf winding around his throat.

I watch him through the window as he approaches the counter to order a coffee, then walks to a table where a young, pretty redhead is waiting.

My chest tightens as I recognize his graduate student, Jessica. She smiles at him in greeting and gestures to a chair, and they sit there conversing for a few minutes.

Jealousy surges through me. *He's mine*, I think, even as the deepest corner of my soul—the one that knows, even now, the truth of my husband—remembers that Dean would never betray me.

My trust is confirmed when two young men and another woman approach Dean, balancing coffees as they unload their backpacks and laptops onto the table. Soon they're all immersed in a discussion, exchanging books and papers and scribbling notes into their notebooks.

Part of me wants Dean to look up and see me standing here. I imagine this great, romantic movie moment when our eyes meet and he pushes his chair back and runs out to haul me into his arms.

But he doesn't. He's busy talking with his students about their essays and research. He leans forward, listens, looks each person in the eye when he's speaking. I can almost hear the steady, measured cadence of his voice, underscored by confidence and authority. Even outside of class, he'll take the time to meet with a group of students and provide whatever help they need. His dedication is boundless.

Just one of the many reasons I will always be in love with him.

The week before Christmas, I arrive at the Epicurean cooking class half an hour before the last class starts. Tyler Wilkes is at his station, getting everything ready for tonight's demonstration. I watch him for a moment, noticing the confidence of his movements, the way he organizes his knives and pans with purpose. He makes it all seem so easy.

"What's on the menu, Chef?" I ask.

His head jerks up at the sound of my voice. "Liv!"

"Hi, Tyler."

He approaches, then stops and glances behind me. "Uh, is your..."

"Dean didn't come with me. He sends his regards, though."

"Oh." He looks perplexed.

I almost smile. "I'm kidding. He won't bully you again, but... well, he's not going to mail you a Christmas card either."

"Understood." Tyler gives me an abashed grin and clears his throat. "So, hey, I never had a chance to ask you how your hand is. Charlotte's been emailing us all with updates, so I knew you were okay but... well, I wish I could have contacted you myself."

"No. I'm glad you didn't." *Really* glad. "I'll be fine. The doctor is a little concerned about nerve damage, but I guess that can heal in a few months."

"Good. I was... I was pretty worried. I'm glad you're okay."

I reach into my satchel and remove the clean, folded chef's jacket. "I wanted to return this."

"Uh, thanks." He scratches his ear. "So what happened with the class? I'm sorry you couldn't finish the semester."

"I talked to Natalie, and she offered me a prorated refund," I explain. "Or she said I can put the money toward next semester's class."

"What are you going to do?"

"I don't know yet."

Tyler looks at the floor. "Did she tell you I'm not teaching the class next semester?"

"She did."

"The instructor is a great chef," Tyler says. "Lila Hampton. She owns two restaurants in Rainwood and one in Chicago. She's a four-star chef. You'd learn a lot from her." He pauses, then adds, "I wish you'd take the class again, Liv."

"You do? Why?"

"You just… I don't know. You seem to have changed so much since that first day. Kind of… kind of blossomed, you know?" He flushes. "And even though I… well, I guess it's obvious I'm attracted to you, but even if I wasn't, I'd be impressed with how you've improved. You've gained confidence. You should have seen the way your face lit up when you made the perfect soufflé."

That *was* a damn good feeling.

"You should take the class again, Liv," Tyler says. "Not for anyone else. For you."

"I'll think about it," I promise. "And if everything you said is true, then it's also because of you. You're a great teacher. I'm glad to have known you."

He smiles faintly. "That sounds… final."

"It is. I came to thank you, Tyler." The tension around my heart loosens a little. "And to say good-bye."

Tyler nods, rubbing one finger against the counter. "I wish…"

Before he can say more, I step forward and take his hand in mine. "Thank you. I wish you nothing but the best."

"You too, Liv."

Our hands tighten for an instant, and then we both let go. I leave the classroom and head through the kitchen store toward the parking lot. Racks of stainless steel pots and pans gleam around me, stacks of white dishes, shiny expensive blenders and mixers.

My breath is easier now, knowing this closure is final. That Tyler Wilkes is in my past.

I stop before a display of baking equipment and pick up a large porcelain dish with fluted edges.

"Can I help you, ma'am?" A salesgirl looks at me expectantly from behind the register.

"Yes," I say. "I'll take this, please."

I walk to the counter and hand her the soufflé dish.

CHAPTER TWENTY-SIX

DECEMBER 22

"These are all returns." Allie blows a curl of hair off her forehead as she dumps another box beside the front counter. "The UPS guy will pick them up tomorrow."

"Hey, have you thought about adding a section for used books?" I suggest. "That might help draw in customers."

"Maybe." Allie puts her hands on her hips as she studies the dwindling number of books on the shelves. "Or I was thinking of expanding the toy section to bring in more kids. Except there's that huge toy store over on the other side of town that I probably can't compete with. Definitely have to come up with something, though."

She heads back to the office while I mull over a few other ideas for her—selling local artwork, adding a café section, working out some programs in conjunction with the library. I do some Internet searches to find out about what other bookstores are doing to improve business.

As usual whenever I'm on the Internet these days, I check my email to see if there's a message from Dean. As usual, there isn't. We haven't even acknowledged that Christmas is just a few days away.

The bell over the door rings. I glance up as a handsome young man with curly, light brown hair enters.

"Welcome to the Happy Booker," I say. "Can I help you?"

"Hi there. Is Allie around? Are you Liv?"

"Oh, you must be Brent. Nice to finally meet you." I give him a quick once-over. "Hold on, I'll get Allie for you. Is she expecting you?"

"Nope. I just got off work and thought I'd see if she wanted to grab a late dinner."

I go to the back office where Allie is working at the computer.

"Brent's here," I whisper. "And he's cute. I approve."

She grins. "Good. How do I look? Do I need lipstick?"

"You're gorgeous. Just get that smudge of ink off your cheek." I grab a few tissues and hand them to her. She does a quick primping before we return to the front counter where Brent is leafing through a car magazine.

"Hey, Allie." He smiles at her, his eyes lighting up with an affection that makes her glow.

It's nice to see. Makes me happy for them.

"Can you take an hour or so for dinner?" Brent asks.

"No, sorry." Allie looks disappointed. "We're open until midnight."

"Go ahead." I glance at the clock, which reads five past eight. Even with the bookstore's extended hours, we haven't managed to attract many last-minute Christmas shoppers.

"The next movie doesn't get out until ten-thirty and the play down the street won't be over until at least eleven," I tell Allie. "Plus we've been slow all evening. I can hold down the fort for an hour or so."

"I don't know, Liv. I hate leaving you alone."

"I'll be fine. We've only had six customers all evening. If we get a crowd, it'll be after the movie lets out."

She's wavering, her gaze going from me to Brent. "Are you sure?"

"Of course I'm sure." I grab her bag from beneath the counter and wave them both toward the door. "Just bring me back some sort of dessert. Chocolate."

"Okay. We won't be long."

Brent beams at me as he holds open the front door for Allie. Their anticipation and happiness reminds me of those early days when I'd get all fluttery inside the minute Dean walked in the door of Jitter Beans.

Ignoring a twinge of heartache, I straighten out the supplies on the front counter, then spend the next hour arranging the books to make the shelves look more well-stocked. I clean up the toys in the kids' section and talk with a couple of customers who come in to browse.

As I'm reshelving a few misplaced magazines, the bell over the door rings. Several male voices boom into the store. A sudden tension constricts my chest.

I move behind the counter and watch as three young men enter. College boys, by the looks of them. Two of them are big, dressed in jeans and sweatshirts beneath their jackets, and the third is tall and skinny with a mop of shaggy blond hair.

I do a quick scan of the store. The other customers have all left. It's nine-fifteen. My heart is beating too fast.

"It was third and twenty-three, dude." The one wearing a King's sweatshirt pauses by the front table to flip through a pop-up book. "No way he should've got that pass off, you know?"

I'm starting to shake. Sweat trickles down my sides.

"Amazing because they're a shit team this year," the other guy responds. He stops in front of the magazine section. "If they'd get rid of Samuels, they might have a shot. Oh, hey, check this out. Fantasy football depth chart."

He tosses a magazine to his friend. "Scott, you going to Chicago for the Super Bowl party next semester?"

"Yeah," the skinny guy says. "Frat's renting a bus. You?"

"Can't. Academic probation. Asshole Dennison failed my last paper."

They all snort with derision. The skinny boy wanders past the counter and shoots me a grin.

"How's it going?" he asks.

Cold freezes the blood in my veins. I force in a few breaths and consciously try to relax the stiffness in my shoulders. My spine feels like it's about to snap in two.

"Hey, look, that's Vanessa Fairfax." The King's sweatshirt guy holds up the magazine so his friend can see a photo of a sexy brunette lounging against a car. "Remember I told you I saw her at the Dax concert? She's so fucking hot."

"Speaking of hot, what happened with that girl you hooked up with last weekend?"

"Oh, man, that was awesome."

Without thinking, I grab my cell phone and speed-dial Dean's number. He answers on the first ring.

"Hello?" he says.

I can't speak past the tightness in my throat. I clench my fingers on the phone.

"Liv?"

"I'm here," I manage to whisper. The college kids are still talking, their voices and laughter growing louder and clashing with the sound of my heartbeat.

"Liv, what's wrong?" Alarm spikes the question.

"I'm..."

"Where are you?"

"B-bookstore."

"Olivia, listen to me." Dean's voice settles into a firm but reassuring tone. "Breathe. I'm on my way." There's a rustling sound on the other end. "Count of two, okay? One, two."

I inhale a breath. My vision blurs, my throat constricting. He repeats the count. I force myself to exhale.

"Hey, do you have the spring semester calendar in yet?" The King's sweatshirt guy stops in front of me and leans his elbows on the counter. His face is too close to mine.

I step back until my hips bump the other side of the counter. "No. Not yet."

"When do they come in?" he asks.

"Liv?"

"Just a... a customer," I tell Dean. A wave of dizziness hits me.

"Keep breathing. Count of five now."

"When do the calendars come in?" the sweatshirt guy repeats.

"Beginning of January."

He straightens, his gaze still on me. "You go to King's?"

"No." *God in heaven, go away.*

"Hey, dudes, look at this." The skinny guy approaches from the kids' section with a topsy-turvy puppet that changes from Little Red Riding Hood to the wolf with one flip. "Little Red has a wolf under her skirt."

Their burst of laughter scrapes my insides like nails. The panic intensifies, tilting the world into a crazy spin. My husband's voice is a steady, deep stream as he instructs me to breathe to the count of eight.

I force air into my lungs. Time has stretched to the point of breaking.

"Stay with me, Liv," Dean says in my ear. "I'm turning onto Emerald right now."

I pray the guys will be gone by the time he arrives, but the three of them move deeper into the store to lift the skirt of the Little Red Riding Hood puppet.

Dean walks in the front door, his stride long and rapid. Tension lines every muscle in his body, and concern burns in his eyes.

I drop the phone with a clatter. He rounds the corner to where I'm standing and puts a firm hand on my shoulder.

"Sit down. You're okay." He glances to the back of the store when the sound of male laughter rings out. His expression hardens, but his voice remains steady as he turns to me. "I'm here. Breathe, Liv. Count of ten."

I inhale on his count, then exhale. Again and again until

finally I'm able to take an easier breath. My dizziness lessens a bit, and the room starts to steady into balance.

Dean rummages underneath the counter and finds a bottle of water. He cracks it open and holds it to my mouth. After I manage a few sips, he nods toward my hands.

"Flex your fingers."

I stretch my fingers out and flex them a few times, the activity a distraction from the tightness in my chest and throbbing heartbeat.

The boys' voices get closer. Dean steps in front of me, blocking them from my view.

"Hey, Professor West, what're you doing here?" It's the skinny guy's voice. "I'm Scott Kenner. I took your class last semester. Cool stuff."

"Thanks." Dean's tone is short and clipped. He tilts his head to the door. "You guys heading out now?"

"Yeah, we're going to a Christmas party down by the lake."

"Good."

The guys hesitate, thrown by Dean's unfriendly demeanor, but then they mumble a goodbye and shuffle out. When the door clicks shut, Dean turns back to me.

I take another swallow of water. The panic is subsiding, like a wave receding slowly from a beach. Exhaustion takes its place, draining my muscles of strength.

Dean reaches out to brush a strand of hair away from my forehead, his fingers lingering against my skin.

"Been a while," he murmurs.

I nod and draw in another breath. I haven't had a panic attack since long before we were married. My throat aches.

"You're here alone?" Dean asks.

"Allie went out with a friend for a quick dinner." I wipe a trickle of sweat from my temple. "She'll be back any minute."

The thought of Allie and Brent returning to find me a total mess is enough to get me to my feet. I go into the bathroom to splash water on my face and brush my hair, then emerge feeling calmer and more in control.

"Triple chocolate fudge cake." Allie waves a cardboard container at me as she and Brent come through the door. "From Abernathy's just around the corner. Oh, hi, Dean."

Even with Brent there, Allie blushes when she looks at Dean. That makes me smile a little. The remnants of my panic fade, though I'm weary to the bone.

I take the sweet-smelling box, aware of Dean speaking to Allie in a low voice. She glances at me with concern.

"Go get some rest, Liv," she says. "I didn't know you have migraines."

Grateful that Dean didn't divulge the real reason for my sudden breakdown, I give Allie a weak smile. "I don't... I don't get them very often."

"I'll stay with Allie until the store closes," Brent offers.

Allie gets my satchel and coat, then ushers us out the door with instructions for me to get a good night's sleep. Although I'm exhausted, part of my brain is prickling with unease and fear.

I can't look at Dean as we head home and go up the stairs to our apartment. All I want to do is throw myself into his arms and cling to him. But I no longer know if I have the right to do that.

I shed my coat and go into the living room. Everything looks the same as it did before I left. Christmas tree, holly-covered mantel, mistletoe. The curtains are open, the town lights shining, the lake an expanse of black in the distance.

"Liv."

I turn. Dean is standing by the door, looking every inch the man I have loved for so long. Dark, rumpled hair, a thick rugby shirt, worn jeans torn at the knee. Those beautiful, gold-flecked eyes fixed on me.

Without a word, he holds out his arms.

A cry breaks loose from the dark pit in my soul. I fly across the room to him, my tears overflowing when his arms close tight around me. I press my face against his chest as sobs wrench my throat and my heart shatters with relief.

He sinks to the floor, never loosening his hold on me, and pulls me onto his lap. The low sound of his voice rumbles in my ear. Tears spill down my face in unending streams. I clutch a fistful of his shirt and cry and cry and cry until my whole body aches.

His arms tighten around me, strong as steel and warm as sunlight. My mind empties of thought, and there is only us again, my body fitting against his, his grip on me unbreakable. All the heartache and fear of the past few months pours out of me, the wrenching torrent of a broken dam, until finally my flood of tears begins to slow.

Dean presses his mouth to my forehead and strokes my tangled hair away from my face. I burrow against his chest and exhale a long, shuddering sigh. My body quakes with lingering sobs.

He shifts and folds himself more securely around me, rubbing his hand up and down my back.

I'm scraped raw, torn in half. We sit there forever. Breathing.

"Dean?"

"Hmm?"

"My foot's asleep."

His muffled chuckle brushes against my hair. We untangle ourselves, and he grasps my hands to pull me up. I work the pins and needles out of my foot before we move to the sofa, where I settle against his side, right into the place I never want to leave.

A deep, dreamless sleep pulls me under. I surrender, knowing I'm safe.

Dean is gone when I wake early the next morning. There's a note on the coffee table saying he went to the bakery. I'm still drained and tired, but the fear has eased.

I push aside the quilt that Dean must have spread over me during the night. I sit up as the front door clicks open and he steps in. Our gazes meet across the room, somewhat cautious, but no anger or uncertainty shimmers in the air.

He pauses beside me, the scent of his soap tickling my nose, and brushes his hand against my cheek. A tingle skims through me at the touch of his fingers.

"You look like you need some coffee," he remarks.

I manage a hoarse laugh. "Yes, please."

"Coming right up."

"Oh, what about Kelsey?"

"I called her last night and told her you were here. She said, and I quote, 'It's about freaking time.'"

We both smile, then Dean goes into the kitchen while I

shove to my feet and head for the shower. I stand under the hot spray for a long time, feeling as if it can wash away all the ugliness of recent weeks. I dress in loose pants and a soft fleece shirt, then go to sit at the kitchen table with my husband.

We're both relatively quiet as we have coffee and muffins, though we cast glances at each other from across the table. Just the sight of him warms my blood—his masculine features that are so dear to me, the strands of thick hair brushing his forehead, the way he picks up his coffee by wrapping his hand around the cup rather than the handle.

We exchange sections of the Sunday paper, commenting on news articles and local events. He reads the sports page. I read the entertainment insert. He refills our coffee. I clip a few coupons. He studies the stock market. I get a pencil and work out a few answers on the crossword puzzle, then pass it across for him to finish. We split the last blueberry muffin.

It's almost eleven before we finally get the dishes washed and the paper stacked for recycling. Dean stands and stretches, his T-shirt pulling across his chest, then comes around the table to wrap me in his arms.

"Ah, Liv." His body heaves with a sigh. "I miss you."

I press my forehead against his chest. "I miss you too. Things sure got messed up, didn't they?"

"They did."

"We've done a lousy job trying to fix it."

"Yeah." His voice roughens with the admission.

I swallow hard and force out my darkest fear. "What if we can't?"

Dean puts his hands on either side of my head and lifts my face to look at him. His eyes are serious but tender.

"We've done it before," he says. "We can do it again."

Fall seven times. Get up eight.

"I don't want to lose you," I whisper.

"You'll never lose me." He slides his hand to the back of my neck. "I want you to come home."

I tighten my arms around his waist. A tentative hope spreads inside me, like a new, green shoot pushing its way up through a layer of ice.

"I want to come home," I say. "And I want you to be here when I do."

"I'll be here, beauty. Waiting for you."

Christmas Eve is cold and bright. A fresh layer of snow covers Avalon Street, and the sun sparkles off it like little jewels. Colorful lights twinkle around lampposts and store windows.

The Historical Museum is having a holiday party for staff and volunteers this afternoon, and Dean and I are going together. Though I haven't yet moved back into our apartment, we're both here getting ready.

I dress in a black, short-sleeved jersey dress with a scooped neckline that displays the cameo necklace Dean gave me as a first anniversary present. The pendant matches my cameo engagement ring, which I'm also wearing. I twist my hair into a ponytail and fasten it with a red bow, then head out of the bathroom.

Dean is knotting his tie in front of the mirror. He slides his gaze to me, and his eyes warm with appreciation.

"Very pretty." He gives his tie a final pull, then comes over to press a kiss against my lips.

My heart flutters. He looks incredibly handsome in black trousers and a crisp, white shirt, the knot of his tie nestled against the column of his throat. I watch as he shrugs into his suit jacket, checks for his wallet, fastens his watch—all those easy, deft movements that have become so familiar to me over the years.

I think I've loved him since he first walked into Jitter Beans. Into my life.

He takes his car keys from the dresser and glances at me. A frown tugs at his mouth.

"Liv?"

Emotions tumble through me, riotous colors, light and shadows, fear and joy. I take a breath.

"Dean."

"What?"

"I'm pregnant."

Thank you for reading Liv and Dean's story!

I am always grateful when a reader posts a review for my books. If you take the time to leave a review for *Arouse*, *Allure*, or *Awaken*, please email me at nina@ninalane.com so I can thank you personally.

Also please consider signing up for the Nina Lane newsletter and liking my Facebook page to receive updates.

THANK YOU!

Liv and Dean's passionate journey continues in
ALLURE, Book Two in the *Spiral of Bliss* series.

"*We both want this so badly. I can feel it resonating between
us like the hot pull of our first attraction, tangible and intense.*"

After lies and betrayal almost destroy their marriage, Dean and
Olivia West reignite their blissful passion. The medieval history professor and his cherished wife are determined to fix their
mistakes and fall madly in love all over again.

Then a family crisis forces Dean back into a feud with his
parents and siblings, dredging up guilt over a painful family
secret. Liv and Dean have battled obstacles together before, but
with bitter family conflicts now endangering their fragile intimacy, they soon must struggle with events that could damage
them in ways they had never imagined.

Liv and Dean's story comes to a breathtaking conclusion in
AWAKEN, Book Three in the *Spiral of Bliss* series.

"*I love that you love me, professor.*"
"*I love loving you, beauty.*"

Since their intense, passionate beginning, Professor Dean West
and his wife Olivia have fought dark secrets and betrayal in order
to save their marriage. Now reeling in the aftermath of a personal
tragedy, Liv and Dean are driven further apart by a vindictive
threat to Dean's career.

Struggling to stand on her own for the first time in years, Liv
is determined to defend her husband and prove herself. Then an
unexpected letter dredges up old insecurities and endangers Liv's
newfound independence. As Dean fights for his professional life,
he is forced to confront his worst fear when he discovers that he
can't protect his beloved wife from her own painful past.

Excerpt from

Allure

BY

NINA LANE

OLIVIA

DECEMBER 24

*W*e're kissing in the coat closet. The *coat closet*. I'm up against the back wall, his hands are braced on either side of my head, and his mouth is locked hot and deep against mine. My ponytail is slipping from the clasp, my fingers are gripping his shoulders, and I'm lost in the sweet, aching cascade of pleasure.

He pushes his leg between mine, moving to pull up my knee-length dress and cup his hand around the back of my thigh. His tongue sweeps across my lower lip. Arousal billows between us, a relief after the simmering tension of the past two hours.

Every time I sought him out amidst the holiday festivities, I found him watching me. Every time our eyes met, sparks of electricity spun through the air. Every time I saw him maneuver through the crowd, my heart beat faster.

We circled each other like prowling cats as we moved through the bright rooms of Langdon House, a historic Victorian mansion adorned with colorful Christmas trees, fresh green garlands, and vintage decorations.

We navigated clusters of people, the women all decked out in sparkly holiday gowns, the men in expensive suits and ties. We drifted in and out of conversations with other guests, then found each other again and exchanged a look of heated promise.

Until he caught me in the foyer beside the walk-in coat closet, curling his hand around my arm as he guided me inside and shut the door behind him. My pulse leapt when he came toward me, backing me up against the wall and penning me into the cage of his arms the instant before his mouth crashed down on mine.

I don't know how long we've been here. I don't care. My world has distilled to this space. There is only the press of his body, the solid bulk of his chest, the mingle of our breath. The scents of pine, cinnamon, and apples cling to the air. A narrow remnant of light shines beneath the door. Laughter and conversation drift through the walls.

I slide my hands over the ridges of his torso, feel the heat burning through his shirt. He moves his mouth to my cheek, down to my neck. My dress is pushed up to my waist.

He grips my thighs, which are covered in sheer nylons. He growls with frustration when he discovers the tight spandex barrier over my panties.

Dean lifts his head, his gaze colliding with mine before he grabs the nylon at the seam and rips it away. My heart throbs.

"Take this off." He plucks at the spandex with a frown of impatience.

"Good thing it's not control-top," I remark breathlessly, pushing the waistband over my hips and halfway down my thighs.

"What the hell is control-top?" He eases his hand underneath my panties and groans. "Oh, fuck. Never mind."

His fingers probe deeper into my cleft. I gasp, clutching the front of his shirt, urgency spooling into my blood. He slides his forefinger into me, pressing the heel of his hand against my clit.

"Come on, beauty," he whispers, his breath a hot trail to my ear.

He presses his lips to the pulse pounding at the side of my neck, then works another finger into my body to stroke my inner flesh.

I arch toward him, straining, my sex throbbing. A cry of pleasure lodges in my throat, poised to escape, when suddenly Dean clamps his hand over my mouth. He pushes me to the right, back through a curtain of woolen coats to the side wall. A second after I realize the doorknob has clicked open, light floods the closet.

I tighten my hands on Dean's shirtfront. He eases his hand from my mouth, our hard breaths thankfully masked by the sound of women's chattery voices.

"Did you try those salmon rolls?" one of them asks. "They're new on the catering menu."

"Oh, yes. So light and delicious. I think we ought to hire the same caterers for the spring festival, don't you?"

I know those women. Members of the Historical Society

board of trustees, Florence and Ruth Wickham are two lovely older ladies who wear designer suits and pearl necklaces and would no doubt be horrified to find me half-naked in the back of the coat closet.

"Do you remember where I put my coat?" Florence asks her sister. "Did I tell you I found it on sale at that little boutique on Dandelion Street? Pure camelhair."

The air is stifling back here. A fur collar from one of the hanging coats brushes against my neck. I push it away impatiently. I'm still throbbing, frustrated at having my arousal thwarted.

Then Dean presses his knee between my legs, spreading my thighs. I jerk my gaze to his lust-filled eyes. A wicked grin tugs at his mouth as he presses his hand against my sex again.

I grab his wrist, acutely aware of the little old ladies still rummaging around for their camelhair coats… but he twists from my grip and flicks his thumb against my clit. I suck in a breath, melting at my core.

He lowers his mouth to mine again, one hand steadying me at the small of my back, the other working me with deliberate intent. I part my lips beneath his and fall into the cascade again. His touch grows more intimate, sliding deep into my opening, his thumb swirling and stroking and…

I can't stop it. I don't want to. It's been long, too long, and even this furtive, hasty rendezvous in the middle of a holiday party is like gulping cold lemonade on a blistering day. I try to suppress a moan and let my head fall back against the wall as his tongue slides against mine.

One more press of his fingers into my cleft, and hot bursts of rapture explode along my nerves. He muffles my cries with the pressure of his mouth. I grip his shoulders, my legs weakening with the force of vibrations flooding me from head to toe.

I pull back and stare at him, my blood pulsing. He's still fully clothed, his heavy erection pressing against the front of his trousers. Though the coats shade the closet light, I can see the burn of his eyes. His dark hair is a mess, a thick swath falling over his forehead, his sharp cheekbones flushed. Though we're both still breathing hard, neither of us moves.

"Oh, here it is! Look, isn't that Grace's coat?" Florence's voice grows distant as she moves back toward the door. "She said it was lynx fur. Can you imagine? Heavens, but it is soft, isn't it? Feel it."

Ruth murmurs her agreement, then finally the light turns off and the door closes.

"We should go," I whisper.

"I'll go first." Dean strokes my cheek. "I'll let you know if the coast is clear."

We straighten our clothing, then fumble around to find my purse and his suit jacket, both of which have fallen to the floor. I manage to get my nylons back around my hips, concealing the rip beneath the swirl of my skirt.

"Wait here." He presses a hard kiss to my lips and ducks out of the closet. A second later, there's a quick knock at the door.

I hurry out, unable to prevent a grin as our gazes meet fleetingly in the foyer. I feel like we're a couple of horny teenagers sneaking out from under the bleachers.

It's a good feeling and not one I've experienced much—the pleasure of a sneaky rendezvous, furtive groping, secret kisses—all so blissful now because I can share them again with my husband.

I cross the foyer to the bathroom and do a quick primping to straighten out my very disheveled self. I comb my long hair back into its ponytail, splash water on my face in the hopes of dimming the heated flush, reapply my lipstick, and try to smooth the wrinkles from my dress.

Dean is gone from the foyer by the time I emerge, likely to deal with his own rumpled appearance. I head for the refreshment table that's been set up in the living room of the house and grab a bottle of mineral water.

"Oh, there you are, dear."

I look up and find myself face-to-face with Florence Wickham, belted into her camelhair coat and tugging on a pair of leather gloves.

"I didn't want to leave without saying goodbye and wishing you a merry Christmas, Olivia," she says. "We've so appreciated all your volunteering with the Historical Museum and the preparations for the holiday festival."

"I've greatly enjoyed it all."

Florence peers at me through eyes adorned with beige eyeshadow and mascara. I hope to heaven that my cheeks aren't still overly flushed. Or, God forbid, that Dean didn't leave a hickey on my neck.

"Don't forget to take a present from beneath the tree in the parlor," Florence continues. "All the gifts were donated by local merchants, and there are some lovely items." She pulls at the wrists of her gloves. "Where is that handsome gentleman you came with?"

"I think he's talking to someone in the kitchen."

"Is he your boyfriend?" she asks.

"He's my husband."

"Oh." Florence arches a delicately plucked eyebrow, her gaze skirting to my left hand.

"It was my engagement ring." I extend my hand to show her the antique cameo on my left ring finger. I wear it only on special occasions, but no other symbol in the world could serve as a more meaningful declaration that I belong to one man alone.

"I love cameos." She peers at the ring. "It's beautiful."

"Thank you."

"If I may be so bold, Olivia..." Florence leans closer and lowers her voice to a conspiratorial whisper. "Your husband is quite dashing, but his adventurous spirit is... well, it makes him just irresistible."

"I... I beg your pardon?"

"My dear, I'm seventy-three years old," Florence says. "And in fifty-one years of marriage, I can only wish that my husband had even *once* shagged me in a coat closet."

She winks at me, then turns and walks away.

ABOUT THE AUTHOR

*U*SA *Today* bestselling author Nina Lane writes hot, sexy romances and spicy erotica. Originally from California, she holds a PhD in Art History and an MA in Library and Information Studies, which means she loves both research and organization. She also enjoys traveling and thinks St. Petersburg, Russia is a city everyone should visit at least once. Although Nina would go back to college for another degree because she's that much of a bookworm and a perpetual student, she now lives the happy life of a full-time writer.

Find out about Nina's latest news and books
at www.ninalane.com or join her on
Facebook at www.facebook.com/NinaLaneAuthor
and Twitter at www.twitter.com/NinaLaneAuthor

ACKNOWLEDGEMENTS

*M*y deepest gratitude goes to Kelly Harms Wimmer of Word Bird Editorial, whose perceptive comments and suggestions have greatly improved both this book and my writing. Thank you to the extraordinarily talented and very patient Victoria Colotta of VMC Art & Design for the gorgeous covers and interior design of the books. I owe my thanks to Martha Trachtenberg for her eagle-eyed copyediting, and to Kim Killion of Hot Damn Designs for her work on the previous covers. I am so fortunate to have found Jen Berg, beta reader extraordinaire whose support for my work has been immeasurable. I am also grateful to readers Jolyn, Elishia, Isabelle, and Pat for their time, and to Michelle, Lori, and Deb for early feedback many moons ago. Thank you also to Cathy Yardley for help with story structure, and to Karen and Michelle of Literati Author

Services for their great support. And I owe a particular debt of gratitude to all the readers who have enjoyed my books. Thank you all so much.

Also by Nina Lane

The #1 bestselling novel about a woman's
intense journey into submission

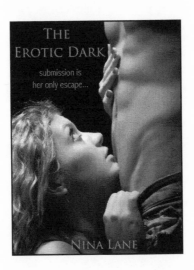

Submission is her only escape... and punishment takes many
forms. Seeking escape from her criminal past, a desperate
woman enslaves herself to a dark trio of men who own an
antiquated Louisiana plantation. Known only as Lydia, she
becomes controlled by three very different men—malicious
Preston, inflexible Kruin, and gentle Gabriel, all of whom
introduce her to a world in which the lines between pleasure,
pain, and shame are irrevocably blurred.

The plantation becomes both Lydia's haven and her prison
as she surrenders to the desires of her unholy trinity. Lydia's submission is fraught with tension and hunger, but what happens
when the outside world enters her dark, anonymous sanctuary?